THE
DESERT HAWKS

Books by James Walker

Husbands Who Won't Lead and Wives Who Won't Follow

The Wells Fargo Trail
   The Dreamgivers
   The Nightriders
   The Rail Kings
   The Rawhiders
   The Desert Hawks

THE DESERT HAWKS

+ + + + + + + + + +

JIM WALKER

BETHANY HOUSE PUBLISHERS
MINNEAPOLIS, MINNESOTA 55438

The Desert Hawks
Copyright © 1996
Jim Walker

Cover by Dan Thornberg,
Bethany House Publishers staff artist.

Map created by Philip Schwartzberg, Meridian Mapping,
Minneapolis, Minnesota 55408.

Published by Bethany House Publishers
A Ministry of Bethany Fellowship, Inc.
11300 Hampshire Avenue South
Minneapolis, Minnesota 55438

Printed in the United States of America.

Library of Congress Cataloging-in-Publication Data

Walker, James, 1948–
    The desert hawks / Jim Walker.
        p. cm.—(The Wells Fargo trail ; book 5)
    I. Title. II. Series: Walker, James, 1948–   Wells Fargo trail ;
bk. 5.
PS3573.A425334D47   1996
813'.54—dc20   96–4503
ISBN 1–55661–700–3 (pbk.)   CIP

This book is dedicated to someone
with the brightest smile under the heavens,
someone who surrounds my life with unconditional love
and has taught me the need to understand and empathize,
my daughter
Jennifer.

JIM WALKER is a staff member with the Navigators and has written *Husbands Who Won't Lead and Wives Who Won't Follow*. He received an M.Div. from Talbot Theological Seminary and has been a pastor with an Evangelical Free Church. He was a survival training instructor in the United States Air Force and is a member of the Western Outlaw-Lawman History Association. Jim, his wife, Joyce, and their three children, Joel, Jennifer, and Julie, live in Colorado Springs, Colorado.

AUTHOR'S NOTES

+ + + + + + +

The Wells Fargo Trail is a series that combines historical detail and rugged action. At times it becomes necessary to depict the raw violence of the West in the 1870s. I try to keep graphic descriptions to a minimum; however, the development of characters that are evil and desperate means that I must at times show their deeds and the results of their behavior.

Like you, I am appalled by the violence of our society. In my books, I work to show the values of the people that oppose this type of conduct. My characters are complex, however—even the ones I want the reader to admire. Like all of us, they are people with mixed motives.

I also want the reader to be stimulated and entertained by the mixture of romance and action. There are examples here that show love—a love that sacrifices itself for others. There are also genuine role models. Heroes are, of necessity, larger than life. They rise above their circumstances. They love the unlovely. They reach out to people that often you and I would not have in our homes. They make an attempt to understand those who seem incomprehensible.

Some explanation of the times in which this book takes place may be helpful. The "ghost dance" was a practice of the plains Indians that spread to most, if not all, the Native American tribes. Missionaries unknowingly lent their teaching of the resurrection to the growing belief that the ancestors of warriors would rise to join them in eradicating the white man. In the end, it was a passionate need for hope that caused those who practiced the ghost dance to have courage about their future and not accept the slavery that the Indian reservations brought.

An author is in the best of worlds when he can write about

7

actual life experience. *The Desert Hawks* has let me do just that. White-water rafting has always been a passion of mine. In the last twenty years, I have rafted down the Rogue River in Oregon, the Nooksack River in Washington State, the American and Feather Rivers in California, the Arkansas River in Colorado, and the Colorado River in the Grand Canyon of Arizona. When I write about the experience of Zac Cobb and his group of fellow travelers as they negotiate the deadly waters of the Colorado, it is something I know very well.

While rafting the Feather River, I actually had a near-drowning experience quite similar to the one I tell about in Chapter 43. There was a peace about it that is difficult to imagine without being there, but I have tried to describe it in a way that allows the reader to feel it, without getting wet!

The landmarks I portray are there, just the way I depict them. The adventure is a real one. The feeling of being totally alive and at the mercy of God and His creation makes the one who dares to take the trip thankful for each and every moment He gives us. I hope you will find in the reading of the events described here a fraction of the sheer joy I felt in living it.

CHARACTERS

+ + + + + + +

Zachary Cobb—Undercover agent and bounty hunter for the Wells Fargo Company. He is ruthless and will stop at nothing to accomplish his mission.

Jenny Hays—Zac's sweetheart. She loves him but is reluctant to pressure him to give up his work in order to "settle down" with her.

Julian Cobb—Zac's oldest brother. Crippled during The War between the States, he has become a vindictive outlaw bent on securing his own wealth at the expense of the Union Army. Zac has not seen him during the last fifteen years and has only heard rumors of his existence.

Drago—Smirking henchman to Julian Cobb. He has been on the "outs" with the law for many years, a career criminal.

Nestor—Treacherous accomplice of Julian Cobb.

Simpson—Young accomplice of Julian Cobb.

Chupta—Apache scout assigned to Zac by the army. He hates all white men, even though he now works on their behalf.

Lawrence Ruggles—Professional gambler. He is a jaded traveler, adept at using his wits and common sense to overcome any obstacle.

Amy Franklin—Fellow traveler with her grandfather, a gambler "down on his luck." She has come to mistrust all men, especially those who gamble.

Tommy Franklin—Amy's young brother by her mother's second marriage. Tommy suffers from a mental and emotional disorder.

Raincloud—Apache wife of Ed Hiatt. Educated by missionaries, she, as well as her baby daughter Sunflower, has been abused by her husband.

Ed Hiatt—A successful miner who throws his money away at the gambling tables and saloons. Although he bought Raincloud from her father to be his wife, Ed has a hatred for the Indian that he puts aside when it is convenient for him.

Mangus—Renegade Yavapai war chief. He is a respected leader of his people and devotee of the new "ghost dance." He is determined to band the Indian tribes of the desert together to drive the white man from their home.

Gandara—Devoted Yavapai assistant to Mangus. He dreams of becoming a leader and studies his Indian hero in the hope of being like him.

Hec Peters—Grizzled stage driver and owner of a new stage line that travels the offbeat paths from Tucson to Lee's Ferry.

Butch Gray—Shotgun messenger on the stage. A young, brash hand on the stage with far too many bad experiences with the Indians.

China Mary—Brothel owner and madam. She runs a brisk supply of vices ranging from drugs to the fair elements of local saloons.

Philip Carol—Son of a very successful mine owner and businessman. He is traveling to Yale, where he is looking to study law.

The Reverend Isaac Black—Itinerant circuit-riding preacher. He is a man who shuns the parish ministry and sees his success in ministry to the "far lost."

Rufus Campbell—Renegade seller of guns and whiskey to the Indians.

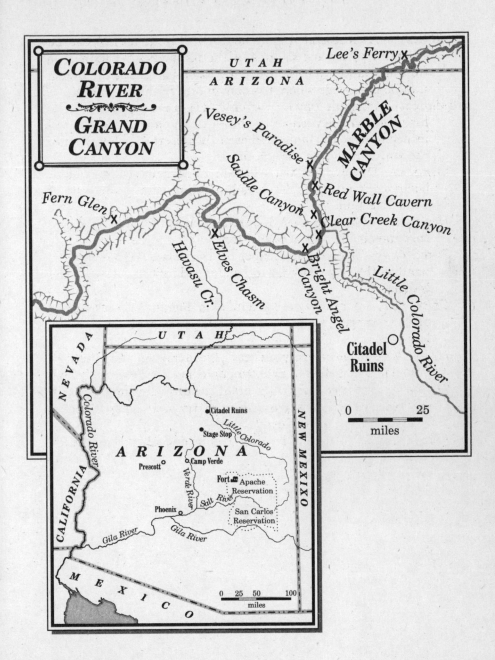

CHAPTER 1

+ + + + + + +

The Acme Saloon, Phoenix, Arizona
A hot Tuesday morning in August of 1878

The wind blew a dust devil down the back street, blasting the saloon's windows with dirt and debris. Not a head turned, except for that of the pretty girl sitting next to her babbling brother. Five men at the green felt table in the back of the Acme stared intently at their pasteboard cards, each striving to maintain his composure after spending an entire night under the flickering lamp. Their intensity made it clear that this was high-stakes poker. A man who betrayed his hand by a look or the way he moved his cards from front to back would go home flat busted.

Overhead, the red lamp swayed slightly, its shadows crawling up the rough, bleached wood walls, then down again. The little boy continued to swing short, spindly legs under the chair and shake his hands as if he were slinging soapy water onto the floor. Repeatedly, he talked in bursts to his silent sister, and then once again began the violent twitching and shaking.

At the table, the children's grandfather peered at the hand in front of him. Dark circles under his eyes curved up slightly at the corners to meet the downward plunge of heavy eyebrows, which twitched like the tails of two curious squirrels. The old man's dark suit and large, drooping, black mustache formed a harsh contrast to his flour white complexion. He gently pulled at a black bow tie and curled pudgy white fingers around his cards, his tight grasp turning his perfectly trimmed nails a lifeless white.

One of the gamblers looked across the table at him. "I reckon the bet is one hundred to you, old feller," he said.

The old man put down his cards and fingered the few remaining

13

bills in front of him. "Arizona, in general, has not been kind to me, I'm afraid, gentlemen. What you see before me is all I have left to get myself and my grandchildren to Utah Territory."

The man who had called on him to exercise a bet continued to show frustration at the delay. "Then I'd suggest you just pick up what you have there and fold your cards."

Another man at the table put down his cards and leaned back, his blue eyes shining. He had a calm look about him that showed a sense of control, someone accustomed to being in charge of his own life and the affairs of others. The man's frame was solid under a black, pressed suit, and his movements at the table were fluid and meticulously rehearsed. Sporting a careful part in a full head of hair, he brushed his dark, thick, neatly trimmed mustache with the tips of his delicate fingers. "There is no reason to be in haste," he said with a smooth Southern drawl. "Mr. Franklin here has been very good to us all night and most of the day."

Franklin pulled out a white handkerchief and rubbed it across his sweaty forehead. He then carefully patted the bald top of his head, a wide swath of gleaming white that dominated his look. Cascading long hair tumbled down the sides of his head. "I thank you for your courtesy, Mr. Ruggles."

Taking up the pile of bills, he laid them on the stack of coins and paper money that littered the center of the table. "I've come too far to quit. This may be the hand that takes my grandchildren and me home."

The two gamblers to his left each folded their hands and Ruggles sharpened his icy blue gaze and placed a stack of twenties on top of the pile. "I will see your hundred and raise you five hundred."

The old grandfather slumped in his chair and the impatient gambler across from them groaned. "I got two thousand sitting in that pile already," the man said. Grunting, he counted out a stack of gold coins and shoved them into the middle of the table. "I guess I'm just gonna have to see them cards."

Franklin reached into his black coat pocket and produced a document. Spreading it out on the table, he cleared his throat. "Gentlemen, this is the deed to our ranch in Utah, over two thousand acres of prime bottom land south of St. George. It's worth many times what you have on the table here, but if you all will allow me, I'll just use it to call."

14

"I ain't got no use for no Utah desert land." The impatient gambler fidgeted in his chair.

Ruggles stared coolly at the old man. "Speaking for my ownself, I'll be more than happy to accept your deed."

"Well, not me. It's cash on the barrelhead, far as I'm concerned. I play cards with people that bet with things I can see."

Franklin mopped his head and looked around at the children sitting in the corner of the room. Nervously, he picked up his cards once again and stared at them. Turning back to the children, he twisted in his chair. He bowed his head as he faced the table, then looked first one man in the eye, then the other. "I will give you a guarantee of my good faith—my grandchildren over there. I will leave them with you, along with this deed. With my daughter's children in your hands, you may rest assured that I will return with the money, should your cards prove the better of mine."

"Young'uns ain't property to be bought and sold," the impatient player shot back. "They's jest gonna be two more mouths to feed, far as I'm concerned."

"Nonetheless, they are a testament to my good faith in the matter."

The gambler grimaced and scrutinized the children across the room. The small boy continued to shake his hands, and the girl raised her head and glanced back at him. She was shapely, even in her well-worn clothes, with a neatly pointed chin and large dark eyes. There was a proud look about her as she raised her chin, a look that belied her circumstances. The man licked his lips and scratched his jaw. "All right, it's a bet. But if you lose, the young'uns are mine to do with as I please."

With that, he didn't wait for anybody but laid his cards quickly on the table. "Two pair," he said. "Aces and queens."

Franklin smiled and placed his cards down one at a time. "There you are—one, two, three jacks, and two tens, a full house." He slapped his hands together and grinned slyly.

The bested gambler gripped the edge of the table, grinding his teeth.

Ruggles, who had been almost forgotten by the others, quietly laid down his cards. "Excellent hand there, Franklin, but I'm afraid it won't best my four sevens."

The old man seemed stunned as he watched Ruggles rake in the pile of cash. He blew a deep breath out of his lips, rippling his mustache with the escaping air. The life seemed to go out of him. Blinking his eyes, he suddenly clutched his chest and moaned.

Ruggles reached for him and held him up in his chair. "Are you all right, sir?"

The girl ran to the table and placed her hands on his shoulder. "Grandfather, are you all right? Is it your heart?"

Ruggles looked at her. "You better go get a doctor."

"I'll do no such thing," she said. "Why should I leave him with you?"

Ruggles looked her in the eye, his sense of calm command returning. "Young lady, doctors are busy people. They rarely leave what they are doing unless someone presses them to do so." He looked at the men around the table. "Would you trust one of these gentlemen to that task, or do you think you might be motivated sufficiently to get that doctor here?"

Her eyes burned the kind of flame produced in a young woman who didn't care to admit to wisdom found outside her own head. "Yes, of course you're right."

Stroking her grandfather's cheek, she left him with parting orders. "You will not die. Do you hear me, Grandfather? You will not die. I will return shortly with the doctor, and together we will find a way to get out of this mess. Do you hear?"

Franklin nodded painfully.

Turning back to the men at the table, Ruggles clipped orders at them, "Someone go with the young lady and help her find the doctor. One of y'all find a room upstairs where we can take this man. Tell them we're going to need a room with a window and some clean sheets." Swiveling around to see the boy, still fidgeting in the corner, he spoke more softly. "See to that child over yonder." He then nodded to one of the men. "Help me pick him up. We'll lay him down for now on the table."

Gently, they placed the moaning man on the table. Ruggles guided his shoulders and, picking up a pillow from one of the chairs, placed it under his head. The other gambler straightened his legs. "I'll go get him some water," the man offered.

"Are you comfortable?" Ruggles asked.

Franklin motioned him closer. "Promise me," he rasped. "Promise me you will take care of the children."

Ruggles's composure disappeared. "I'm single, a gambler, and not fixed to care for children. I look after myself . . . I have no time to take care of others."

"Tommy is a simple-minded boy, but Amy is a fine young woman. She's almost eighteen. She is quite smart and has her own mind, but she will obey when she sees the wisdom of a thing. I've had them ever since their mother died of the yellow fever. I'm afraid I've failed them in my desire to become a rich man at the expense of others at the gambling tables. They will have no one now."

"Don't speak about such nonsense. I couldn't possibly consider such a thing. I'm somebody who needs a clear head, and children are nothing more than a bothersome distraction to a body like me. Being a gambler yourself, you must understand my position. Y'all will be just fine just as soon as we find a doctor."

"I am afraid that is not true, sir, and I find . . . myself in the awkward position . . . of having to place all my trust in . . . in you, and the future of my grandchildren, as well."

The words came haltingly, punctuated by gasps, as both speaking and breathing became increasingly difficult for him. "Please . . . please, reach into my coat pocket and . . . t-t-t-take out the little bag I carry there."

Feeling the man's pockets, Ruggles produced a small velvet bag. Franklin's eyes narrowed. "Open it up," he said.

Loosening the drawstrings, Ruggles spilled into his palm a glittering diamond the size of a robin's egg. His mouth dropped open.

Franklin smiled. "That stone is worth multiple tens of thousands of dollars." He gulped and wheezed. "Many have killed and been killed to . . . hold what you are holding now." Swallowing hard, he went on. "All I ask is that you use it . . . to look after my grandchildren's welfare, to see that they are cared for, and that Tommy . . . will know no want. Apart from that, you may have . . . what is left."

Ruggles eyes were glued to the diamond. In his short thirty years, he had never seen nor heard of such a stone, and in spite of the enormous value the old man seemed to place upon it, he was sure the diamond was worth even more.

Franklin reached out his chalky fingers and grabbed Ruggles's ruffled white shirt. "You are a gentleman from the South, sir, and I must trust you." The old man twisted in pain. "I fought for the cause my ownself, and you cannot deny me this last request. Will you promise me on your honor as a gentleman?"

Ruggles looked straight into the dying man's eyes and nodded.

CHAPTER 2

✦ ✦ ✦ ✦ ✦ ✦ ✦

The Sonora Desert
Late Tuesday afternoon

Over fifty miles to the southeast, the six troopers and the lieutenant had left Fort Apache and been on the hot desert trail for three days. They would be in Fort Wingate in two days and each of them looked forward to a cool bath and a chance to find some daytime shade.

For days they had complained about leading their horses in the sun. It was a policy designed to save the animals and keep the fatigue factor low, but the Apache had been peaceful as of late, and none of the soldiers could see the sense of it. Besides, they weren't transporting rifles or ammunition. There was nothing much they had that the Indians would be interested in stealing. The payroll for Fort Wingate and the rest of the army supply posts in the area seemed to carry little temptation for the Apache.

Julian Cobb and two of the men who had been trailing the soldiers watched from the rocks as the group made camp for the night. They had left Drago with the animals on the other side of the rocky outcropping. Julian squinted with his right eye and studied the bluecoats as they stripped the saddles from the backs of their horses. He beat the stump of his left arm on the sharp rock beside him, drawing the attention of the two men beside him.

He wasn't a man who took well to questions, in spite of his peculiarities. Since losing his left arm and eye at Gettysburg, he often felt the clinching of his missing hand. It was worse in the cold, but he'd discovered long ago that sharp pain was better than the numb deadness.

Simpson gave him an inquisitive stare. Julian shot a hard look back at him.

"Sorry, it's jest that I ain't knowed many men with one arm and one eye afore."

"Back where I come from, there ain't many men my age that have two arms, two legs, and two eyes. Everybody still breathing 'tween the ages of thirty and forty is missing something."

"Guess it don't make you none too friendly to people who wear them blue uniforms," Nestor chimed in and paused, "like them men down there."

Julian didn't respond. He simply turned his head and watched the soldiers begin to light their cook fire.

Hours later, the stars blinked brightly overhead. The watch at the camp had been changed twice, and dawn would be coming in a couple of hours. Years of training in the hardness of war had taught Julian that the predawn strike was always the most effective. Having at least three of the seven cavalry men already missing sleep seemed to be the wise way to have an edge.

Julian and the men took off their boots and put on the moccasins they carried. The softness of the footwear would warn them of twigs underfoot before they put their full weight down. The moccasins would also leave the kind of tracks Julian wanted to leave at the ambush site—the tracks of an Apache war party.

They made their way down the rocky slope toward the sleeping group. Julian moved with the quick, fluid motions of a panther. He had none of the awkwardness of a horseman's walk. He moved through the darkness like a hunter—which he was, a hunter of men. Each man knew he would have to kill one trooper on the first rush, and if Drago could get the sentry, the others would be easy pickings.

The four outlaws separated near the foot of the rocky outcropping, each circling to their agreed-upon positions. Near the camp, they watched the sentry silhouetted against the starry sky. They'd been used to sneaking up on soldiers' camps before. In the three robberies they'd done in New Mexico, there had never been a slip up.

✦   ✦   ✦   ✦   ✦

The lieutenant turned in his bedroll and looked up at the night sky. He was one of the few who had a wife waiting for him at the fort, and for some reason he couldn't get her out of his mind. He listened to the soft snoring of the men around him. The corporal, who had just returned from his late watch, was fast asleep, and the sound of his heavy breathing joined in the chorus.

A quail peeped in the distance. The fire had long been cold, a precaution they always took in Indian territory. Even though the Apache had been penned up in their reservations, it gave the young man comfort to feel the lump of the .45 underneath his blanket. Tomorrow he would be home—not much of a home, but right now it was all he had.

He closed his eyes. He knew that even if he couldn't sleep tonight, he would sleep well enough tomorrow night. That would be some consolation. His memory of his last evening at home had been a sweet one; a hot meal, a special dessert his wife had prepared for him, and the good-bye kisses she had showered him with made being thousands of miles away from their home in the East something he could live with, at least for now. His mind drifted, and he deliberately shut his eyes.

At the sound of a grunt from the sentry, his eyes jerked open. He heard the movement of running men all around him. He fumbled for the revolver under his bedroll and brought it up, quickly swinging it around to find one of the dark shapes running into the camp. Shots were fired, and he could see the flashes of the muzzles. Taking aim, he fired several rounds at one of the running men. He watched the man pitch forward. It was the last thing he saw.

✦ ✦ ✦ ✦ ✦

Julian continued to fire round after round into the bundled lumps on the ground. Each of the men in turn approached several of the soldiers who were still giving out dying sounds. The bark from their revolvers silenced the soldiers at last.

"Is that sentry done for?" Julian asked.

"Durn tootin'," Drago responded. "Deader'n Julius Caesar."

The moan at the edge of the camp turned their heads.

"That's Simpson," Nestor said. "Might as well shoot him here and be done with it. We can't be nursin' no wounded man through this desert."

Julian holstered his pistol and grabbed the man's shirt. "We'll take the kid with us fer a spell. I won't leave anybody they can identify."

The three of them approached Simpson and watched him squirm.

"Got myself belly shot," Simpson whimpered.

"You got to ride outta here, kid," Julian said. "You best let us get you into a saddle, otherwise you'll be toted outta here slung over it. Drago, you get one a them bedrolls out, pile the guns and gear into it. When Nestor and I get back with the mules and horses, we can scalp and strip them Yankee soldiers. I want this to look like 'paches done this. Little bit a confusion goes a long ways out here."

Over an hour later, the dawn was rosy over the edge of the mountains. The group was finishing tying down the equipment. Drago and Nestor cinched their lines tight. "How much you figure we got?" Drago asked.

"Near as I can see, we took in about ten thousand in currency and another thirty thousand in gold," Nestor responded. "That what you figure, Cobb?"

Julian ignored the question and continued to let Simpson sip from his canteen. The faint light of dawn showed Julian's rawboned look. What once had been a bright red shirt had faded to the color of a muted rose. At first glance, he was a man who placed little value on his life. Besides missing his left arm and eye, he had a scar that meandered down his clean-shaven face from the edge of his right eye to the corner of his chin.

His pale green eye looked like a peeled grape planted in his sun-browned, leathery face—a narrow, rough-cut face, angular and hard. He studied the swim of the sun on the hills to the east. He had the look of a man who knew the desert. His tall, broad-shouldered frame was testimony that he had spent many a day in the saddle. Tied down to his side was a Smith and Wesson Russian .44.

He nodded at the pile of clothes the men had taken off the soldiers. "Bundle them things up. We got to get them outta here and bury them, along with the gold. We need to travel light for a spell. Scatter them army mules and horses, too. I want it to look for all the world like a bunch a hot-heads off the San Carlos done this."

"Them mules are mighty valuable out here," Nestor said.

"Maybe so," Drago grunted, "but if someone spots us with anything that has that there U.S. brand on it, it's gonna make some questions traipse across their mind. 'Sides, the 'paches love mule meat the best."

Nestor mumbled to himself as he finished cinching the packs on the mules. Tying off the rope, he straightened himself up, placed his hands on the small of his back, and stretched as he squinted at the rising sun. Frowning, he watched Julian continue to let Simpson sip from the canteen. He was the type of man who could rarely abide anything he saw as a waste of resources. For Nestor, things were something to be used by him alone, or by others who might offer him some protection.

Sauntering over to where Julian nursed Simpson, Nestor kept up his complaints. "That water's gonna be scarce, Cobb. Why is you wasting it on the kid anyhow? The boy's been gutshot. Bad fool luck it was, but he's done for. Anyway, I ain't never seen nobody walk away from a slug in the innards."

Simpson blinked back tears. "Is that right?" he asked. "Ain't there no way then, even if'n we meet up with some doctor?" The boy grimaced in pain and clenched his teeth.

Julian slowly handed the canteen to Drago and whirled around, landing a loud slap to Nestor's jaw with the back of his knuckles. The force of the blow caught the big man off guard, jerking him upright and stunning him. Julian stepped into him and landed a haymaker directly into his chin.

Nestor fell to the ground, fluttering like a wounded butterfly. After a moment, he twisted onto his backside and moved his hand, ever so slightly, to the strapped gun he carried.

"Go ahead," Julian said. "I don't know about belly wounds, but I ain't never seen a man walk away from crossing me."

Nestor slowly lifted his hand, then joined his hands together in the air over his head. He remained seated on the desert floor. "Okay, Cobb, you done proved your point. You can be whatever kind of fool you aim to be. I ain't about to try and outdraw you. Why would I want to, even if I could? I was jest tryin' to save on that there water of ourn. 'Sides"—he skinned a forced grin—"you know where all the gold is buried. Man'd be a durn fool to go up against you, now, wouldn't he?"

Julian reached around and took the canteen from Drago. He took several swigs before placing it under his left stump and pouring some into his cupped right hand. After taking a long look at the prone gunman, he rubbed his hand over his face, mixing the water with his sweat. "I been around these parts for years. I know where there's water in spots where men have died within reach of it. We'll come out of this thing together; otherwise, I'll walk out of it my ownself."

✦ ✦ ✦ ✦ ✦

The Apple Tree Cafe, San Luis Obispo, California
Six days earlier

The light breeze blowing into San Luis Obispo carried with it the crisp scent of salt from the Pacific. Zac Cobb watched the leaves on the oaks ripple outside the window. He had passed the point of dreading good-byes; at least that was what he kept telling himself. It seemed as if every time he had to say good-bye, he had to go through the explanation of why he continued to do the job he was so good at. It was a ritual he tired of.

He sat in Jenny's small restaurant, probing the remainder of his apple pie and listening as Jenny put away the pots in the kitchen. Most of the customers had left. He never tired of watching the way she moved. There was a deliberate, determined femininity to Jenny Hays. Each step, each movement, and each word meant something.

Now, with the idea of leaving her once again in his mind, he felt lonely. It was a disposition he had grown accustomed to since the war. He remembered the sensation of standing over his ma's and pa's graves out back of their place after he walked back from the surrender. Only then did he know what the word lonely meant. He had lived with the feeling in some way every day since. He thought about how very funny it was that his loneliness hadn't bothered him until people who loved him entered his life once again.

As Jenny came through the swinging doors from the kitchen, she pushed at her golden hair with the back of her hand. She cast a glance at the bedroll and gear Zac had placed against the wall. His carefully bagged Sharps rifle stood upright in the corner. Forcing a smile, she held up the coffeepot in her hand. "How long will you be gone?" she asked.

"Hard to say." He pushed his cup forward. "Might be a month or better. Gotta be back before we start to calve on the ranch."

She sat down and poured a cup. Leaning forward, she smiled once again at him. "I'm glad you were able to find your brother."

He sipped the steaming cup of coffee. "It was an added ease to the trip."

"And for you to be at his wedding, it must have felt like being part of a family again."

"It did have a queer feelin' to it. Guess I've been so used to just being by myself for so long that sitting down with somebody that knew me in diapers made me feel a might funny."

She poured herself a cup, her eyes dancing as she sipped it. "I say something wrong?"

"No, it was just the thought of you ever being in diapers that took me by surprise."

"Well, I wasn't born in buckskins with a knife between my teeth."

"No, I don't suppose you were." She took several sips and eyed him carefully, as if trying to drive off the thought of her man in diapers. Helplessness was something she found very hard to associate with Zac.

"He did give me a picture of the family that I'd forgotten about."

"Can I see it?"

Reaching into his shirt pocket, he took out a small photograph in a tin-plated frame and handed it to Jenny.

"Which one are you?"

"I'm the youngest," Zac said, "the scrawny little kid with the frown on his face."

Jenny studied the picture, smiling as she looked at the Zac Cobb of long ago. His long, angular look had always appealed to her. The sharp features of his face and the large black mustache he sported these days showed him to be a formidable man, but Jenny knew better. The large dark brown eyes that expressed a depth of feeling gave him away, and that part about him hadn't changed in the least. She handed the photograph back to him. "You know, sometimes I think the thing I'd want most in life would be to have a long talk with your mother."

"You'd have liked her."

"I'm sure I would have. Any woman that could have reined in you four boys must have been some kind of woman."

"She did it with a kind hand, most of the time. I suppose our respect for her and Pa was the thing that kept us in check." He smiled. "'Course, Pa's razor strap may have had something to do with it, too."

"You boys were beaten?"

"We were never beaten." He paused. "But we got ourselves some good old-fashioned whuppin's, and we deserved it more times than we got it. Pa would take us aside, and we'd have to be the ones to explain what we had done wrong and why we deserved a whuppin'."

"That seems odd. Surely he knew why he was punishing you."

"Oh, he knew all right. He just wanted to make sure we did. And

24

he'd lay it on good and hard, too. But I must say, I can't never remember him being angry when he whipped any of us. 'Course, Julian probably got him the closest to it."

"Why was that?"

"Well, Julian was the oldest and I guess Pa just expected more from him. I reckon it would be easy for a man to raise a boy and expect him to do all the things he never did his ownself. You know, try to make up for his mistakes by making sure his children don't make their own. Sometimes I feel that way about Skip, and he's not even my own. A man gets older and learns the best way to live, and all of a sudden he wants to plant it straight into the mind of a child, without the child having to learn it in the same way. That's not right. A youngster has his own right to a childhood. He shouldn't have to deal with all the finished thinking of being a man too soon."

"And do you think Julian resented all of that pressure being put on him?"

"He did have quite a lot of it. Pa coming back from the Mexican War with only one leg pushed a lot of the work on Julian. I think it put a lot of hardness in him, too, sorta steeled him up for life. I looked up to him a lot, too. Him being the oldest of us, the rest of us couldn't get far away from admiring him."

Zac sipped on his coffee. "Sometimes on a cold night in north Georgia, a night when there was snow on the ground, I would wake up. The moon would shine through the window and put a cold white square right on the wooden floor. Those were the times I'd see Julian sitting up in his bed, looking out the window. He'd just be staring out into the night, almost as if he was somewhere else. Me, when I stayed awake, I'd try to read. Julian would sit up and imagine."

"You two must have been very close."

"No, he always said that, my being the baby, Ma sorta coddled me. She taught me with real gentleness and gave me a love for good books and music."

"That must account for you and the violin?"

"I reckon it does at that. The violin is an instrument that takes loving attention to learn. I think it was her excuse to spend more time with me. Sometimes on a night at the ranch when I have it under my chin, I can feel myself drifting away to places I have never gone, places I've read about but never seen or touched."

"Maybe it's only the violin you can show your true feeling to."

He removed his pipe from his pocket and took out a buckskin bag filled with his special mixture of tobaccos. Even though she hadn't said it, he could tell that what was coming just might be some notion of him settling down. Long ago Zac had learned to use his pipe to avoid the uneasiness of conversation. Biting down on it might just help him avoid words he would feel sorry for later.

Stuffing the pipe bowl, he raked a match on the leg of the chair and lit it. Clamping his teeth around the stem, he puffed it to life. Fastening his eyes on her, he grimaced his words around the smoking pipe stem. Even as he said them, he knew they would produce more of what he was trying hard to avoid. "Being with the people I love has a great deal of appeal to me. The hankering grows every day. I reckon, though, I still got too much of the Georgia coon left in me." He pulled out his watch and opened the lid. "You gonna walk with me to the station?"

"Don't I always?"

Reaching across the table, he picked up her hand and gently squeezed it. "I appreciate you most in times like this for the things I know you're thinkin' about but won't say."

"I don't need to. It's all been said before."

"Maybe that's what makes you so different from most women I've run into. They all seem to think that by keeping on with the talking, they'll get it said better, and you just say it by the way you look at me. Girl, sometimes I'd swear you were staring right down into my soul."

"Maybe it's because I know you. You have always found your own way. You don't follow anyone very easily."

"All the same, it's the look in your eyes that says it best for me. I ain't gonna go through all my excuses again, and I ain't gonna make no promises I can't keep. This will all end and if you're not here for me when it does, I'll understand. There ain't nothing special about me that should keep a woman like you hanging on."

"Zachary Taylor Cobb, you know full well that I'll be here for you. I love you, and you know it. Love isn't something you wait to get. It's something that makes you want to keep on giving."

He pulled his hand away and straightened his pipe. "You've given enough already. Sometimes I'm afraid that when and if I get through with what I do, there will be little left for you but the pain of a broken body to put up with."

"You mean like your mother had to deal with?"

"Yes, something had changed about Pa, at least that was what people who knew him before he went off to Mexico told me. Mother fell in love with the man who marched off but had to live with the man who came home."

"And because you had this deep love for your mother, you want to spare me from a similar experience?"

"Yes, I suppose so."

"It appears to me that you're treating me just like Skip. Because of the lessons you've learned, you want to take away my learning. Well, I'm not a child. I have my own life to live, and I hold myself fully responsible for the way I choose to live it. If I decide to love you and wait for you, it's my decision to make. I'm not a glass vase to be protected and placed on the highest shelf in your life. I'm a grown woman."

"I suppose I just worry that you might not know just what you're getting into, or that you might be holding out hopes for something that will never happen."

"At times in the past I know I loved you not for what you are or for what you do, but for what I knew you could become. Now though, I think I'm settling into the comfort of knowing you for the man I love now. It's not my job to ever change you. That's God's work. My job is just to love you for what you are."

Blushing, he took the pipe out of his mouth and started to speak.

She reached out and put her fingers to his lips. "Don't say it. I don't ever want to hear you say it until I know you're ready to do something about those feelings of yours. Some men say the words so easy, a girl gets the feeling they've all been said to others before."

"You know, I ain't never said those words since I said them to my momma when I went off to the war. I suppose I didn't ever think I'd even recollect the thoughts again. The killing and the dying I've seen since I was fifteen just tends to choke them right out of me."

"I know."

"If I had my choice of what to be, I'd want to be the man in your mind, somebody you could depend on, somebody who could give you back everything you give, and then some. But the only thing I am is the man you see before you. It's not the only thing I'll ever be, but it is what I am right now."

Placing her hand back on his, she gently rubbed his fingers. "The man you are right now is the man I love. I hope you find what you're looking for, and I know that when you do, you're gonna discover that it's the thing you've had beside you and the person you've had in you all the time. Until that happens, I know you have to be the best at what you do."

He pulled the pipe from his mouth. Silence passed between them. "You don't know how that makes me feel," he said. "I've got enough on my mind when I work, and to have you say something like that just puts my mind to case."

"Just do your job and come home." Her eyes seemed plaintive. "I know you all too well, Zac. No matter what those people send you to do, you always find something else besides that pricks your conscience. It's one of the things I admire most about you and the thing that scares me to death. Surprise me this time, though. Do only the job you were sent to do and get back early, please—for me."

CHAPTER 3

+ + + + + + +

A small valley north of Prescott
Tuesday evening, shortly after sunset

The moon shone bright in the Arizona sky. Mangus signaled to the warriors riding with him. The sound of this many Indian ponies could easily echo across the rocks and might mean the death of one of the men who rode with him. He didn't have to say a word. A sign from his hand was enough to tell them what he wanted, that and a look from his sharp black eyes. Speaking to men without words was a skill he had developed from childhood. His wide face and the lightning-bolt eyes that darted their glances at others had always been able to betray his heart to the people around him.

The white man could never understand this. To them, noise and words, gibberish that spoke only about the emptiness of their souls, were the only ways they could make sense to one another. Too much talk was a white man's disease. Many times he had even seen them stare at scribbles on paper and pretend to know another human being's thoughts. He had seen the missionary man read from the big black book and claim to read the thoughts of God. No one could read God's thoughts but the Indian, and these were things not found in the paper scratches of the white man.

The ghost dance had taught him much over the last several months. The holy man had called them out to dance the dance. He had lifted his face to the wind and spun around the fire circle all night. The dance had changed him on the inside, making him see things that he had never seen before, and now he believed. Perhaps even the God the white man talked about, the Christian God, would help the Indian get his land back. It could be that this God's resurrection power would bring the old warriors back. Perhaps there would be this thousand years of peace on the earth, peace where he and the other men of his people would be allowed to roam.

The old medicine man Nochaydelklinne had spun his tale of the end times with much power and had warned what would happen if the people of the sun did not listen to the new medicine. The old man talked hypnotically. The drums beat, and the tribe danced.

Nochaydelklinne had envisioned the hour of the white man's disappearance. The white man would go away, and once again the Indian would roam freely with the resurrected bodies of all those who had died before. Mangus knew of this thing; even the missionary had taught him about the resurrection. It had happened before, and it would happen again; all it needed was a man like himself to believe and take the step of faith.

He looked down the hill at the store. It had always made him feel weak to walk into the white man's store, but that was before. Now he felt strong. The white men would snicker at the Indians in their stores and then cheat them out of what they owned. They stole from them the same way they had taken their land. The strength these men held over the Indian was only the power of the gun—the gun and the pony soldiers that came by the multitude. Mangus knew that. The white man's strength did not come from within; he could not tell when the rain would fall as his people could.

Mangus no longer feared the white man. The thing he feared worse was the death inside him he felt when he saw his people bow their heads to the strangers. That he would live out his life and no longer be a man, that he would become one more of the pony soldiers' Indian cattle—these were the nightmares that made him awaken in the night.

This would have to be the time when he and the other men who were still men rose up and struck down the white-eyes. General Crook's words were no longer listened to by the white-eyes' chiefs in Washington City. He had promised them they could stay on their lands for as long as the hills stood, and now the new agent wanted to move the Yavapai to San Carlos and make them no longer a people. To mix with the Apache in the pens of the San Carlos would be to lose their place on the earth. The two-hundred mile walk would kill the old people. He could not allow that to happen as long as he had breath.

He would ride down with Gandara and another to the white

man's store below. There were only twenty of them now, but he knew that if he could find more rifles, other men would join him. The people respected him. Even when he stood in the white man's lines to get the worm-eaten flour and spoiled beef, the people all watched him. It was as if they knew that one day Mangus would finally rise up, and when he did, they would all be waiting to join him.

He nodded his chin at Gandara—only half an inch, but it was enough. His glance at the other man kept him on his pony. Together the three of them slowly rode down the side of the hill to the dimly lit store. By now, the white man would have eaten more than enough to feed an Indian family for a week and was probably smoking his tobacco. But when the sun rose in the east, the people could step around the bodies of the man, his white squaw, and his bleached children and get whatever they wanted. No one would be alive to tell them what they could not have. The people would take the food and blankets from the store's shelves and remember Mangus. They would remember and they would know that a real man walked among them once more.

The big English box in the back of the store banged out its foreign music into the desert night air. Mangus had heard it many times before—a gay, lively, foreign music swimming between the dark hills when the sky was black. He had often thought it to be the spirits of a thousand white-eyes bragging about how they had conquered his people. The woman would sit in front of the big box and make the foreign spirits play in a land that didn't belong to them. Tonight he would make the noise stop, make it stop so that the people would once again hear only the music of the night wind as it slipped around the mountains.

The three of them padded their horses up to the front of the store and slid to the ground, allowing the reins to drop. He held up his hand and the two warriors froze in place. Moving silently around the store, he peeked into the shiny glass window. There they were, the white squaw behind the big box and the two little white girls beside her. The three of them seemed lost in the spirit noise that came from the thing. Across the room, he could see the keeper of the store reading the book of gibberish.

Mangus rejoined his men. They mounted the steps with long, silent strides and slightly pushed open the door. Mangus took hold of the bell above the door, stopping its noise before it sounded out, and held it as Gandara and the other warrior slipped in.

In the far end of the cluttered room, he could see light creeping around the edge of a closed door. The white man's noise continued to sound and the men skirted around the counter, taking down several rifles that stood in the rack. When the other warrior reached for a jug of whiskey behind the bar, Gandara touched his arm and shook his head, making the man return his attention to what they had come to do.

Each of them grabbed for the rifle shells in the boxes under the rack. Carefully, they loaded the weapons, one round at a time. Each of them jacked shells into the chamber. Slowly, they moved across the big cluttered room toward the noise.

Reaching the door, Mangus straightened himself to his full height. The streaks of red and white paint ran from the corners of his eyes, widening down his cheeks and ending at the edges of his jaw. When he had put the paint on that day, he had thought of his tears, tears of pain now turning to tears of pure hate. There would be no tears for the white man and his women, only shouts of victory. He turned the brass knob and pushed the door open.

The white squaw sat behind the box with her two small girls sitting beside her. When the woman saw him standing there, she gasped and stared at him, unable to speak or move. The two little girls continued to play, each lost in the making of the white man's noise. "What are you doing here?" the woman finally asked.

The storekeeper, who sat at the back of the room in a chair, put down the book of the white man's scratching and jumped to his feet. "Now, see here, it's too late to buy anything." He marched toward the three Indians, waving his arms. "You'll have to come back in the morning."

As he neared the three men, Gandara pulled out his knife like a snake poised for the kill. The man continued toward them, seemingly more taken with the fearful females than watching the looks on the faces of the three warriors. Gandara struck him suddenly with the knife, launching the point of the blade up deep into the man's belly. He watched the shopkeeper's last breath pass out from his lips, but the sound of the man's dying gasps were quickly drowned out by the screams of the three females.

Mangus looked at them calmly. He felt no panic as he watched them shiver and scream. Studying them carefully, as a man looking at a new horse, he saw that each had hair the color of honey, long hair that would make fine prizes for the top of his lodge.

His chest swelled with pride. This would be the way he lived the remainder of his life. He no longer had any desire to be one of the old men shuffling through the white man's line for bread. To live that way was to lose his soul forever, to send his spirit crying into the night in search of what it meant to be a man of the people. No—he would die a man, a young man with pride.

✦ ✦ ✦ ✦ ✦

On a hillside near Jerome
Later that same night

Miles away, Raincloud waited with her baby girl. She had busied herself all through the day, doing what was expected of a white squaw—like the women in their underthings whose pictures were plastered on her husband's walls. The shirts were washed and folded neatly, the way he always wanted them. She gently patted the fry bread and laid it carefully in the skillet. Listening to the popping noise made by the oil, she once again glanced at the paper money that was stuffed into the old jar, sitting up high on the shelf.

She had gone with him to the store and watched as he gave it to the man to buy whiskey and the few things she could beg him to buy for the baby. This paper money was the strength of the white man, and she knew it. It was a power that could never belong to her. There was no power left for her. She had traded what had been in her to the man who kept her for his pleasure, and his pleasure was now in the beating and stain of humiliation he gave her every night of her life.

She sighed deeply as she thought back on her life. Her years at the missionary school had taught her much. The missionary's wife had taught her to speak and read the white man's tongue. What she could never understand was the white man's mind.

She turned the bread and looked out the window at the sky. Clouds were running away from the golden moon. She breathed out a heavy sigh, longing to be one of the clouds—to take wing and fly away from the valley, the dirty mine, and the dirty man who beat her. He had become the deepest regret of her life.

She could no longer go back to her people. Her husband would find her there. Her father would give her back, and she would have to return to her husband in disgrace, in shame—and then he would beat her bare back until she was sick with pain.

There was no love left in her for her own life, only for that of the baby. She had seen the man kick the girl as he walked out of the house and knew that soon her pain would also be the pain of her daughter. It made her heart sick to know that the dishonor she felt, the girl would feel too. He had called the baby a "half-breed." In fact now he only called her "breed."

Raincloud took out the bread and laid a slab of carefully sliced bacon into the bubbling oil. It popped and spit at her, stinging her arm. Shortly, she would no longer have the beauty everyone had said belonged to her. She knew that. The man would beat her and drive away her unblemished complexion and radiant smile. She ladled a spoonful of the oil into a cup and blew gently on it.

Turning the bacon, she walked to the counter that held her few things in a piece of yellow cloth. Taking out a smooth tortoise-shell comb, she walked back to the counter where she had placed the cooling grease. Carefully dabbing it onto the comb, she stroked the mixture into her long raven black hair. The slick grease would make her hair shine. To give some attention to herself, even if just a few moments with a comb, might give her back some pride. Gently, she pulled the comb through the black thickness, one stroke after another.

Taking the bacon out of the pan, she removed the skillet from the fire. She would have to wait for him to come back before she could eat. He would come back drunk—she could hope for nothing different—and the white man's money he had taken with him would be gone forever. He had no power over that. His only power seemed to be the one he had over her now, over her and over the baby.

The child began to cry. She walked hurriedly over to the baby's bed and picked her up. Sitting in the rocking chair, she lowered her dress and allowed the child to suck.

Several hours passed before she heard the sound of the man. She could hear his cursing long before she heard his horse. She stood beside the now sleeping child and straightened her dress. From his sounds, and from what she had experienced many times before, she knew that it was best to go out and face him on the porch. That way there was a better chance that he would beat her there, away from their sleeping child. She took one more look at the baby and, opening the door, stepped out onto the dark porch.

The man weaved in his saddle as he pulled up to the house. Struggling to get his feet out of the stirrups, he collapsed and fell to the ground with a loud thud. His moans and curses were followed by angry shouts. "Get over here, woman. Get over here and help me up!"

Scrambling to his side, she heaved and hoisted him onto his feet.

"Lousy injun squaw! Far as I'm concerned, you is a cloud with no rain."

"I have food fixed for you inside, bacon and fry bread."

"Lousy injun squaw." He leaned on her shoulder, the smell of liquor filling the night air.

"The baby is sleeping," she said.

"Lousy breed. If'n I can't sleep, ain't no lousy breed gonna sleep neither. You put my horse away, woman." He staggered, blowing his angry breath into her face. "Put my horse away and come on back in the house. I'm gonna show you what I do with lousy injun squaws and their breeds."

"I am sorry. What have I done to you, my husband?"

"You do enough to me just by breathing, woman. Ain't no decent woman 'round for miles, so I gots to hold up with some 'pache squaw. Folks 'round town keep callin' me the squaw man, and I is plumb tired of it. I is tired of it, ya hear?"

She nodded, then leaned him against one of the posts that held up the roof of the porch and backed away from him.

He swung his powerful arm and sent her flying to the dirt with the force of his blow. His own sudden movement made him lurch and grasp at the roughhewn timber that held him upright.

Raincloud scrambled to her knees and bowed her head. If she could just take her beating out in the open, away from the baby, that was all she wanted. He was already so tired and drunk, she knew he couldn't stand up much longer.

"That's just the start of it for you tonight," he yelled. "If'n I can'ts get no pleasure from you no other ways, I'm gonna beat you till you turn white. If'n I dust you all over with some of that flour, it might make you easier to look on."

She crawled toward him to make the beating easier to manage.

"Afore you know it, woman, I'm gonna make you one of them dead injuns. Folks in these parts admires the dead ones lots better than the ones still breathin'." Sending a powerful kick in her direction, he lost his balance and crashed to the ground.

She crouched beside the saddled horse and watched him roll over onto his back. He moaned and began to curse. The whiskey had taken its toll on his consciousness, and in a matter of moments, his curses were followed by silence and then by the sound of a gentle snore. She got to her feet. Lifting her head to the sky, she watched the clouds continue to move slowly away from the low-slung moon.

Hiking up her dress, she moved around the sleeping man and into the house. Hurriedly, she took a bag and stuffed the food she had prepared into it. She picked up a sharp knife and stuck it behind her belt. Taking dried beef and flour and some of the dried apricots she had begged him to buy, she filled the small sack.

Glancing around the room, she racked her mind for what she might carry. She snatched up the small bundled cloth that contained her personal things and placed it in the bag. Picking up the pitcher of cool water, she filled a gourd. Then, taking the canteen, she filled it to the brim as well. Moving around the room, she stopped and began rummaging through the trunk. She found a change of clothes for her and two for the baby.

She would be ashamed no longer. She would trade her shame now for the fear of running. As she looked around the room, she saw nothing in the place that was hers. The pictures of women that he had taken out of the catalog were posted everywhere, plastered up for all to see. She hated everything her gaze fell upon, everything that reminded her of what she had become.

Scooping up the sleeping child, she quieted the baby with her finger. She laid the child upon the Indian carrying board that her husband hated. He hated everything that was Apache, and that was what she was, an Apache, the object of her husband's hatred. Lacing the board up, she slung it behind her and gently bounced up and down to quiet the sleepy child. "We go now," she whispered. "We go where he can never find us, someplace where you will know no shame."

Picking up the bag and the water containers, she started for the door, and then she stopped. She looked back at the jar on the shelf, the jar with the white man's money. Reaching up, she took it.

Hurrying out of the house, she stepped around the still-sleeping man. He lay content in his drunkenness upon the ground, lost in his whiskey.

Her heart pounded with a mixture of fear and long-forgotten pride. He would be behind her now. She would go someplace where his money would buy her something to live with, someplace away from her people, away from where he could find her. She and the child would make their own people now. They would be with each other forever, two birds flying away with the moon together. He would sleep until the heat of the day awakened him, and by then she and the child would be far away.

She placed her moccasin in the stirrup and mounted the horse. Walking the animal from the house, she reined it to the north and urged the animal into a trot. The quiet night desert stretched out before her. In the distance she could see the moon and the clouds that continued to scatter from its presence.

CHAPTER 4

+ + + + + + +

Phoenix, Arizona
Wednesday morning

The children marched stoically from the cemetery. Ruggles had paid for the plot and the necessary arrangements. He watched them as they walked in the bright sunshine, the boy shaking his hands and winding his head around as if to see a bird in flight when there was none. Both of them seemed accustomed to funerals and, surprisingly, even more accustomed to the feeling of being alone in the world.

"My grandfather died, and we had to bury him before he got stinky," the boy said.

Amy reached out and touched his hand, seemingly more concerned about the continued movement than what her brother had said.

"You two will be wanting something to eat," Ruggles said. "We can meander over to the hotel. They put on a mighty fine spread over there."

"You needn't bother any longer," Amy shot back. "You've done more than enough already." The sarcasm was not lost on Ruggles.

"My grandfather died, and we had to bury him before he got stinky," the boy continued to chant.

Staring straight ahead, Ruggles deliberately ignored Tommy and continued to walk. "I made a promise to your grandfather."

"Yes, and I know what a gambler's promises are worth."

"And what would that be?"

"What they've always been worth—the turn of the next card."

"You always make it a practice to judge a man you don't know?"

Amy stopped in her tracks and looked him up and down. "My

38

daddy died during The War between the States, and my mother married Tommy's father. We moved to New Orleans, where I spent my childhood. I've seen more gamblers in my life than you could ever hope to know. Not the casual kind that goes into a saloon with a notion of luck on his mind, but the kind like you, one who prides himself in what he thinks is a scientific knowledge of the next card. You all end up the same way because you are all the same."

"And how do we all end up?"

"Like my grandfather back there, full of notions that there are untold riches just ahead and finally laid to rest in a coffin purchased with borrowed money. Lady luck is a harlot. There is no love in her."

"You seem a might too educated for a slip of a girl."

"I've been everywhere and done just about everything. I'm almost eighteen, but sometimes I feel like I've lived a hundred years, especially when it comes to men like you."

He ran his hand over his chin. "It seems you have me pegged, little sister. Maybe I've got a lot to learn from someone like you. This firsthand education of yours will give us something to talk about on our way up north to that ranch of yours."

"You forget, it's no longer our ranch. I've only barely seen it twice. Grandfather won it in a card game from an out-of-luck Mormon."

"That may be, but I swore to him that I'd see the two of you settled, and that's what I intend to do. Besides, I have no intention of holding on to a ranch of any kind, especially one in Utah. I've made some special arrangements, and I'll see you there and make sure you're cared for. Then I'll get on about my business and leave you to yours, I can promise you that."

Amy took the boy's hand and walked off. "Promises," Amy said as she walked away, her voice full of ridicule.

A short time later the three of them were seated in the hotel dining room, trying to enjoy a noon meal. They ate in silence, except for Tommy, who continued to talk. "My grandfather died, and we had to bury him before he got stinky." He slung his hands and waggled his head. Ruggles leaned over and with his knife and fork cut the boy's meat.

"He will eat when he's hungry," Amy said.

"I'm sure he will, but I won't have him eating with his fingers."

She cocked her head at him and narrowed her eyes. "And what is it that makes you want to be so helpful?"

"It's just the way I was raised. I was born and brought up in Spartanburg, South Carolina, trained at the end of a switch to be a gentleman."

"Humph." She popped a piece of meat into her mouth and chewed vigorously. "I think I've had my fill of Southern gentlemen."

"Besides, like I said before, I promised your grandfather." He laid down his knife and fork and looked her in the eye. "I can tell you one thing, though, it isn't your charming company that is taking me out of my way. Let's get this straight. I've got my own life to live. I plan on taking you and Tommy here to that ranch and getting you two settled, or you can come on with me to Denver. I'm heading that way to gamble."

"We do have a great-aunt who lives there, but she's never seen us, and I have no desire to drop in on long-lost relatives with the notion of them adopting us and the trouble Tommy would bring."

Ruggles watched the boy swing his head around and look at the ceiling, not at any part of it in particular, but at all of it at once. "Hopefully, we can leave on the stage I hired tomorrow," he said. "Most stage lines only stay in business for a few years down here and none of them go north where we want to go. I had to find a man who's buying a coach and offer him plenty to take us north to St. George. We ought to have little company, and you should be comfortable. Now, your experience with men in general and gamblers in particular is something you'll have to carry around with you in your lifetime, but it has little to do with Lawrence Ruggles."

She placed her hands in her lap. "I am sorry. Whatever else I am, my mother did raise me to be a lady. You have been more than generous. Your winning of my grandfather's money was with his full consent. Had it not been you, it would have been someone else."

A large, round-faced man wearing a high hat and duster walked in the door of the dining room. He surveyed the room before laying eyes on Ruggles. After striding over to where the three of them were eating, he stood at the table. "I'm Hec Peters," he said as he wiped his mouth. "I'm driving that northbound stage outta here tomorrow afternoon. Understand you folks paid for it?"

At the table next to theirs, a red-haired man in a beat-up stovepipe hat leaned over as if to get a better listen. Amy's eyes caught the man's, and he smiled and pulled away slightly. Ruggles put down his knife and fork.

"My grandfather died, and we had to bury him before he got

stinky." The boy looked up at Peters and once again gave out the story of his day.

Ruggles barely cast a glance in Tommy's direction. "Yes, that's right. The three of us are going to Utah Territory tomorrow and then I head on to Denver."

"Well, I come in here to tell you folks 'bout the trouble. Seems some Yavapai renegades jumped the reservation northwest of here. This here injun ghost dance business has got everythin' in a tizzy 'round here. Now, I got me a shotgun messenger, and a fine one at that, and the army's s'pose to be meetin' us up ahead. We contracted to haul some ammunition for 'em. You might just wanna consider waitin' 'round here fer a spell, though, till this all clears up."

Ruggles looked at Amy, who shot out her lower lip. "You can stay if you like, Mr. Ruggles." The look of disdain was hard to wipe off her face, in spite of the recent apology. "But my brother and I have no desire to remain in Arizona. The sooner we leave, the sooner we can get on with our lives."

Peters scratched his jaw. "Well, I can tell you, ma'am, if me and Butch didn't have this job, we wouldn't be goin' our own selves. This Mangus feller that has them Yavapai warriors of his runnin' 'round is a bad one. I seen him once, meaner'n a teased snake. Now I hear he's even hooking up with some southern Paiutes. This ghost dance religion is bad business."

"And are you sure he's between us and Utah?" Ruggles asked.

"Hard to say. The telegraph 'tween here and Prescott has been burning with talk of him. He burned a ranch north of here two nights ago and last night killed a storekeeper and his family, took a bunch a rifles and ammunition. With all them new guns, he's got more hotheads joining up with him every day. And that bothers me a mite more. The army's got the stage carrying more ammunition for the patrol that's s'pose to meet us. Kinda makes us a temptin' target. We got us some gold on board too, but I tell you, that Mangus bunch has got everybody's nerves on edge. I don't reckon we're gonna find no highwaymen venturing out 'round here."

"And you think that Mangus is still north of us?"

"Lord only knows where he is by now. I'd say though that once we got passed Lee's Ferry we'd be okay. That's the edge of Ute land. Don't think Mangus would be raiding the Utes or them Navajos, either. 'Course it's gonna take us a week to ten days to get there."

"We do appreciate your warning," Ruggles said. "We'll talk it over between us and make up our minds."

Peters pulled on the brim of his hat. "Suit yerself, then. The boss has gots to pay for that new stage, and I got myself a few more passengers to find 'fore I can eat. Just wanted you to know all the likelihoods before you go."

As Peters walked out of the dining room, the red-haired man next to them laid down his napkin and he, along with the Mexican across the table from him, got up. Amy caught his eye once again, and he tipped his hat to her and smiled.

"I don't like that man," she said.

Ruggles smiled. "I'd say there aren't many men you do like."

Her eyes narrowed, and he quickly brought the conversation back to the issue at hand. "Now, about this trip, what's your pleasure? Like I said, there aren't any stages that go north. If we don't get this new one, we'll have to buy horses and ride north ourselves."

"Traveling all that way by horseback has little appeal for me."

"I like horses," Tommy said. He clutched at Amy's arm. "Can we ride the horses?"

Ruggles smiled. "He does listen when he wants to, doesn't he?"

"Yes, Tommy has a very selective attention. I, for one, however, would prefer to take the stage. For all we know, it might be a month before the army has things back in hand. Besides, if we wait around here, you may have all of that money of yours lost at the tables."

The tip of Ruggles's mustache dipped down. "You do have a point there."

"No, I'm for leaving tomorrow. The quicker you get us to that ranch, the quicker you can be gone."

"You sound like you're anxious to be rid of me, like you're the one that won *my* care in a poker game."

+ + + + +

The next afternoon saw a cloudburst that swept into the streets and back out again. The three of them walked out onto the boardwalk in front of the stage and handed their bags up to the driver. Ruggles had his coat off, and Amy noticed that he was now wearing a Colt .45 strapped to his hip. "Are you any good with that thing?" she asked.

"A man in my profession has to be good with his hands, and you will find, should it become necessary, that I am very proficient in the use of firearms." As he handed up one of the bags, she saw a derringer strapped to the inside of his left arm. She couldn't help but notice that the apparatus around the gun had a coiled spring beneath the stock. The springed apparatus could place the little gun in a man's hand instantly.

A lanky older man with a high forehead walked out of the stage office and handed up his carpetbag to Peters. His eyes were deep set and a large mustache swooped down his face to a point just below the jawline. Out of his mouth hung a twisted cigar. He bowed slightly at the waist and smiled at Amy. "Morning, ma'am. May I present myself? I am the Reverend Isaac Black, serving as an itinerant pastor to the people scattered about and an occasional missionary to our Indian brethren."

Amy extended her hand. "Pleased to meet you, sir."

Ruggles reached over and took the man's outstretched hand. "Name's Lawrence Ruggles."

Amy glared at him, her offered hand hanging in midair. Quickly, she dropped it to her side.

Reverend Black's eyes were immediately drawn to the sight of Tommy, who was now climbing onto the top of the stage. "You be careful up there, son. This thing bounces all over the road and we wouldn't want to lose you."

The boy ignored him and began to swing his head around and survey the sky.

He continued to watch the boy, who smirked and droned from the corner of his mouth. "Little boys who fail to listen to the advice of old men also fail to live to be young men." He took out the cigar and flicked ash to the boardwalk.

Ruggles cleared his throat. "This is Miss Franklin and up there is her brother, Tommy."

The man smiled and nodded at Amy.

"I know few men of the cloth who smoke," Amy said.

"Then welcome to the West, miss," the man said as he clamped the cigar back into his mouth. His lips creased into a wide grin at her. "I believe in the moderation of all things, which is why I refuse myself the privilege of smoking in my sleep."

From the station, a tall, thin man walked out. On his arm hung a woman with thick, blotted rouge and brightly painted lips. He wore a low-slung six-gun and wheeled a large double-barrel shotgun. His smile was toothy and broad and his hat was cocked back, showing a grease-slicked full head of sandy hair that swooped down his forehead.

43

"Let's go, Butch!" Peters called out. "We gonna be at it all night till we get to the wells."

He leaned down and planted a lingering kiss on the woman. "Gotta go, Suzie Q. Gotta pro-o-o-o-tect these folk from the wild 'pache and desperadoes hereabouts. Some men gotta be heroes, ya know, and some men just gotta be plain old folk."

The woman pushed up on her toes to kiss him back. Then she giggled.

Ruggles opened the door to the coach to assist Amy inside. She glared at him and pulled back her arm. He smiled and stood aside as she climbed aboard, followed by the Reverend Black. Standing by the door, Ruggles's attention was immediately drawn to a large group of people marching down the boardwalk. A tall man with a star on his vest held a large Chinese woman by the arm, guiding her along the walkway as several women haughtily paraded behind them.

The stout woman's straight black hair was pulled up in pigtails and wound into buns on each side of her head. Her heavily made-up face, the dark-lined eyes and bright cheeks, did nothing to hide the fact that she had long ago lost the bloom of youth. Her foreign-looking, bright blue silk dress hung to her side and rustled when she walked.

"China Mary's going with you, Hec," the man called up to the driver. "There ain't no way she can stay 'round here no more."

"Going with me?" Peter blustered. "We're headin' north to Utah. There ain't nothing up there for China Mary, and them Mormon folk won't take well to her, no ways."

"I don't rightly care where you're goin', just so Mary here goes with you."

Ruggles stepped aside as the lawman put the woman on the stage.

"This here's a special fare," Peters barked down. "Boss is just starting this northbound up and it'll cost plenty."

"Town council will pay her fare," the lawman called up to Peters. "Wherever she lands, just you make sure she don't come back to the Arizona Territory, ya hear?" The starpacker crossed his arms and stared up at Peters. The gaggle of women surrounded him on each side, their eyes filled with contentment at a job well done.

Ruggles followed the large woman into the coach and had barely seated himself when Peters swung his whip, sending the stage barreling down the street. It was going to be a long but interesting ride.

CHAPTER 5

+ + + + + + +

It had taken Zac almost a week to get to Fort Verde. At Prescott, Ken Trasker, the agent for Wells Fargo, met him. Trasker was a man of the soil come west, a man who felt uncomfortable out of overalls but wore a suit anyway. After a night's rest in noisy Prescott, he put Zac's things in his wagon and the two of them headed out to the fort. The sun was just beginning to rise when the two men started their drive. In the desert, there was no better time to get down to anything than at early sunlight.

Zac sat and stared straight ahead as Trasker talked.

"We heard lots about you down here, but didn't think we'd ever see you. Heard tell that you was quittin' and settlin' down to ranchin'."

Trasker made the statement and looked at him, expecting an answer, but Zac continued to look straight ahead. Trasker went on. "Well, it don't make no nevermind, we is just glad you showed up. We ain't got no idea of what we is up against here—might be injuns, then again, might not. And what with this ghost dance business, the army jest ain't got no time to run around chasin' hold-up men. We've had ranches burning north of us fer the last four days. Folks is spooked, sure 'nuff."

Zac gazed toward the mountains to the north of them. They had a commanding view of the Verde Valley. One man and a pair of binoculars could just about keep tabs on the whole of this part of Arizona. Trasker continued to talk.

"We've had two coaches hit and the army has lost three payrolls in New Mexico and eastern Arizona. By the time a body runs up the

45

bill on that, it mounts up to over a hundred thousand dollars. Man, I can tell you, money like that would tempt the apostles. The U.S. Marshal has been lookin' abouts on it, but he ain't worth spit when it comes to chasing down a bunch a men across the desert. He's one of them poh-lit-ee-cal appointees."

The sun was high in the sky when they rolled into the fort. A row of whitewashed structures lined the parade field, and behind them, small bluffs dotted the floor of the valley. It was land suitable for farming, which was why the army was closing down the Yavapai reservation and moving them onto the arid land of the Apache to the east. There was nothing fair about it, but that didn't seem to matter much to Washington. It made no difference that the Yavapai had been traditional enemies of the Apache. They'd be together now. After all, Indians were Indians.

Trasker steered the team to the front of the headquarters building and pulled up rein. "Colonel Decker will be waitin' for you in there. I'll introduce you and he can lay out what yer facin'."

After the introductions were made, the colonel picked up a bottle of whiskey and offered some to Zac.

"No, thank you. I don't touch it."

Decker signaled toward a chair. "Please be seated. Then, what are your vices, Mr. Cobb?"

Zac sat down and carefully surveyed the man. There was spit and polish to him; few rose to the rank of colonel without that. There was also an informality that spoke of a man who had bumped up against real life. The colonel's tunic was unbuttoned to the waist, hanging open and exposing the unstarched white shirt beneath it. Zac glanced over at Trasker. "Work, I reckon. Friends of mine would say that leaving home and saying yes to this outfit would be my greatest vice. I am kinda partial to buttermilk as well."

"A man of duty; I like that in a man. Well, I can tell you this, we are more than a little concerned about what we're up against here. These payrolls that have disappeared have come with loss of life. You couldn't have come at a better time, though. This morning we found our payroll patrol. You ought to still have some sign out there. It looks like Apaches did the deed, but I, for one, don't believe it. Injuns ain't got much use for money." He leaned forward. "And I can tell you, with this ghost dance business starting up, the last thing I want to do is take a company of cavalry into the reservation to conduct a search for the army's payroll."

"Seems, then," Zac said, "that taking money from the army is easy pickin's."

"Right now, that's about the size of it. That's why we sent for you. The Secret Service says you're about the best retriever Wells Fargo's got, and just now, we need the best. A man like you can do what a company of men in the field could never hope to accomplish."

"I know a lot about chasing men, but I know next to nothing about this territory."

"That's why I'm sending one of my best Apache scouts with you. Chupta is a good tracker and he knows all the water holes, which around here is the difference between life and death."

"And what makes you think this Chupta is not mixed up with the ghost dancers?"

Decker scratched his chin. "We don't know for certain. You never know about the Indian. That's why I'm talking to you ahead of time, without him present. I suppose that's a chance we're taking."

"No, Colonel, that's a chance I'm taking, and it's generally why I prefer to work alone."

Decker paused and smiled. "I understand. But that's why Wells Fargo is paying you a five-thousand-dollar bonus, plus your usual fee of ten percent of the recovered money. That's an enormous bonus, but it's worth it to the government if we can put an end to all this." He swore. "Man, I can tell you, the army would be history for me with that kind of money in my pocket."

"Durn tootin'," Trasker chimed in.

"I've only been in Arizona for three years," Decker went on, "but I can tell you, you'd be taking a greater chance out there all by yourself. I wouldn't give John the Baptist more than four days out there without a knowledge of this here territory."

Trasker laughed.

"Now, Chupta will take you to where the last payroll was stolen, and hopefully you can pick up the trail from there. You'll have to be very prudent. Mangus has taken a bunch of his Yavapai out of the reservation west of here, and they are creating some kind of roaming war. They don't normally get along well with the Apache, but with this ghost dance we don't know what might happen. Chupta can steer you clear of trouble with the Apache, but if you meet up with Mangus, you'd better have your skeedaddle clothes on."

"I always do."

A half hour later, Zac had chosen his mount, a large, sixteen-hands-high buckskin mare with white face and stockings. He put his Sharps in the rifle scabbard under the saddle, and Decker had the quartermaster give him three canteens, over a week's supply of dried beef and flour, and some dried fruit.

He walked the buckskin out to the parade ground and spotted Chupta right away. The Apache was a smallish man in a blue tunic with corporal stripes. His legs seemed bowed, with moccasins that covered his calves. His long black hair was shoulder length and a red bandana was tied around his head. Zac thought his face resembled that of a vulture, with wiry features, polished black eyes, and a narrow, beaklike nose. There was no smile, and Chupta seemed to be doing just exactly the same thing as Zac, taking the lay of the man he would be spending his time with. Chupta spoke up, "You Cobb?"

Zac nodded.

"Good, we go now."

The two of them rode hard the rest of the day and the better part of the next morning before they reached the site of the ambush. Both Zac and Chupta uncinched their saddles and proceeded to look over the area. The victims' bodies had already been removed, and the wind that had blown for the last two days made it difficult to find any sign of the perpetrators' trail. Zac looked out on the grassy desert plains to the south of the site. A rocky outcropping lay to the north of them, its boulders pockmarked by greasewood.

"Let's take a look on the other side of that," Zac said. "Right now, I'm more concerned with how the men who did this thing came up on them without being seen."

Chupta grunted. "Apache come out of the desert. He not be seen."

"That may be, but you don't think it was the Apache, do you?"

"Don't know."

"Why would the Apache take on army payroll escorts?"

"Too many white-eyes to kill all at one time. Better to kill a little at a time."

Taking the horses in hand, the men circled the rocky slope to the north. As they walked, Zac couldn't escape the feeling of being watched. The desert was a lonely place, but in no way did he feel alone. It was as if he had walked into a dark room with someone watching his every move in the twilight. It made the hair on the back of his neck stand on end, and he continued to pan the rocky horizon for any movement that might give away the watcher.

Meandering to the backside of the rocks, Zac stopped at some brush that looked to have been grazed upon by some animals. Pointing, Zac commented, "They picketed their animals here."

Chupta nodded.

The wind had long blown away any horse tracks, making it impossible to tell if they had been shod or unshod like Indian ponies. Zac and Chupta turned over several piles of horse droppings. Zac began to separate one of the piles with his fingers. "I don't speck you folks feed your animals oats."

Chupta shook his head.

Zac threw a stirrup over his saddle and tightened the cinch. "Then, what we're after is a pack of white wolves. You better take me to the closest water hole and we can look for signs there. We may have to go to several of them before we can find out the direction these fellers headed off in."

Near the end of the day, as they approached the second watering spot they had come to, Chupta signaled Zac to dismount and keep low. Dropping the reins of the horses, Zac poured water from his canteen and swabbed the mouth of the buckskin. He crouched low and followed Chupta to the edge of a rocky ledge.

Below them, they could see two Indian ponies. The warriors who had ridden them were down on their bellies drinking out of the flat, low-lying pool.

Scrub oak sheltered the area, and had it been the heat of the day, Zac knew they might have been in for a long wait. But given it was near to evening, he figured they wouldn't have to wait long. No intelligent outlaw would remain close to water for long. On the desert, these places were the crossroads of anyone who might be traveling. Anyone who might recognize desperadoes on the lam.

An hour later, when the two Apache had ridden off to the east, Zac and Chupta took their horses and picked their way carefully down the rocks. They dropped the reins and let the horses drink freely. In a matter of moments they had found a spot where many animals had been picketed. Again Zac found the telltale sign of oats in the horses' droppings.

Chupta signaled Zac from across the pool. Zac moved quickly around to where the Indian crouched. "Man bleed here," Chupta said, pointing to the dried blood.

"Good, that ought to slow them down a mite. We'll camp up there a ways and keep a good view of the water. Seems they're headin' north. We'll light out of here long before the sun comes up, and you can take us in the direction of the next water to the north of us."

"Umm," Chupta nodded his head.

It was close to midafternoon when they both heard the sound of a lone shod horse ambling across the rocks toward the water below. The sound was quickly followed by the noise of a crying baby.

CHAPTER 6

+ + + + + + +

The grassy desert east of Prescott
Late Wednesday afternoon

Raincloud tried to quiet the baby. It was the first time all afternoon that little Sunflower had cried. The sun seemed to have beaten the child's will down, just as it had hers, and because it took energy to cry, the child had stayed silent through most of the day. Raincloud sat down by the pool, and before she drank, she attempted to nurse the baby. Even a little bit of nourishment would allow the child to sleep, and then maybe Raincloud could eat and sleep.

The land had been a lonely place during the day, and that was just the way she wanted it. Often, she had stopped and attempted to look back down the trail, in search of some bit of dust that might be her husband. Ed Hiatt was a relentless man; she knew that much about him. If for no other reason than his hatred of Indians and his need to be brutal, he would try to find her.

Her heart felt heavy as she considered her life. There had been joy at her wedding. She had believed the money her husband had and the mine that he was taking the yellow gold out of would bring her happiness, but it had only brought her pain and sorrow. She thought that when her belly swelled with the newness of the baby, Ed would love her; but he didn't. She had become useless to him, and the baby had been a girl.

How could she have been so foolish to think that she was rising above the misery of her people with this marriage to the white man? They could no more live together than a bird could live with a snake. The bird and her eggs would always be food for the coiled reptile. The snake could not love the bird. The snake could only take the eggs from the bird and eat them, and then at last eat the bird itself. The thought sickened her inside. She had been a foolish and giddy child, but now she was growing into a sadder but wiser woman. She was like a bird that could no longer fly. She couldn't go back to her people. She had no one left but little Sunflower.

She reached into the bag and withdrew the jar that contained the money. Wads of bills were crowded into the glass, and, at the bottom, several large gold nuggets rested with ten to twenty glistening gold pieces. *This will have to be enough*, she thought.

After eating, the baby fell asleep. Raincloud laid the child down, gently, and crawled over to the pool to drink. The water was cool and refreshing. She drank, paused, and then drank deeply again. Reaching into the bag, she took out the food she had prepared the night before. She tore the bread off with her teeth and chewed it vigorously. It would give her strength. She consumed part of the cooked bacon and then turned to the dried apples. They were sweet to her lips.

She didn't know how long she could remain at the water; perhaps until the horse had rested himself. Then she knew she would have to leave. There were too many people who gathered at the water, to say nothing of any mountain lions that might be nearby. She felt vulnerable and all alone. Perhaps God saw her. He alone could see her and help.

She looked up into the darkening sky. He did see her, she knew. This kind and compassionate God some of the white men spoke of was a God who would watch her. The missionary man had told her, "God is love." The thought overwhelmed her. He had said that God knew the number of her hairs and that He cared about everything in her life. That she could be so special to someone so powerful was a strange but wonderful thought.

A noise made her look up from the pool. It was then that she saw the two men: an Apache scout in a blue tunic and a lanky white man. She sat up, scooted back to the sleeping baby, and reached into her belt, pulling out the sharp knife.

"We don't aim to do you no harm," the white man said to her.

She knew English perfectly well, but in no way wanted to speak it. Feigning ignorance of the language might give her an edge. She barked back at the man in nervous Apache, "You leave me and my baby alone. I will kill you if you try to touch me."

"She is much afraid," Chupta said to Zac.

"Tell her we mean her no harm, that we are looking for bad

white men that kill the pony soldiers and steal army money. Ask her if she has seen any men nearby. Ask her if she has seen a man with a bad wound."

Raincloud pretended ignorance as she watched the white man speak to the scout. Chupta relayed the questions to her in the Apache tongue, and she followed each line as if it were her first time to hear the language. Shaking her head, she responded in Apache, denying any and all knowledge of the men they were seeking. Even had she known, she would have said nothing. "I know nothing of the men you seek," she said. "All white men are alike to me. They are all bad and should be taken away from here."

"Ask her who she is and why she is here," Zac said.

Chupta led out in an exchange between the two of them, and Raincloud lied.

"Woman say her name is Running Moon. She say she is here because her father cast her out for being unmarried and having baby. She say she is ashamed and looks for a new home north of here, a place away from her people. She say she not want her father to cut her face in shame."

Zac nodded. He knew of the Indian custom of disfiguring the face of a permissive woman. "I can understand why she's out here all alone," Zac said. "Tell her we mean her no harm and will not molest either her or the child. Tell her we arc headed north of here and will leave in an hour so we can travel while it is dark and cool. Tell her she is welcome to join us for protection, if she can keep up."

After Chupta relayed the message in Apache, Zac went on. "Tell her we will pass near a white man's stage stop, and she can take the coach if she likes. Tell her she cannot remain with us because we may have to fight the white men we seek and want no harm to come to her."

Raincloud could tell that these men were in fact who they claimed to be. She knew enough about the men who traveled the desert to know that many men were scavengers, like the buzzards that circled over the weak and the dying. Right now, she was one of the weak, an easy mark for prey, and even these men, if they knew about the money she was carrying, might take what she had and leave her to die. She could trust no one with her name and her story. They might tell Ed, if they saw him. She listened to Chupta and nodded in agreement.

An hour later, when they had finished drinking their fill and re-
plenishing their water containers, Raincloud strapped the baby to
her back and mounted the horse. Riding with the men across the
desert would mix her tracks with theirs and that would confuse Ed.
He could not tell the difference between the horses' tracks, and she
would wait to find a place to slip away. The next day she would find
a place of hard rocks and let the men sleep in the shade while she
ran. They would not bother to look for her, and she would have
made a confusing trail. Maybe Ed would follow their horses and not
hers.

The men rode ahead of her in silence. Chupta stretched out his
lead and would occasionally step down from his pony and look over
the next rise in the desert slope. The moon now hung low and full,
casting a gloomy light over the desert floor. Mesquite trees stood
sentinel and dotted the harsh terrain. Their arms seemed to beckon
her on. She rode behind the white man in silence, a slight breeze
brushing her face like a gentle fan.

The white man lifted a hand in her direction, then placed his
forefinger over his mouth to signal silence. Up ahead, Chupta had
dismounted. He seemed to have heard something and dropped his
reins to scoot closer to the next rise. She dismounted and followed
the white man warily. As he lay beside the scout, he looked back
to her. She could tell he was nervous—not about her, but about the
baby. She nuzzled her finger into Sunflower's mouth and crept forward.

Coming up to the rise, she could see the reason for the man's
alarm. Below them, on the desert floor, a large group of mounted
warriors rode in the direction from which they had just come. She
looked and began to count. When she got past forty, she gave up.

The three of them lay on the grassy hillside and watched the
string of Indian warriors ride toward the south. She figured they
would remain by the water long enough to rest their horses and
leave again when the moon rose high. It worried her. Even if they
were Apache, she was traveling with an enemy, and this was obviously a party bent for war. They would need no woman with child
to slow them down, and they would want no one left alive to tell
what they had done.

Raincloud could only hope that Ed had followed her closely and
would soon meet the warriors in trying to find her. The thought
sent a rush through her, and then a twinge of pain. He was, after all,

her husband—her husband and the father of Sunflower. She wished him no harm, and it shamed her that the thought had even crossed her mind. She squinted and said a silent but confused prayer for his protection.

Raincloud watched the scout and the white man lie still, their breathing barely noticeable. The scout slowly reached out and, touching the white man's arm, pointed up the hill off to their left. There a lone rider sat on his Indian pony and surveyed the war party as it rode through the valley below. With a group this large, it would be wise to have one or two outriders to keep prying eyes away. How long they could remain in the moon shadows and not be seen Raincloud could only guess. She froze; the warrior was slowly riding in their direction.

CHAPTER 7

+ + + + + + +

The Sonora Desert
Wednesday night

Zac touched Chupta's arm and pointed off toward the lone Indian. Chupta nodded and, drawing out his knife, slowly circled toward the rider. It was a moment Zac needed, to see firsthand the loyalty of the Apache scout, but it was one he hadn't thought would come in this way. Chupta was, after all, Apache. Zac didn't have the experience with Apache scouts that the army had. They seemed to place great stock in the men and no one seemed to question their loyalty, but that was before the ghost dance.

Zac hugged the ground low and watched Chupta move silently up the hillside. Zac was still in his boots. He always brought along soft moccasins for just such an occasion, but there was no time to change. If they were to escape without alarming the war party that rode below, it would have to be Chupta who did it. Moments later, the scout disappeared into the shadows.

The moon was high now, but clouds had begun to meander over its face, casting the desert floor in intermittent shadow. Zac watched the lone rider slowly move toward him and the woman. The rider still seemed to have no idea they were there, and the horses in the draw below them hadn't made a sound. He knew enough about horses to know, however, that the silence wouldn't last. They were the best night watchman a body could have; the first sign of an intruder would bring their heads up, followed by a snort or a nicker. At any moment the sound of the approaching rider would cause everything to come unraveled. The breeze was blowing uphill from the horses, which was the only thing that protected them so far.

Every muscle in Zac's body tensed as the rider approached. He had to be ready; he had to be ready to move fast.

There was a sudden scramble from the hillside as Chupta ran for the man. Chupta took a leap and knocked the man from his saddle while Zac bounded out of his position and ran toward the struggle.

The man's horse began to run. If he got away, he would run toward the group moving silently through the valley below. There was now only one chance, and that was to grab for the horse's reins. If he failed, Zac knew their position would be given away just the same as if the outrider himself had let out a cry.

He listened to the men struggle and grabbed for the spooked horse's reins. The Indian pony stomped on the ground and swerved around him, knocking Zac to the ground. Rolling over, he scrambled to his feet. The Indian woman had been right behind him. She grabbed for the reins and held the animal firmly as he tried to break free. Zac ran to her and took the reins from her hand. Only when he had the horse under control did he turn to see what had happened to Chupta.

The scout knelt on top of the fallen sentinel, and Zac could see that he was taking the man's scalp. Zac and the woman marched over to him, the horse firmly under their control.

"He Yavapai," Chupta said. "Me take scalp for reward money. Buy things for my woman."

In a few minutes, they had remounted and ridden down the hillside to the valley below. It would be morning before the rider would be missed, and Zac wanted to make sure they backtracked through the hoofprints of the war party. If they could ride to where the group had come from, at least for a while, they might be able to confuse their pursuers. The shod horses they rode would be noticeable, but mixed with the number of recently left Indian hoofprints, it just might work for a while.

More than two hours later, they saw the dying flames of several buildings in the distance. It would be dawn shortly, but they had followed the tracks of the war party straight to what they had been up to the night before.

"It stagecoach place," Chupta said. "They no come back here."

"Why is that?" Zac asked.

"People see come daylight, and army here. Yavapai no come back to face army patrol, I think."

"Let's hope you're right about that." Zac touched his spurs to the flanks of the buckskin and bolted ahead in the direction of the burning buildings.

Minutes later, he pulled up rein at an empty corral. He sat his horse and watched the last of the flames lick at the collapsed roof. The adobe bricks held strong, but the wooden part of the structures still sent smoke up into the twilight that came before dawn.

As Chupta and the woman rode up, Zac dismounted and dropped his reins by the water trough. Walking toward the smoldering main building, he kicked at the debris that littered the yard. He pulled his neckerchief above his nose and mouth and went inside.

Moments later, he walked outside with a shovel in his hand. "We got graves to dig," he said. "There's three men, a woman, and two children in there. It ain't a pretty sight. You better check over the barn and see if there are others. I'll start with the shovel."

"Better let them lay," Chupta said.

Zac cocked his head at him. "Why? You already said you didn't think Mangus was coming back."

"If he does, then he know we here."

"Well, let's just hope you were right about that and wrong about this."

The dawn had bleached the sandy desert with light when the three of them finished the graves. Zac patted down the soil mounding the children's graves and took off his hat. "Lord, we commit these souls to you. We don't rightly know who they were, but you do."

"We go now," Chupta said. "Men we seek are north." He pointed in the direction of the valley. "They be at the wells. Best water close by."

Zac replaced his gray hat and pulled it down tight. "Yes. We'll ride along the stage road for a spell. I'd feel a bit better if we mixed our tracks with any that might be left on the road. Then we can cut across to the valley again. You better tell the injun woman that it's her choice. She can stay here and wait for an army patrol or the stage, but that bunch could double back to find us. I don't really want to take her with us."

He glanced over at Raincloud and the child she was now feeding. She was listening to his every word. "I'm feared that at just the wrong moment we're gonna have a crying child on our hands, and I am counting on surprising them folks we're trying to find. I ain't about to tell her that, though. I got enough to live with at any rate, without leaving a woman and a baby out here on the desert with Mangus and them Yavapai prowling about. Put the choice to her, though, only don't say anything about the baby."

Chupta grunted and nodded. Turning to Raincloud, he explained the choices to her in the Apache dialect. He spoke in slow and deliberate tones and she listened, watching Zac the whole time.

"Woman say she not want to go with us anymore. She say she and baby will wait for the army or the stage. She say she have enough food and we no have to care for her."

By the tone of her voice and the way she looked at Zac, he could tell there was more to her message than just the little bit Chupta was relaying to him. "What else did she say?" Zac asked.

Chupta stuck out his lower lip. "Woman say she know we go to do murder. She say she not want to be any part of a killing business. She say if Chupta were real Apache that he would not go to do this dirty work and be a running dog of the white man."

"And what did you say?"

Chupta's eyes narrowed. "I tell her she is right. I also say that Chupta hunter of men, just like you. Not take job and quit."

"I appreciate that."

"You a-a-appreciate," he formed the word carefully, "even more when we finish. Without Chupta, you will die."

Zac ignored the challenge. "Tell the woman that I thank her for her honesty. Tell her we wish her and the baby well."

Minutes later the two of them rode off. Zac turned in the saddle and looked back at the woman. There was something about her that spoke of loneliness. No matter what they had been doing, he was certain that she would have chosen to go on alone.

After leaving the stage road, they headed east, hoping to cut the trail of the men they were following. These were not the type of men who would be seeking the comfort of a well-traveled road. To keep from being spotted, they would be leaving as little to chance as possible. They wanted no one to see their faces, of that Zac was sure. If this was the same group that had been responsible for the string of army holdups, they'd want and need the namelessness of the open grassland.

One other thought bothered Zac as he rode. *Why the army?* he wondered. There were easier targets to find in Arizona and the New Mexico territories. He struggled with the thought. Ten years earlier it might have been easy to blame the robberies on former Confederates bent on revenge, but now? *No one would be so bitter as to nurse a grudge this long, would they?* he thought.

It was easy to let his mind linger over the thought. He always wanted to know as much as possible about the men he was hunting. Understanding what made them tick made his job all the easier. Would the man back down when faced with a gun? Was there a tendency to quit somewhere in the man's background? Was the motive greed or hatred? From all Zac knew about men, the answer to those questions made all the difference.

Zac looked up from the ground and saw Chupta watching him. "You know these men?" Chupta asked.

"No, but I've known men like them. I saw some of them during the war. The bitterness and the anger got to be too much for them. When a man thinks he's right and then loses . . . Well, that man never forgives."

"All these white men say they Christian, but they hate."

Zac scratched his chin. "It's the lost cause, I reckon. When a man is caught up in a dream of what ought to be and sees that dream shattered, the ought-to-be never dies, even when the dream does."

"Yes," Chupta responded. "Apache right, and he lose. Mangus right, and he lose too."

"And now both you and me are working for the Yankee army. I guess that don't make us very different."

Chupta looked at him carefully. Like Zac, he was a man unaccustomed to agreeing to anything he hadn't thought over. "We are different," Chupta said finally.

"How's that?"

"You white man, no matter what you say. You can come and go. Chupta must stay here and be a whipped dog."

Chupta jerked on his reins and galloped off toward the south, to the edge of the rise. Zac continued toward the east and watched the scout dismount and inch his way toward the overview. Within minutes, Chupta made his way to his horse, mounted it, and rode back in Zac's direction.

"I wrong," Chupta said. "Mangus send twenty warriors," Chupta flashed ten fingers at Zac twice, "back to the stage house. They try to find us there."

"And when they don't find us?"

"They find graves."

"I guess we shouldn't have buried them folks."

"No, we better to leave them lay."

"Okay. You were wrong and so was I. I only hope we weren't wrong to leave the woman and her baby back there."

CHAPTER 8

+ + + + + + +

The stage road southeast of Prescott
Thursday morning, just before dawn

The stage rolled on through the night. The blackness of the sky was such that anyone looking into it might expect the dawn to produce a new world, one that carried with it a sudden surprise bathed in the light of a new day, one without the harsh bitterness of the desert. Amy held her head out the window and blinked into the gathering dawn. In a matter of moments, she watched the magic of the first rays coming over the mountains to the east of them and onto the desert floor.

"Whoa!" Hec Peters pulled back on the traces. The team lurched to a slow walk, then ground to a complete stop.

Peters cranked open the handle on Amy's door. "Okay, folks. We is gonna take us a leg stretcher. Don't go to wanderin' off too fer, 'cause we ain't gonna be hereabouts fer long."

The members of the suddenly thrown together party seemed to be lost in their own individual worlds, as if the confinement of the coach were something that needed to be escaped from, even if only for a few minutes. Ruggles helped Amy and Tommy down from the coach, and then wandered off.

The Reverend Black took out another cigar. He struck a match on the side of the coach and puffed his weed to life. Taking out his Bible, he walked off facing the sunrise. Finding himself a comfortable rock, he sat down to read.

China Mary clasped her hands behind her and marched off toward the rise in the hill that overlooked the road ahead of them.

Tommy began to run around the stage, making an ever-wider circle. He shook his hands, as if to draw off some untapped source of

61

energy, all the while making rattles and shrill guttural sounds. Amy watched him and her eyes narrowed, as if she were trying once again to understand what made him the way he was.

"Is that kid brother of yours tetched or somethin'?" Butch Gray, the shotgun messenger, scratched the back of his head while he asked the question. Obviously it was a sincere query, but one Amy had heard many times before. She simply looked back at the befuddled man and ignored him.

Amy walked up next to the Reverend Black, carefully peering over his shoulder. "It's so very nice to see a man read his Bible, something I'm not accustomed to."

He looked up at her and then over to young Tommy, who was now running wildly around the stage, arms waving like a bird in flight. "Miss Franklin, you do seem to have your hands full. If there is anything I can do to help you control him, you have only to ask. I know it's none of my concern, but sometimes an older man can help, where a sister can't."

Amy nodded. "Thank you, Reverend."

"It's been some time since I had children to care for."

" I do appreciate your offer, and I'm sure Tommy would do quite well with you. It's just that I've been taking care of him practically his entire life. He just gets all pent up inside and feels like he's got to race around and make a general scene until he can calm himself down."

Butch Gray had been unable to take his eyes off her, and Amy lifted her head to see him once again staring in her direction. She smiled at him and batted her eyes. Turning her head, she could see Ruggles peering straight through her. He had a smirk across his face. Narrowing her eyes, she glared at him, but her nasty look merely made his eyes twinkle and his smile broaden.

"Please excuse me for a moment," she mumbled out of the side of her mouth to the Reverend Black before she sashayed her way over to where Ruggles was seated. "And just what do you think you're staring at, Mr. Ruggles?"

"Oh, nothing much," he smirked.

"It most certainly was something. You were acting like a man with four aces playing with somebody else's money. There's something about you and those looks of yours that make a person feel uncomfortable."

"It's just my job to know people," he said.

"And you presume to think that you know me?"

He looked her up and down. Her pretty yellow-and-white checked dress made the gold highlights in her brown hair sparkle. "That's a very pretty dress you're wearing today."

"And what of it?"

"Well, I was just thinking, that tattered, dirty dress you wore when you sat near the poker table the other day, the day your grandfather died, that was just for show, wasn't it? Just to make folks feel sympathetic."

Her face turned red. "What if it was?"

"Nothing. I was just wondering how much of the rest of you is for show and how much is real."

Her fists balled at her side and she swallowed hard. She lifted her chin, ever so slightly. "A fine thing for you to say, a man who makes his living showing people what isn't real, and then hoping they don't find out until it's too late."

"I make my living allowing people to believe what they want to believe. When I look at you, though, I can't help but think that someday soon, you might make a mighty fine gambler yourself. You've got a strain of larceny running through you."

"I would never stoop to a thing like that."

"Oh, you wouldn't, would you?"

"Never!"

"I suppose you wouldn't at that," he leered, obviously insincere. "You remind me of a hothouse orchid plant I saw one time in New Orleans. It was only for show, kept in a glass case, of no earthly good whatsoever that I could see. It just sat there to turn the heads of whoever passed. Oh, you're a head turner, little sister, but you'll never feed the hungry."

"What I am and who I talk to is no concern of yours."

Ruggles looked over at the young Butch Gray. "It might be. I was just watching the light in that man's eyes over there as he looked you over. Just maybe he might make my job a whole lot easier. I might not have to take you as far as I planned."

She narrowed her eyes and wrinkled her nose, looking for all the world as if she would erupt, but she held herself in check. "Mr. Gray is just doing his job and seeing to the passengers." She clinched her fists still tighter. "And you are a most disagreeable man."

He chuckled. "I would imagine any man you can't wind around your finger would be disagreeable to you."

"A man like you most certainly is, a man who only wants to see what he can get when we finally arrive at the ranch."

Ruggles nonchalantly crossed his arms. "I suppose only time will teach you what I've been telling you all along. Sorry to disappoint you, but I have no interest in you or in that ranch of yours. My only desire is in fulfilling a promise I unwisely made to your grandfather."

"Lawrence Ruggles, I've known men like you all my life. The only thing you and your kind are interested in is what puts them in silk sheets with no labor involved."

"Little sister, you can keep that cynical view of men you possess and take it with you to the grave for all I care. I made a promise and I've never laid down a bet yet that I couldn't back up with the cards in my hand or the money in my pocket. I travel alone and the one thing I've learned about living life alone is that a man has to be able to face himself in the mirror every morning and like what he sees."

"Well, I for one, Mr. Ruggles, will believe in the purity of your motives when you wave good-bye and leave us with just enough to eat. What other motives you may have where I am concerned will bring you only frustration and continued loneliness."

Looking her up and down, he laughed. "Don't kid yourself, baby sister. You needn't worry about any interest on my part. You are like a tall head on a glass of beer. You attractively take up the space, but you're undrinkable."

Hec Peters gave out a whistle that brought up the head of every passenger. "Let's get to goin'!" he yelled.

Amy scampered off, madder than a wet hen.

Ruggles shook his head as he watched her saunter away in a womanly gait. This was a girl desperate to become a woman, or at the very least be treated like one. She was trying hard, and she didn't need to. He had seen the sight before. When people tried hard to be what they already were, they usually embarrassed themselves for their trouble.

He loosened his collar and walked past the Reverend Black. The man closed his Bible and stopped him. "Ruggles, I've been watching you two mighty careful-like. Half the couples I marry act smitten with ecstasy. They roll their eyes back in their heads and coo uncontrollably at one another like a couple of moonstruck calves. Makes a body sick to watch them."

He puffed his still-lit cigar. "The other half seem to be at each other's throats and at first glance a man wouldn't dare put a knife between them, let alone a bridal bouquet. Yet, time after time, it's those scrappers that always seem to work out better in the long run."

"Well, you can forget about that, Parson. That gal's a slip of a thing at seventeen, and I'm a man of almost thirty."

"Shucks, that ain't nothing, son. My own daddy was forty years better than my mother." Black took the cigar out of his mouth and stared at the wet end. Smiling, he popped it back in and bit down. "You best be careful. You keep on insulting that girl, and she's gonna slap you. When that happens, your goose is cooked, sure 'nuff. There ain't nothing more attractive to a man that is overconfident than a woman that hates the sight of him."

When all of the passengers got seated, Peters sent out another shrill whistle, followed by the crack of his whip. The team lurched forward on the road, spilling Amy directly into the lap of Lawrence Ruggles. She quickly stiffened and clumsily retook her seat. The two of them exchanged looks.

Across the coach, Black cleared his throat and winked at Ruggles. He closed his eyes and drifted off to sleep.

Several hours later, the coach took a turn in the road. Ahead of them was the army camp they were looking for, the place they could leave the ammunition. "Camp Verde!" Peters yelled out. "We're coming into Camp Verde."

The parade field was empty, and sheets flapped lazily on lines strung between the houses. As the stage pulled in front of the headquarters building, it was plain to see that something was wrong. There was no one there to greet them.

Peters jerked open the door. "We best have a look around," he said. "I don't like this. I don't like this a-tall."

There were no horses in the stables, and the only sound that came from the place was that of the sheets gently flapping on the line. The travelers fanned out, Ruggles drawing his revolver and walking over the boardwalk, followed by Amy. Posted on the door was an announcement, "Dinner party tonight for all officers, given by the KOW." The poster was dated two days earlier.

"What is a KOW?" Amy asked.

"That would be the commanding officer's wife," Ruggles said. "They substitute the letter C with a K out of courtesy. Although, from what I hear, in this case it would be most appropriate."

THE WELLS FARGO TRAIL

"You don't like women very much, do you?"

"Most of the time I find them a necessary bother."

They walked into the building. Papers were still scattered about the room, as if the wind had blown them off the desk.

Suddenly, under the floor, they heard a loud thump. Ruggles pushed Amy back with his arm. He kicked over a rug, exposing a ring that held the door to the cellar. "All right," he yelled, "come on out."

Slowly the trap door hinged up. Ruggles reached down and yanked it open.

There below, a young man with long dark hair and a cherubic face blinked into the sudden sunlight. He held a shaking revolver. "I-I-I'm Philip Carol, Philip Carol from Prescott. I was going to go with a patrol to Santa Fe and catch the train east. My father's sending me back to Yale." He unsteadily climbed the stairs.

"You better put that gun away, Philip Carol, before you hurt someone."

"I couldn't sleep last night, and so I rode out early to get here. There were ranches burning all along the way, and I guess I kinda got scared."

"You had a right to be," Ruggles said.

"When I got here this morning, the whole place was empty."

"They must have had a good reason to clear out so fast," Ruggles said.

"They might have gone to Fort Wingate. I must have passed them in the dark last night."

Ruggles holstered his revolver. "I'd say you picked the wrong place to be at just the wrong time, Carol."

He turned to Amy. "We'd better tell Hec to put some distance between us and this place. Things don't look too healthy for white folks around here."

It was more than two hours later when the team once again slowed. In the distance were the ruins of the smoldering stage station.

"Folks, you better get on out while we water the team," Peters yelled.

Ruggles jumped out of the coach and proceeded to help the rest of the passengers. Amy shunned his arm and stumbled. Ruggles smiled and picked up Tommy, placing him securely onto the ground. "You better watch the boy," he slurred the words at Amy.

66

Peters and Gray unhitched the team and led them to the water trough. "We ain't gonna be here long," Gray shouted to the group. "Don't wander around. Be ready to jump back in when we give out the word."

The eerie silence of the station was punctuated by the morning breeze as it stirred up the dust around the still-smoking ruins.

Ruggles found the well and lowered the bucket, drawing up a load of cool water. "You folks had better drink your plenty and start filling up whatever canteens and containers you can find. It's going to be a long, hot day."

"The man's right," Peters called out. "It's gonna be a ways till we get ourselves to the next water."

The passengers clustered next to the well, each taking a turn at the tin ladle and drinking freely. Ruggles continued to let the bucket drop into the deep well, each time drawing it up and filling the canteens and flasks the people carried to him.

Black produced two empty buckets he had found next to the burned-out barn. "That's smart thinking, Parson. You'd do well to start your praying now," Ruggles said.

"Oh, I intend to. The Lord can provide streams in the desert and a way in the wilderness. He also had the wisdom to provide the Apache."

"Well, let's just all hope He allows us to find the army before we meet up with the ones that did this."

The reverend straightened his coat and walked toward the smoldering adobe station.

China Mary stood with her hands on her hips, watching Peters and Gray water the horses. "We going back?" she snapped.

The men ignored her, which seemed to make her all the more insistent at being heard. "We going back?" She asked the question in a louder tone.

"Ain't no way to tell if'n they is behind us now or out in front of us," Peters quipped. "We'ze jest as likely to find them waitin' fer us on the road back there."

"Well I, for one, would just as soon go on," Amy joined in the discussion.

"If Miss Franklin here wants to go forward," Gray said, "then I reckon that's exactly what we oughta do."

Ruggles cracked his now familiar smile at Amy. He circled the little finger of his left hand with the index finger of his right.

She lifted her chin and, turning around, marched back to the coach.

Peters and Gray took the horses and, ignoring the discussion, proceeded to hitch the well-worn team. Slapping on the last of the harness, Peters glanced at the group. "The closest water is out in front of us. I'd say that about settles it, as far as I'm concerned."

"We have company." Black's announcement brought every head up as he walked into the open from around the far side of the burned-out adobe building. He was leading a saddled horse and beside him walked an Indian woman with a baby in her arms. The woman looked up at them but continued to soothe the child, wiping a cold compress across the baby's forehead

"I speak the Apache language," the reverend said, "and this woman calls herself Raincloud. She says she got here shortly before we arrived."

"She's more'n likely one of them that done this," Gray quipped. "That horse she's got is too good fer the likes of her. More'n likely it's stolen."

"I doubt she's with them," Ruggles shot back. "Does she want to come with us?"

Black exchanged words with the woman, who rocked the child gently in her arms. There was a soft resolve on her face and a natural beauty for all to see. In spite of the devastation all around, there was a calmness about her. It was as if she had walked into the camp of an enemy, determined to make sure that her baby would survive, even if she didn't.

She suddenly reached out to the reverend, took his arm, and squeezed it as she spoke to him. In spite of the whiteness of his skin, it was obvious that she thought this man different from the rest. It was more than the kindness that showed underneath his wrinkled skin and drooping mustache. He had taken the trouble to learn her tongue.

Black turned back to the group. "Gentlemen, I don't care if she is Apache, this woman and her little one are God's own, same as the rest of us." He looked back at her. "She says it was Yavapai that did this; says it was Mangus. She says she will ride along behind us, if we will allow her."

"I don't want no 'pache at my backside," Gray quipped.

"It's a free country," Peters said in a huff. "If she can keep up, she's welcome to fall in. We won't be pushin' this team very hard, so she shouldn't have any problem."

As Black started to explain what the men had said to the woman, they all heard the horses, a sound that brought every eye to quick attention. Down the slope, behind the station, they could see a group of riders. The dust cloud that trailed behind the Indian ponies told all of them that the group riding toward them was a sizable one.

"Get in!" Peters yelled. "We got to hightail it on outta here and fast."

Ruggles grabbed Amy's arm. "Where's Tommy? I can't be watching out for the both of you."

CHAPTER 9

+ + + + + + +

Amy's look of panic made him instantly feel guilty for having said what he had. She screeched out Tommy's name. Running toward the smoky barn, she continued to scream frantically.

Ruggles took over the situation immediately. It was as if being in command was second nature to him. "Get on that stage!" he yelled at Mary. To Peters and Gray he shouted, "Get that team ready to haul out fast and you"—he pointed directly at Gray—"bring that shotgun and the rifle in the boot and climb down here." Turning to the Reverend Black, he snapped quick instructions, "Get my rifle from the coach and follow me." As he ran toward the station, he shouted back at Peters, "You sing out when she comes back with the boy."

Moments later the three men stood in the gray light of the smoking adobe building. Ruggles took the rifle from Black's hand and the shotgun from Butch Gray. "Here, Preacher, use this scatter-gun. You shoot when we shoot." Turning to Gray, he ordered, "Don't you fire till I open up. If we can take down a few when they ride close, then we'll get them off their horses. It might just buy us some distance on them. Do you understand?"

Gray nodded.

With each of them positioned at a window, they heard the clear call of Hec Peters from the top of the coach. From the corner of his eye, Ruggles saw Gray and Black hesitate and pull back from their positions. "Stay right where you are," he said. "We got to get them off their horses to give us a running start."

"And if they just keep coming and go around us?" Gray asked.

70

"Then, more than likely we are all dead," Ruggles barked back. "So, I'd just suggest you make those shots count."

He crouched low, behind the windowsill and watched the approaching band of renegades. Training his sights on the man who seemed to be in the lead, he followed him with his aim. Each second that ticked by brought the group closer. They were well within rifle range now, but still Ruggles waited. They would have to get closer for the shotgun to be effective.

Outside, Peters yelled once again. Ruggles could hear the nervousness in the man's voice. In the heat of battle, it was near to impossible to tell everyone what the plan was. He only hoped that for the sake of the three of them, Hec Peters wouldn't make a foolish decision all on his own and ride off and leave them.

Turning all of his attention back to the trail of steel that led from his eye down the Winchester's barrel, he sighted the lead rider. They were close now, maybe too close. If they got suspicious as to why the stage was waiting for them in front of the ruins, they might be able to pick out the weapons that were pointing in their direction. He was counting on Peters and the stage to distract them just long enough to make their volley count. "Pick out some secondary targets," he barked at the two others, "just to the right or left of the first man you pull the trigger on."

Carefully, he watched the lead rider. The man was closing fast, bent on getting to the waiting coach and whatever booty they might be able to find. Ruggles had long ago learned the proficient use of firearms. He relaxed as his finger curled around the trigger. Taking one last shallow breath, he exhaled slowly and squeezed the trigger. The Winchester bucked, sending the rider spilling to the ground.

Jacking round after round into the chamber, he continued to lay down rapid fire as he listened to the sound of the shotgun in the reverend's hands boom out across the desert. He could hear the regular reports of Gray's rifle put out a steady killing field of fire.

Through the smoke and fury, he could see four or five riderless ponies. It was more than he had hoped for. The Indians were not used to taking many casualties; they had too few men to begin with. They had dealt with the white men long enough to know that in the long run, numbers were seldom to their advantage. They simply could not afford the losses of a pitched battle. The three of them had stung them good, and Ruggles well knew it. "Hold your fire!"

he yelled at the other two. "They're down from their horses now, we better get."

The three of them backed out of the station and began a dead run toward the still-waiting stage. Black and Ruggles piled inside the door and Butch swung himself topside as Peters wheeled his whip over the heads of the stationary team. Ruggles watched the Indian woman kick frantically at the sides of her horse as the stage bolted out of the yard and down the road. At best, they had bought themselves only the few minutes it would take for the Yavapai to gather and mount their horses—unless they decided to treat any wounded they might have.

There was another factor that might make a difference. Ruggles knew the Indian mind well enough to know that they took directions well. Of course, someone had to be there to give it to them. If one of the warriors they had grounded had been the man in charge, it would take them longer to decide what to do next. He looked up from his position on all fours on the coach's floor and watched Black silently murmur his prayers.

The team was running wildly now but that wouldn't last long; they had traveled all night. There just was no chance at all of out-running the Indians if they decided to give chase.

He got up on his seat and looked at Amy. She was holding Tommy in her arms and shaking like a leaf. "I'm sorry I spoke to you the way I did back there. You're doing the best you can with the boy. I'm going to go up top. Maybe I can do some good at a distance with this Winchester."

"Are you sorry about everything you said this morning?"

"Sometimes I find myself sorry the words travel the distance from my mind to my mouth, but it rarely changes what I think." Reaching into his sleeve, he produced a double-barrel derringer. "Here, you hang on to this. If they catch up with us and take the horses down, feel free to use it any way you see fit."

He handed the rifle to the reverend. "Here, Parson, when I get on top, you pass this up to me." He clamped the man's hands down around the barrel of the gun. "Just don't drop it. It's irreplaceable."

Moving to the window, Ruggles scooted out onto the top of the opening. Reaching up, he grabbed on to the iron railing that ran around the lip of the coach's prow. The stage bounced and he held on, tightening his grip on the wrought iron. Swinging up, he slid his legs from the opening and pulled himself up toward the roof of the bouncing stage.

Butch saw him and, reaching out, took his wrists and pulled him up. "Whatcha doin'?" he asked.

Ruggles flattened himself onto the deck of the coach. "Thought you might need another gun up here. If they get close enough to take one of them animals down, we're done for."

"You got that right!"

The coach came to a severe drop in the roadbed and a sudden downward grade sent its back wheels into the air and then down again with a nerve-shattering thud. Ruggles pitched forward, his head banging on the ammo boxes in front. He paused a moment to gather his senses and turned to crawl back to where he could take the rifle from Black.

Reaching his hand down to the open window, he grabbed for the rifle the preacher held up in the air and latched on to it. Moments later, he found himself nestling the Winchester under him as the stage continued to bounce down the road. He pointed the rifle back in the direction of the swirling dust.

"I got to slow these horses down, or we're gonna lose 'em right here," Peters yelled back at him.

Ruggles nodded and Peters leaned back on the traces.

"They might not foller us so close," Peters said. "T'ain't no mystery 'bout where we got to go. They might just as well circle 'round and be a waitin' fer us when and if these animals reach them cottonwood wells. If'n they do that, they might just do to us what we did to them back there. That would be the smart thing to do, if'n I wuz them, and I ain't never know'd no injun to be dumb about desert fightin'."

A short time later, the horses had slowed to a steady pace. The coach turned on the road and stayed on the lip of a rocky curve. To their left, the hills had blossomed to an abrupt series of sheer cliffs. If the Yavapai had decided to ride to the left of the coach's route, they would be invisible until the last possible moment. Ruggles cautiously swept the cliffs above them with the muzzle of his rifle, looking for the first sign of the hostiles. He might not get off the first shot, but he sure wanted his chance at the second. "When do you think we'll pull into these cottonwood wells?" he asked.

"Not before dark, I'm afeared. By then, that bunch could be well hid. We wouldn't see them till it was too late to do anything about it."

"Isn't there any other water we could find besides the wells at the cottonwoods?"

"There might be. Off to the east of us, in the valley, there's some tanks I know of from my prospectin' days. I knows lots from them foolish days of mine. Poor innocent that I was, comin' from Missouri, I listened to all the talk, all them rumors 'bout other people's dreams of glistenin' silver and glitterin' gold. Little did I know, I was getting myself drunk with the smell of somebody else's cork." He paused and looked off toward the east. "With all this heat, though, them tanks might be dry by now, then again, they might have some left in 'em. Them injuns could foller our tracks real easy, though."

"They could if they came up the road. But if they know where we're going, why should they? Just like you said, they might just circle 'round hoping to find us where they know we're going."

Peters continued to work the traces, thinking on the matter. "Might just work at that. 'Course, it would be a downright gamble."

"That's what I do best," Ruggles replied. "From where I sit, I think I'd rather gamble than shoving all my chips into the middle of the table against a full house."

"You got a point there, young feller. But if them tanks ain't got no water left in 'em, then we're gonna be afoot, afoot with no water fer the horses and durn little left fer us."

"I'm for the gamble," Gray joined in. "If I had my druthers, I'd jest as soon pick a dry spell over injun arrows and gunsmoke."

"All right, it's my call, I figure, as the driver of this here thing, but you boys is talkin' sense. When we clear this here hilly area, we'll light a shuck fer the tanks."

"I'd say we'd be better off to do that before we clear all the hills," Ruggles said. "They might just be waiting for us up there, and these horses are too played out for another run. When we hit the next wash, just take us on down."

"All right, we'll do it your way. It'll be rough going, and if they are up there a ways, we won't fool 'em fer long."

Ruggles swung around to the rear of the coach. He could see through the dust that their back trail was empty. "We got another problem," he yelled. "That Apache woman and her baby aren't with us anymore. If we turn off, she might not know where we've gone."

"That's her leeway," Gray said. "Maybe if they find her, they'll leave us be till they finish up with her."

CHAPTER 10

+ + + + + + +

The Sonora Desert
Thursday afternoon

Simpson had hung on, putting up quite a fight in the heat of the desert. It had been hard to leave the sheltered pool the day before, but they all knew that well-traveled watering holes like that one just invited too many people and far too many questions. In the last six months they had been taking the army payrolls, no one had been left alive that had seen their faces, and that was just the way Julian liked it.

"Kid's got sand," Drago said.

Julian tightened his cinch and looked over his saddle at the young man lying on the rocks. "That he has."

"I s'pose when this here life is all that one has left, it makes a body kinda reluctant to say good-bye to it."

"But it ain't all," Julian said. "Some things are more important than livin' and dyin'." He drew out the words in a deep, raspy voice. The tone of Julian Cobb's voice had always put the fear of God into anyone who heard him. It was a menacing voice. There was no bluff in it, only truth—deadly truth. Drago had imagined it to be the voice of one of the devil's demons summoning someone down into the depths of Hades.

"What's more important than living and dying?" Drago asked.

"Honor," Julian paused, "and love of country."

The thought, coming from Julian, took Drago completely by surprise. He blinked. "I don't get it."

"Comin' from California, I don't reckon as how you would. Been my experience, people from thereabouts have little in the way of roots. When you don't know where you come from, you don't know who you are."

Simpson began to moan and Julian unwrapped the strap of the canteen from the saddlehorn. He shot Nestor a glance.

Nestor turned away. The man had been keeping his distance ever since the incident at the ambush. Some people didn't take kindly to being knocked to the ground. Julian knew the kind well—he was one of them.

Julian walked over to where the kid was moaning, more softly now. He knelt down beside him, lifted Simpson's head, and placed it on his knee. Unslinging the canteen from around his neck, he bit the stopper off the opening and held it to the man's lips.

"Thanks," Simpson croaked.

Once again, Julian held the canteen to his lips and poured slowly.

"I'm feelin' better now, kinda drifty like."

"That's cause you're dying, kid. You won't make it till sunset."

The boy closed his eyes, blinking back the tears. "Will you see my folks get my share?"

"Kid, I don't run no charity ward. 'Round me, nobody gets what he doesn't earn. Next time your momma rides with me and pulls a gun, she'll get her share, same as the rest."

"What you s'pose is gonna happen to me after I die?"

"It all depends on who you believe."

"Who I believe?"

"That's right." Julian nodded in the direction of Nestor, still brooding beside the pack animals. "You can believe somebody like Nestor over there. He says when you die, you're just dead like a dog. Or you can believe somebody like my ma and pa."

"What did they believe?"

"They was Christian folk."

"What do you believe, Julian?"

"Don't rightly know. I used to, but I don't no more."

The kid coughed. "You know," he said, "you believe like them folks of yourn. If'n you didn't, you'da left me lay where I was gutshot. I guess a man don't get off too far from his own people."

"I don't think a man's people have much to do with it when it comes his time to go. What happens then will be between him and his God." Julian poured another sip of water into the young man's mouth. "Besides, I had my own reasons for not leaving you back there."

"You don't fool me none. You've said more to me here than I've heard you talk in the year since I started follerin' you."

"No man deserves to die all alone."

"Maybe so, but that don't answer it all. You may act one way on the outside, but on the inside you're somebody else."

"Kid, you're justa lookin' at a shell, or what's left of it. There ain't much left on the inside, I suppose. There's just the leavin's of the war and all the wars I done took on after my own was all over with. You're looking at a man that believes in Julian Cobb now, or at least in what's left of him."

"I'm afraid that ain't gonna be enough for me, not now." With that, the kid squeezed Julian's arm and closed his eyes in death.

Julian held Simpson's head and then, scooting back, laid it gently on the rocks. He got to his feet. "Nestor, you and Drago get them two shovels. We're gonna dig a deep hole right here."

"Why a deep one?" Nestor murmured. "The kid's past caring."

"We'll dig a deep one for the gold, and put Simpson on top of it."

Drago pulled on his black and gray streaked beard. He had a stocky build with broad, heavy shoulders. His bare forehead showed off heavy salt-and-pepper eyebrows and a pair of large, twinkling brown eyes. He ambled awkwardly over with a shovel in his hand. "Put the kid on the gold? Why do a fool thing like that?"

"This is just the spot I had in mind to bury the gold." He pointed to the rocks that had given them shade. "Up in them rocks is a tank with water in it. I know this place. When we get back to uncover it, we'll have water close by. If somebody follows us and finds where we been digging, all they'll find is the kid. They won't go no deeper."

"That why you didn't leave the kid back there?" Drago asked.

"I got my own set of reasons thought out for everything I do, and sentiment never enters into it. I don't carry no dead weight. Every man and every thing has its purpose, even the dead and the dying."

Both Nestor and Drago knew enough about the desert to know that in certain areas the rocks formed a catch basin that served as a watertight compartment for the rain that fell all during the year. These desert tanks could remain well hidden to all but the Indians and a few prospectors that occasionally stumbled across them. When the monsoon rains swept the area in July and August, most of the moisture would be lost to the sand. But the deep tanks on top of certain rocks would be filled with deep, cool water. Little if any vegetation gave away their location, and a man who had a knowledge of them was valuable indeed.

"Put your hole right over there, in the V-shaped dirt between the rocks. Any runoff that comes will put that ground back to shape."

Drago and Nestor stripped off their shirts and began to dig. The sun was high now, and the shade of the rocks was a thing of the past. The two men dug through the rocky surface and spaded the dusty, dry soil in a heap beside the growing hole. In just under a half hour, the dirt turned a deeper color and showed signs of moisture. "Is this deep enough?" Nestor asked.

"I'll tell you when it's deep enough," Julian responded.

Nestor kept up the spade work alongside Drago. He stopped and planted his shovel into the fresh dirt. Leaning back, he ran his hands through his sandy-colored hair, pulling it straight back. He glanced back at Julian. "I s'pose there's some benefit to only havin' one arm," he said.

Julian looked him in the eye. "I don't get where I am by having two arms and two eyes. I get where I am by using the brain God give me."

Both Nestor and Drago stood in the hole, now up to their armpits. "Even so, this here hole is already plenty deep enough. Lots deeper than we need for that gold and the kid."

"Now who said you were digging that spot for just the gold and that kid?"

Drago's eyes widened, and Nestor's color disappeared. He stammered. "W-w-why else? You ain't a planning to bury them mules too, are you?"

"No, we're turning two of them loose and keeping the other two. I was figuring on planting you right about where you're standing now."

Nestor dropped his hands to his side and Drago backed up to the edge of the hole.

"Drago," Julian drawled, "you better climb on outta there. I wouldn't want any strays to take you down by mistake."

Drago scrambled out of the hole, and Nestor raised both hands, motioning them in Julian's direction. "Now, there ain't no call to do that. It don't make no sense. There's plenty enough here and with them other payrolls to keep all three of us in silk sheets for some time to come. 'Sides, yer not through. I know you and you ain't about to stop. Yer gonna need me."

"I kept you breathing long enough to help dig that hole. Like I said, I don't carry no dead weight. Every man and every thing has its purpose, even the dead and the dying. Besides, already got to find another man with the kid gone. Might as well get two same as one. Only thing is, this time I'll find one that won't give me no lip, one I can close my eyes on now and again."

"You can trust me." Nestor spat out the words.

"I can trust you to put a bullet in my back when I got it turned on you."

With that, Nestor dropped his hand to his side and fumbled for his revolver. Julian's hand stood straight out, the Russian .44 an extension of his arm quicker than the strike of a rattlesnake. He squeezed off several rounds, forming a tight group in the middle of the man's chest and dropping him into the bottom of the hole.

Holstering the .44, Julian spoke calmly to Drago. "Put the gold beside him, it was what he wanted. Lay down a foot or two of dirt over that, then we'll wrap the kid in a blanket and put him on top. After you fill the hole up, we'll scatter what's left of the dirt. I don't want to leave no mound. If folks find this here grave, we're gonna make 'em look for it."

Drago hoisted the saddlebags containing the gold over to the grave site and laid them inside. He picked up the shovel and proceeded to spade in the hole. "With injuns hereabouts, we might have found ourselves in the need of another gun," Drago said.

"Maybe so, but I'd much rather face the Apache than have a Judas gunning for my backside."

"And what makes you think I wouldn't do the same thing?"

"I know you, same as I knew him. You're a man with limited ambition. You ain't the kind to go after the whole hog, Drago—you get by in life by finding the sparest amount of pain. You want a sure thing at easy living, not an unsure thing with quick dying. 'Sides, you ain't no hothead like Nestor. I can't abide a man that thinks with his belly."

With the ground prepared, they wrapped Simpson in a blanket and gently laid him in what remained of the hole. Julian swept some dirt over the boy and then pointed at the shovel. "Fill it up and make it smooth."

Loosening the cinches on two of the mules, Julian gave them a swat. They watched the two animals stampede into the valley be-low. "Unless they got them a very good tracker, they're gonna foller them mules. If the 'pache finds them first, all they're gonna come up on is what remains of an Indian supper."

"What makes you think we're being followed?"

"I can feel it in my bones. 'Sides, I like the chase. It's stimulating to the mind of a man to know he's being hunted. It makes him a better hunter when he's on the prowl himself."

"Don't nothing scare you?"

"Nothing on this side of the grave."

CHAPTER 11

+ + + + + + +

The rocky outcropping overlooking the valley
Early Friday morning

When the clear dawn broke over the desert floor, Chupta and Zac got off their horses and walked along, studying the ground. The trail of the men and the group of horses and mules was clear now. The places where rocks had been turned over by the animals' hooves showed a clear path northward toward the wells and tanks that Chupta knew well. They mounted their horses. In the daylight, this trail would be easy to follow.

"They seem to be going slow," Zac said.

"Wounded man make them stop," Chupta replied.

Zac pointed out the rocks to the west. "Let's circle 'round. I don't like being out in the open here. It might have been all right for them, traveling in the dark and all, but it makes us too easy a target."

Chupta grunted and nodded. "We go," he said. "We find trail again when they come close to water."

Zac mounted. "It shouldn't be too hard," he said.

There was no way a group of men could be expected to conceal the trail of horses and heavily laden mules. To Zac, it seemed all too easy. The army, being what it was, could be expected to follow them, and if the Indian situation hadn't been the way it was, that would be exactly what they would be doing right now. They wouldn't be needing him.

He turned the matter over in his mind. The only hope these men had for escape was speed, but here they were nursing a wounded man. Why? Either this bunch was short on sense or long on misplaced compassion. Or maybe they had something else on their minds. Maybe they had a place to store the loot. It would be something to consider. If that was what they planned, then he and Chupta would have to throw caution to the wind and try to follow their trail more closely. His job was not just to find the men who had done this, but to find the stolen army payroll as well. He would have to think on it. He had tracked men enough to know that following a man meant following his mind.

The two of them rode to the rocks and wove in and out of the boulders that shadowed the desert. A bee flew by them and Chupta stopped near some white sandstone and dismounted. Wedging his moccasins into the cracks in the rocks, he began to climb. At the top of the rocky finger, he stooped low and came up, his face dripping with water. He signaled for Zac to come up.

Zac slid off the horse and dropped the reins. Scuffing his boots on the rocks, he climbed up the sandstone. At the top of the rocks, a deep bowl had been carved out by the elements, forming a large pool of fresh water. "You drink here," Chupta said.

"We'll pour out a couple of hatfuls for the horses when we get back down," Zac said. "Then we can refill our canteens up here." Taking off his hat, he plunged his face down into the cool, clear water. He shook the water from his face and then got down on his knees and drank deeply. Sitting up and taking handfuls of the water, he splashed his black hair and ran his fingers through it, allowing the liquid to trickle down and cool his back.

"Every other place a man goes, he learns to look for water in the lowest spot he can find, but I can see the desert here is just the opposite."

Chupta grinned. "You learn quick, for a white man," he said. "Better to learn quick and stay alive than learn slow and die."

Zac beamed at him. "I can see I'm fortunate to have a man like you that can teach me. You know of other places like this?"

"I know many places for water. Apache not need soldier canteen. Apache live here."

"That's right, this is your home, and before we're through I want to learn everything about your home that you can teach me."

"I teach by doing what I do. I don't explain. You watch and learn."

Zac caught Chupta's sleeve and pointed off to the north. Chupta swung around and saw the group of Indians riding swiftly down the rocky face to the north of them. The group was a large one, more than a dozen warriors. "Are we sitting on their canteen?" Zac asked.

Chupta crouched low and watched them. "No, they ride back to spring we were at last night. They ride fast, not take time to find our trail."

"Let's just hope for our sake they don't stumble across it."

Chupta pointed out a number of horses with men draped across them. "They go bury dead, then they come back. They ride hard now."

"They must be in a hurry to get on with their burials so they can get back to what they were up to."

"These with Mangus. They not Apache."

"Then they've got themselves some killing and burning to do. Let's water the horses and be long gone before they get back to here."

Chupta nodded and the two of them slithered down from the rocky outcropping. Filling their hats with water from the canteens, they watered the horses. Chupta took the empty containers and once again began his climb up the rocks. Within minutes they were in the saddle, circling to the west and away from the hard-riding renegades.

✦ ✦ ✦ ✦ ✦

Raincloud rode slowly up the stage road. She had stopped following the coach when she saw they were not being pursued. Figuring the war party had circled them and would be waiting, she wanted little part of what was to come.

The baby needed her, needed her alive to care for her, and the white-eyes were riding on to their deaths. She would go slow until she heard the gunfire, and then she would go around them.

The horse moved slowly down the road, its hoofprints mixing with that of the stage. She was still concerned about Ed. She knew he would follow her, at least until his need for liquor or his desire to gamble once again came over him. When and if that happened, he might just give up the chase—at least that was what she told herself. She didn't really believe it, however. She had taken too much of his money, and his hatred for her was too strong.

The baby began to cry softly. It was time to feed little Sunflower, but she dared not stop along the road. The war party may have held up temporarily, and before she could hear them coming, they might be upon her. Ed could be riding the road as well. It was too much to hope that the warriors would meet up with him and attack him. The thought had crossed her mind and saddened her that she had allowed the thinking to take possession of her. She wanted to be free of him, but she had no desire for him to suffer. He was, after all, her husband. She had sworn to love him, and it sickened her that she was betraying her vow, even if it was one arranged by her father for the price of five horses.

She rode to a place beside the road that contained a rocky outcropping. There, she could take the horse off the road and perhaps leave little in the way of tracks. The animal's iron shoes clicked across the surface of the rocks and she looked down the slope. It was steep, but the baby was crying. Pulling on the reins, she kicked at the horse's sides. The animal hesitated, as if resisting her urging, and after another kick moved forward. Lunging down the rocks, he clattered over the stones, slipping and bracing himself against a fall.

Moving from one low ledge to another, she meandered down the rocky face to the bolder-strewn hillside below. Weaving in and out of the rocks, she craned her neck back to see if she could see the road. She was out of sight. Breathing a sigh, she dismounted. She could still spend a few moments with the child in the cool morning air before the sun climbed high.

A short while later, she began to walk the horse through the greasewood and around the mesquite. The thorns on the brush pulled at her. Suddenly, she stumbled over a rock and fell to the ground in pain. The baby on her back began to cry. Trying to get up, she watched the horse run off with their water and food supplies. She felt helpless, pain racing through her ankle.

Unslinging her cradle, she took the baby out and rocked the child in her arms. "Hush, little Sunflower," she whispered in Apache. "They might hear you cry."

She kept up her rocking motion and allowed the child to suck on her finger. "You will be all right. Mother will take care of you and see you come to no harm." She only wished that she could believe her own words.

It was some time before she could quiet the child and begin to hobble along the trail of the runaway horse. She grimaced with each step as the pain shot through her ankle. Overhead, the merciless Arizona sun shone brightly. She had to find the horse; she had to get to the water before the day was full upon them.

Hours passed and still there was no sign of the animal. Raincloud's mouth was parched. Reaching down, she picked up a small, smooth pebble and placed it in her mouth. The act of rolling it around in her mouth would make her saliva flow. It would help keep her mind off the dryness of the land.

She sat down beside a large rock and, taking out her knife, cut a strip from the bottom of her dress and wound the cloth tightly around her throbbing ankle. She could not die, not now, not with little Sunflower.

In a short time, her mind began to drift from the pain and the heat of the day. Perhaps this was a better way for both of them to die. At least they were free from the fear she had felt with Ed. If she and Sunflower died on the desert, they would die the death of free Apache. Better to die an Apache than live as the white man's slave. She closed her eyes against the sun and prepared to wait for the night. Maybe then she could bear to walk.

She didn't know how long it was, but the next thing her mind became aware of was the shadow of a man crouching low over her and the baby. She squeezed her eyes tightly shut, praying that the man behind the shadow was not Ed.

"Are you all right?" The man asked the question in Apache.

Popping open her eyes, she strained to see him. His figure was outlined in the bright sunlight, but she could see that he was a massive man, much larger than her Ed.

"Here," he said, "you'd better take a little water." He held a canteen to her mouth and poured a little of the cool liquid through her lips. Taking the cradle from her arms, the man wet his finger and touched the baby's mouth. The little one began to cry.

Raincloud sat up straighter. Taking hold of the baby, she held the cradle steady. She took the man's offered canteen and slowly let a few drops of the water fall into the child's mouth. She could see the man clearer now. His hair, sticking out from the sides of a weather-beaten hat, was the color of mowed hay. His head was large with a square jaw, and his blue eyes shone with a light all their own. There was a kindness in the man's face that she hadn't expected— the kindness of a white man looking on an Apache.

"I found your horse," he said, still speaking in her tongue, "and followed his trail back to you and the baby. You'd better come with me. My wife and I can see that you get cared for, until you feel ready."

"Thank you," she spoke to him in English.

"That's what folks are for." Taking her under her arm, he helped her to her feet. "I'll just help you onto your horse and take you to our place. It ain't far, and we can get you fixed up with some food and rest. My name's Harry Potter."

"I am called Running Moon," she lied.

It was over an hour later when Harry led her down into a canyon that contained an adobe house. He paused. "It ain't much by certain standards," he said, "but to me and Emma, it's heaven on earth." He called down to the house before he led them up to the front door.

Emma came out from the house with two children, a boy who appeared to be about seven and a girl of nine or so.

"Here now," he said, "let's get this lady inside where she can be tended to. She's twisted her foot up something bad, and she could use some vittles."

Inside the hut, Emma stirred a savory-smelling pot on the fire. "I've had these beans soaking since last week," she said. "You tell her there's plenty to go 'round, Harry."

"She speaks English," Harry said.

"That's fine." Emma scooped up a plateful of the beans and picked up a spoon. "I don't speak Apache so well," she said to Raincloud. "Leastwise not like Harry here." The little girl had changed the baby and was playing with her. Walking over to where Harry had made Raincloud comfortable on a cot that served as their bed, the woman placed the plate on her lap. Raincloud stared at the beans, and then at the two of them.

"We don't have much," Harry said, "but you're sure welcome to what there is."

"Why you do this?" Raincloud asked. Kindness at the hands of whites was something she had grown not to expect.

Harry grinned. "At the end of a man's life, the only thing he can expect to find over there is the things he's given away over here."

Raincloud blinked in puzzlement and began to eat.

CHAPTER 12

+ + + + + + +

A small valley southeast of Prescott
Friday afternoon

The heat of the day had taken its toll on Ed Hiatt. He knew that no matter how hard he tried, he couldn't possibly overtake Raincloud and the gelding she was riding. Only his determination and the knowledge that the woman would have to stop to care for the baby kept him riding in the direction he knew she had taken. No matter what, the woman wouldn't stop at a town. She knew better than that. He knew that she had already learned that going back to her people wouldn't help her much, either. The Apache were funny people about making bargains and then keeping them, and he had made a deal with the girl's father. He had already brought her back from there one time, and the beating he had given her afterward would have been enough to teach her not to do that again.

He rode the mule steadily onward, the canteen and the pot he carried clanking together. This time she had gone too far. The five hundred dollars he had managed to save was something he could not stand to lose. To lose it at poker was one thing, but to have it stolen by that Apache squaw was something he would not tolerate. No matter what it took, he would find her. And when he did, he would make sure she would never run away from him again.

The fact that she had run away from him gnawed at his soul. Ed knew he could never be mistaken for a handsome man. His sandy hair was always unkempt, and the buckteeth that gleamed through his mustache had made him the object of many a joke as a boy. There was nothing to his average height that commanded respect at first glance, and in every way, from his droopy eyelids to his weak chin, he could never have been expected to turn a woman's head.

But that was no excuse for her to run away.

As he thought about Raincloud, he knew she was a beautiful woman, even if she was an Indian. Maybe that was why he had always made sure she dressed in rags and in the things that came from the church hand-me-downs for the poor. It wasn't that he couldn't afford better—he could. It was just that he didn't want other men turning their heads when she walked by—she was his.

That would change now. He would make sure of that. There were plenty of men who would pay to have her, and he would make her pay back every cent she had run off with, and then some.

He reached back into his saddlebag and took out one of the bottles of whiskey he carried. It was almost empty, and he turned it upside down as he poured the remains into his mouth. The angry liquid roared down his throat and into his empty stomach. It burned, but he had long since stopped worrying about how it made him feel when it reached his insides. Now all he could think of was blinding himself from the feel of the hot sun overhead and doing what it would take to keep moving on.

He threw the empty bottle down and kicked the sides of the mule, urging him on. It would be some time before he got to the Mongolian Rim, and that was where he would begin to look for her. She was unlucky for him, always had been, but now that would change. His luck puzzled him. He always seemed to do well when it came to taking things out of the dirt. He'd sold a silver mine, and for a lot of money, and now the gold was coming out. How could a man be so lucky with the dirt and be so unlucky with cards? The thought was a puzzlement to him.

In the distance, he could see a cloud of dust kicked up by the hooves of a number of horses. It bothered him, not so much that he might meet up with someone he couldn't handle, but that somebody might find Raincloud and the baby before he did. He pulled the mule up next to a large set of rocks and got down. He would wait and see who the riders were before he moved on.

Squinting through the sunlight, he could see these riders were not whites. They were a band of Indians, and they were riding fast to the southeast. He edged his way around the rocks and squatted down, watching them in the distance. Try as he might, he couldn't make out any of the horses they rode as being his gelding. Surely, if they had found Raincloud, they would have taken the horse.

Several hours later, with the sun settling above the mountains in the west, he came to the spot he had been looking for. The towering rocks above him would have fresh water for both him and the mule. His gaze fell on the shelf of rock that lay next to the desert floor and on the scuffle of hoofprints around it. There was something strange indeed about the disturbance of the ground. Someone had recently been here before him, someone towing a string of animals.

Ed walked the mule over to where the ground appeared to be darker than the desert sand around it. Sitting on the flat rocks, he studied his worn-down boots. The day had been hot, but now the desert would cool off. He reached into his vest and took out the flat bottle of whiskey he carried there. Pulling the cork, he swirled the liquid around, studying its dark amber color. He raised the bottle to his lips and surged down several swallows.

"E-e-ehhh." The expression was followed by the smacking of his lips. Lifting up his hat, he held it up against the low sun. *It won't be long now*, he thought.

Once again, he looked down at his boots. Setting the half-empty bottle on the ground and swinging his right calf over his left knee, he reached for the boot and wrenched it off. He repeated the process with his left boot. Setting the boots aside, he looked at the dark socks that Raincloud had darned for him, not more than a week ago. He pulled them off and wiggled his toes in the dirt.

The exercise of drinking and then wiggling his toes seemed like a strange thing for a man to do, but for Ed it was natural. It reminded him of his boyhood, a simpler time. For a brief moment, it helped him set aside his bitterness.

There was something odd about the feel of the ground under his bare feet. It was almost cool to the touch, something he wouldn't have expected. He dug his toes into the loose soil. Looking down at the dirt, his puzzlement deepened.

It was plain to see that some of the ground had been dug, dug deep, and then scattered. He might not know about a lot of things, but dirt was something he worked with best, and somebody had been working this dirt. It might have been a bunch of greenhorns trying to find water in the desert, but then why would they have taken the trouble to cover it up?

He turned around and looked over the rocky shelf. It wasn't exactly the lay of the land to find silver, but what if somebody had found gold? Refilling the hole that had been dug wasn't the way of a prospector who had come up empty. It just made no sense.

He got to his feet and hobbled over to the mule. Taking out his shovel, he ambled back over to the softened earth. Had he been a day later, the sun might have made the dirt dryer and concealed the digging. Whoever had dug this hole had done it earlier that same day or late the day before. If they had discovered a strike, then he just might be able to beat whoever had dug this to a place where he could file a claim on it. *Maybe I am the right man in the right place, after all*, he thought as he began to dig.

Twenty minutes later, his shovel struck something solid, but soft. He dug a few more spadefuls. It was a body. Somebody had planted someone here and then rode off. *But why no marker?* he wondered. *Is it an injun?*

His mind raced. Part of him wanted to leave whoever it was alone and ride on, but then there was that part of him that was naturally curious. It was the curious part that made him a good miner. He moved the dirt aside and uncovered an army blanket, just the kind an Indian might use for burial. The army was giving such things away to the Apache. Moving the dirt aside, he grabbed the edge of the blanket and pulled it up.

Blinking, he stared down at the fresh corpse. The dead man was no more than a boy. He could see the results of bleeding from a stomach wound. He walked around the body in the hole, checking the man's pockets for anything the would-be undertakers might have left. Anybody else would have just ridden on and left the boy to the night critters of the desert, but Ed's curiosity far outweighed his sense of decency.

With the soles of his feet, he could feel the ground give way beneath him. There was more to this hole than the boy's grave. If he'd had his boots on, he might not have been able to feel the softness of the earth underneath the boy. To Ed, the thing just got curiouser and curiouser. Laying the shovel aside, he heaved the body out of the hole and once again began to dig. In a matter of minutes, his shovel hit other foreign objects. One was another body, which aroused his interest further. It took several minutes more for him to uncover what lay below.

His mind raced and his smile beamed as he tried to lift the saddlebags. From the weight of the bags, he could tell they contained gold. Given the U.S. brand on the sides of the leather, he knew why the people who had done this thing had buried them among their dead. This was stolen army loot! Once again, he had proved his point. He was unlucky at cards, but very lucky in the dirt.

+ + + + +

Friday night

Raincloud studied the man and his wife carefully. The way he treated his woman was a mystery to her. She watched him as he carefully helped her with the water, but the thing that made her the most curious was the way they both smiled so freely at each other. There was a bond of love between them that was a strange thing for Raincloud. At times she had seen it between certain couples among her people, but it was rare. She didn't believe such affection was possible among the whites.

The woman walked over to Raincloud with the fresh, cool water. Stooping down in front of her, the woman began to carefully unwrap Raincloud's ankle. Raincloud marveled at the sight of this white woman stooping down in front of her. *What is it that is different about these people?* she wondered.

"Here, you'll be needing your bandage changed. Let me bathe your ankle for you before I wrap it again."

Raincloud defensively moved her foot back. The man saw her.

"Here, little lady, you just let Emma here do some doctoring for you. She's always had the touch of an angel for me and the children. She's fixin' up animals and such all the time."

"Harry, you hand me that alcohol and the cayenne, too." Emma looked up at Raincloud. "This will cool off the swelling and make your pores open up. I learned the alcohol part from my mother, and the pepper part from an Apache medicine man. So you see, a body can get the best from both places and do themselves just fine."

"Why do you do this for me, a stranger?"

"There ain't no strangers out here in the desert," Emma said. "We're all out here together, all part of God's own way of dealing with this here place."

"I'm sure you'd do the same for us or for one of our young'uns, if we was hurt and needin' care," Harry chimed in.

"We just won't let you go hobblin' off unattended to," Emma said. "That wouldn't be right."

"You have no fear of being out here all alone with the Apache?" Raincloud asked.

"Naw," Harry said. "Why should we? We treat them as neighbors and they let us farm what little we can and tend the few cattle we have. Besides, we ain't exactly alone."

"No, indeed," Emma joined in. "God brought us to this place and He's the one that said, 'I will never leave you or forsake you.' "

"His word on the matter has always been good enough for us," Harry said.

Across the room, Raincloud could see the children continue to play with Sunflower. They had each made the baby a doll out of corn husks. The little white girl had made a dress for her doll out of a piece of torn gingham.

"Someone comes to look for me," Raincloud said.

"Whatever put you out on this desert alone is nobody's business but yours," Harry said. "Your own thinking on the matter is plenty good for us. We won't be sayin' nothing to nobody 'bout you, 'cept God."

CHAPTER 13

+ + + + + + +

A spring east of the desert
Friday afternoon

Mangus took the news of the stage fight without blinking an eye. He stared straight ahead and said nothing. The Yavapai who had delivered it blanched and uttered a string of excited shouts, as if by appearing angry and brave, he could drive out the shame and fear he really felt. Mangus had seen it many times before. Men died a little bit inside when they had to admit defeat or fear, Mangus knew. The man was brave. He didn't have to persuade Mangus of that with his waving arms and his angry shouts.

Three men had been killed and three more wounded; that was the hardest blow—that and the sting of defeat which might mean bad medicine. The news of bad medicine would travel fast if something were not done to bring back the flush of victory. He wanted the Apache to join him. The ghost dance was powerful, and to dishonor the dance was to stop the stamping out of the white-eyes before it had even begun.

He was also troubled by the disappearance of the wolf scout. Whatever had happened to the man had been done in silence. The wolf had been killed and the band of dog soldiers had followed the killers to the stage stop. If the killers had been scouts for the army, even now the white-eyes might be close by.

That was four dead now. Four dead and two of the three wounded unable to ride. It was bad. It left him with only about forty effective fighting men. He would have to gain many more small victories before he could expect to bring in the Apache.

Mangus had said nothing as he listened to the sounds of the beaten leader. His gaze had been straight ahead after the initial

93

glance at the man. Now, he looked the man directly in the eye, his gaze silencing him.

He slowly got to his feet and walked toward the pool. Every eye in the camp was on him. Bending down, he cupped his hand and drank the crisp, clear water. The liquid felt like cold steel seeping down into his belly.

He looked down at the water and studied his face. His broad, round face was marked only by the tear lines of the paint. It made him look more sad than fierce. It also made his heart proud. The sadness made him more of a man. To send men to their deaths required sadness. Any young man with no woman to care for and no children to ask where he was could afford to be fierce. He could not blind himself with hate only. Hate would be in his eyes when he rose his hand to kill, but now he must think carefully. All of the men were watching him, and he wanted to make sure they would see only the face of a man ready to die for the right to breathe free.

He slowly walked back to the same place where he had been sitting and sat down. It was as if nothing had happened. From the corner of his eye, as he walked by the man, he had caught the expression of iron will on Gandara's face. Such a man would do well as a leader. Gandara could use his strong tongue to speak but, until he did, he tried to keep his thoughts unreadable. But Mangus could. Mangus knew him well. Gandara was such a one as he, a man whose words and actions did his talking. He, too, was a man the people followed. It was good that Gandara was with him. When the warriors were puzzled as to what to do next, they would always look to Gandara, and Gandara always made sure to affirm Mangus's thoughts. Gandara was his strong right hand.

As the men began to mix and exchange words in whispers, Mangus knew they would learn. They would soon learn to trust him with their lives, even when he said nothing. They led the horses bearing the bodies of their fallen comrades away and rode off into the hills for the burial ceremony. It was good that they knew what to do next without him speaking. They knew his mind well.

Over an hour later, when they rode back down to the pool from the hills, they found him silently sitting in the same spot. It was as if he had passed the time without moving a muscle. Soon enough they would know why they were waiting in this place. There were signs of the white man all around them, signs that they could follow, and there was a stagecoach to take revenge upon, but that could wait until he had finished the business he had brought them here to do.

The sun had run its course when two of the wolf warriors Mangus had sent out to keep watch returned. He got to his feet. He saw their excited but puzzled expression and knew what they would say. As he listened to the report, he walked with them to the edge of the camp. Climbing up the rise of greasewood and cactus, he looked out to the desert floor.

The wagon was coming in his direction, just as promised. Its dirty canvas cover wagged back and forth, the rose color from the low sun painting the streaks of white that still remained in the material. A team of four tired mules plodded along, their ears pitched forward from the strain of pulling the vehicle through the sandy soil. From the back of the wagon he could see a stovepipe that pointed at the sky. It was the way these men chose to cook their meat.

He would never understand these people. Why the white man came to the desert and built houses with wood they stole from the hills and why they would cook on iron instead of the ground—these were mysteries of the spirit to him. Why would a man live on soil he hated? Why would someone feel the need to separate himself from the sky and ground? To Mangus's thinking, it showed weakness, an inability to live in the place they claimed God had brought them to. It was a sign they would not last long here, not as long as the people.

Gandara walked over to Mangus with the rest of the warriors. They fanned out, forming a semicircle to greet the approaching wagon. There on the bench seat, behind a team of mules, sat a man in a black stovepipe hat and long, flaming red hair cascading down the sides of his head. Seated beside him was a Mexican in a large sombrero.

Mangus walked back to the pool. He would wait for them to come to him. Forcing the wagon to drive between his men would make them understand who they were dealing with. It would put fear into them, and fear was his friend. He watched the expressions on the faces of the strangers as they drove the wagon down the hill. The band of warriors walked beside the clattering gig, eyeing the men and the team of mules they drove. Mangus silently approached, staring up at the two interlopers. His calm manner put the warriors at ease.

"There you are," the redheaded man said. "It took us longer to get here than I expected, but Rufus Campbell be a man of his word. And I didn't come empty-handed nor empty-headed."

Mangus nodded, slightly.

Both men climbed down from the wagon. "I got me some mighty fine rifles back there, enough to equip a whole army. Took me durn near two weeks in Prescott to round 'em up, but I know you're gonna like 'em. Repeaters they are, mighty fine Winchesters, mighty fine."

Mangus looked to Gandara, who followed the Mexican and several of the braves to the back of the wagon. In a matter of moments the sound of yelps and squeals told Mangus that the man had indeed delivered on his promise. Gandara brought him one of the rifles. Mangus levered the action of the gun and then squinted down the length of the barrel.

He was pleased. The weapon was shiny and new. Its action was covered with a bright copper. Once again he squinted down the barrel and squeezed the trigger. The snap inside told him that the firing pins were in place.

"See, just like I told you. You couldn't buy a finer weapon anywhere else in the world. You bring the gold like we agreed?"

Mangus looked at Gandara, who walked to the camp and came back with several heavy cowhide bags. Gandara dropped them at the redhead's feet.

Dropping to their knees, both Campbell and the Mexican began to finger the gold coins. "Whew-eeeee, you must have done some passel of dirty business to get all this in one pile. There's been lots of talk 'bout you boys in town. Word is spreadin' all over the territory. Jest about everybody is scared. I gotta admire your sand, though. Can't many folks come up with a pile like this. I won't ask you how you got it," Campbell said, eyes gleaming. "I'm just glad you did."

The Mexican had started to count the coins, but Campbell stopped him. "We won't bother to count it. I'm sure you're a man of your word, two hundred of these here twenty-dollar gold pieces just like we agreed on."

He stood up and squashed down his hat. "Here, Paco, you put this away under our seat back yonder whilst I tell our friend here the news."

The Mexican hefted the bags and Campbell grinned at Mangus.

"I got me some news you're gonna like, somethin' we hadn't counted on, but somethin' you're gonna be needin'. There's a stage left Prescott day before yesterday, a stage that's carrying ammunition, and you'll be needin' that for this here war of yourn."

Mangus and Gandara exchanged glances.

"All we're asking is for the gold and money that there stage is carrying. I'd say that was fair enough to give you the ammo you need. It'll be plenty easy pickin's fer the likes of you boys, I'd say. There's just the driver, the shotgun guard, a preacher, and a greenhorn to deal with. That and a kid and some women. Your braves ought to make quite a sport outta them."

Several of the braves who spoke English began to pass the word to the others. It was obvious to the white man that this news held more to it than they had originally thought.

"That stage is heading north. I think they're trying to meet up with an army patrol and get that ammo off their hands." The man took off his hat and scratched his head, fluffing up his red mop. "With you on the loose, them army boys is runnin' 'round like chickens with their heads cut off. So it may not be likely that coach will find the patrol they is supposed to. You boys had better get a move on. You'll be wantin' to find them before the army does."

Mangus signaled with his hand and the warriors started to pack their things and break camp.

"Now we brought us some ammunition with us, but it ain't near enough to give them boys of yours much practice with them guns. Shooting the best rifle made ain't gonna do you no good, if'n you don't know what you're gonna hit."

When Mangus turned to walk back to his horse, the redhead followed him like an excited puppy dog. "Now don't you go to killin' them womenfolk. That would be a terrible waste. Paco and me will just take what's left when you're through."

Mangus ignored the man, tying his blanket to the back of his paint horse. Ignoring a man was something he did best, and the Indians he rode with knew it. They respected his ability to stay in control, but he knew full well that his behavior would only drive the white man crazy.

The man's excited talk continued. "We'll follow you just as best as we can, and you can find us when you're all through. Have we got ourselves a deal? I brung you the news as soon as I could and you'll be needin' us and what we learn from now on. We can even bring you boys some mighty fine whiskey the next time we see you. You and yourn will like that, sure enough."

To speak to this man would be a waste of Mangus's breath. Such men were like the weeds that blew in front of the wind. The wind moved them and finally made them go away. He would push them where he wanted just as long as he wanted to use them, then he would kill them just like the rest. They were like the rolling weeds and he, Mangus, was the wind. These two men had no right to live while better men than they died. Mangus mounted his horse.

"Now looky here, we is partners," the man went on. "When you do well, we all do well. You just sit yerself close to old Rufus Campbell and I can give you whatever it is that you want. You just keep on dealing in cash money and Rufus Campbell can give you all of Arizona."

It was just like the white man to promise what he could never deliver. The land didn't even belong to the people. The people belonged to the land.

CHAPTER 14

+ + + + + + +

The Arizona desert
Friday afternoon

The wind blew through the windows of the coach—a hot, dry wind promising no rain, only dust. The carriage bounced furiously, pitching forward and then with abrupt suddenness reeling backward. Where there were no roads, Hec Peters did his best to make a smooth one. It was next to impossible to do so, but he swerved the team from side to side on occasion, just to make sure he avoided the worst spots on the grassy desert floor.

Everyone inside the coach braced themselves against the frame and windows, trying hard to keep from being thrown against either the brass knobs or the other passengers. They made little attempt to shield their faces from the blowing sand, as it would have meant letting go of what grip they had on the handholds they had managed to secure.

Ruggles had joined the people inside at their last stop, switching positions with young Tommy. He now envied the boy. On top and away from the cramped conditions and flying knees and elbows of his fellow travelers seemed like the perfect place to ride. The sun was low now, so even the heat of the day would not have been a factor.

Ruggles sat on the floor with his head down and his back pressed into the door. His hat was pulled low and he tried to keep to himself, in spite of the other people's chatter and the sandy dust blowing in through the window. He had seemed the perfect gentleman by taking his place on the floor, but that was just how it appeared. He was a man used to caring for himself. He was his own keeper and had always taken smug satisfaction in being the master of his own fate. Just because he had given his place up to Tommy didn't mean he had stopped watching out for himself. On the floor, he could stretch out, something no one else could do.

"Are you going to school in the East, young man?" The Reverend Black asked.

"Yes, sir, I am—to Yale. Eventually I would like to study law here in Arizona. At least that is what my father thinks would be best for me."

"Well, I'm sure your father has thought it through for you."

China Mary giggled near the far window.

Young Philip looked over at her. "Do you know my father?"

Once again she giggled and then stifled a laugh with her handkerchief. "I solly. China Mary know every man near Prescott, know them sooner or later." She dabbed the perspiration from her lips and stuck the white linen back in her pocket.

"Then I take it my father does business with you?"

"He pay his men, and his men pay me and the girls who work for me. In case of your father, China Mary know him sooner and later. I know him when he came into town looking for gold, and I know him when he own mines and hire men to dig his gold."

It was a line Philip had no intention of pursuing, but Amy's curiosity had been aroused. She followed it up. "Do you do housecleaning for these men?"

The Chinese woman squinted her eyes in a flash of anger. "No," she said, "I not do any man's dirty work."

Ruggles tipped his hat back and looked across at Mary. "Don't let Mary over there fool you none. Between her and young Philip Carol's father, we practically have the owners of Arizona riding with us in here. China Mary there supplies most of the labor in the territory. The Chinese work off their passage and pay her, and no one has a job 'round here without her say-so. She supplies every bawdy house with her celestial beauties, every restaurant with her cooks and clean-up people, every laundry with the equipment and coolies to do the wash, and many of the mines with their dirtiest swampers. On top of that, she has all of the opium trade and smoke-filled dens in Arizona. I hear she's got quite a place dug out underneath her home in Prescott, lots of opium-filled tunnels with mats all around. This woman is a virtual Cornelius Vanderbilt in a silk dress."

"Is that right?" Amy asked.

Ruggles could see in a flash that Amy was not so much insulted at the vices and sin that the woman promoted as she was impressed by the power that was being wielded by someone in a dress.

China Mary nodded.

"Then, why do you have to leave Arizona?" Amy continued.

Ruggles kept on answering the questions, even if they weren't directed at him. "She had to leave because two young boys died while on the opium underneath her house. One boy was just twelve and happened to be the governor's son. Those folks were all too happy to put Miss Mary here on the first stage leaving the territory."

"You wrong, gamble man," Mary spat out. "You not know nothing. I don't even know them boys that died."

"You see, little sister," Ruggles added, directing his words to the stunned Amy, "you play your cards right and you too might someday become the queen of the cowboy's nightmares, the cowboy's nightmares and all of his fanciful illusions to boot."

"You should be the last man on earth to criticize the peddling of illusions," Amy said.

"At least I give every man that goes up against me a fair shake." Ruggles noticed the Reverend Black studying each face. Ruggles smiled and his voice dripped with cynicism. "And you, Reverend, aren't you the lucky man? You see before you every ill known to the territory—sin and vice, corruption, tomfoolery, naive obedience, and raw ambition. Quite a crew you have displayed here. This is some congregation for a man of the cloth to have as his last one."

"I wasn't sent to minister to the spiritually well off. If I'd wanted to do that, I would have stayed in St. Louis, where the problems revolved around why Mrs. MacIntyre wasn't speaking to Mrs. Jones at the picnic supper. Heaven is filled with the wrong kind of people. I should think," the parson went on, "that before we're through, we'll all learn to depend on and appreciate each other."

"If Mangus has his way, we'll all learn to bury each other."

"The army can protect us," Philip said. "We are supposed to meet up with a patrol."

"I'd say, young Mr. Carol, that it was time for your education to begin. If the army was going to join us, they would have met us along the road, not in this direction. Besides, those boys in blue have their hands full with stomping out the fires that Mangus and his people have already got going. You should have learned that when you rode into Camp Verde and found it empty. They're not going to have much time to hunt down a dislocated stagecoach that is overdue."

"Are you saying that we're all alone in this?"

"By George, son, you do catch on fast. You just might make it at Yale yet. That's exactly what I'm saying."

Amy joined in. "If the army can't find us out here, then, why did we leave the road?"

"Because Mangus and his people knew where the road was going to take us. They don't know we're here, or at least they didn't when we turned off. They probably will, though, before the day is over."

"Then, tomorrow, they will come to find us. Is that what you're saying?" Amy asked.

"We've bought ourselves one more day, one more day to enjoy each other's company." He smirked. "If you look off toward the east, you will see a range of mountains. If Mangus has one of his scouts anywhere on them, then, they are watching us right now. We're sorta hard to miss out here. And these horses won't last long if we don't find some water soon."

Ruggles pulled his hat back down and listened to the silence his talk had created. The corners of his mouth lifted in a smug expression. That was something that popping the mental soap bubbles of people's ideas always seemed to do for him. To him it was like the work of bringing light into a dark room. In a way, he saw himself as a minister of enlightenment. His work was that of making a gentleman more educated. He did it every time he turned over the last card. It was a feeling of power, the power of the mind. If nothing else came of the talk, at least he could have a little silence. The people on the crowded coach all seemed to be locked in their own thinking now. He had seen to that.

The smugness inside of him was punctuated by a more sobering thought. If what he had told them was true, then this indeed might be the last day any of them would spend on this earth. It would be the last sunset he ever saw and the last people he would ever know. He tried hard to drive the thought from his mind. After all, he was a gambler, and as such, optimism was part of his stock and trade— but only a small part. He depended on his knowledge of the odds even more. Many an optimist had gone broke at the poker table.

The team had slowed down, and Ruggles could only imagine the exhaustion of the horses. There were no plaintive cries from Peters, and the whip would be useless with a worn-out team. Moments later, the coach came to a halt.

Peters jerked open the door opposite of where Ruggles lay. "All right, folks, we'll have to walk a spell. The sand along here is getting too deep for these horses to keep up the pace."

They each piled out of the stage. "How far we have to walk?" Mary asked.

Peters pointed up ahead to a flat area of the desert surrounded by massive pillars of sandstone rock. "We're walking to them rocks yonder. If I'm right and remember this country, there'll be water in them rocks. I don't know if there'll be enough, but it'll have to do."

With the coach empty, the team of horses walked much more easily through the sand and dry creosote. Butch led the team by hand, with Peters walking along beside them and the rest of the group falling into line behind. The sandy soil gave way under their boots with each step, making it plain why the fatigued horses would have found the going difficult.

Amy's gaze wandered off to the mountains to the east, making it obvious that she was thinking about the prospect of being watched. She walked faster, placing her slightly behind Ruggles. "If we aren't staying on the road, where are we going?" she asked.

"Lee's Ferry. It's where we would have wound up anyway. It will take us into Utah Territory and near that ranch of yours, and it will take me on my way to Denver."

"That remains to be seen."

Ruggles looked at her and then up ahead at the young Philip Carol walking beside Mary. "To what do I owe the pleasure of this company? I would have thought you'd want to share your good humor with the young man up there, the one with the wealthy father."

"A lady learns not to throw herself at a man she's attracted to. It's best to force him to go out of his way."

"Oh, I see. Then I suppose that makes me something to be used to solicit young Philip's jealousy, force him to make his move before it's too late."

"I might as well put you to some use," she said.

"You do have tender treachery, little sister. But at least you don't disappoint me."

Amy watched Tommy play as he ran laps around the coach. Occasionally the boy would stop to inspect the ground, as if making a new acquaintance with some scrub or lizard. "Sometimes I actually envy him," she said. "He has no worries, no thought about tomorrow, and no notion about a future."

"He always been this way?"

"Yes, he was lost inside himself even as a baby."

"It might be a blessing for him before we're through."

"How is that?"

"The Indian has regard for people with thinned-out know-how. They see them as someone touched by God—don't view them the same way white people do. Folks like Tommy can come and go as they please among the Indians, take food off of people's plates, pretty much have the run of wherever it is they want to go."

"That seems odd."

"Not if you know Indians. You see, anything that has been touched by God is, in a sense, untouchable by the Indian. That's why the land as it stands is sacred. That brother of yours has an innocent purity in his empty-headedness that the Indian respects."

Amy walked on a ways, thinking about the new idea. "I guess the white man has improvement in mind. We want to make things better, and if we see someone with limited possibilities, then we treat them with disfavor."

Ruggles smiled at her. "Women look at men that way, too. When a man sees a woman, he says to himself, 'I like that a whole lot,' but when a woman casts her scruples on a man, she thinks, 'It'll take some work, but with my help, he might even amount to something.' 'Course with some of us, the enterprise just isn't worth the effort."

She looked at him. "No, it isn't." Walking on, she looked over the desert. "I suppose life for the Apache is quite simple."

Ruggles gestured toward the valley. "The Indian sees what already exists as that which has ultimate honor. To him the land is just right already. It needs no improvement. The way God made it is the way God wants it. I think they see themselves as people that way, too. They have no desire to improve on themselves; they just live with who they are."

"That thought seems so strange to me."

He walked beside her and looked at her. "I'm sure it does. I think you look down on who you were and where you came from. You've smelled some of the good life as a child and want it back. You see yourself and aren't the least bit satisfied. And the worst part is, you don't even see the gifts and possibilities you already have."

"If you mean to say that I'm unwilling to live the life of gambling I've known all my born days, you're exactly right. Just because my father gambled his life away on the Southern cause, and my stepfather and grandfather did it on the green felt table, doesn't mean I have to throw my life away too. I do know cards, and I know the men that play them, but that doesn't mean it's the life I want."

"You got to play the cards dealt you, little sister. You want the finer things. You long for the glitter of New Orleans and San Francisco, and don't tell me any different. With what you want and what you know, I could make you into the queen of the Barbary Coast. You'd never know another day of want in your whole life. A blind man could see what you're capable of, and I'm not blind."

"That's the last thing I want."

"That's all you want, little sister, and that's just what you are. The sooner you come to accept it, the sooner you can get on with living the life God made you to live as you are."

"That's where you're wrong, Lawrence Ruggles. I believe we were put here to rise above what we are, not give in to it."

Ruggles smiled. "Then, I suppose your thinking isn't any different than any other white man. Now me, I've just learned over the years to come to terms with who I am. I'll never be any different. There's no hope for me to be anything more, and I wouldn't want it if there were."

"I couldn't live without hope."

"Maybe you're right, little sister, maybe you're right to go after marriage to a man of wealth. That way, you can have the things you need, money to keep you happy, and a man to improve on to boot."

"I just want the things any other woman wants—a home and a family. Frankly, I think that men like you that are single and have no wife and children are the parasites of our society."

"Oh, bloodsuckers, are we?"

"Yes, you and your type contribute nothing. You are takers, not givers. It's only when a man holds his own children in his lap that he sees the value of building something for the future."

"You are quite the social philosopher."

"Perhaps you think a woman shouldn't be allowed to think seriously."

"Well, you would anyway, no matter what I thought. You need to know, little sister, that no matter what you think of me, I am giving you one thing."

"And what would that be?"

"I'm living up to the promise I made to your grandfather. I may be a parasite, but I still am, in the final sense, a gentleman and a man of my word."

CHAPTER 15

+ + + + + + +

A valley southwest of Prescott
Late Friday afternoon

Ed rode the mule down the road. He had managed to pick up the trail of the gelding at the burned-out stage station. At first he couldn't believe it. He'd gone to the place to see if anyone had seen her, only to find it burned out and deserted, and then he had spotted her tracks. He had shoed the thing himself, and he knew he could find his own mark, even in the midst of other tracks. The wind had been picking up, and he wanted to make sure he could determine Raincloud's direction before the tracks were all gone.

He trotted the mule along the stage road, looking down at the distinctive prints. They were there, all right, mixed in with the tracks of the stage horses. It was obvious she had been following the coach, as her prints at times were on top of those of the other horses. Whatever had happened to her, she hadn't tied the thing on the back of the coach and ridden inside. It would have been the thing to do with the baby and all, but for some reason, she hadn't. He wondered why.

Within the hour he had lost the tracks of the gelding. He moved back and forth from one edge of the road to the other. *She has to be here someplace*, he thought. *That horse didn't just sprout wings and fly away*. Some time later, he saw where the stage had turned off the road and headed down the slope to the desert floor below.

He pulled up on the reins of the mule and sat up straight. Ever since he had first come upon her trail at the station, he had stopped his drinking. There was something about being so close that made him want to be sober. He didn't want to take a chance of losing her, and the whiskey just might make his luck change, as it had so many times before.

The mule was winded from carrying the extra weight of the gold. He swung the animal around and slowly walked back along the road. The sun was getting low, but he could still make out the prints of the stagecoach horses and the deep, fresh grooves of the wheels.

A short time later, he found the tracks of the gelding. Swinging the mule around, he got down. Maybe he could follow them on foot before the wind erased them forever. Carefully, he paced up the road to the place where they disappeared. She had left the road here. He stared down the shelf of rock descending down to the floor of the desert below. More than likely, he wouldn't be able to find her tracks on the slope, but that was where she had gone, all right. With reins in hand, he ambled down the rocks.

Several hours later, he spotted the simple cabin. The darkness was setting in, but several lights shone from the window and from the cracks around the handmade door. A thin wisp of smoke came from the adobe chimney. He tugged at the mule and made his way down the valley. If nothing else came of it, just maybe he might be able to find a home-cooked meal.

A short time later, he called out, "Hello the house!" He had learned over the years that it was never a wise thing to get too close to a camp or a house without giving the people inside plenty of warning. There was no response, even though he could see shadows moving around on the inside. Taking out his Colt revolver, he checked to see that it was loaded and then put it back into his baggy pants pocket.

The door cracked open, sending out a shaft of light. "Who are you?"

"Just a prospector passin' through. Saw your light and hoped you might have some hot food."

Then the door swung open wide and a large man stepped out into the light with a shotgun cradled under his arm. "We always have hot food for a stranger passin' by. Come on in and my wife can spoon some up for you. You can water your mule in the trough over yonder ways."

Several minutes later, with the mule tied and watered, Ed lifted the heavy bags and blanket and took them to the porch. Laying them beside the door, he covered them over with the blanket and stepped inside.

The man's wife had set the table for one and a large cup filled with water was sitting beside a blue tin plate. "Sit down," she said. "It'll be a pleasure to serve you."

Ed noticed the two children move to the other side of the room. Each of them appeared to be somewhat nervous. He moved to the table and took his place.

"Here now, you two go on outside and play," the man said.

Ed sputtered. "I'd appreciate it if'n you left my things be out there. And that mule of mine is just as likely to kick your head in as to look at you."

"You see to it, you two," the man said. "People don't take kindly to having their things tampered with."

The children quietly slunk away and ran out the front door to play. "My name's Harry Potter," the man said. "And the lady with the beans and beef is my wife, Emma."

Ed nodded and smiled as Emma scooped beans onto his plate. "I'm Ed Hiatt."

"And how in the world did you ever find us out here? We're not zackly smack dab in the highway of life."

Ed spooned the beans eagerly into his mouth. "Knew somethin' was down here. I followed me a set of tracks for a ways." He made sure he didn't look too interested in their response.

"Well, like I said, we ain't in the crossroads here, but strays do pass by once in a while."

"And am I the only stray you've had lately?" Out of the corner of his eye, he caught the man and his wife exchanging a quick glance. He didn't know what their answer would be, but he knew that somehow, some way, Raincloud had been here. Maybe she was still here hiding out someplace. Certainly she had passed close by. He'd followed the tracks of the gelding to the edge of the valley before it had gotten too dark to see the ground well.

"We've had a number of folks pass by lately. The missus and me has been wonderin' if we need to set more vittles aside." He spoke rapidly, as if trying to subtly change the subject. "We are blessed to have a spring on the place, and that keeps it green and gives up water to spare."

"I was looking for a woman I saw up the trail, an Apache woman and baby. You seen anybody like that?"

"She somebody to you? Would she have been looking for you?"

Ed stuck some more beans in his mouth and thought about how

to answer. He swallowed. "Naw, just saw her and thought you mighta seen her come by."

Looking over on the bed, Ed spotted a cornstalk doll. He reached over and picked it up. "Seems to be kind of a young toy fer that little girl of yours," he said.

"She likes dolls," the woman said.

Ed turned it over and inspected the simple string tied behind the doll, holding it together. "Maybe so, but this looks like somethin' fixed up fer a baby."

Emma reached out and took the doll out of his hand. "Once you have children, mister, I reckon you'll find out they play with almost anything. Out here, toys is hard to come by."

When Ed finished his meal, he pushed his plate back. "I thank you, folks. I suppose I'd better move on and find someplace to bed down."

"You're welcome to throw your bag somewhere out near the spring. The kids will be coming in soon and you can sleep. In the morning we can feed you some breakfast before you move on."

To Ed's way of thinking, Harry seemed all too anxious to have him stay. He wondered if the man was running a bluff on him or telling him how he truly felt. If Raincloud was still here, the man might be trying to get him to move on quick. If she'd already left, and he wouldn't be able to tell until the sun came up, it just might mean that he would lose a night's travel in his chase. The man was large, quite a piece of work if he planned on a tussle. There was the Colt in Ed's pocket. Maybe if he pulled the revolver and threatened to use it on one of the kids, maybe then he could get the plain truth.

+ + + + +

Raincloud crouched in the mine tunnel as she fed Sunflower. She felt safer alone here and out of the way. She had left the house at the end of the day, in spite of the white people's objections. With Ed chasing her, she felt so much better on the move. She had ridden the gelding for some distance before she found the place the man named Harry had told her about. The mine tunnel was a place where she could keep the horse out of sight, somewhere that she could find shelter and water. She had found it in the dim twilight, below the cliffs, just as Harry had said she would. She was happy there was still some faint light from the west so she could see the dim hole in the earth.

She laid Sunflower down and began to play with her, shaking the doll with the gingham dress at her. Sunflower smiled at the doll and, reaching for it, fingered the bright cloth. Raincloud handed over the doll to the cooing child.

Fumbling in her bag, she produced the stub of a candle she had brought with her. She struck a match and lit the blackened wick. Holding it up, she got to her feet. Maybe she could find a larger room farther back in the mine, someplace away from the opening. If she was to have some light from time to time, she could not risk it being seen from the outside. Perhaps Ed had grown tired and stopped chasing her. Maybe he even felt bad because of the type of husband he had been and had decided to allow her to be free from him. She hoped so.

She looked back at the baby, playing with the doll in the gathering twilight. *She will be all right for a little time*, Raincloud thought. She held the candle high and peered over the back of the gelding and into the darkened tunnel. Stepping around the horse, she held out the candle.

Several stacks of tools sat beside the wall of the mine, and to one side, she could see a pile of unused torches and a tin jug marked "coal oil." *Should I light one of these things?* she wondered. *No, I don't want to chance any stray light out on the desert.*

She picked up two of the unlit torches and poured some of the liquid from the jug over them. Tucking both of the ready-made flames under her arm, she cupped her hand around the candle and moved deeper into the mine. The candle flickered slightly, almost as if a breeze were coming in her direction by a passageway she had not yet discovered.

She swiveled her head back, listening for the baby's cry. Sunflower's cries might echo far, given the place she was lying. But all she could hear now were the playful, contented gurgles of the child. It was good.

She lifted the candle. Up ahead she could see the wall of the mine split in two directions. She edged her way to the right. A meandering tunnel wandered off into the darkness and a sharp, almost hidden shelf of rock concealed yet another passageway. She veered into the sharp cutoff to her left. With only nine or ten steps, she was once again in the main tunnel.

Peering around it, she could see a wooden scaffolding standing in the middle of the main opening. *Could this be the place of the well water?* she wondered. She moved back toward the entrance and was satisfied when she saw the gelding still standing in place.

Turning around, she walked back to where the scaffolding was concealed. She paused to turn her head occasionally and listen for the baby. Moving around the corner and toward the structure, she thought that it might now be safe to light one of the torches. She held one out and positioned the candle underneath the soaked cloth. It exploded into flame.

Raincloud blew out the candle stub and placed it in her dress pocket. Moving forward, she peered over the edge of the shaft with the torch. It was dark and very deep. Below her, some ten to twenty feet down, she could see a large, flat ledge. The rocks stood out from the edge of the shaft and formed a platform. She could only guess it to be the place where Harry had stood while he deepened the hole. *The man only pretends to be a farmer*, she thought. He wanted no one to know about this place, but why had he told her? What was there about her that made this white man trust her? He had no reason to.

Waving the torch back and forth over the dark hole, she wondered if this was the well of water. Maybe Harry hadn't intended it to be. Maybe he had been chasing gold when he struck water instead. The rope went down the shaft and disappeared into the darkness, but still she had to know.

She lit the second torch with a fluff of flame and smoke and held it out over the hole. Letting go of the flame, she watched it plunge into the black below. Down it went, far down, until at last she heard the sizzle that told her there indeed was water below. She had watched the flame pass massive rock walls until at last there was nothing left but the blackness of the water.

It was then that she heard Sunflower's cry. The baby had obviously become aware of the fact that she was alone. Turning quickly, and not bothering to light the candle, Raincloud hurried back to the crying child. She laid the torch down beside the baby and picked her up. "Hush little one, it is Mother. You needn't cry anymore. I am here."

Without bothering to snuff out the torch in the entrance of the mine, Raincloud rocked the child back and forth, softly singing an Indian lullaby. She walked with the little girl in her arms and spoke softly to her in Apache. "Mother will watch out for you all the days of her life. You will have the brightness of the noon day, and the soft voice of the summer's wind."

Raincloud walked over to the gelding and stripped off his saddle. Taking hay that the white people had given her for the horse, she laid several handfuls on the floor of the mine and watched the animal eat. "You see, little one, you will have the swiftness of the horse, the beauty of many fine horses."

For some time, Raincloud walked and talked with the baby as the torch burned low. She knew that travel by night would be best in the desert. She thought perhaps she should wait here through the night and all during the next day, but she decided to move on that night. The sooner she left, the sooner she could make a new life for herself and the baby.

She laid the child on the carrier and laced her tightly in place. She would brush off the gelding's back with a handful of the hay before she once again saddled it. Animals needed to know they were being cared for, just like people needed to know they were loved. Gently, she began to massage the horse's back. Her head snapped up when she heard a familiar voice.

"Hello, little darling. I been lookin' for ya."

CHAPTER 16

✛ ✛ ✛ ✛ ✛ ✛ ✛

A mine northeast of Prescott
Friday night

Ed Hiatt stepped into the light of the dying torch. "It's so fine to see you again, gal." He laid down his gear and took off his jacket. "I just come from that nice family down there. It sorta made me recollect our happy family." His mouth creased into a sneer. "And it hurts me somethin' fierce, gal, that you would run away again from the home I built you."

Raincloud backed up as Ed stepped forward.

"And now here you done gone injun on me again. How many times is I gonna have to beat the notion into your head that you ain't no injun no more. You is Ed Hiatt's woman." Ed squatted and scraped debris into a small pile. He tossed several scraps of wood onto the pile. Picking up the fluttering torch, he lit the pile of firewood.

He stood up straight and, unbuttoning his shirt, pushed up his sleeves. "Now, little girl, I'ma gonna have to learn you a lesson 'bout running out on your husband. And when I finish with you, you're gonna thank me. I'm gonna take you back with me and sell you to some men I know. You gotta pay me back for all this here trouble you been."

Raincloud shook her head, trembling.

"You is lucky in a way. I ain't gonna beat you so that beauty of yours is harmed—no, why would I do that? It might make you less kindly to look on and that would cost me money. But I am gonna make you hurt some, girl. I might even take some of this here fire to that breed of yours, so's you can watch her cry and suffer. That would learn you a lesson, now, wouldn't it?"

Raincloud stiffened. To be hurt by him was something she had

113

grown to expect, but she would sooner die than allow him to hurt Sunflower. She backed up beside the gelding.

Ed stepped toward her. "Not only did you run away, but you stole my horse this time. In some parts around here, that's a hanging crime. Do you know that?"

"Do anything you want to me, but please don't hurt the baby. She is your baby too."

"'That breed don't look nothin' like me. How do I know you ain't been entertainin' some roving bucks whilst I been out digging? No, she don't look nothin' like me. 'Sides, she's a girl. What do I want with that? That's just another mouth to feed; can't get no work outta her ever—just a bother to a man. I keeps her around just to have a whip hand over you."

Raincloud cast a glance around her as Ed approached. There seemed to be no place to run to, nowhere to hide. As Ed took another step toward her, she reached up and gave a hard slap to the backside of the gelding. The horse bolted right toward Ed, sending him tumbling to the ground. Immediately, Raincloud turned to the darkness and ran.

Taking off the carrier, she swung it around and put her finger into Sunflower's mouth, stifling the child's cries. She bounced the baby gently as she turned into the right corridor and darted behind the shelf of rock that contained the hidden passageway.

Ed roared behind her and began to curse. The angry words filled the dark mine. She could hear him get to his feet and take another torch. From behind the rocky shelf, she could see the glow of the light as he moved slowly toward her position.

Somehow, she had to keep Sunflower quiet. She had to circle around and run out the main entrance. She didn't know how long she would be able to hide.

Ed came closer. She had the baby quiet for the moment, but her heart was pounding. *Oh, little one,* she thought, *I need you to be very quiet and still. I need you to be an Apache in the dark.*

The flicker of Ed's torch was closer now. He had seen her run to the right and she knew that this was the direction he would come. If he saw the narrow passage, all would be lost. She only hoped that for a moment the baby would be quiet as her father passed by them.

She heard the creak of his boots on the rock. Only if he went far into the blackness of the right tunnel could she hope to circle around through the main entrance. It was her only hope.

She dared not move as he came closer to her. If she accidentally kicked a stone on the ground, it would be all over. She would find the gelding and ride bareback as fast as she could.

Her heart beat faster.

Never again would she stop, no matter how hurt she was. The kindness of the people had lulled her to sleep on the inside. That would not happen again. She could depend on no one but the Apache in her.

She held her breath.

She could feel the heat from Ed's torch now. He was only inches away, just slightly around the edge of the cuts in the rock.

The passage had been narrow, obviously a place where the vein had veered off and Harry had dug. No matter where it had died out, he must have just decided to join the two tunnels, forming a narrow triangle of air in the midst of solid rock. She had almost missed it herself, and if she hadn't decided to turn her head and listen for the baby, she would have never seen it.

The baby! Oh please, Sunflower, please remain quiet, just for a few moments more.

"It won't do you no good to hide down there in the dark."

Ed was talking to the darkness of the tunnel. If only he could keep talking, keep talking loud, then maybe a chance noise by Sunflower wouldn't be heard.

"You best just come on out and it'll go easier on you. You make me come way back there and look for you, and I'm just gonna give you more hate tracks on that back of yourn."

Raincloud held her breath.

He was walking forward now. He thought she was in the darkness of the trunk tunnel, and he would soon be past her, unless he turned to his left and looked back.

She hoped and prayed he would continue to move straight ahead. *Move quickly!* she thought. *If you want me so bad, just come and get me.* She thought the words deliberately, as if by thinking them they might travel through the walls of the cave, enter his mind, and deceive him. It was Apache to think that way and she knew it.

Go into the darkness, white man. You are a man of the darkness, not fit for the bright sun of the day, a creature of the dark earth.

Just a few more steps and he would be past her. Then she could slowly move out of the passage and back into the main tunnel. From there, she would run.

He continued down the dark corridor. "Don't hide from your husband, woman. I'm warnin' ya. If I have to come down there, it's gonna go very hard on you."

He moved past her, waving his torch back and forth into the darkness, probing the darkness ahead with the flame.

Raincloud slowly inched her way through the dark passage, sliding her feet sideways. She knew there would be a faint light in the main tunnel from the fire Ed had started. And once she came out into the main tunnel, the area toward the well and beyond was bound to be in total darkness. As she moved down the narrow passage, she could hear him still talking in the darkness of the tunnel.

She planted her feet clumsily and stumbled. Sunflower began to cry.

Raincloud ran for the main tunnel, holding her finger in the baby's mouth to try to quiet her.

When she came out into the main passageway, the baby quieted down. Sunflower was a good baby. She did not cry long or hard. Maybe she was just too tired to cry.

Raincloud could hear Ed from around the corner, running back toward the direction of the entryway. If she tried to run for it now, Ed would see her and overtake her. Squatting down, she picked up a rock and, rounding the corner, threw it in the direction of the dimly lit entrance. It was all she knew to do. She had to make him think she had run that way. She had to once again take refuge in the darkness of the mine. Maybe he would leave. Maybe he would try to find her outside and then she could slip away. Maybe the kindly white man who owned the mine—Harry—would come to her aid before Ed could find her.

She backed up into the darkness as Ed rounded the corner with his torch. He had heard the rock near the entrance of the cave and was running toward the sound.

Inching back into the mine, she felt for the edge of the scaffolding around the well. She didn't want to fall into it.

Sunflower whimpered.

"Shhh, little one," she whispered. "You have been so good. Don't cry now. Make Mother happy with silence."

Waving in the darkness behind her, she touched the scaffolding. She put her hand to the rope.

Remembering the ledge below, she tested the rope. It would be a good place to hide. If she could keep Sunflower quiet long enough, they might be able to go undetected.

She ran her soft hand across the baby's face. Sunflower lay against her chest, the carrier turned in front of her. "Stay quiet, little one. Trust Mother."

She held on to the rope and lowered herself and the baby into the hole. Keeping her feet braced against the side of the shaft, she lowered herself hand over hand.

Stopping to catch her breath, she could feel the pull on her arms. The rope burned on her hands. It was biting her. She had to go lower. The ledge must be just below her. Scooting her feet lower, she felt nothing. Once again, she transferred her hands and dropped. Each movement sent pain through her arms and hands.

Finally, pointing her toes straight down, she could feel the shelf of rock. She released her grip on the rope and dropped to the shelf.

Sunflower began a soft cry and Raincloud once again ran her hand over the baby's face. She pressed the child's face close to hers. "It's all right. Mother has you with her," she whispered. "Stay very quiet for Mother."

The edge of the rocky surface was something Raincloud did not want to venture too close to. She had watched the torch drop a long distance before it went out in the water. She crouched close to the wall of the well and waited. There was no way to tell how long she would have to wait. Maybe Ed would need a drink and come to the well to draw water. Raincloud shivered to think of the possibility. He would be very angry indeed. He had been so close to catching her, and now she was gone. Near the entryway of the mine, she heard him pass by and curse. His angry voice rang through the tunnel.

She bounced Sunflower slightly to comfort her.

Ed's voice was now getting closer. He was talking to himself.

He cursed a reference to her. "I'll kill her, I will. No 'pache squaw is worth the trouble she's been." He continued a string of curses, each one growing more violent and explicit.

Raincloud held the baby close. The child began a soft cry and Raincloud blew a soft breath onto Sunflower's face. There was little more she could do now. There was nowhere else to go.

Ed's ranting grew silent.

Raincloud looked up, wondering if he had heard. The light from above her was growing brighter.

Raincloud's heart beat faster. With each look at the ever brighter light above, she seemed to die inside.

She gently bounced the baby, running her hand over the child's mouth and allowing it to suck on her finger.

Above her, the torch was bright. *He must be at the well*, she thought, terrified that he would be curious about what was inside.

Ed held the torch down over the well.

She could see his face.

Could he see hers?

"Look at you. Where you gonna go now?"

Her heart sank. There would be no escape now. She kept her silence.

"I done told you it would go worse for you and that breed if'n I had to find you."

Raincloud thought that if she could just wait down where she was, then maybe someone would come. Perhaps the nice man would be curious about how she was doing in the mine he had told her about.

"You better climb on up here, woman. Get yerself and that whelp up here where I can see you better."

Raincloud froze. She was not going to move. She wouldn't climb back up to be beaten. She would rather he shoot her right where she was.

"Yer gettin' me plenty angry." He said the words with a sneer followed by more curses, each one louder than the last.

Sunflower began to cry. She would let the child cry now. It would do no good to try to hush her. *Cry louder*, she thought. *Cry out to the rocks and the wind outside. Mix your tears with that of the other Apache.*

Ed vanished from the opening of the well. The blackness was a welcome sight. Moments later, the light once again lit up the roof of the mine. Ed poked his head over the side.

"You ain't gonna just sit there. I ain't got the time no more to waste on you."

He held out something and she could feel the splashes of thick liquid on her. It smelled, reeked of petroleum. He continued to pour it out. In moments, both she and the baby were soaked with the substance.

"I done found me some coal oil back there." He held the torch over the opening. "If I drop this thing on you two, both of you will light up like the biggest fire you ever saw. You think you're gonna like the smell of that little girl's burnin' skin?"

CHAPTER 17

+ + + + + + +

The Arizona desert
Friday

Earlier in the day, Zac and Chupta had spotted the vultures from a distance. Things die in the desert, and vultures were the scavengers of the territory. They worked hard to keep the place looking as God had intended it; so to see one or two was not all that unusual. This was a larger group than that, however, much too large for the remains of a small animal. The fact that the war party had passed near them only made Zac's curiosity more keen. The two men exchanged glances and kicked their horses into a faster gait.

Minutes later, as the two of them rounded the hillside, they spotted the bodies. The two men lay beside a freshly dug hole, next to a shelf of rock. Chupta recognized the place at once. It was near there that Chupta was going to begin his search for water. From the looks of the site, it appeared that the men had tried to dig for water and died of thirst. They would have to see.

Several of the brave buzzards were perched on the bodies, but the approaching horses sent them reluctantly into the air.

As Zac and Chupta slowed down and trotted up to the bodies, it was apparent these men were not victims of thirst—they were gunshot. Chupta was quietly relieved. It wasn't that he rejoiced in the manner a man died. It was just that the thought of having two men die of thirst within shouting distance of the tanks bothered him. He had seen it before, more than a few times. The desert in the valley of the sun never forgave a man for ignorance. It showed no mercy. And for the white man that belonged in the East and came to Arizona to find riches, ignorance was something that abounded.

Zac and Chupta dismounted. Zac rolled the bodies over to inspect them while Chupta walked up the rocky shelf to look it over closely. Moments later Chupta walked back and found Zac standing in the hole.

"Seems we got ourselves some sort of puzzle here," Zac said. "We trailed our people to this spot. From the looks of them, the kid over there might have been the one that was wounded. Kind of a slow, angry way to die, I'd say."

Zac got out of the hole and walked over to the two men. "This one's been shot several times. Kind of a tight pattern, too. I'd say whoever did this knows what he's about with a six-gun."

"Ummh," Chupta grunted.

"From the size of the hole and the dirt scattered on the bodies, I'd say that hole was the grave of these two fellas. Now, you tell me, my Apache friend, you ever know buzzards to dig up folks in order to eat them?"

The crack of a smile appeared on a corner of the Indian's mouth. He shook his head slightly.

"Well, somebody dug them up. Somebody planted them and then somebody either forgot to clean out their pockets and had to dig, or somebody else came along and dug these boys up. Now the question is, who and why?"

"We follow the men who rob army here to this place," Chupta said.

"Right, and we can figure that the youngster over there was the one whose blood trail we've been following. There's lots of tracks still left around and plenty of signs. I'd say before we plant these fellas again, we'd better have a look around and see what there is to find."

Where Chupta was involved, Zac found himself talking more out of necessity than anything else. He was sure that what he had in mind was something that was already running through the mind of the scout, but he said it anyway, just to make sure.

The two of them spent the better part of the next half hour walking around and through the camp in circles. Each of them formed their own opinions of what had happened. They met at the hole to talk.

"I see five sets of boot prints on the ground. I can only reckon that two of them belonged to these fellas. I don't see where anybody was dragged."

"Two men ride out alone," Chupta said. "Have two pack animals, mules. Send off three other mules." Chupta pointed out toward the valley. "Mules run off that way. Mules get here with full packs, leave empty. Mules men take with them have heavy loads."

"You're good," Zac said. "That's the way I see it, too." He took off his hat and scratched his head. "What about fella number three?"

"He not like other men. He ride mule. He not go with others. He ride off toward stage road. Other men ride north around valley."

"Both of them are heading north. We just don't know if they met each other here. We know one thing, though."

"What that?"

"The two fellas with the pack animals are most likely the ones with the gold."

"Only one thing," Chupta interrupted. "Man who come in on mule, ride out with heavy load." He pointed to the tracks. "Deeper tracks go out than come in."

"You do have a sharp eye." Zac paused and looked at the two bodies. "I guess we'll cover these boys up a second time and then for my money, we follow the two men with the mules."

Chupta nodded in agreement.

＊　＊　＊　＊　＊

The mine
Friday night

Raincloud shook more out of anger than fear. Her hatred for the man swelled up inside of her. He was her husband, the man she had pledged her life to, but he was also her blood enemy. Ed Hiatt only wanted her for revenge, revenge against the failures of his own life, and he would not let her go. Nothing she did seemed to be enough to satisfy the man.

She was beaten. Inside, she knew that she could do only one thing. She would give her body to the man, as she had done many times before, but she would send her soul away. She would send her soul to cry alone for her in the desert. That way, her spirit could remain pure. No matter what he might do, and no matter what he would subject her to, she would remain untouched inside. He could never reach her soul crying in the desert.

"I will come up," she called out.

"I ain't gonna pull you up, woman. Yer gonna have to get up the same way you got down."

She swung the baby into the carrier on her back. Grabbing the rope with her hands, she planted her feet on the sheer face of the well. Sunflower cried harder now, making the effort not only difficult for her arms but for her soul as well. With each pull, it seemed the child was crying out for her, knowing what was to come. As she strained hand over hand, the ropes continued cutting into her flesh.

The time that passed as she climbed back up the rope seemed much longer to her than when she had climbed down into the shaft. With each bawling scream of the child, Raincloud's desperation grew. She still had the knife in her belt. Could she use it on her husband? She didn't think so. Better to suffer than to become the kind of person she hated in him. To bow before his blows was something she had done before. The only thing that could drive her to murder would be if she thought the baby was in danger. She was Ed's wife, but she was also a mother. This was a sacred charge to her from God. She could not, while she still had breath, allow any harm to come to the baby.

Placing her elbows on the edge of the hole, she scrambled to get a grip with her feet. Ed reached down and, grabbing her dress and the carrier with Sunflower, he hauled her up. She scooted to the wall, breathing hard. Sunflower continued to cry.

"Now, woman, you is gonna pay." Ed unbuckled his belt, sliding it from around his waist. "And you is gonna continue to pay fer the rest of your sorry, miserable life for what you done to me."

"Take me back to my father," she said. "He will give you back what you paid for me." The thought of going back to her people this way was one that held great disgrace for her. But it was something she could live with.

"No, woman, you belong to me. I'm gonna get everything I paid for you out of yer hide." With that, he sent the belt lashing down across her face. The next two blows went to her back. Sunflower cried harder. One of the blows had glanced across the baby as well.

Raincloud lifted her hands plaintively. "Please, don't hit the baby. Hit me."

Ed grabbed her by the dress and dragged her toward the entrance of the mine. Her dress tore and Sunflower kept up the loud crying. Ed continued to strike them both as he dragged them toward the fire.

Raincloud prayed. Her head was swimming with the thoughts of what might happen to her before the night was over. Would she live to see the sun again? She didn't know.

She scooted toward the wall when Ed released her torn dress. Turning her back to the man, she sheltered the crying child.

One after another, the lashes of the stiff leather belt fell upon her. Then suddenly they stopped. She heard Ed grunt.

Turning around, she looked up and saw another man behind Ed. The man's face danced with the light from the fire. He had the sharp features of a hawk, with a black patch across one eye. The man had placed his knee to Ed's back and was pulling on his shirt collar, bending him backward. Ed twisted in pain and the man slung him to the floor.

Stepping quickly toward her fallen husband, the man placed his boot on Ed's throat. "You just lay there and let the lady be," the man said.

"She's my wife," Ed croaked.

"That don't make no difference; she's a woman."

"She's Apache."

"She's a woman."

Raincloud sat up and took the child out of the carrier, holding her close. She looked at the man in amazement, unable to take her eyes off him. He was like nothing she had ever seen before. His left arm was missing above the elbow, but he didn't move like a cripple. There was anger in his eye, a brooding boil like the scorching sun in the noonday heat. She had never seen the man before and couldn't imagine why he had pulled Ed off her. Looking down, she could see the fear in Ed's eyes as he squirmed under the man's stiff boot.

A second man with a large black beard and shining dark eyes entered the cave. He blinked at the scene and his mouth drooped open. "He's got our gold on that mule of his," the man said.

The man with the hawklike nose took his foot from Ed's throat and drew his revolver. "For a while today, we thought you were following us. We watched you, couldn't figure you out. You'da been the first bounty hunter to chase somebody down on a mule."

Ed sat up and slid over to the wall. He held up his hands. "I just found that gold in the desert. Didn't know whose it was. Thought it might belong to the army."

The man with the large dark eyes spoke. "S'pose we could just kill him here, Julian. It would be a favor to us, and a mercy to the woman."

Raincloud had never seen Ed so helpless. He had been the object of her hatred for many months now. She had left him, she had wished him dead, but now she couldn't bear to see it happen with her own eyes when she might be able to prevent it. She hesitated and then spoke up. "Please don't kill him. He is my husband. He is the father of my child."

Ed glanced over at her, his eyes filled with surprise.

Julian cocked his revolver. "He's a miserable cur dog," he said. "Man like that just isn't fit to live."

The bearded man spoke up. "Listen, Cobb, just put one in him and let's be done with it."

Julian looked at Raincloud. For a woman in fear, a woman who had been beaten, she was also loyal. It was something he admired. He eased the hammer on the revolver back into place. "Drago, I don't suppose this woman here wants to remember the sight of her husband dying. No woman wants to see that in her mind for the rest of her life." Pointing the gun at the cringing man, he waved the barrel up. "Get to your feet. We're gonna take a short walk to the back of this mine."

Ed staggered to his feet. "There's a well back there. You can leave me in there. I won't be following you no more. You can have her and the breed."

Drago helped Raincloud to her feet. "This woman smells like coal oil," he said. "Maybe he was thinking 'bout settin' her and the baby on fire."

"Is that right?" Julian asked. Ed's silence and the stillness of Raincloud told him all there was to tell.

"Drago, you take what's left of that stuff and wet our grave robber down. Make sure he gets it all. I want him scared to death of a spark." Looking at Ed, his eye sparkled. "We'll see how you hold up with the same medicine you were going to give out. Wet down several of them torches first, Drago."

After applying the liquid to four of the torches, Drago emptied what was left in the can on top of Ed. He picked up one of the cloth-wrapped sticks and touched it to the fire, igniting it in a bright blaze.

Drago gave out a smile. He was the type of man who always seemed to be able to smile at anything, especially a funeral. There was a sadistic streak to him. "Cobb, I don't zackly know when I seen a more compassionate killer of men. You musta had a real soft momma. Now mine was a hard old lady. She taught me to swim by throwing me in the river. She'd just say, 'Boy, someone that was born to hang need have no fear of the water,' and I reckon she was right."

"There ain't no ounce of pity in what I'm about to do to him. I'm gonna let him think about his dying for a while."

Julian watched Ed back up slightly, his hands in the air. He signaled with the muzzle of his revolver. "Now, you move right smartly back there. You've seen your last day."

Ed turned and walked back into the main tunnel of the mine, followed by Julian and Drago.

Raincloud followed with the still-whimpering baby. "Please do not kill him," she said. "Put him in the hole, but don't burn him."

Julian was silent. His eye was locked on to the cowering man as he walked ahead.

Drago went on. "You trust us, gal. I'm a plenty merciful man myself, just like my momma. On our place we had us a herd of cats. Momma would drown the new kittens, but she'd always warm up the water first."

When they got to the scaffolding over the well, Julian once again signaled. "You get on down there," he paused, "and be quick about it."

Ed grabbed the rope and hurriedly shinnied down it to the ledge below. He obviously didn't want to remain in the gunsights of the one-eyed man for long.

"Drago, you light them torches and plant them all around this side of the well. We wouldn't want that man to be left here in the dark, now, would we?"

Drago weighted the torches down with rocks. They were positioned above the well, glowing above Ed's head as he stood on the ledge.

"Now, we'll just see how long you can dodge the sparks," Julian said. "You're going to blazes eventually. It remains to be seen if it starts right here. Come on," he barked at Raincloud, "we'll be taking you with us for a spell."

With that, the two men turned to go to the entrance of the mine. Raincloud looked over the edge of the well at Ed, and then securely lashed the rope to the scaffolding. If Ed was to climb out, she didn't want him to fall.

125

CHAPTER 18

+ + + + + + +

The Arizona desert
Friday afternoon

Zac tossed the bag of jerky to Chupta. The scout reached in and produced several long, twisted strips of peppered beef. He clamped his teeth on one of them and pulled. Zac watched him closely. It was hard to judge an Indian's age; he had already discovered that. For people who spent as much time in the sun as they did, the skin of the man seemed remarkably smooth. It was plain to see from the way Chupta pulled the hard beef apart with his teeth that age had not diminished his ability to chew. If he had been forced to guess by appearance alone, Zac would have said Chupta was a man in his twenties, but the men at the fort said he had been an Apache scout for over ten years, and that would have made him at least thirty.

Chupta's glance as he ate told Zac that this meat was not the man's favorite staple. It made Zac curious. He thought how nice it would be to actually visit Chupta's family and see what they prepared for him. To know another man in his home was to really know him. Many times Zac had watched visitors to his home stand in amazement as he played the violin. It seemed so out of place for a man who made his living with the gun. But then as far as Zac Cobb was concerned, there were so many things out of place.

Most of the times he visited San Francisco, he made it a point to hear the symphony. He envied the musicians. He knew there was little or no money in it for them, yet they all seemed so happy just to be sitting there in a group, playing beautiful music. Zac loved the violin, but he realized he was too much of a loner to just sit in a crowd and blend in. Still, it always gave him great joy to watch folks do what they did best.

126

Right now, Zac knew that what he did best was work with his wits and his gun. Maybe later he could learn to satisfy himself with cows and his violin. He doubted it, but he could hope.

Chupta got up and walked over to one of the low-slung cacti Zac had been inspecting earlier in the day. The desert was south of them now, and the sandy soil of the bluffs was only occasionally marked by cacti. Small buds of pink flowers sprouted into chains of fruit, each with a slick, green, glossy surface peppered with brown spots. He took out his knife and sliced several of the pods from the cactus. He worked on them with the knife, carefully peeling back the skin. Then he placed one of them in his mouth. He smiled.

"Are those good?" Zac asked.

Chupta repeated the procedure with another cactus and took the pulp to Zac. "You try," he said. "They called jumping cholla. This good time to eat them."

Zac inspected and then tasted the slice of cactus meat. "They aren't half bad," he said. He took out the pouch of dried apricots he was carrying and handed several of them to the scout. Chupta chewed one with interest and then his face turned sour. He spat it out into his hand and dropped it to the ground.

"No like," he said.

Zac smiled. "If you're ever invited to eat at a white lady's table, just make sure you don't do that with her food. You have to eat what they give you and grin about it."

"Why?"

"Because it's just polite."

"White men lie and be polite?"

"No," Zac chuckled, "white men lie to women and be polite."

Chupta shook his head. "I never understand white man. Apache women no like man who lie."

"I suppose with us, it all depends on what you lie about. If you were drinking and lied about it, the women don't much like that. But if you tell them they look pretty when you've seen them looking better, they'll never believe you, but they'll like you all the same for saying it."

Chupta continued to shake his head. "I never understand white man. How can Apache understand a white woman?"

"Well, since both of us are men, we won't have to worry about lying to each other. You don't like the way I look or smell, you just tell me right off."

"No care how you look or smell."

Zac laughed. "Like I said, since we're both men, it doesn't much matter." He began to chew on some of the apricots. "Meanwhile, if there's ever anything you or I want to know, we'll just make it a practice of telling each other the truth. That good enough for you?"

"Apache hear that before. Only few of the older men remember believing it then. White men tell lie and his eyes show him not know the difference between the truth and a lie."

"I make no excuses for the white men you've known. I only speak for one man and that's Zachary Taylor Cobb."

Chupta's face hardened. His coal black eyes seemed to bore through Zac's, as if he were trying to read the white man's mind. Chupta got to his feet. He walked over to Zac's horse and put his hand on the rifle bag. "Tell Chupta about big gun," he said.

Zac joined him and slid the gun out of the scabbard. Unwrapping it, he dropped it in Chupta's arms.

The Indian held it in his hands as if weighing it. "You no use Winchester."

"No, I like this here Sharps Creedmore."

"How many shots?"

"One."

Chupta continued to bounce the gun in his hands. He lifted it to his shoulder and squinted down the long octagonal barrel. "This rifle heavy. Only one shot? It not enough."

"It is if you hit what you're aiming at, and I hit what I'm aiming at just about every time I squeeze the trigger."

"Two triggers?"

"Yes, the one in front is a set trigger. When I pull that, I slip my finger to the other one and then all I have to do is squeeze real gentle-like. It goes much farther than a Winchester. A man would have to be a durn fool to charge me when I got this thing up. For that matter, a group of men would have a tough time. I could reload and fire a great many times before they got in close enough to use their puny weapons. I never try to shoot fast, and I make it a point never to shoot at a man more than once."

"You different. Most white men not careful."

"I try to be smart," Zac said. "The people I hunt sometimes travel in packs and the ones that go by themselves are usually faster with a six-gun than I am. It always pays to have an edge, and that weapon there has been an edge for me many a time."

"You hunt men like a wolf," Chupta said.

Zac took the rifle and scooted the bag back over it. He replaced it in the scabbard. "No, more like a lion, I think. Wolves travel in packs. They snip at their prey to disable them first, then they go in for the kill. When the lion pounces, he goes for the kill right off."

Chupta narrowed his eyes and looked at Zac as if inspecting him. Both of them had started the trip together suspiciously wary of the unknown in each other. They had seemed to be sizing each other up, not so much as a man looking on an enemy, but as a man testing out a new piece of equipment, one that he might need someday.

"I think you right," Chupta said. "You like lion, Apache like wolf. I think it better to be wolf."

Zac smiled. "One thing's for sure, the wolf life ain't near as lonely." He began to pick up what was left of their meal. "Right now, though, the army has joined up a wolf and a lion to do their hunting for them. I used to hunt them boys in blue my ownself; today I do their hunting for them."

Chupta grunted and nodded. "Chupta too."

Zac reached out and put his hand on the scout's shoulder. "Then, we're both doing something that's strange for us, and I, for one, am glad you're with me."

Chupta shrugged Zac's hand from his shoulder. He straightened himself to full height. "Don't think soft about why I with you. Chupta is with you because he has to be. That is all. That is all there will ever be."

They mounted their horses. It would be dark soon, and both of them wanted to squeeze every ounce of the daylight into the process of following the strange trail of the men in front of them.

✦ ✦ ✦ ✦ ✦

Late Friday night

Hec Peters walked through the group sitting on the ground. He passed out what little beef jerky he had left. "This may be all we have for a spell," he said. "Twern't zackly counting on missing our stops; we didn't have much time to look around at the stage stop."

Ruggles spoke up. "I spotted some bighorn sheep while we were walking today. When we get to a place where we know they go for water, I'll bring one down."

Philip Carol sat next to Amy. He patted her arm. "This may be kind of rough. You may not be able to trust everyone here," he said, looking up at Ruggles, "but you just stick close to me. When we get to a place with a telegraph, I'll see that my father takes care of you and your brother."

"Thank you," Amy said. "That would be much appreciated. I don't know when I've ever felt more helpless or lost."

"I felt that way my first day at school last year. There I was, and no one knew who I was or where I came from. It took me a while to remember what I was there for, but after that, I was fine. There's great strength in remembering that you have a family and a father backing you."

"I would suppose so," Amy said. "But that's a feeling I haven't known in years."

Carol looked longingly into her eyes. "As long as you're with me, my father is backing you, too. He will do for me just exactly what I say. He always has and he always will."

The Reverend Black pulled a wad of cigars from an inner pocket and held them up. "We do have a little vegetation to draw upon here, the blessed barley of Virginia. If you get some water started, I could crumble these up and make some good old bright leaf stew. It would make you plumb sick, but then you wouldn't be hungry anymore, now, would you?"

Each of the people in the group looked on the outspoken preacher with doubt. Some already had the feeling that he was crazy to live and minister in the desert as it was, and the fact that he spoke Apache and smoked cigars didn't go very far in removing the doubts they had about the man. Ruggles could see it in their eyes. Amy and Ruggles looked at each other. "Parson, these folks here don't know when you're funning them and when you're serious."

"It's not important for them to know, but it's terrible important for me to know," he said. "I've always taught my congregations to take nothing I say as momentous until I open my Bible. Trouble with folks is, they take themselves too serious, and God not near serious enough."

"Shouldn't we view ourselves solemnly as human beings?" Philip asked. "My professors at Yale tell me that man is the noblest creature on the globe, and as such we have obligations to history."

"Creature?" Black's mouth turned down. His heavy salt-and-pepper eyebrows dipped over glaring eyes. "Boy, you best be getting it straight just what man is supposed to be. I can assure you, it's much more than you're being taught in school, but not nearly so special as most of us thinks we are."

"Weren't we made special?" Amy asked.

"The good book says that man was made a little lower than the angels. The difficulty with us is, we don't know how lowly an angel's thinking truly is, and we place too much stock in our own. The best of the angels have only been taught to follow orders. They ain't had an original thought in them since the world started spinning. The ones that did think on their own went over to the other side."

"Don't the obedient angels think for themselves?" Amy asked.

"To a small degree, they do. They think, 'What did the Lord say?' And then they think, 'Am I gonna fall into line and do it?' Frankly, that about sums up what ought to be the best of our thought life as well."

"All the same," Ruggles said, "I think we'll have to pass on your tobacco stew."

Black replaced all but one of the dark cigars back in his pocket. He bit off the end and spit it out on the ground, striking a match to it. "Suit yerselves," he puffed. "You all had your chance and now I'll have mine."

Amy got up and walked to the edge of the rocks. Ruggles joined her. "Disgusting, isn't it?" he asked. "Somehow, men never turn out the way you want them to be."

"You don't mean that."

"No, I don't. You know me too well." He looked back at the group and at Black enjoying his cigar. "I kinda like him, though. He's got just enough wrong with him to make me want to listen to what he has to say. Some of the preacher types I've known are so puffed up with themselves that a man would have to be ten feet tall to scrape their underbelly. At times a man can be so full of pretending, he doesn't have any room left for living."

The wail of a coyote brought every head around. It was followed by the soft peeping of an elf owl.

"The horses are watered and rested, and I think we better be moving on," Peters said.

"Why must we go on?" Mary asked. "We need to sleep."

Ruggles walked back to join in the discussion. "I think Hec here is right," he said. "We need to put as many nighttime miles as we can between us and the Indians to make us all the harder to catch."

"You got that right," Gray added.

"I don't want to be anywheres close to here come dawn," Peters went on. "If I knew about the water here, they sure 'nuff do. When they come our way, they'll make a beeline for these here rocks."

"Where's Tommy?" Ruggles asked.

Black got to his feet, puffing on his cigar. "The last time I saw the young man, he was running around those rocks over there. I'll go get him. You folks just get on the stage."

Black walked toward the rocks, his frock coat blending into the darkness. He caught Tommy as the boy rounded the formation. "Whoa, son, just hold on there."

The boy struggled in the man's arms and then stood passively.

"Don't you want to go with us?" Black asked.

"No!" The boy vigorously shook his head. "I like the dark and I like to run."

"Son, I can tell you one thing, many was the time I thought I was running in the dark myself. But when I stopped running, I found out I was just in the darkness all by myself. That's a bad place to be—not the darkness, just the loneliness."

CHAPTER 19

+ + + + + + +

The desert, a cool wind blowing from the south
Friday evening

Mangus rode at the head of his men, his eyes flashing forward across the darkening valley. They picked their way around the greasewood and large cactus sentinels that stood in the gathering twilight. From what he had been told, the white man's wagon would be at the cottonwood wells. The horses at the station had been taken in the raid and without fresh animals to pull the thing, it would not go fast. The one thing he must make sure of, however, was that he would not lose any more men.

As he rode, he signaled to two of the men who were riding beside him. Gesturing with his hands, he sent them riding off in opposite directions. They would be his wolves. The two of them would flank the band and keep a watchful eye for any sign of the army. Both knew where Mangus and the rest of the warriors were going. It would be no problem to scout the darkness of the desert and still arrive at the wells along with the rest of the band. They must avoid temptation, however; they could not stop to hunt.

The mountains stood like giants on their toes, their tops leveled by the weather and their bellies flattened like young warriors painted for a raid. Mangus could almost hear their voices call to him, these strange silent ones that stood and watched him ride. "Mangus," they would say to him. "We are watching you, Mangus. You are a child of the desert. You belong to us."

Off to the north, he could see the rocky spire that sprouted from the mesa and rose into the sky. The Indians called it "the finger of God." It spoke to him like the mountains, pointing its finger at the lanterns of the evening sky. Seeing it reminded him that it was God who kept the people of the desert. God did not depend on his war with the white man to protect his people. Mangus must instead depend upon God.

The rocky black finger stood against the ever graying sky. Overhead, the lights in the dark sky were beginning to come on. They twinkled a soft glow on the northern horizon.

The night that was gathering all around Mangus as he rode made him proud that God had made him one of His people, a human being. Overhead, he saw several bats swooping down to claim fresh morsels of flying insects. These creatures were swift and sure, the kind of warrior Mangus wanted to be. They flew to their prey and snapped the flying bugs up, vanishing and then appearing again to feed.

An elf owl flew from its burrow in a giant cactus. With a torrent of wing strokes, it interrupted its glide to the ground just long enough to pick up prey it had spotted from its perch in the cactus. Pounding its small wings against the air, it whirled around and flew away to find a spot to enjoy its evening meal.

All around him the balance of the desert reassured him of the rightness in what he was doing. God had made the creatures and He had also made the men of the desert. The creatures showed no mercy; neither would he.

Mangus had long ago learned to be alone with his thoughts, even in the midst of people. In the silence of his mind, Mangus could see what few could, and he wanted to see everything there was to see. It was in the still silence that he heard all of the sounds that God had put here for him to hear. The land, the wind, and the animals talked to him. These were the voices of God to Mangus. The voices of men came from themselves; they did not come from God.

Many times he had heard the missionary man claim to read the voice of God from the black book he carried. It was something Mangus had listened to. He respected the man. Unlike others, the missionary had not come to the desert to take from it, so Mangus listened to the words. He told himself that if the man believed these words enough to live with the Indian, then, perhaps they were worth the hearing.

The God of the book was a strange one to Mangus, though, a God who had a son that walked the earth to know men. This was indeed different. Mangus wondered about such a God.

How could such a powerful God as the man had read about humble himself to walk the earth? It was a puzzle to Mangus. To him, pride was the distinguishing mark of a man. How could God be any different?

Several times, Mangus noticed the wolf he had sent off to the south ride back over a rise and wave his arm. The one he had sent north made no such appearance. *Perhaps he has seen sheep*, Mangus thought, *fresh meat for the fire of camp. He should not take the time to hunt.*

+ + + + +

Friday night

The lone wolf riding to the north had smelled a strange smell in the night air before he heard or saw anything. It was a smell that did not belong in this place. Had he not known better, he would have thought it to be the smell of the desert flowers blooming in the night air.

He had ridden in the direction of the rocks, the ones that he knew had the high places with cool water. It would be good to take a drink from the high places and bring back water for his spotted horse.

The horse had been with him for three years now. His father had given it to him when he became a man. The old man had been sad when he had ridden away to join Mangus for the ghost dance and war with the white man. As he had ridden away on that day, he saw the sadness in his father's eyes and wondered whether he had been sad to see him leave, or sad to no longer be able to look upon the horse. Whatever the case, the animal must be cared for. He would not have him tired and without water.

As he came closer to the rocks, he walked the horse slowly through the tall cacti and around the small brush that blanketed the desert floor. As he got closer to the big rocks, a rabbit scurried away from him. The strange smell drew the man. Then he heard the noise—the sound of people talking, white men!

He slid down from the back of the spotted horse and slowly led him forward. The noise came from the rocks. Nearby, he heard the noise of a quail, followed by the peeping of an elf owl from his high perch on a cactus. It was as if his desert friends were warning him of the danger up ahead, telling him to take care. They were the same words Mangus himself would have told him. He walked the horse slowly forward.

He dropped the reins of the horse. It would not move from this place. There was plenty of brush to graze on and keep him occupied; besides, he had trained the animal well. As a man of the desert, he and the horse were one. Others, especially the Apache, would ride their horses into the ground and then eat them. Stolen horses were sweet to the taste, but he could not bear to part with his father's spotted horse.

Leaving his new rifle, he took out his bow. He slung the quiver of arrows over his shoulder. It was a thing he trusted. He had not yet had enough time to make his way with the new rifle. Crouching down, he moved toward the sound of the white men's words.

Suddenly, up ahead, he saw the small boy running around the rocks. There was an aimlessness about the man-child that he watched carefully. The boy took several steps and then swung his head around, as if trying to see all of the sky at one time. Then shaking his hands, he would walk several more steps and begin to run again. The man-child belonged to God; he would not kill him.

The wolf stayed close to the ground. He continued to listen to the white words he did not understand. He knew if he went farther, the chances were good that he might be seen by the boy. He watched as the child circled around the rocks and then moved out of sight. It was then that he heard the metal sounds on the other side of the rocks. Something was back there, something large.

He heard the horses and then the creaking of a wagon. Getting up, he moved quickly to the side of the boulders. The white man's stagecoach pulled away, slowly at first, but then with greater speed. It was moving off toward the north. This was the thing Mangus was trying to find, and here it was.

He walked into the place where the white people had stopped. There were many tracks still in the sand. He stopped and once again smelled the air. Now he remembered the smell. Only once before had he caught the scent of a white woman. He had watched a woman in the store splash on some smelly liquid from a colored, polished bottle. It had the stink of many flowers, dead flowers. There were women on the wagon of the white man! These women with their light hair would make a prize for any man.

+ + + + +

Friday, about midnight

Mangus and his men had ridden for several hours before they approached the wells of the cottonwoods. The smell of woodsmoke lingered in the night air, a smell that only meant one thing—white men!

Through the trees, he could see a fire. Only white men lit fires in the darkness. The Indian lit a fire to cook; the white man usually had one to keep the darkness away. It was a silly thing to do. A man at night commonly found his eyes drawn to the fire. When that happened, if he had to suddenly look off into the darkness, he would be momentarily blinded. It was just another thing that told Mangus the whites did not belong in the desert. They belonged in their places with the wooden walls and noisy streets.

Mangus signaled for the men to dismount and circle the camp. He got off his horse and watched the men fan out on either side of the campsite. Moving quickly through the brush, he came closer to the camp. There he saw three men—three men but no stagecoach. Two men lay under their blankets and a third sat beside the fire. The noise of the running water behind them, the cool water that came down from the mountains, was mixed with the sound of the crackling fire.

Across the stream, he could see three horses busily grazing on the grass. Ordinarily, had he been alone, these horses would have been easy to steal. The breeze was blowing toward him and his men; otherwise, the animals might have picked up their heads and warned the men of his approach. He watched them paw at the grass.

The man who was supposed to be on guard sat with his head slumped forward. He looked to be asleep. One of the two men on the ground suddenly threw back his blanket and got to his feet. The man walked over to the fire and, squatting down, took a pot from an iron grate and poured a cup of steaming liquid.

Mangus signaled two of the men beside him. He pointed to the man with the cup and made eye command to one of the warriors. Looking at the second warrior, he gestured toward the sleeping sentinel.

The two Indians each drew back their bows and with clear twangs in the night air sent two polished shafts straight toward their respective targets. Each of the arrows landed with painful suddenness, spinning the man with the cup to the ground and pitching the man who sat sleeping directly backward.

With quick yelps, the warriors all around the camp ran into the firelight, quickly finishing all three men with their bare knives. In a matter of moments, the camp was full of the Indian braves. Scalps were being taken and men were ransacking the possessions of the dead.

Mangus walked slowly through the camp. He picked up the blue metal cup and poured some of the steaming water into it. He was curious about everything to do with an enemy. Holding the cup to his lips, he sipped the liquid. It was bitter. He threw it down with disgust. There was nothing the white man had that he wanted, except for the rifles and ammunition.

Mangus sorted through some of the spoils of war the men were tossing aside. He held up a small paper picture. Walking over to the fire, he waved it close to the flame. The paper showed the image of a woman and two small children. The woman was dressed in black with lace around her throat. She held a baby in a chair with her. Beside her, a small, grim-faced girl-child stood with a hand on the woman's shoulder. Mangus imagined their cries when the news that their man would not return reached them. It was good. Maybe then they would go back to the place where they belonged and leave his land alone.

Mangus noticed Gandara. He had taken a scalp and now stood and waved his coup in the air for all to see. Gandara wanted to show his fierceness to all. He was like many of the others in that way— to stand over the body of a fallen enemy was to once again be a man. Gandara still had much to learn. If he was to lead the people someday, he must be willing to stand aside and allow the young bucks to summon up courage. A leader must show that he already had what it was the men who followed him were seeking.

Mangus watched him. He knew that Gandara was part of his mission before he died. Mangus was a maker of leaders, not just a leader. To be a leader meant to look out for the future. It was not enough to take revenge on the whites and enjoy the kill. He had to leave something behind, something the people could take hope in. The men who went to war with him would be men who could tell the stories of conquest long after he was gone. In a way, these men were more important to Mangus than the small victories. Gandara continued to wave the scalp and shout into the night air. His gaze then fell on Mangus and he stopped. One look from Mangus was enough to tell Gandara that his bravado was not appreciated.

To take revenge on an enemy was a good thing; it smelled of victory. But this had been too easy and Mangus knew it. There would have to be many more such triumphs for the white man to go away. News would have to travel to the Indian people as well, good news of hope. And before long, Mangus knew, he and his men would have to stand over the bodies of the white pony soldiers and their Apache scouts. A few lone farmers and prospectors killed would not be enough. Only when the soldier man died would the people know that it was safe to live again.

That would take many more men leaving the white man's reservation-prison to join Mangus and his war on the whites. It would take many more guns also and the ammunition he had been promised.

A short time later, the missing wolf returned to the band. He had news, news he was sure Mangus wanted to hear.

CHAPTER 20

+ + + + + + +

The mine
Saturday morning, past midnight

Ed craned his neck, watching the flames overhead. The torches burned brightly—glowing balls of fire suspended over the well of darkness. Ed could smell the coal oil all over his body. If one of these torches fell and landed on him, he'd never be able to bang the flames out. The ledge was a fair size though, almost four feet by six feet. It had been a place for whoever had dug this thing to stand on while he worked on digging the level below. Unfortunately, those men had placed the torches directly above the ledge, and not just one torch, either, but four.

Several showers of sparks fell down the shaft. Ed pressed himself into the rocky shelf and held his breath. He watched the sparks fall toward him, then past him by only inches.

"Raincloud!" he yelled up into the flame-lit shaft. "Raincloud darlin', don't you leave me here. I is sorry." There was a sense of desperation to his voice. "I'm the father of that baby. What you gonna tell her about her father when she gets older? How you gonna 'splain the way he died, and that you coulda helped him but didn't?"

He listened carefully. Silence was all that greeted him. He had hoped that they would have stayed in the mine for the night, but maybe that was too much to hope for. Traveling by night and holding up during the day was sure a lot safer, especially for men on the run—and these were men on the run, sure 'nuff. These were men that he in no way wanted to try to face down. Both of them looked plenty tough, especially the one with one eye. He looked to be a man who would more likely kill you than shake your hand.

"Raincloud! Don't leave me down here. You can't do that to me, darlin'."

Several sparks again fell, floating down the dark shaft. Ed moved quickly to the other side of the ledge, narrowly avoiding them. Realizing Raincloud was gone, he knew he had to get up this thing.

He looked carefully at the hanging rope. He knew he could climb it; after all, Raincloud had and with the baby on her back. What worried him most was being on the thing if one of the torches gave way. How could he avoid the falling flames while hanging on to the rope? And if he stayed where he was, would the flames burn the torch sticks and then all fall into the hole, catching him on fire for sure? He couldn't afford to wait. He had to try to climb out and do it now.

Reaching out, he grabbed the rope and pulled it closer. He tugged on it, testing the give on the line. Leaning out, he spun off over the darkness of the well. He would have to climb quickly. It was, after all, only twenty feet or so to the surface. He began to pull hand over hand up the rope.

Overhead, the torches began to shower more sparks. Ed quickly put his feet to the wall and pushed off, spinning away from the falling fire. His grip loosened and he grabbed for the rope. Spinning now out of control, he careened back into the path of the showering sparks. His hand slipped again. He was losing his grip. He let go of the rope and fell to the ledge. The impact of landing on the rocky shelf sent pain through his ankle. All around him, the sparks fell. He pushed his back to the wall. All he could do now was hope.

+ + + + +

The desert floor
Saturday morning, two hours later

Raincloud followed the men on horseback. She had left the stagecoach and gone off on her own. Maybe she had been right in doing that; after all, Mangus was near and his men would have taken no thought at all in making sport of her. She didn't want to leave these men, though. She didn't know why, but she trusted them; at least she trusted the man with one eye. Maybe she was attracted to his strength.

It was the way she had been taught as an Apache to evaluate a man. He seemed like a hard man, a hard and desperate man. But from what she knew of the desert and the men who roamed it, this was a man she knew she had to trust. He could protect her and Sunflower; he had already shown that.

The three of them rode on in the darkness. Raincloud was tired, but she had no intention of slowing the men down. An hour later, Sunflower started to cry from hunger. Raincloud knew that she, at least, would have to stop.

The man with one eye turned his horse around and trotted back to her. "We're gonna rest for a spell," he said.

"I don't want to make you stop," she replied.

"I'm not stopping for you. These horses and mules need a breather. You just tend to what you got to do when we pull into those rocks up ahead."

A few minutes later when they rode into the rocks, the men dismounted. Raincloud could see Julian watching her as she got down from her horse. He walked over to her. "We won't be here long," he said. "You best do what you got to do and be ready to travel. We'll ride most of the night and stop a couple of hours before sunrise. That way we can get a little sleep before we try to find some place out of the sun."

"You are very kind to me. I am not used to that."

"I'm not being kind at all. Don't go to fooling yourself about that. I just don't want you following us and turning up where you're not wanted, that's all."

"You saved me from my husband."

"I just scraped some scum offa my boot, that's all. You're well off to be rid of him."

"He is not always that way. It happens to him when he starts his drinking and card playing."

"Cards and whiskey don't make a man bad. They just show what a man always was."

Julian kicked aside some rocks on the ground and smoothed a patch of dirt for Raincloud to sit down on. Pulling out his knife and reaching down, he stabbed the ground and lifted a large scorpion on the point of his blade. He flicked it away. "That ought to make it a might more comfortable for you."

She sat down and, turning around, lowered her dress to feed the baby. Time with Sunflower was the most precious thing in her life now. It was all she had to remind her that she had a future to consider. It was the baby who made her go on when she might have just wanted to stay and take whatever came her way. But she would go on. The two of them had a life together, and it was a life she wanted.

When she finished feeding the child, she turned around to watch the two men. They were eating out of a bag, passing some dried beef back and forth. They talked quietly. She could only imagine what they were discussing about her.

Julian got to his feet and walked toward her with the bag. He tossed it. "It ain't much," he said, "but you better take some. It'll keep you going till we can get something better."

"I have flour and bacon," Raincloud said. "When we stop tomorrow, I will fix it for you."

"You hear that?" Drago spoke up. "The lady's gonna rustle us up some breakfast in the morning."

Julian turned around and looked back at the man on the ground. "I heard."

Drago grunted, "That oughta be real fine, don't you think, Cobb?"

"Just so she don't get too used to our company," Julian responded. "We got us some distance to make up for, and I don't intend to be no traveling nursery."

"I have money," Raincloud said. She was hesitant to tell the men about the cash she was carrying. It was a lot of money and she knew it. Men would kill for what she had and these men were obviously thieves, but the money would do her no good if Ed caught her alone again.

She could not count on him dying in the mine and something told her that he would never quit until she and Sunflower were dead. The thought that he might live troubled her. Right now she didn't know if she was a widow or a wife. "I know a woman is much trouble for you," she went on.

"You might be right," Julian replied. "Women are trouble and a woman with a baby is more trouble than she's worth. You just make sure you keep up with us. You can keep your money, though. You just might need it."

Drago spoke up. "You know, Cobb, if we meet up with some Apache, it might be her that pulls our fat out of the fire."

"And if we didn't have her, we wouldn't have to worry about bein' seen or having that kid of hers cryin' when we're trying to give someone the slip."

Raincloud didn't like being thought of as a bother. "I can keep her quiet. You don't have to worry about her." She still could not read the man. From his outward appearance, he was obviously someone not to be trifled with. His words were harsh, but his actions showed that he did care about what happened to her, no matter what he said. Her face showed her puzzlement. She chewed on a piece of the dried meat. "You are kind to me, all the same."

"I wouldn't leave you to the scorpions, neither the kind under the rocks or the two-legged kind."

+ + + + +

Drago walked up to Julian and the two of them wandered off. "The woman just might come in handy for us, for all we know," he said. "Cobb, you beat all, though," he snickered. "You can't fool me none. You'd soon kill a man too quick to blink an eye, to say nothing of leavin' that there woman's husband down there to die, but you know yourself that you take in every stray cat and orphan you come across. It beats all I ever seed."

"Guess it's my poor upbringing. Every time I think about what my momma might do, it just gives me cause to think. I might make war on the Yankees, but I just ain't got no quarrel with a woman and a baby, not just yet."

Drago dusted himself off. "I ain't got no quarrel with the woman either. In fact my eyes hunger to look on a woman, and even if she is Apache, she ain't too bad to look at. I'm like you in one way, though, I don't want nobody slowin' us down none."

"You just let me worry about that. If we find that she and the kid are hanging up our pace, we'll leave her flat when we cross that road."

"And when is that? Will you be listening to that head of yourn, or will you still be a-listenin' to that there momma you left?"

"My momma's not here; so I reckon I'll have to listen to my ownself."

After some hard riding, the four of them bedded down for a much-needed sleep. Julian kept a watchful eye on the woman for a while and then he, too, went to sleep. He was up before the dawn crested the mountains, but much later than he had intended.

He roused the woman. "We need to make up for some lost time. You best be keeping up."

She nodded.

The rough, hilly area, sprinkled with cacti and sharp spiny plants, made the going rough. Blind turns and sharp drops could have turned a group of tenderfeet all around, but Julian kept his eye on several prominent points to the north. As they rounded a turn that spilled out into a small valley, they spotted something they hadn't counted on—an army patrol of over twenty men heading their way.

Both Julian and Drago stiffened their spines in the saddle. Raincloud could tell at once that this meant trouble. They continued moving north. To change direction to avoid the patrol would arouse suspicion, and there was no way they could hope to outrun them. Julian surveyed the mules. The army pouches they carried were still covered with canvas.

The patrol pulled up in front of them. In the lead was a weather-beaten captain that looked to be a man with some time in the saddle. His wrinkled tan face was covered with dust and a graying mustache drooped down from his upper lip. "You folks lost?" he asked.

"Naw, we ain't lost," Drago shot back. "Are you?"

Julian rode up next to Drago. The last thing they wanted to do right now was stir up trouble with the army. "We're heading north," Julian said. "Doing some prospecting."

"There ain't much in the way of strikes north of here," the captain quickly replied. "We don't even patrol to the north—it's colder than blazes in winter."

"That's why we're headin' that way," Julian responded. "Ain't much call for a body eating off of somebody else's plate."

Several of the soldiers walked their horses up to the pack animals and Raincloud, who had been trailing the group. "We're patrolling and looking for hostiles. This place ain't been too healthy for white folks of late. There's men hereabouts, too, that robbed an army payroll. Robbed it and killed seven men."

"Sorry," Julian said, "we ain't seen nobody."

The three soldiers continued to walk their horses around the pack animals. "Why would you want to be out with Mangus on the loose?" the captain asked.

Raincloud rode her horse forward. "That's why I come," she shouted out. At the sound of her voice, every head snapped back and looked at her, including Julian. "He didn't want to leave me and the baby alone with all that happening. Indian not bother squaw man."

Raincloud nervously took the child from her back and rocked it in her arms. One of the soldiers rode over to her and looked at the now crying child. "Baby looks to be part white," the man called out.

"My baby belong to my man there," Raincloud said. "He not

want to leave me and the baby all alone."

Julian swallowed and blinked at her while Drago let out a slight smile.

"No, I suppose not," the captain replied. He looked at Raincloud carefully. Her long black hair hung down her back and her sparkling black eyes highlighted a strikingly beautiful face. "Well, we're turning north from here too. You can just ride along with us."

"Oh, that's not necessary, captain. We've been riding all night to make us some distance and were just about to set ourselves aside for a spell to rest the animals and the baby."

"We're due for a rest too. I think we'll just accompany you folks a ways and make sure you're all right. After all, that's part of our job out here."

CHAPTER 21

✦ ✦ ✦ ✦ ✦ ✦ ✦

The desert floor
Late Friday night

Chupta slept on the sandy soil while Zac kept watch. The scout dozed quietly, as if he expected to spring to his feet, ready for battle, at the slightest noise. It gave Zac great comfort. Most of the time, if he had his druthers, he'd just as soon work alone. There was less to worry about that way and more time to concentrate on whomever he happened to be chasing without having to worry about the welfare of a partner.

Working with the Apache scout was different, though. The man was entirely self-sufficient and obviously had little love for Zac. To care one way or the other about Chupta would be a waste of one's sympathy. Still, whatever else he was, the man could carry his own weight as a partner. Zac knew that if he could keep Chupta with him for the rest of his Wells Fargo days, he'd have a better chance of living to be an old man.

Zac looked over to where the man's rifle lay. Chupta had studded the beaten stock of the Winchester with brass tacks arranged in the outline of a cross in the midst of a circle. It seemed to be the custom of the Indian to alter whatever he received from the white man. Zac had seen it many times before—as if taking something directly from the white man and using it as is would be to acknowledge that the new way of doing things was right. It would be the white man's rifle and not the Indian's. Customized, his rifle became a part of him. Chupta would not belong to the Winchester arms company—the Winchester would belong to him and only him.

Zac admired the self-sufficiency of the Indian. Being kept by the white man and looked after by the Bureau of Indian Affairs went contrary to everything inside these people. Standing in a line for rancid meat was a dehumanizing thing. No one deserved to be treated like that. A man might have pets, but people couldn't be kept in a pen as if they were the army's pets. It wasn't right.

Zac lifted his chin up. There was nothing like the nighttime sky. He soaked it all in, allowing his mind to drift away to the things that were important to him. Somewhere right now, Jenny and Skip were sleeping under these same stars. Skip wasn't his, not by blood anyway. Still, the boy looked to him as a father, even if he was a poor substitute. Jenny might never be his. He might never be able to let her close enough to act on the feelings he carried around for her.

He'd lived for years thinking only about himself and what was good for him; he doubted if there was any room for thinking about another. Yet here he was, doing just that. Sometimes he surprised even himself. There were at least two people he cared about. He looked up at the sky. The lanterns of the night were keeping watch over them at home as well as him out here on the lonely sands.

It was a music kind of night, and he imagined what it would sound like to have his sweet red violin tucked under his chin. Everything about the soft breeze from the south and the lights of the night spoke to him of music. God had arranged the notes in the heavens, and he wanted to play them. It was a man's job to play the notes God arranged.

The stars reminded him of one of the lessons his mother had taught him, the one about the witnesses that had passed on. It was as if each one of the glowing lights in the darkness represented a hero who watched him. Heroes had always been important to him. His reading and his study of history had taught him that only when men were extraordinary, only then could they expect to leave their mark. Perhaps it was one reason he found it hard to quit and just raise cattle. He had studied and fancied his heroes since boyhood. He'd grown up wanting to be like them, and then the war came. The war's end had left him a hero without any witnesses to acknowledge it.

Of course, he always knew that real heroes put on their pants and went to work day after day, with never any limelight, never any thought of anything beyond the ordinary. Faithfulness was heroic. A man's ability to keep on doing what was right was the thing that made most men heroes. The thought of being a farmer, however, was something that stuck in his craw.

The war had been something he understood; the raw nerve of facing one's death made life all the more worth feeling. If there was one thing that brought heroics into the light of day, it was the daily death and dying of the war. Courage was more than likely a last-minute feature of desperation, even to a hero. The more he thought about it, none of the heroes he had ever seen or studied about would have chosen the part they played. It had been something forced upon them. Maybe becoming a farmer was being forced on him as well.

He had been fortunate enough to see General Lee up close several times during those years. There had been sadness in the old man's face, even when the army had been fresh from a victory. One could tell at a glance that he would rather have been curled up next to a fire reading a good book with a grandchild on his knee than leading an army. There was no ambition to him, none at all. Lee, like the other heroes he had read about, had no desire for the spotlight of history. Men like him didn't seek the opportunity to be heroes, but the circumstances found them and revealed what they were made of, all the same.

Often he had thought of these men who had been his heroes. Now he wondered what they might think of him. Would they just look at what he did, or would they take the time to examine his soul? He killed people for a living, hunted them down like one of his hounds back in Georgia, treed them, and killed them. Many times he had told himself that he was just bringing about justice and punishing evildoers, but it worked out to killing men for a living, all the same.

A man could rarely judge the motives of another. Most of the time, Zac didn't even know the real reasons he did the things he did. He knew one thing, though; he had no apologies for his actions, but he had a lot to improve on in the whys of what he did. His heroes hadn't chosen to become what they had been, but everything he did was based on his own choosing. It was a difference that made him uncomfortable.

The nighttime stop was one of the few times he could afford the luxury of his own thoughts. He'd always said the thoughts a man had when there was no one around to share in them were the true measure of any man. One thing did bother him about stopping at night; he knew the men they were chasing would be moving and moving fast. The trail had been one that would have been easy to follow, even in the dark. That wouldn't last long, though. Now he and Chupta would have to travel in the heat of the day. They would have to approach the men in broad daylight, too. It just might make him and the scout an easy target for ambush.

The men up ahead had two mules in tow. That was to his and Chupta's advantage. They couldn't ride both night and day. They had to rest sometime. He knew they wouldn't stop for long, though. They could make good time all through the night and travel in the cool of the morning and evening light. He and Chupta would have to stop when the sun set or face losing their trail. Someway, somehow, they had to find a way to make up the time.

Zac slept when Chupta took the last watch of the night. Feeling the man give him a slight shove just before dawn, he sat up.

"Sun come up in one hour," Chupta said.

"Good, then we better eat and saddle up. I want to be well on down the trail before we see the light."

Chupta nodded.

"We got to close up on them before this weather changes and we get some rain."

"It rain today," Chupta said. "Can smell it."

Zac opened one of the food bags and tossed Chupta a corn fritter. The biscuits were hard, but still edible. Taking a handful of dried fruit, he crammed it in his mouth and took out a strip of beef. Both men saddled their horses while they ate. Within minutes they were riding hard.

The sun was high overhead when they stopped to give the horses a drink. There would be no rationing of the water, and Zac drank freely. He knew enough about the desert to know that men who drank sparingly would not operate at peak power. Men like that might have a half-canteen of water but be slowed down, meandering aimlessly through the heat. He couldn't afford that. He could see that Chupta knew that fact as well. The man was lifting his own canteen and drinking.

"We not find more water soon," Chupta said.

"Then we'll have to ride thirsty," Zac replied.

Several hours later, they followed the trail directly to the foot of an overhead series of bluffs. A set of rocks made following it difficult, and in the sky, storm clouds were building. Chupta picked his way around to the left of their stopping point, and Zac moved his horse to the right. He got down and stooped low over the ground. Even if he couldn't pick up the prints of a horse's hoof, snapped brush and overturned rocks would be a clear sign.

A half hour passed before Chupta joined him. "They went up this way," Zac said.

"I find more tracks," Chupta said. "Same mule tracks from grave."

Zac pushed his hat back. "Maybe this was where they joined up."

"Chupta find horse tracks, too. All tracks go up hill."

"Must be a cave up there, or maybe a mine."

Overhead, several thunderclouds had gathered. The air had the smell of gun metal to it—rain was coming soon. With the threat of a summer storm, trailing these men would be more difficult. They didn't have much time to waste, but maybe the rocks would offer some shelter till the thing passed on. There might even be something the men had left behind.

Their horses in tow, the two men began to climb the hill. After a hundred yards of climbing, they both spotted the mine. Outside of it, they could see a mule grazing. They continued to climb, and standing outside the mine, they dropped their reins.

Suddenly, the sky grew darker and the wind picked up.

Zac drew his Colt and stepped inside. The light filtering in showed the coals from a dead fire. Zac put his hand over them and pressed the burned wood. "It's still warm," he said, "not more than a day old, I'd say."

"Why man leave mule?" Chupta asked.

"Good question."

They both got to their feet and cautiously moved into the cold darkness of the mine tunnel. Finding a burned torch, Zac picked it up and struck a match. It blazed up, a bright flame that caused shadows to dance across the walls of stone.

The two of them inched closer, walking toward the spot where the tunnel separated. "We won't go far," Zac said. "I don't want to waste too much time in here; we still got some distance to make up when that storm blows over. If they left any sign, I want to know about it. The more we know about them, the safer I'll feel."

Staying in the main tunnel, the two of them walked forward. Zac poked the torch ahead of them, illuminating the floor of the mine. Up ahead, they could see an opening in the floor and scaffolding built around it. Zac and Chupta cautiously approached it. Standing above the dark hole, Zac waved the torch over it. Below them, they could see a man lying still and silent on the ledge, the rope from the scaffolding running past him and into the darkness.

Zac picked up a small rock and dropped it. It hit the man in the shoulder.

"Unnh," the man grunted.

"He's alive," Zac said. They both watched the man shift his position, slowly moving his legs.

"I better go down and get him," Zac said. "I'll tie the rope around him and then when I climb back up, we can pull him up together."

Chupta nodded.

Zac shinnied down the rope and, landing on the ledge, began to check the stranger for broken bones. It was some time later when Zac and Chupta hoisted him to the surface. They picked him up and carried him to the entrance of the mine.

"Water," the man croaked out, "there's water down there."

"See if you can't haul us up some water," Zac directed Chupta.

Moments later the scout brought a bucket of fresh water. Zac sponged off the man's forehead, then lifted his head and gave him a sip. It took some time for the man to gain his senses. He blinked at the two men.

"They gone?" he asked.

"Who are you taking about?"

"The one-eyed man . . . the one-eyed man and my wife."

Zac gave the man a few more sips of water. "We haven't seen anybody. What did these men look like?"

"One was a dark-eyed fella with a black-and-gray beard, kinda heavyset. The other one"—the man's eyes turned ghostly and wild—"the one with one eye was tall and kinda lean lookin'. His left arm was missin', too." The man suddenly grabbed Zac's sleeve and pulled himself up slightly. "He was spiteful, too, had an evil green eye, one that showed he'd just as soon kill you as look at you."

Zac laid the man down and sat back.

"Did he speak like a man from the South?" Zac asked him.

The man nodded slightly.

"You know this one," Chupta asked, "the one-eyed man he speak about?"

Zac paused in thought. He didn't want to admit what he was thinking, even to himself, and he didn't want to speak the words.

It was almost as if the words themselves would make his worst nightmare a reality. "I might," Zac responded. "I just hope it's not the one I'm thinking about, though. If it is him, this feller here is lucky to be alive."

"Who is this one?" Chupta asked.

"Somebody who's bound to hate every Yankee soldier he sees, worse than any renegade Apache or Indian I've ever come across."

"That not possible."

"Oh, it is." The more the thoughts swirled around in Zac's mind, the more real they became. He didn't want to ever be on the other side of a battle against any of his brothers, especially Julian. There would be no mercy with Julian; he had never know any from him, even as a boy. Zac could show mercy, but Julian could not.

"How that possible?" Chupta asked.

"The Yankees took from him everything he held dear in life. Then they took away part of his manhood to boot. Hatred drives this man."

"How you know him so well?"

Zac looked Chupta straight in the eye. "From the sound of it, it could be my brother Julian."

The eyes of the man on the ground opened wide. "That's him, his name was Julian, Julian Cobb."

"This right?" Chupta asked Zac.

"It would be hard to find another man fitting that description. I spoke to one of my other brothers a short time back, one that had seen Julian after the war. He told me Julian lost an eye and an arm during the war. Last thing he'd heard from him, Julian was off in Mexico fighting with Maximilian for money."

"He sound like dangerous man," Chupta said.

"Very dangerous."

Outside, lightning cracked.

CHAPTER 22

+ + + + + + +

The hills east of the desert, near a spring and flowing creek
Saturday noon

Finding the shelter of overhanging rocks, the cavalry patrol dismounted and began to loosen their cinches. Julian signaled for Raincloud and Drago to follow him to another nearby location, a shady place that was somewhat removed from the soldiers.

After dismounting, Julian took the cork out of his canteen and began to drink.

"Don't you think you should offer your wife a drink first?" Raincloud asked.

Julian took the canteen from his mouth. He looked back at several soldiers, who were watching him. One of them was talking to the other, obviously about him. He could see that in spite of what they had been told, the soldiers were still suspicious. Word of Mangus had been all over the territory. A man would have to be a fool to travel at a time like this. They still hadn't found the time to bury the gold, and if the captain decided to check the mules, it would all be over.

Raincloud's eyes darted over to the watching soldiers. Julian handed her the canteen.

Raincloud slowly sipped the water. Pulling it away, she spoke in low tones. "We must look married," she said. "We have to make soldiers believe." Once again, she sipped on the canteen, and then pulling it down, she handed it back to him. Reaching her hand up, she gently touched his face. She spoke softly. "I think you should kiss me."

Drago cleared his throat and stepped back, smiling.

Julian shot him a wicked look.

"The lady's right," Drago said in a low voice. "You wanna get us outta this, you best do what she says. Speaking for my ownself, I'd be glad to do it, but I ain't married to the woman." His grin widened.

Julian stepped closer to her. His hand shook slightly as he touched her face. Leaning down, he gently kissed her cheek. Then, pulling back slightly, he looked her in the eye. "Are they watching?" he asked.

She nodded slightly and smiled.

Lowering his head, he pressed his lips into hers, a long, lingering kiss.

Raincloud felt herself melt inside. It was a kiss for show, she knew that, but it had a power and a passion to it that she had never known before. She wrapped her arms around his shoulders and kissed him back.

As he pulled away, she spoke softly. "I think you should pick up and hold the baby. Then maybe walk over to the soldiers and talk to them. Be friendly."

She had given him good advice and he knew it, even if it was to do the two things he least wanted to do at that moment. "All right, I'll do it."

He stood beside her as Raincloud took the carrier with the baby off her back. She carefully unlaced it and, picking the child up, handed her to Julian. "What do I do now?" he asked.

"Just hold the baby close. She does not break."

Sunflower was not crying. Raincloud leaned over her and tickled her chin. "Now," she said, "we will walk to the soldiers and talk nice to them. Then they will go."

Julian walked toward the men, carrying the child with his only arm. He forced a smile.

"Looky here!" a sergeant spoke up. He got to his feet and held out his arms. "I ain't held me a baby in a coon's age. Can I hold it?"

Julian nodded and the man scooped the child from his arm and began to cuddle it and show it to the rest of the men.

The captain walked over to Julian. "Can't say I agree with the wisdom of traveling about with your family, what with Mangus running loose."

"A body's got to make himself a living," Julian replied. "I got a grubstake, but it won't last us forever. People that loan you money get real impatient when you're setting about waiting for the army to bring a bunch of injuns to heel."

The captain blew on his mustache. "I can assure you, sir, the army is doing the best it can with what it has."

Julian knew when he had said it that it was the wrong thing to say. There was no sense in antagonizing the man, and showing his true feelings about the army was the height of foolishness.

"I'm sure you are. I, for one, want to thank you boys for being out here. You just don't know how much safer it makes me and my partner back there feel, to say nothing about my missus."

"Looks like she's cooking something up for you boys," the captain said.

Julian looked around and saw that she had built a fire and was making dough out of her flour, slapping the tortillas back and forth with her hands.

"I'd say you were a lucky man."

"I guess I am at that." He watched the captain out of the corner of his eye as the man studied Raincloud.

The man cleared his throat. "Normally," he said, "my men and I ought to search your things. Like I said, there's been an army payroll holdup."

Julian's heart sank. He dropped his hand to his side, next to the Russian .44. He knew that even if he and Drago emptied every round into the men, there were just too many of them. There would be no way out of a search. To play a bluff might be his best chance. "You're welcome to look over anything we got, Captain."

"I said normally," the captain went on, "but the type of desperadoes we're looking for wouldn't be carrying a family with them, and two men just couldn't have massacred that whole patrol. Besides," he grinned, "that woman of yours would probably take out after us with a frying pan."

Julian nonchalantly scratched his chin. "She just might at that. But you can search all you want; we got nothing to hide." Julian knew that running a bluff was never his strong suit. He just hoped the man meant what he had said. "'Course," he went on, "you might just dig into her cooking supplies or the baby's clothes and if that happens, I wouldn't want to be you."

The captain continued to watch Raincloud. She had taken out a pan and was now frying breakfast. He took off his hat and ran a cloth over his balding head. "Well, with the grease from that bacon she's cooking, we just might take casualties."

"You just might at that." Julian forced a smile. "I guess I better get on back to her. She never likes to have to call me for a meal. You know how these women are."

"I certainly do."

Reaching out, the captain nudged Julian's stump. "You best be careful now. Those men are desperate."

"We will. I got myself a lot to protect over there. How many injuns did you say was on the loose?"

"We don't rightly know. I'd suspect no more than a dozen or more, but that would be more than enough for the likes of you folks, so be watchful. These people are Yavapai and that Apache woman of yours won't do you a whole lot of good with them."

"Thanks for the lookout. We will."

With that, he walked over to the men playing with Sunflower. "Sorry, boys, we got ourselves some hot vittles waiting for us over there."

"We can see that," said a soldier.

"And smell it, too," the sergeant joined in. "Smells mighty fine, to boot."

Julian held out his arm and took back the baby. Now he had to just concentrate on not looking too out of place while he carried the child back to Raincloud. He walked back over to the cooking fire, catching Drago's smile with each step.

"Yer gonna make yerself a right proud papa," Drago smirked.

"Just wipe that smile off your face and get to eating. You still got me to deal with when them Yankees ride on outta here."

Raincloud took the baby. "I serve my husband first," she said. "Sit down." Rolling some bacon into a fresh tortilla, she handed it to Julian. She sat back and watched him sample it.

He took a bite.

"Good, ain't it?" Drago said.

Julian nodded.

"I'd say it was mighty good to get some hot vittles out here in a place like this. Yes sirree, this new wife of yourn is gonna work out just fine after all."

As they were finishing their meal, the soldiers began to mount. The captain rode his horse over to them. "Well, folks, it's time we got on with our patrol. You folks take care, you hear?"

Raincloud had prepared a bacon-filled tortilla for herself, but she sprang to her feet and carried it to the officer. She smiled a broad, engaging smile. "Here, you eat this, mister soldier man. I made this for you."

"Well, bless your heart, missy. I don't mind if I do." Reaching down, he took it from her hand and took a bite. Holding it out, he smiled. "Now, that's about the best thing that's happened to me in days, I'd say."

He shook the partially eaten tortilla at Julian. "I'd say right off that you were a lucky man, mister, a mighty lucky man."

"That's what I keep telling him," Drago joined in.

The man reined his horse around and galloped off to join his departing troops.

Drago watched him ride away and got to his feet. He looked at Raincloud. "That man is right, sure 'nuff. We is mighty lucky indeed."

✦ ✦ ✦ ✦ ✦

The desert floor
Early Saturday afternoon

Zac and Chupta had picked up what little trail they could find after the rain had passed. It was hard to conceal the leavings of that many animals for very long. They at least knew enough about the general direction to head off at a pace that would allow them to make up for some of the time lost.

Ed Hiatt had insisted on coming along with them, and Zac saw that as a mixed blessing. They would have to slow down for the mule, and the man was not in the best of shape to travel. Still, one more gun just might come in handy, especially now that Zac knew who they were following. He fully expected one thing, though; Julian would not want to be kept waiting for a woman and her baby. They would find her before they found the men. When that happened, they would have a problem with Ed Hiatt.

"That woman done gone and stole my money." Hiatt kept up the talking to the two men as they rode. "She ain't never been no good to anybody in her whole life. I just thought marriage to me might learn her some duty. Foolish, childish thought that was. How can a man teach an injun to be upstandin'?"

Zac watched Chupta as the man continued to babble on. The man's words were hitting him like daggers, he could tell. But for all the insults, Chupta maintained a stone-cold expression. Zac knew just how the Apache felt. After the war, he had endured many a drunken insult by Northern men fresh from the flush of victory. There was never anything pleasant about being the object of a man's haughtiness, especially when it was accompanied by downright ignorance.

"Them squaws ain't good fer much," Hiatt went on, " 'cept'n fer bearing squealing young'uns. Can't sew. Wouldn't know what to make. Can't talk worth a durn. What would a man want to talk to any woman about, to say nothing about it being some 'pache gal? And she just left me there, didn't hardly try to stop them two a-tall. Just left them do to me as they durn well pleased and rode off with them."

Near midafternoon, they pulled up next to some large rocks and dismounted. Chupta looked around. He could see a gathering of ants. Reaching down with his knife, he stabbed the ground and then held up their meal. "Man kill scorpion last night. They stop here."

"Yes, but they didn't stay long," Zac replied. "If I know that brother of mine, they won't stay long at any place they hold up."

Ed was checking the loads on his revolver. He murmured to himself, but both Zac and Chupta could clearly hear him. "When I find that Apache witch, she's gonna get one of these planted in that sweet little head of hers."

Chupta's eyes narrowed and he frowned.

Zac spoke up. "Mister, you're gonna keep that six-gun of yours in that holster where it belongs until I give the say-so. Is that understood?"

Hiatt lifted his head and, squinting his eyes, gave a blank stare.

Zac stepped toward him. "I said, do you understand? Because if you don't and you draw that horse pistol and fire before I tell you to, the next sound you hear will be your last. 'Cause I'm gonna shoot you right where you stand."

Hiatt lowered his pistol. "You don't mean that. That there woman is my wife, all bought and paid for. If'n I wants to kill her, then I got myself a right."

"Fella, there's something you ought to know about me. That brother of mine and me have at least two things in common, besides our name; neither one of us has ever said anything that we didn't mean, and both of us tend to hit just what we aim at. Now, you just put that thing away and don't ever pull it out until I say so."

Turning to leave the man to think the matter over, Zac wheeled back around. "One more thing," he said. "You keep that yammerin' up and my friend here is gonna slit you from belly button to jawbone. You wanna stay with us and keep healthy, you best stop the palaver about the Indian."

Zac walked back and started to tighten the cinch on his saddle. Chupta edged up next to him and spoke in a low tone. "Man no good. We should kill him now. He try to kill woman when we find. You see. His promise no good. He like white man that want to buy my land. I say to them, 'How Chupta sell you what he not own?'"

Chupta proceeded to cinch his saddle tighter. Zac was listening closely to him. It was far more than he had ever said before, all at one time. He went on. "How can Indian sell the place that have the bones of his father and his father's father buried in it? The earth is made of the bones of our ancestors. It not belong to us. The woman not belong to that white man either. Chupta just kill him now. He no good."

"No matter what I do for a living," Zac said, "I don't take to murdering folks."

Chupta nodded his head slightly. "I know. You ride on, and Chupta join you later."

CHAPTER 23

+ + + + + + +

Mangus listened to the news about the stage with an impassive stare that made the young wolf obviously uncomfortable. He watched the young man's chest swell as he told the story. It was plain to see the young man thought the news about finding the coach would be pleasing to Mangus, so much so that he forgot the fact that he had strayed and been late. Mangus continued to look at him, as if expecting a further explanation.

The young man lowered his eyes, casting his gaze at the ground and slumping his shoulders forward. Mangus knew he would rather die than disappoint him. The boy's father had pointed to him and told him to return a hero like Mangus or die in the trying. Only then had the old man been willing to part with the horse the boy rode.

Mangus still refused to say a word. A man had to search his own heart. His silence would allow God to speak to the young wolf. Many times since his own boyhood Mangus had discovered that God's voice to the heart was much more powerful than man's voice to the ears.

"I hunt for fresh meat," the young man said to the ground at Mangus's feet. He spoke in the clear and melodious Yavapai language. "Thought that warriors would like taste of sheep. I was wrong." He lifted his head up, looking Mangus in the eye. "Then I smelled the dead flower smell. I go on and saw white boy touched by God."

Mangus's interest was suddenly piqued. "White boy touched by God?"

"Yes." The man bobbed his head, becoming excited at Mangus's interest.

161

The young wolf began to swing his head around in all directions and shake his hands as if he were air-drying them after a bath. Then he looked Mangus in the eye and put both hands up to the sides of his head. Shaking his head back and forth with his hands firmly clasped to his temples, he said, "Boy wander in the mind. He belong to God, not know anyone else. He get on stagecoach with others and go away."

Mangus motioned with one hand to Gandara, who quickly came to his side. "We must ride," he said. "Take this young wolf and one other and go on before us. Watch for soldier man."

Gandara nodded and shouted orders to the others. Some of the men had begun to eat what was left of the white men's meal supplies. They stuffed the half-eaten beef and fruit into their shirts and went to hunt for their horses.

+ + + + +

A short time later, the wagon that had been following them pulled into camp. Campbell and the Mexican got down, then walked up to Gandara and Mangus. "Coach wasn't here, I take it," Campbell said.

Mangus was silent. His head never moved.

"No," Gandara said, "but know where it go. We ride now."

The Mexican nudged Campbell and pointed with his chin to Mangus. "He never talk. Don't he speak Anglo? If he speak Spanish, I can talk to him."

"Mangus here was educated by Christian missionaries," Campbell said. "He speaks both English and Spanish perfectly well. He just does this to aggravate me. Won't lower himself to speak our tongue."

Mangus turned without saying a word and walked away.

Campbell watched his rigid gait. He put his hands on his hips and turned to Gandara. "We'll foller you when you light on outta here. We wanna be close by when you come up on that stage. We want what it's carryin' besides that ammunition." He grinned and scratched his chin, eyes flashing. "We'd like any women on it after you boys is finished with 'em. No sense killin' off perfectly good womenfolk. They'll fetch a pretty price in places I know. 'Sides, they'd just slow you boys down. Now, we wouldn't want that, would we?"

Gandara turned and walked over to Mangus and the men who

were bridling their horses. "Don't like the way dees men don't make talk," the Mexican spat out.

"Don't pay no nevermind to Mangus," Campbell said. "He's been like that for as long as I've known him. Takes a pride in only mixing with his kind, but he ain't long for us, not for this world anyway."

"What make you say that?"

"Gandara tells me Mangus dreams of his death, and the closer he gets to it, the more he dreams about it."

Campbell studied Mangus across the camp. He didn't like the man, but he admired him all the same. "Nah, we ain't gonna have to worry 'bout old Mangus fer long. Gandara's our man. We stick close to him and we're gonna be rich men afore long."

Campbell walked over to the littered campsite. Articles of cookware, personal effects, and paper were scattered all over the ground. The three dead men lay partially clad next to the still-burning campfire. In all likelihood, the missing pieces of men's clothing were now on a scattered collection of the warriors who were mounting their horses with Mangus.

"Hey, I know this feller!" Campbell exclaimed.

He circled one of the scalped corpses to get a better look at the man. Pointing his finger, he signaled for his partner to walk over and take a closer look.

The Mexican ambled over.

"This is that fella we met up with in Prescott a couple of weeks ago. The one whose wife and kids were shopping with him to buy supplies for his prospectin' trip. You know. He was the nice fella that gave us directions and was so proud of his kids." Campbell took off his hat and wiped his forehead. "Who'd a thunk we'd been seein' him again this way. I guess I just didn't reckon on seeing people we know'd kilt like this."

"Compadre, before we is finished here and if dees Mangus gets hees way, we is gonna see lots of people we know."

"You reckon?" Campbell asked.

The Mexican nodded.

Campbell's head came up at the sound of the horses leaving the wells. "We better get ourselves on that wagon," he said. "We don't want to lose them boys, least not till we get the rest of that gold we come for."

+ + + + +

The sun had been up for more than an hour when Gandara galloped back to the rest of the band. He skidded his horse to a standstill in front of Mangus. "Place where wagon stop in rocks back there. You, come and see."

Mangus urged his horse forward and the rest of the band followed. When they reached the rocks, he dismounted and walked to where one of the warriors he had sent with Gandara stood. Pausing, Gandara watched Mangus as he looked up ahead, possibly looking for the young wolf. Mangus always seemed to watch out for the well-being of others. Gandara admired that.

The signs from the place would have been easy to see, even from a distance. Scattered over the ground were droppings from a number of horses, a mixture of footprints, and the deep sandy ruts of the coach. The blind could follow this coach in the desert. Walking around the camp, Mangus examined the different sets of prints. They had to figure out how many people they were up against. Gandara knew that losing too many men in the process of capturing this ammunition would not be worth it.

Mangus signaled several of the men to go up into the rocks to get fresh water. After the recent rain, the rock tanks would be full. They would rest for a short time and make sure the horses were watered and fresh for the ride ahead.

The sun was creeping higher in the sky, its hot rays covering the landscape. The horses had been watered when the young wolf came riding hurriedly back from the tanks. He was out of breath, and his horse was winded. Leaping from the horse's back, the young man proudly ran up to Mangus.

"Soldiers, pony soldiers ahead of us. They ride down through the valley."

"How many?" Mangus asked.

The young man held up both hands and flashed all ten fingers twice.

"Mmmm," Mangus grunted.

Gandara stood beside him and watched the expression on Mangus's face. It was a look of study he had seen many times before. Mangus never did anything without much thought. He knew Mangus didn't want to risk great losses before the band grew. Gandara also knew that it would take a victory over the white man's pony soldiers before all the people could hope that things would change.

The ghost dancers had predicted that the soldiers would all fall, their bones bleaching in the sun, vultures filling the air. The shaman had spread his arms while he danced and sang about the buzzards picking on the bones of the pony soldiers. Was this to be the fulfillment of the man's dream, the promise of the dance? Only then would the old warriors rise from the dead and join in the campaign. Mangus knew this as well as Gandara did. He had seen the dance too. It was not the place of Gandara to say the words. Only Mangus himself could speak them.

The stagecoach would get farther ahead of them if Mangus chose battle, but it would not get away. With the noise of the victory in the people's ears, they would need the ammunition that had been promised even more. Many young men would ride to join them. As well as the fallen ones the shaman had told them about. This new resurrection would mean many warriors of the past rising to join them, rising with bodies that could never be killed again. Perhaps even the great Cochise would be among them.

Mangus looked the young wolf in the eye. "It is good thing you have done," Mangus said.

The man looked for a moment as if he would die at the spoken words of the war chief. To hear Mangus say anything was an unexpected blessing for the listener, and for those words to be ones of praise was an event a man might not be able to contain. The young man grinned with pride, his chest size swelling by inches at the sound. *His father would have been very proud*, Gandara thought silently.

"Water and rest horse," Mangus said.

The young man almost tripped over himself as he stumbled to back away from the war chief. He walked quickly to his horse and took the bridle from the animal's mouth.

Gandara watched as Mangus drew his knife. Probing the point of the blade into his own arm, Mangus traced a stream of blood. He lifted the knife to the men around him. "No more will our blood run without vengeance," he said. "We ride to strike down the pony soldier. All will perish before our eyes." The blood dripped from Mangus's wrist onto the desert sand.

Gandara raised his two fists into the air and let out a bloodcurdling scream. "Paint faces," he yelled. "We will kill. We kill all the soldier man."

The warriors checked their weapons and loaded the new rifles they had been given. Several began to mix the paint. Within sight of a half hour, the Yavapai rode out of the rocks. Forming several bands, they rode their horses in a canter—the entire group heading in a northeasterly direction to intercept the soldiers the young man had spoken of.

+ + + + +

Before long, Mangus, Gandara, and several of their best men had stepped down from their horses and approached the overlook to the valley below. It was just as the young man had said. Below them a column of cavalrymen were riding north, two by two. The soldiers were riding the length of the long valley, and Mangus would want to spread them out for the attack. Together, the pony soldiers might still be dangerous. Separated, they would make easier targets.

He spoke to one of the warriors. "Take five and ride to the opening of the valley. Wait for me there. I will send you down to the pony soldiers. Make them see and chase you."

The man eagerly nodded his head and, choosing the five, rode off.

Turning to Gandara, he spoke softly. Mangus's orders for Gandara were always words between the two of them. They were secrets to be shared by no one else, a power bound by friendship. "Ride down fast to the north," Mangus said. "Take the men and scatter them among the rocks on either side of the valley. When pony soldiers are inside your killing field, fire your first shot. Kill them. Kill them all."

Gandara slapped his chest with his fist and circled his hand to the riders behind him. Mangus watched them ride off. Allowing Gandara to make the attack would build the man's spirit. The kill would make the man feel invincible to the white man's bullets. He would soon become the one to lead all the people, and Mangus wanted to make sure his spirit was ready.

There was more to being a leader than strength of body—Gandara had that. A leader must think. He had often made sure that Gandara watched him think. There had been times that Mangus wanted to speak, to act in a more forceful manner. A leader's confidence was built in the heart, not the body only.

It would be good to die and leave the rubbing out of the white man to Gandara. Many times Mangus had dreamed of the manner of his own death, and it puzzled him. He would awaken from his sleep wrestling, his arms in the air. The dream frightened his wife. She would watch him toss and murmur in his sleep and back away from him. The struggle was violent and his death was sure. He had seen it and felt it, but still, he did not understand it. The possibility seemed too remote for him to comprehend.

He touched the trickle of blood on his arm. There would be no blood in his death. He had seen that clearly. He shook his head. The thought for him at that moment was a puzzle in the stars. They knew of it, but they had not shown him all that they knew.

A short time later, Mangus joined the six warriors at the head of the valley. The rocks and turns in the passage through the mountains would make it impossible for the pony soldiers to see what was only a short distance in front of them. He looked to either side of the long stretch ahead and could see the rocks bristling with Gandara's rifles.

We will take many scalps today, he thought, *many scalps, many horses, many rifles for the ones who join*.

Motioning to the warrior with his still-bleeding arm, he sent them at a gallop. It would be only minutes until they would come riding back toward him again—fast and with smiles on their faces.

CHAPTER 24

+ + + + + + +

The desert floor
Early Saturday afternoon

In spite of the sudden drop in temperature, Tommy had taken his usual position on top of the coach, where he was content to swing his head around and continue in his attempt to take in what there was to see, all at one time. He began to sing, "Dutch brown maiden, thou hast a bright blue eye for love. Dutch brown maiden, thou hast a bright blue eye."

Butch Gray turned and watched as the boy continued his ritual.

"The bright blue eye is thine love. The look in it is mine love. Dutch brown maiden, thou hast a bright blue eye."

Gray jacked his thumb back at the boy and nudged Peters. "That kid is cracked as a body could be. He's liable to do or say anything. Now, where you reckon a kid that age picked up one of them sea shanty songs?"

"No telling. We'll have to keep a watch on him, though," Peters said.

"You got that right. Fer all we know, he might get up and walk hisself right off the top of this here stage just to see what the fall would feel like."

"Hadn't thought along them reasonings, but you might be right at that. You better see if you can at least get the kid's attention."

Gray shrugged his shoulders and reached out for one of the bags on top of the coach, a worn, dark brown leather bag with deep scratches on its soft side. Emblazoned across the front of the case, in between the straps and buckles that held it together, were the gold initials LDR. "I'll use the gambler's bag here. Can't rightly use that China woman's bag; she never lets it outta her sight."

Tommy continued to sing, seeing all of the world and none of it at the same time. "The ruby lips are thine, love. The kissing of them's mine, love."

Gray slid the bag across the top of the coach, up against the boy to get his attention.

Tommy was startled. For the first time in Gray's memory, the youngster stopped his head movements and stared back at him. His mouth turned down and suddenly anger flashed across his face. Picking up the bag, he flung it from the top of the coach.

Gray grabbed Hec's shoulder. "Better pull up. That kid threw that bag overboard."

"What?" Hec Peters suddenly hauled up the leather ribbons between his fingers, bringing the team to a sudden halt.

Ruggles stuck his head out of the window. "Why are we stopping?" he asked.

Peters yelled down. "You better tell that little lady to get this kid down offa here. He done gone and thrown your bag off."

Moments later all of the passengers had taken the opportunity to stretch their legs among the cactus plants and sage. Amy stood beside the coach and called out to Tommy. "You come down here, mister. You have been very bad."

Ruggles had spotted his suitcase and was walking back to where it lay.

Taking the child firmly by the ear, Amy steered him toward Ruggles. The man walked on ahead of her, toward the suitcase, ignoring the cries of the child.

"I hope you haven't damaged anything," Amy shouted at the boy as she shook him.

Ruggles stooped down and began to unbuckle the valise.

"I'm so sorry, Mr. Ruggles. I do hope nothing has been damaged. Sometimes the temptation to do things is just too much for my brother. He doesn't mean to do harm; it just happens."

Ruggles looked up at her and the still-wrestling boy. "The trouble with temptation is, a body gets what he wants right away. To do the right thing takes a longer time to enjoy."

He lifted the lid on the valise, uncovering neatly pressed white shirts, carefully laid out and folded. Several ties and socks were meticulously laid in a row, alongside a wooden-handled hairbrush and a freshly broken bottle of bay rum. The spicy scent of the liquid rose to greet them.

"I'm sorry about that," Amy said. "Tell the man you are sorry, Tommy."

Ruggles cocked his head up. "Miss Franklin, if it isn't the boy's idea, he isn't really sorry."

"But now your clothes are ruined."

"Not ruined. I won't be able to sneak up on a glass of milk with these till I get them laundered, but they aren't ruined."

Lifting one of the shirts, he pulled out the small velvet bag that had been tucked beneath it and felt the contents.

"That's my grandfather's."

He slipped the bag into his coat pocket. "Your grandfather owns nothing now." He stood up and patted his pocket. "He gave me this to use in order to look after you and your brother there."

Her face turned beet red. "You stole it from him. I wondered what had happened to that. That diamond has been in my family's care since the War of 1812. He would never have parted with it. Certainly not to a total stranger."

Kneeling down, Ruggles laced the straps back into place. "Baby sister, when that grandfather of yours died, he parted with everything."

Picking up the bag, he began to walk back to the stage, followed closely by Amy who was dragging the boy by his ear.

Ruggles stopped and looked her in the eye. "When a man is dying, it's amazing how straightforward things become."

"I sorry," Tommy blurted out. "It was wrong thing to do. It not happen again."

Ruggles reached over and peeled Amy's hand from the boy's ear. "Apology accepted, son." He looked at Amy. "Things become crystal clear to a dying man, and I'd say that grandfather of yours trusted me plenty. He had confidence that I had more horse sense about your welfare than you did. God knows I wish he hadn't."

Amy blinked her eyes as Ruggles marched off. Tommy ran after the man and jerked on his coattails, stopping him in his tracks. "Will things be clear to me when I die, like they were to my grandpa?"

Ruggles set down the valise and, kneeling, put his arm around the boy. "I reckon so, Tommy. I think things will be clear to all of us."

Philip Carol walked up cautiously to Amy. "Don't blame yourself," he said. "A man should never travel with fragile items on a stagecoach." He shot Ruggles a wicked look as the gambler handed up his suitcase to Peters. "A man ought to know better," Carol said.

"I still feel partially to blame," Amy said. "Sometimes, Tommy just gets frustrated and out of control."

Carol put his hand on her shoulder. "We all feel a little frustrated out here, it's not your brother's fault. Are you okay?"

"You're very kind. I'll be fine."

Peters called down to Ruggles. "You better get up top. I'd feel a whole lot better with the boy inside."

Mary smiled at Tommy. "That's nice. We have the handsome gentleman inside with us women. All handsome men should ride with the women."

Tommy blushed slightly, momentarily forgetting the slight from Hec Peters.

Looking at Tommy, Ruggles spoke softly. "You ride inside for a while. I'll get you back on top with me before long."

Tommy nodded and walked to the stage. Ruggles pulled his rifle out from inside the coach as a silent Amy climbed in. Their eyes met and held for a moment, each one wanting to speak, but everything had been said, and they both knew it.

In a matter of minutes, the stage was busting over the sandy grass and brush. The stink bush around them gave off an aroma that was unmistakable. "You got a place in mind to stop?" Ruggles asked Peters.

"I know a spot. It's spooky as all get out. It's a place where people the injuns call 'the ancient ones' used to live. The injuns want nothing to do with it, but it's got plenty of shade and there's water thereabouts."

"Sounds good. I don't like the idea of us traveling through here in the daylight. We make a real inviting target."

Peters slapped the reins against the backs of the horses, urging them on at a faster pace. The desert was heating up and the hills ahead looked cool and inviting, a blue-yellow softness in the distance. It would be two hours or better before they came to the shelter of the rocks and could stop. The three men on top continued to eye the horizon, searching out the land for any sign of distant riders. The dust from the back of the coach rose high in the air. It wouldn't take much for someone to see where they were in the bright daylight, and a blind man could feel the dust they were kicking up from five miles away. Ruggles was sure of that.

"I'm powerful hungry," Gray said.

"I think everybody feels the same way," Ruggles said. "Maybe tonight, before we start off, I could sneak off and kill us a sheep."

"That would be plenty welcome," Peters joined in. "I've seen plenty of bighorn out here."

"It wouldn't be easy. I'd have to use something besides a gun. The sound of a shot at night would travel ten miles or more."

An hour later, Peters pulled the team to a halt.

"Why we stoppin'?" Gray asked.

Ruggles sat up straight and craned his neck in all directions. "You hear that?" he asked.

"I don't hear nothin'," Gray responded.

Peters shot Ruggles a worried look. "I ain't seen nothing moving or flying since we stopped back there. You thinkin' what I'm thinkin'?"

Ruggles nodded his head. "I've seen one only one time before. Hoped I'd never be around to be in one again."

"What are you two talking about? I don't hear nothin'."

"That's right," Ruggles said. "No birds, no insects, no noise of any kind, just silence. You can't see a thing, not even a lizard move. And feel that air."

"It do feel kinda strange," Gray said, "kinda prickly on the skin."

"There it is," Peters shouted as he pointed toward the southwest.

The three men stared off in the direction of what should have been mountains. A golden-brown haze hung low over the desert, reaching up with its fingers into the clear blue sky. The sight of it sent fear into the men. A sandstorm on the desert would sweep away everything in its path, and both Ruggles and Peters knew it. Insects and animals alike located the deepest shelter they could find. Birds refused to fly. Horses rolled their eyes in fear and pain, running in all directions.

A man's senses are a fragile thing. To know where one stands on the earth and where one needs to go is something all people are so accustomed to, it's nearly impossible to imagine not knowing. But in the blinding sand, the sun and earth seem to simultaneously disappear. There is no longer a right place to go and a wrong place to stay. A man needs boundaries, a horizon to see, rules that will tell him where to stand and which way to walk. And the fear, the fear of being cut off from all that had been familiar, along with the feel of electricity as it whips through the air, is enough to send the strongest man wildly running to his injury, or even death.

To anyone caught out in the open, the blowing sand brought a biting agony. There was simply no place where it did not hurt. The force of the swirling wind would toss a man back and forth, making him stumble about like someone in a drunken stupor. If a man fell to the ground, he did best to just hang on and wait for it all to pass. The blinding sand burrowed its way into a man's eyes, ears, and mouth, lashing him like the swords of millions of tiny wind-borne horsemen.

"What do we do?" Gray asked.

Peters climbed down, with Ruggles right behind him. The old driver signaled to Gray, who was still mesmerized by the approaching storm. "Get on down. We got to unhitch this here team."

He turned to Ruggles. "You best go in there and get the preacher, young Carol, and that Amy girl on out here. I hate to do it to her, but we got to have one person with each of them horses. I'll lash them horses' tails together, but we still got to try and hold them. Better tie things down in there for that China woman and the boy, too."

Ruggles cranked open the door. "Collect every bit of loose cloth you can find," he yelled. "We got a sandstorm coming and we'll need to blind the horses." He looked at Amy. "Sorry, baby sister, but we need you out here, along with the preacher and young Philip. You best bring something to wrap your head in, that and most of your face. Philip, you and the preacher try to tie them curtains down. Mary, you get Tommy here on the floor and hold him down if you have to." He reached over and took the boy's chin. "Partner, you just lay still and do like Mary here tells you. All right, now all of you, let's move."

Peters and Gray had unhitched the team, and now Peters was tying a tight knot to the tail of the lead wheel horse. "We'll tie 'em tail to head, two by two, and team up to keep them in place beside the coach," he said.

Ruggles reached out and grabbed Philip's shoulder. "Young Carol and I will hold on to these two."

Philip Carol pulled his sleeve clear of Ruggles's grasp.

Peters went on, noticing the way Philip resisted the notion of being coupled with Ruggles. "Gray and the preacher will take those and Ruggles; you and the girl can handle those last two. I'll take the lead team with young Carol here. All you folks hang on to them halters. From here on out, it's just you and the horse you've got hold of."

"We're getting something for blinders," Ruggles yelled.

"Good."

Ruggles turned around and watched as Amy lifted her skirt. She had hiked the dress and was tearing strips of the petticoat from around the bottom. He looked up at the approaching storm and ran over to her. "Hang on to that dress!" he yelled. With that, he grabbed the edge of her petticoat and yanked it down to her ankles.

Amy gasped and fell to the ground in a faint.

Ignoring her, Ruggles pulled the petticoat free and tore off a piece and ripped it into long pieces. He ran to Peters and Gray, handing each of them long sections of the material. Taking a piece of rope from Peters, he tied the tail of his horse to the harness of another. Leading the two animals back to where Amy now stood, he motioned her forward. "I saved one of these for you. You better wrap your head and make it so it covers your ears, nose, and eyes."

"That was the rudest thing I've ever seen anybody do."

"I wasn't on my best party manners there, baby sister. I'll admit that, but we have no time. I'll wrap the eyes of these two horses and you better hang on to a harness. If they get away, just let them go. I'd rather be without horses than have you dragged across this desert."

"Well, that's a surprise!"

Carol dropped the traces of the horse he held and dusted Amy off. "Gamblers are born to be rude," he said. "They have little respect for ladies because they've met so few of them."

Ruggles took out a white handkerchief and tied his hat tightly in place. He looked over at Carol. "Youngster, you better grab that horse of yours and hold on. There'll be plenty of time to be a gentleman later. We don't want to have to go looking for the horse you were supposed to hold."

In a matter of moments, what had been total stillness erupted with a tornado-like force. Ruggles backed their animal in next to the stage and tried to stand as close to Amy as possible. He heaved his shoulder into the beast, driving it against the coach. Catching the fear in Amy's eyes, he looked back toward the approaching storm. He pulled his hat down and clinched the handkerchief even tighter.

The wind was like nothing any of them had ever heard or felt before, filled with the solid mass of a wall of sand. It made a loud popping sound as it hit the coach's wooden sides, and it pushed the stage slowly from side to side, rocking it like a cradle and moving the horses skittishly away. Mary's and Tommy's screams could only be heard faintly.

The noise of the air absorbed everything. It was deafening, choking out all sense of life as they had known it. Brush bounced near them and several times Ruggles swung his arm to deliver a glancing blow at the flying debris. Sand seemed to fill the air, choking the breath out of all that dared to face it. The solid, smothering air surrounded them from every angle, stifling their every breath.

Fear raced through the hearts of everyone—a gnawing, blinding fear of suffocation. The air seemed no longer breathable to man or beast. The noise of the wind and its effects were beyond human understanding. It went past the boundaries of what anyone might expect to experience in a lifetime.

The horses stamped violently, trying to turn their backs to the howling rage. The problem for the animals was the same as for the humans; there was nowhere to turn without facing the rampaging bites of the sand. There was no sun, no heat, no desert, no earth itself, only the blinding fury of the wind-borne frenzy.

The coach rocked back and forth violently, its wheels leaving the ground, first one side, then the other.

Ruggles turned his attention at once to the dark, swirling figure of Amy.

She screamed, her hands clamped to her ears.

Ruggles reached out and grabbed her, throwing her to the ground. He held on tightly to his horse's harness as the animal Amy had been holding swung around and began to kick.

In a teetering motion, the stage tipped toward them.

Ruggles reached out for Amy and pulled her and the horse away.

The stage landed with a crash on the ground.

Ruggles pulled her toward him. He looped an end of the harness around one arm and, stooping to the ground, held Amy with the other. Time stood still for them. There was no future, no past, no here, no now, only the wicked wind and the two of them.

How much time passed he did not know, but suddenly a stillness came over the desert, a stillness of sand.

Ruggles got to his feet and, dropping the reins, pulled Amy upright. The sand fell off her like water from a waterfall.

"Tommy!" she gasped.

They both ran to the coach and climbed up its sides. Opening the door, Ruggles lowered himself inside.

There below, Tommy lay in Mary's arms. Ruggles gently picked him up. The boy sputtered and opened his eyes. He clamped his arms around Ruggles's neck and squeezed hard.

"He's okay!" Ruggles yelled. "He's scared like the rest of us, but he's okay."

Sitting the boy down, he brushed the sand from Mary's face. He stooped down and listened to her heart. There was no sound. Lifting up a portion of her sandy shawl, he covered her face.

CHAPTER 25

✦ ✦ ✦ ✦ ✦ ✦ ✦

The desert floor
Saturday afternoon

The burial service for China Mary was simple. There would be no marker, no sign that she had ever been on the earth, except for the memories she had left behind. From the way she had been hustled onto the stage in Prescott, Ruggles was sure that the people who would miss her most were those now standing around the lump of sand covering what was left of her. Had it been he lying there instead of she, he was dead sure that would have been his eulogy as well.

In the end, that was the most that many people could expect. Houses owned, horses, bank accounts, businesses, the rewards of occasional recognition, all of that went into the hole with a man. Ruggles had never spent much time thinking about his own death. It was the finish; the end of torture, the end of trying to make a place for himself, the end of warm sun, clean shirts, women who smiled, spicy food, and the satisfaction of winning a hand of poker. In some ways, his own life seemed pointless. Perhaps the only thing he might be able to look back on now would be a promise kept to a dying man.

Only Tommy was crying. Mary had done her best to shelter him from the blowing sand. The storm had been too much for her heart, and the stage falling to its side had been the thing that finally put an end to her wayward life. Amy crouched down beside Tommy and held him in her arms.

"Why did she have to die?" Tommy asked.

"It was just her time," Amy said. "Everybody has a time."

The Reverend Black finished his words. "The Lord giveth, the

Lord taketh away, blessed be the name of the Lord."

The men had righted the stage, and Peters and Gray hitched the horses back in their traces. Hec Peters walked back to the group. "We'd better be moving on. Can't stop here. Got about an hour left to go before we can pull up and sleep for a spell."

The group walked back to the coach, and soon they were moving north once again. Only Tommy poked his head out the window to watch the spot behind them disappear.

In a short time, the shade from the hills covered them, providing a welcome relief from the bright sun on the desert floor. Peters wound the team down a steep canyon, the sides of the hills echoing with the sound of the coach and the horses' hooves.

Up ahead, pockmarks on the bluffs marked the place of an ancient people. Apartments were built into the sides of the limestone cliffs. The holes in the canyon walls seemed to watch them, ageless guardians of time and place. The sight made the hair on the back of Ruggles's head stand up and bumps rise on his arms.

Peters pulled up on the reins and brought the coach to a stop. Wrapping the ribbons to the brake handle, he took off his hat and wiped his head. "We can't stay here for very long. We got just enough time for some sleep and maybe, if we can, to round up whatever food we got on us. We'll take the horses to Beaver Creek down there and let them drink."

Ruggles climbed down and cranked open the door on the coach. "Watch yourselves here." He looked at Amy. "We don't want Tommy here to go to falling down some hole, and there's plenty of them to find."

Tommy bounced out of the coach and ran off to climb the hill to the houses in the rock overhead. "You be careful," Amy yelled after him. "Don't go getting into anything."

Ruggles smiled. "We just have to watch him real careful-like. No matter what we say to him, there's that little boy inside that shouts just a little bit louder. I listened to it when I was his age, and so will he."

"Whew-eeee!" Gray screeched. In his search for spare food, he had begun to go through China Mary's bags. He held up a wad of greenbacks from one of the carpetbags. "That gal had herself a peck of cash."

"Put that back," Ruggles barked. "We can't eat cash!"

"That's a first," Amy said gently. "A gambler who seems disinterested in money."

"You have to live first before you can worry about living well." He looked up at the shotgun messenger, who continued to rummage through Mary's bags. "Some people's eyes get dazzled by money they don't work for, so blinded they can't see what's right in front of them. He'd probably overlook dried beef looking for jewels."

"And you think you earn the money you get?"

Ruggles narrowed his dark eyes and looked down at her. "Baby sister, it just galls you that you can't quite place me, doesn't it? You got yourself a group of narrow boxes in that pretty little head of yours, and the problem is the thing you hate most is the fact that your father and that grandfather of yours were just the kind of men you take me to be. I understand that. I don't take what you say personally. I know it's not me that you have your problem with. The trouble is, the men you really want to give your mind to are both dead."

He started to walk away, leaving her standing with her mouth open. Suddenly, he stopped and turned. "The money I win comes at risk. I study the people at the table, and I've worked with cards and probability all my life. I deserve every nickel I pick up at the tables. Money earned has very little to do with the value of a man's sweat. It takes time, heart, and someone's ability to know what to do. What makes you think what I do is any more wrong than a railroad owner who sends a telegram and earns a hundred thousand dollars in a back room deal? Do you think his steaks taste better or that he sleeps more peaceful? I doubt it."

As Ruggles walked away, the Reverend Black stepped up to Amy and put his arm around her. "Don't take what he says too hard. No man likes to be doubted, especially by someone he's attracted to."

Amy whirled around, her mouth open. "Attracted to? How can you say that? He calls me his baby sister."

"That's his way of not telling himself the truth, darling, the truth about how he feels about you. That man is going to a whole lot of trouble to take care of you and your brother, more trouble than any normal person would go to in a matter that doesn't concern him. Now, either he places more stock in that promise he gave to your grandfather, and you don't believe that to be possible, or he has a deeper interest in you. I'd suspect the latter."

Black watched Ruggles stomp over to help unhitch the team. He went on, " 'Course, don't sell him short on his hankering to keep that promise of his, either. He strikes me as a man who values his word."

Amy's eyes were fastened on Ruggles. She was speechless.

Black simply smiled at her. "You folks have quite an attraction to each other, from what I see. Just watching the sparks fly off between you two somctimes makes me want to laugh out loud."

"We hate each other," Amy said.

"Ha! That ain't hatred, darling, that's deep-down raw emotion. He does something to you that makes you feel weak and disarmed on the inside." Black shook his head. "No, from what I see, God has, in His providence, put two people who need each other in the same place at the same time. You need someone you can count on, a strong man, and he needs some tenderness."

"I hate that arrogance of his."

"Miss Franklin, that isn't arrogance, it's a man who has a lot of confidence because he knows what he's talking about. You're woman enough, girl, but you're still a teenager and your world is smaller that his. He's been to the places he talks about, and he's done the things he claims knowledge of. That's not arrogance, it's boldness. That man is like a lion walking around in a chicken coop."

+ + + + +

When Ruggles finished with the horses, he tossed a rifle to young Philip Carol. "You know how to use one of these?" he asked.

"Yes, I handle myself fairly well with one."

"Good. Then take this and get back to the mouth of the canyon. Keep a sharp eye out. If you see something, don't shoot. Just hightail it back here with the word. You understand? We don't need no battle between you and the Indian nation."

Philip frowned but nodded and trotted down toward the mouth of the canyon.

Ruggles spoke to Peters. Gray had not shown himself to be a man who could be counted on. "Why don't you take all the food you can find and put it together. We can't exactly count on finding anything here. I'll go down to the stream and check for any paw prints. If there are some animals that come down to drink, I'll stake myself out and wait. Right about now, we could use even a fresh batch of lizards."

"Sounds good," Peters said. "When we get something fixed up, we'll fetch you back."

Ruggles walked back over to where Black and Amy were talking. It was obvious from the way the conversation suddenly ended that he had been the subject of all the talk.

"Tommy's gone off exploring those cliff houses," Amy said. "I best go make sure he's not going to get into any trouble."

Ruggles picked up a rifle. "I better go with you," he said. "No telling what you might find up there." They walked over to the cliff in silence. Scaling the rocks, he stopped and held out his hand for Amy.

"I can make my own way. I've been doing for myself for years now."

"Suit yourself," he said, "but you just watch where you put your hand. There just might be some critter that don't take too kindly to getting his afternoon nap disturbed."

She thought for a moment and then held out her hand for help.

Sometime later they stood at the entrance to a set of houses dug in the wall. "Tommy!" Amy called out. "You in there, Tommy?"

They could both hear the boy running and playing inside. Stooping slightly, they walked in.

The dark walls were charred by smoke, the leavings of a thousand cooking fires. It was almost as if the place had been vacated the day before by people who expected to return at any moment.

"Do you believe in ghosts?" Amy asked.

"No, only the kind a man carries about in his own mind. The Indians around here do, though. That's why this place would be one they fight shy of."

Amy walked through the room, lightly running her hand over the wall. "This place seems strange, all the same," she said.

"Well, it isn't from ghosts."

She turned around, leaning back against the wall. "Then, why the strange feeling, and why do the Indians stay away?"

Ruggles walked toward her. The enigmatic smile on her face carried with it a playfulness that she hadn't shown him before. But after all, she was just a girl. He touched the wall at a spot that contained several drawings. "Memories, I'd say. This place is like every other home; it makes memories, then keeps them all to itself."

"Is that why you don't want a home? You don't want the memories?"

"I haven't had enough time to make memories just yet. I spend too much time thinking about the future to worry over the past."

"Don't you think that a future should have pleasant memories to look back on? I should think you would want that."

The way she batted her eyes made him feel uncomfortable. Women had a natural way of flirting with a man, even one they said they didn't like, and that made him edgy. Most women he had known made their intentions all too obvious. This one was different, however. With her, he could never tell. She was too much of a girl to be thought of by him as a woman, but far too much of a woman to be dismissed as a girl.

"I think about a home and memories as much as the next man," he said. "I just haven't had a great deal of reason to think seriously on the matter as of yet."

"Well, maybe it's about time that all changed for you, Mr. Lawrence Ruggles. Maybe serious thinking is called for in your life."

Something was different in her thinking. He could see that in an instant. Women had always appeared so moody to him. One minute they would be spitting like a leopard and the next purring like a kitten. Wiser men than he bragged about how to produce such mood changes, but unless the woman was someone he faced across a poker table, he'd never bothered to explore the subject. Two things were certain to him now, though; there were different wheels spinning around in Amy Franklin's head, and he hadn't been responsible for them. For whatever the reason, the comfort of the place had suddenly left him. "I think I had best be going to find us some fresh food. That stream in the valley down there might even have some fish in it."

"Must you go just yet?"

He tipped his hat and smiled. "Oh, I think I should. You and Tommy can just play here for a while till we have some food ready." He knew when he said the word "play" it would strike a cord in her that she'd rather not hear. *But land sakes*, he thought, *she's only seventeen. What am I thinking about?* The smile left her face, just as he had hoped.

"I've been past the point of 'play' for the last seven or eight years. I have no dolls."

"Well, whatever it is now that you do, I'll leave you to it and go fishing. You might think about getting some rest. It's going to be a long, hard drive tonight."

He couldn't leave the cliff dwelling fast enough. In an instant he was out the door, and with a bounding gait, he moved down the rocks to the valley below. Picking up his pace, he walked down to the running stream. Scrub oak dotted the stream bed. He took out his knife and cut several saplings. Carefully, he smoothed two makeshift arrows, cutting sharp tips into each one. In a matter of minutes, he had fashioned a bow and arrows. If there were small game or fish in the stream, he wanted to be ready.

The sun was still high and warm when over an hour later, Ruggles had managed to spear two small fish. He cleaned them and laid them on a flat rock.

A short time later, he heard the rustle of leaves behind him. Swinging around, he watched Amy hop from rock to rock. "We have some food ready," she said, "if you can come and get it."

There was a simple grace in the way she moved. As she neared the bottom of the rocks, though, something else caught his eye.

"Don't move!" he shouted.

"Why?"

"You've got a large snake at your feet. Just freeze right where you are."

The snake at Amy's feet buzzed with a set of healthy rattles. It coiled to strike, pointing its head at Amy's ankles.

Ruggles pressed his arm to his side, springing the derringer directly into the palm of his hand. The spring-loaded rig strapped to the inside of his arm made getting a gun into his hand a matter of simple movement. Snapping his arm forward, he fired it with a loud bang. The round from the palm gun caught the rattler midstrike, jerking it into the air.

Ruggles drew his knife and jumped to the rock. Amy stood there, shivering.

The snake continued to tumble. Placing his boot on the serpent's head, he sliced it off with one clean stroke.

He took her in his arms. She shook and hung on to him, pulling him closer. Moving her back from him slightly, he stroked the tear from her cheek and pushed her brown hair aside. "You're all right now. Just calm down, you're all right."

She held him closer and laid her head on his chest. "You saved my life. I wasn't even watching where I was stepping."

"You'll do, baby sister. We'll all get through this together. I'll make sure of that."

Lifting her head, she looked him directly in the eye. "I think you will. I don't know why, but I just think you will." With that, she stood on her toes and kissed him.

The kiss took him by surprise. He held her tightly and kissed her back. He could hear her swoon and feel the give in her tight embrace. It stirred him and made him, for a moment, even forget where they were.

She smiled. "You can stop calling me baby sister. That wasn't a kiss a man would give his baby sister."

"No, I suppose it wasn't."

They started back toward the camp. The fish and snake he carried gave him an excuse not to hold her hand. He wasn't quite ready for that, and he wasn't prepared for what people might say. Very rarely had Lawrence Ruggles ever been unprepared for anything. His ability to carry himself in a confident way into every situation was a badge he had always sported proudly. Now he felt a bit sheepish. Allowing this young girl to break into his heart embarrassed him.

He held up the snake and the two fish. "We do have some fresh meat." He grinned, holding up the large rattler. " 'Course, we weren't exactly looking for this one."

Moments later, they had the fish cooking on a flat rock. The snake had been cut into small pieces and skewered onto the two makeshift arrows. Ruggles and Amy turned them over the top of the coals.

"Butch here and I had some sleep," Peters quipped. "We'll be ready to go come dark. That storm we had us helped rub out our tracks, I'd say."

"That'll only help for a short while," Ruggles said. "It will buy us some time, though."

"We're gonna need it," Peters interrupted as he stepped forward. "That fall the stage took back there cracked the axle. It got us here, but we ain't about to get much farther till we get her fixed."

CHAPTER 26

✦ ✦ ✦ ✦ ✦ ✦ ✦

The spring east of the desert floor
Saturday, midafternoon

Julian and Drago lay in the shade for several hours. The sun was hot and they wanted to wait for the heat of the day to pass before they moved on. A short nap would keep them going for the rest of the day and into the night. Raincloud worked to fill the canteens and prepare a meal to be eaten later. She fed Sunflower and watched the two men sleep.

The canyon was quiet. Several birds flitted from the branches of the scrub oak and cautiously drank from the small stream that meandered down the valley. The quietness of the place was seductive. It gave the appearance that all was right, and Raincloud knew full well that all was not right. There was death in the air, death and hatred.

Julian roused himself, stood up, and stretched. "Don't you sleep, woman?"

"Raincloud slept a little."

He watched her feed the baby. "I guess that young'un tells you when it's time to wake up. Not much you can do about that."

Julian pushed Drago awake with the toe of his boot. "Let's get rolling. We're burning lots of daylight."

Drago sputtered and turned over. Blinking himself awake, he rubbed his eyes. "Which way do we go from here?"

Julian stooped down and smoothed out the dirt. With a small stick, he drew a map. "We still got to move north. I figure we're about three days, maybe more, from Lee's Ferry. We'll cross the Colorado there. We might as well follow them Yankee soldiers as long as they're heading that way. There's enough of them to blend our

185

tracks with. Ought to confuse anybody coming along behind us."

"We taking the woman with us?" Drago asked the question with a smile on his face. He had seen the way the woman had handled herself with the soldiers, and what was more, he had seen Julian's startled reaction.

"We might as well. She does cook."

"That she does."

"Besides, I wouldn't want to leave her behind to shoot off her mouth to whoever's following us."

"Think she'd do that? I'd be willing to bet that there husband of hers is trailin' us."

"I doubt that. I think we fixed his wagon."

Drago looked over at her. "Somehow, I don't think she'd be willing to bank on that. You shoulda killed the man when you had a chance to."

Julian looked down at the sandy map and murmured, "Can't very well kill a man in front of his own wife, no matter what he's like."

Drago got to his feet and shook the sand out of his pants. "Cobb, you got a soft spot left in you yet. Wouldn'ta bet on it unless I'd seen it with my own eyes."

Julian stood up and stretched himself to his full six-foot-three height. He glared at Drago. "You saw what I did to Nestor, didn't you? When I catch a man in my sights that needs killing, I won't even blink."

Minutes later, the three of them had saddled their horses and were towing the mules behind them onto the trail left by the soldiers. They followed the shallow, dying stream down into the valley north of them. The mountains rose high to the east, and a series of shadowing bluffs to the west cast a blue hue in front of them. The sky formed a narrow, pale blue roof over rich gold rocks.

Some time and several stops later, they spotted the flock of vultures swinging lazy circles in the narrow sky. What they were circling had to be something more than a dead animal, and they all knew it.

"What in the blazes could that be?" Drago asked.

"Either them Yankee soldiers found Mangus or Mangus found them."

The three of them rode forward, rounding a bend in the valley. There before them the soldiers lay littered over the ground. Buzzards were scattered over the blue-clad bodies, and at the sight of the three riders, they began to fly off. The men galloped forward, swinging their arms and yelling.

Dismounting, they poked their way through the fresh bodies. A small clump of bodies lay in the center of the group. It was there they found the captain.

"Good thing that woman spared us from taking this ride," Drago said.

"You notice something about these bodies?" Julian asked.

"Besides being scalped?"

"Yes. Only a few arrows in these bodies. Mangus had plenty of rifles to go around and now he has twenty more."

"Lots of their jackets are gone, too," Drago said.

"Yeah, them injuns like those blue coats, for some strange reason."

"This place gives me the spooks. We better clear on outta here."

"And ride right into Mangus?"

"Well, we gotta stop soon, and I ain't about to lay in here."

Julian looked over the bluffs. "I'd say we better find some high ground." He pointed to a trail that led up the hillside.

"Let's head up that way, then," Drago said. "Mangus won't be staying 'round here. We can stay up there for a while and rest the animals. We'd best be moving hard and fast, though, during the darkness. Maybe we can even get a jump on him and get ahead."

Julian nodded.

The sun had started to set when the three of them found their way to the top of the bluffs. Since Raincloud had already fixed their meals earlier in the day, they didn't even need to think about a fire. Julian spread a blanket for Raincloud.

"Mangus is very bad," Raincloud said. "I saw him once at the store. He says very little, except with his eyes."

"Now, how can an injun talk with his eyes?" Drago asked.

"Many men say more when they talk less," Julian responded. "But that's something you wouldn't know much about."

"Whatcha mean by that?"

"The more a man talks, the less he gets listened to. And you, Drago, sometimes you say whatever comes into your head. In fact, sometimes you say it long before the thought gets in there."

Drago scratched on his beard. He glanced over at Raincloud.

"Then, maybe I got myself a lot to learn from this Mangus feller, ya reckon?"

"You just better hope it's not him that does the teaching. From what I hear, they teach white folks mostly how to scream, seldom how to talk."

The sun had gone down, and Raincloud turned over to sleep. A short time later, the rattle of vultures' wings below gave way to a snarling sound. "Guess the coyotes are taking over from the buzzards," Drago said.

Raincloud tossed slightly. The eerie sound from the coyotes would have made sleep difficult for anyone. Julian watched her and knew what she must be feeling.

Drago took a flat bottle of whiskey from his saddlebags and pulled the cork. He slugged down several gulps.

"Put that away," Julian said. "We need clear heads out here."

Drago frowned. "I like my liquor strong, 'specially with all that noise down there. Fact is, I like it strong 'nuff to make a jackrabbit spit in a bobcat's eye. I ain't never seen you drink much, though, Cobb. What's the matter with you? You some kinda temperance critter?"

"I was raised to keep a level head and a keen eye. Never had a drop till somebody gave me some shine during the war. I guess by then, it was just too late to develop a taste for the stuff. Frankly, I never saw the sense of it."

"I think a body would need a drink to stop his ears from that noise down there. That woman of yours could probably use some."

"She's not my woman. She's on her own."

"Didn't look that way to me this morning."

"Like I said, Drago, sometimes you hatch out words before they get laid. I think we ought to move out, though. The sun's long down, and I don't reckon any of us will sleep here."

Julian walked over to where Raincloud was trying to sleep. He stooped down and put his hand on her shoulder, shaking her gently. "You can stay here if you've a mind to, but I think Drago and I will get on."

Raincloud reached up and put her soft hand on his. "I will go with you. This is a place of death."

The touch of her hand startled him, but he didn't pull away. "You think the baby can travel quiet tonight? Mangus might still be close by."

"Sunflower is a good baby. She will be very quiet when we move. I know the desert air carries sound. We will keep silent."

Julian pulled his hand away and stood up. "All right. If she needs feeding, you can do some of that now. You make sure you drink up too. I'm going to ride on ahead and make sure we don't come up on anything by surprise. You can follow with Drago and lead one of the mules."

Julian walked back to Drago, who was tightening his cinch. "Wait for the woman," he said. "The three of us and the mules make so much noise in this quiet nighttime air that I'm going ahead for a ways to make sure there's no one there to hear."

"Good idee."

"You just make sure the packs on those animals are tight. Last thing we need tonight is a buckle that bangs or a pack that slips."

Julian threw his saddle on the back of his horse and tightened it down. He swung up onto the animal and looked down at Drago. "You give me about a half hour before you start off. Follow the valley north." He leaned down to get closer to the man and spoke in a soft voice. "Make sure there's no singing or drinking on your part, you hear? Or Nestor will have company." With that, he spurred his horse into the darkness and toward the fingernail moon.

Almost two hours later, he smelled a faint scent of smoke. The wispy moon hung low over several small hills. Julian dismounted and picketed his horse. Wrenching off his boots, he hung them on the horn of the saddle and slipped on his moccasins. He would move quickly and silently to see what he had to see.

With fluid, catlike motions, Julian moved through the low brush. He kept low. Even in dim moonlight, there was no sense in skylining himself. Nearing the top of a small ridge, he flattened himself to the ground. By now, his eyesight was well adjusted to the dark. Having only one eye made his vision from side to side somewhat hampered, but he slowly swung his head around, making sure he saw everything there was to see.

Beside one of the rocks in the distance, a subtle movement caught his eye. The figure was too small to be a horse, but it was something. The light breeze continued to bring him the aroma of faint woodsmoke. He knew enough about Indians to know that they rarely kept a fire going at night, especially renegades on the run. They would cook in the daylight and allow the fire to go out. But given the fact that it had only been a few hours since sunset, the smell might just be left from their cooking fire. Mangus could have traveled this far from the ambush site before he stopped for the night. They had done enough killing for one day. Perhaps their bloodlust was satisfied.

He didn't know how far he should go, but he did want to see for himself what lay ahead of the path he had told Drago to follow. If indeed it was Mangus, they would have to swing wide and be careful about laying down a trail. He would need to move quickly. He knew he had at least a half hour on Drago and the mules, probably more, but he didn't dare take a chance on hearing those mules clang up behind him.

Keeping low, he circled to the west of the movement he had spotted. He would have to be swift and yet restrained. If it was Mangus's camp, it would be the first watch of the night he would come up on. The man would be fresh. He would be alert.

As he got closer to the rock, he stopped. There, not twenty yards away from him, an Indian was relieving himself. The man swayed slightly, and Julian saw the bright gleam of a bottle, probably one of the spoils from the day's fight. Leaning back away from the rock, the sentry took several long swallows.

As the man walked away from him, Julian drew his knife. He would need one swift strike across the man's throat, a deep cut that would silence any cry for help.

With a sudden explosion of speed, Julian raced across the open ground. He lanced violently and deeply across the man's throat. Kicking the sentry to the ground, Julian straddled him and delivered the final blow to the man's heart. Then all was silent and still.

Edging his way around the rocks, he could make out the still-smoldering coals of the cook fire. Scattered around the fire were the rest of the renegades. He only hoped they had been drinking, too. But from everything he had heard about Mangus, that would be too much to hope for. In all likelihood, the sentry had found the bottle and kept the discovery quiet. Perhaps being able to drink it all himself had been the man's motivation for volunteering for the first watch.

Julian quietly moved around the rock. He wanted to see the whole camp. Picketed beside the rocks were Mangus's horses. Spooking them would buy him and Drago time. They wouldn't have to worry about covering their tracks for a while. Besides, the trail of three riders towing two mules would be hard to hide from a tenderfoot, much less a band of desert braves. There would be another sentry on the other side of the camp, Julian knew, and if one of the horses shied or nickered at his presence, all would be lost.

He edged closer to the horses, and a large paint picked up his head. Julian murmured a low, soothing sound. "That's fine, boy. It's your new owner come to get you."

Moving past the first three, Julian began to cut the picket lines. All along the line, he reached out and calmed the horses, moving with rapid determination. When he had severed the last horse's lead rope, he moved back to the first three and tucked their horsehair lead straps behind his belt.

Grabbing on to the mane of the large paint, Julian swung himself on top. Placing his knife back in its sheath, he clamped the paint's lead rope between his teeth and drew his .44 revolver. He kicked the sides of the big horse, driving it and the two he had in tow into the standing string of ponies and then fired several shots into the night air.

From across the camp a shot rang out, sending shards of the rock behind Julian flying. He kicked the big paint and, holstering the revolver, took the lead strap out of his mouth. The pony string was running wild as he drove them into the darkness. He gave out a long, guttural rebel yell, making the animals think the devil himself was fast on their tails.

Several minutes later, he circled back toward the south. He'd find his horse and take the prizes he had seized back to Drago and Raincloud. Having fresh animals to ride would refresh their horses and make the trip to Lee's Ferry all that much quicker. He felt a deep sense of smug satisfaction. In one night and all alone, he'd accomplished what the entire Yankee cavalry had been trying to do for the last two weeks.

A short time after mounting his horse and riding south, he came upon Drago and Raincloud. He galloped up to them and quickly dismounted. "Here," he said to Drago, "tether these horses real good. I'm sure Mangus was mighty proud of them, and I wouldn't want to lose them."

Drago laughed out loud. "Cobb, you beat all. How you people ever lost that war I'll never know."

CHAPTER 27

+ + + + + + +

The spring east of the desert floor
Monday, midafternoon

Zac followed Chupta north, down the slope. He could see the small stream that ran along the perimeter of the cliffs. The greenery of the scrub oak, dotted by Yucca plants, their spikes pointing in all directions, showed the clear outline of the water's edge. Rocks draped massive shadows over the stream and across a large patch of desert in front of the men.

As he picked his way down the hill, Zac watched Chupta ride a wide circle around the shady patch of desert. The scout leaned down from his pony and steadily stared at the ground. *The man sure is thorough,* Zac thought. *He doesn't want to lay down any tracks until he sees what's there.*

Riding out onto the desert floor, Zac pulled rein on the buckskin and stepped to the ground at the edge of the afternoon shadow. He squatted down to look at the leavings of what had been a cooking fire. There to the side, he could see that grease had been poured into the sand. Ants were working the soil for every precious drop of grimy nutriment that could be found.

Chupta rode up to him. He pointed at the line of oaks next to the stream. "Soldiers stop there," he said. "I think was army patrol."

"How do you know it was soldiers?" Zac asked.

"Dung in straight line where soldier man tie horses up. Indian keep his pony next to him during the day. Besides, shoe prints."

"How do you know they stopped during the day?"

"Sign only one or two day old. Ground too hard for soldier man to sleep on, too many rocks and spike bush there. No place close have sign of men lying down."

Zac stood up. "You are a wonder, my man. You can see a lot, even from a cold trail." He pointed at the dead coals. "This must have been where Julian and his bunch pulled in. If they weren't here with the army, then, they were close behind them."

"Umm," Chupta nodded.

Behind them, they heard the noise of Ed Hiatt's mule. Mules were surefooted and had the staying power of any horse, even if they didn't arrive at the same time. Zac turned and watched Ed pick his way down the hillside. "Why you let that man live, I'll never know," he said.

"I not know either. He make much trouble to us."

Ed rode up to them. "I thought I was going to lose you two," he said.

Ignoring him, they both continued to look at the tracks.

Ed pulled out a bottle of whiskey and downed several swallows. Replacing the cork, he took off his hat and pointed to the clumps of hair that were missing from both sides of his head. "You see what that brother of yourn done to me the other day?" He grabbed Zac's sleeve. "The man's a menace. He like to have kilt me."

"You don't keep that yap of yours shut, and he'll do just that. I would have killed you myself. He just made it so that scalp of yours isn't nearly as attractive as it might have otherwise been." Zac gave off a sly smile. "It might just save your skin before we're through."

Chupta stifled a grin.

"All the same," Ed grumbled as he put his hat back on, "he's a menace and not to be trusted 'round decent white folk."

Zac put his hands on his hips. "Hiatt, you calling yourself decent is a stretch to any man's ideation."

Ed ignored the insult. "She been here?"

"They have been here," Zac responded. "Remember, it's not just your wife we're chasing. Frankly, I'm not at all clear why Julian hasn't cut her loose long before now."

Ed's eyes narrowed. He squinted at Zac. "Womenfolk can be powerful entertaining if they take a mind to."

Zac stepped in his direction. "Julian's not the sort of man to be taking advantage of a woman, your wife or any other woman for that matter."

"He's a cold-blooded killer, sure as I'm sittin' up here. Looked to me like he had ice water runnin' through his veins. So why wouldn't he do what he wanted with a woman?"

Zac walked away from him, ignoring the swipe. He took his canteen from around the horn of his saddle and gulped.

Ed was not to be denied. He stepped the mule forward. "Well, he is a killer, isn't he?"

"You wouldn't understand."

"I knows a gunny when I sees one, and that man looked like a man that always stays one tick ahead of unraveling cartridges."

"He's the toughest man I've ever known, but he's always had some scruples."

"Tougher'n you?"

"We'll have to look to that. When it comes to Julian, he's flat-out capable of anything, except taking advantage of a woman. He was raised better than that. Now, enough of this conversation. You're starting to bore me, Hiatt. We got distance to make up for."

The three men watered their animals and topped off the canteens from the stream. It was a queer feeling for Zac to be this close to a brother he hadn't seen in more than fifteen years. Everything he'd heard about him in recent times had been mostly rumor mixed with a smattering of legend. The Mexicans hated him for fighting alongside Maximilian; he was wanted in four states, rumored to be dead, and now hunted by the army. It made Zac ponder about the job he'd been called to do. *What if I'd known it would be Julian I was to chase?* Zac wondered. *Would I still have come?*

They started out toward the valley that lay to the north of them. There were still plenty of trail markings left by the patrol. Zac rode on the western side of the basin, the one next to the bluffs, and Chupta walked his horse near the mountain on the east. If Julian and his group hadn't destroyed the tracks left by the patrol, either Zac or Chupta would spot them. It was hard to cover up the trail of three horses and two mules.

Zac's mind drifted back to the dinner table at home, to the time when they would all perform Shakespeare or read poetry after Mother had read the Bible. Julian had had a hard time with what he called "playactin'." He was more serious. Everything always seemed to be a matter of duty and work to Julian. There just wasn't any room for fancy. Of course Julian, being nine years older, hadn't given Zac any chance at all to know him as a child. Julian had always seemed so grown up. When their father came back from the

Mexican War with only the one leg, Julian had been forced into adulthood long before he was ready. Zac's mother had told him that.

Zac saw the first vulture about an hour later. The bird did very little circling. He seemed to know right where he was going and wanted to waste little time in getting there. With each passing minute, more of the big birds appeared, cutting circles in the blue desert sky. Zac and Chupta both picked up the pace.

Rounding the bend in the valley floor, they pulled up rein. Scattered across the basin were the remains of the patrol. Fragments of leather and blue cloth were intermingled with what was fast becoming a boneyard above ground. Zac kicked the sides of the buckskin and waved his hat, sending the buzzards aloft once more.

Having dispatched the vultures, Zac shook his head and dismounted. The stench of this place seemed to simmer and thickly paint the summer air; the rancid odor shimmering in the heat hung there for the three of them to inhale. Zac pulled his neckerchief above his nose and walked the buckskin forward. The animal shied and pulled back. The smell of death was repulsive.

Zac looked over to Chupta. "You know who this was?"

"Yes. Captain Vickers. He go out with patrol eight days ago."

"This here Mangus must have took them by surprise."

Chupta nodded. "Now Apache come to Mangus."

"Mangus is Yavapai, isn't he?"

Chupta nodded once more. "Mangus, ghost dancer. If he show Apache his medicine strong, Apache men come and ride with him. The sand will run blood just like this place."

"The man's got more guns and horses to give to those who join up with him now. He could kick up quite a fuss for the army out here."

Zac turned and spotted Ed Hiatt. Holding a cloth to his face, the man was rummaging through one of the corpse's pockets. "What do you think you're doing?" Zac asked.

Hiatt held up a gold watch. "This here feller was an officer. He ain't about to tell the time no more."

"Why don't you take the gold out of his teeth, then? He ain't gonna eat no more, either." Zac could tell the notion was far from repulsive to Ed Hiatt.

Zac poked his way carefully through the string of bodies, looking each corpse over very carefully. If there was one thing he needed to know, it was that each of the cadavers wore a uniform and had two arms. After all, they hadn't been sure if Julian and his group had been with the patrol or were just following in their tracks.

He turned to Chupta. "We got to put what's left of these men under some ground." He pointed toward a wash in the middle of the basin. "We'll use our ropes and drag these bodies over there. When we get them piled in the wash, we'll collapse the sand over them."

Chupta took out his rope and swung it over his head. "You too, Hiatt," Zac called out. "It's high time you earned that watch."

For the next hour, the three men dragged one carcass after another into the depression. They spilled the sandy walls of the wash into and over the pile of bodies, quickly making the place level with sand. Now all that was left of Vickers' patrol were a few of the blue caps that blew across the basin's floor and the remnants of a camp deserted.

"Julian and his bunch were riding behind the patrol. It was a smart idea on his part, hoping to lose all his tracks in those of the army. Hard to say how far behind, but it was far enough not to hear the shooting, because they rode right up on this place."

He looked at the now empty valley. "We better fan out and see if we can cut a trail. I shouldn't think they'd have waited too long to clear out of here. I don't expect Julian would have been too anxious to catch up with this Mangus fella after seeing all this. He'd have wanted to put some distance between him and this."

It was only a matter of minutes before Zac spotted a place where the hillside bore evidence of horses and mules that had climbed them, heading west. He let out a low whistle and signaled Chupta and Hiatt in his direction.

The three men rode up the slope and shortly thereafter found the place at the top of the bluffs where Julian and his group had stopped. Soon, they were following the trail north.

Zac pointed to the tracks. "I'd say they weren't exactly traveling together. There's a set of hoofprints moving off to the side, and from the way they're digging into the ground, I'd say whoever it was happened to be moving in more of a hurry than the others."

"Umm," Chupta grunted approval.

"Makes sense," Zac went on. "If I had a woman, a baby, and two heavily loaded mules with me and this Mangus nearby, I'd want to get on ahead and make sure of no surprises."

"Umm."

"Then, that woman of mine is still with them," Hiatt chimed in.

"Oh, she's with them, all right."

An hour or so later, they came to a place where a group of unshod ponies and one horse with iron shoes had rejoined the followers. From there, the trail abruptly turned northwest.

A short while later, just as the sun was beginning to set, they saw a wagon. The dirty canvas bounced in the glow of the setting sun, its stovepipe protruding from an opening. "It's cutting the trail," Zac said. "Let's go ask if they've seen anybody."

After a few minutes, they rode to within shouting distance. One of the men on the wagon had leveled a rifle and was squinting down the barrel at them.

"Hello," Zac called out. He held up a free hand. "We mean you no harm. We're on U.S. Army business. Can you answer some questions for us?"

The man lowered his rifle slightly and motioned them forward. The three men rode up to the wagon. "Howdy," Zac said. "Name's Zac Cobb, and this here is Chupta. We're on army business." He nodded toward Hiatt. "That there is Ed Hiatt."

"I'm looking fer my 'pache wife," Ed joined in.

"Name's Campbell," the man with the rifle offered. "And this here is Garcia, my partner."

"We're looking for two men and a woman with a baby," Zac said. "They had two mules and a string of horses with them and they were heading your way. You might have run across them."

Chupta scrutinized the two men. Zac thought he saw both recognition and dislike on the scout's face.

"No," Campbell said. "We ain't seen nobody like that. Ain't many people travelin' 'bout these days, not out here, at least. Mangus is on the loose and he's got folks plenty worried. Whatcha boys lookin' for these folks for?"

Chupta let out a low grunt; Zac looked over to see his face harden. Turning back to Campbell, Zac motioned toward Hiatt. "This here fella's wife is run away with his baby. She joined up with the other two, and we need to find them to ask them a few questions."

Ed started to speak, but Zac cut him off. "Can you describe your woman to the man?"

Hiatt paused for a moment. "She's 'pache; big black eyes, long black hair, nice to look on—fer an injun."

"Naw, ain't seen nothing like that." Campbell grinned. He scratched his peppered red beard and gave off a toothy smile. "Believe me, we'd remember a gal cut like that."

"Well, I aim to have her back," Ed blurted out. "I done bought and paid for her."

"Women are mighty perculiar creatures," Campbell offered. "Mighty perculiar. A body can never tell what fool notion creeps into their minds and how."

Chupta's eyes focused on the desert in the distance. A small dust cloud had risen, obviously being kicked up by the heels of a number of horses. He grunted and, lifting his hand, pointed them out to Zac.

The men fixed their eyes on the strange group of riders bearing down on them.

CHAPTER 28

+ + + + + + +

The desert floor
Monday, early evening

"Indians," Zac said. "Looks to be a dozen of them or more."

"We're done for, then," Ed mumbled.

Zac got down from the buckskin. "Not necessarily."

"They Apache," Chupta said. "Warriors painted for war."

Reaching into the boot of his saddle, he slid out the large, beaded buckskin bag. He then pulled the rawhide strings loose with his teeth, slipped out the heavy Sharps, and broke the action open. Extracting a long heavy cartridge from the bandoleer slung around his waist, he chambered it and snapped the rifle shut.

"How you 'spect to hit anything that far away?" Campbell asked.

Zac laid the rifle down on the edge of the wagon and set his windage sight erect. They watched him as he set the forward trigger. Taking careful aim, he slowly exhaled and gently squeezed the back trigger. The weapon exploded with a loud bark, rocking the rifle backward.

The men watched and waited.

Suddenly, in the distance, one of the horses tumbled forward, spilling its rider.

"You hit a horse!" Campbell yelled.

"I hit just what I was aiming at," Zac snapped back.

He had chambered another round and once again laid the rifle down on the edge of the wagon. Before taking aim, he watched the riders. "I wanted to give them a chance to stop."

The Indians continued toward them at full speed.

"Now we'll take out their leader." With that, he squinted down the octagonal barrel and set the trigger. The flame from the rifle spat out another heavy round.

Every eye focused on the band of screaming Indians in the distance. Seconds passed; most of the men thought the shot to be a clean miss. Spectacularly, the leader of the charge pitched backward into the rising dust.

Campbell jerked off his hat and rubbed his eyes. "I ain't believin' that. How'd you do that?"

"A matter of the right weapon at just the right time."

"I can sure believe that."

"Time of day helps too. There's less glare to interfere with a good aim." Zac chambered another round. "When a man's outnumbered," Zac said, "he best not be outgunned."

"Well, mister, when it comes to distance shootin', you sure ain't outgunned."

In the distance, the charge had stopped. The Indians gathered in the still-swirling dust to see to their fallen leader.

Zac turned and surveyed the bluffs to the west of them. "I'd say we best find some high ground," he said. "It won't take them long to come up with a better plan, and they won't be riding head on to us, neither."

He bagged the rifle, slid it into the boot, and mounted the buckskin. "That draw over yonder looks to be the best spot for the wagon and team. We can make it there, and Chupta and I can take the high ground and make our shots count. We can make this a mighty expensive proposition for them before we're through."

Both Zac and Chupta turned their horses and galloped toward the draw, riding fast. Getting the best position for the coming attack would be crucial and they both knew it. As he rode, Zac yelled at Chupta. "We gotta find a good spot to give covering fire for the wagon, someplace where we can see the whole valley."

It wasn't until they had ridden almost to the foot of the rocks that they turned back to check on the wagon's progress. It had turned, but still sat almost in the same position as where they had left it. Ed had remained at the wagon and the three men were talking.

Zac pulled the big rifle from the boot and came off of the buckskin on the run. He and Chupta took positions on either side of the draw and waited.

"Now, just what do you suppose got into their heads?" Zac asked.

Chupta looked at Zac from across the draw. "Two men down there trade guns and whiskey to Apache. They stay, make deal."

"And why in tarnation would Hiatt throw in with them?"

"He marry Apache woman. He speak Apache pretty good."

"Durn fool! He may be used to dealing with the Apache of last year, but this ghost dance thing changes everything."

Chupta nodded. "It change much. Indian ready to die. Better to die a human being than live under white man's feet."

"I can understand that," Zac said. "No man's prepared to live until he's ready to die."

They watched the Indians ride up to the wagon while the three men below raised their hands and began to talk.

Zac rested the Sharps on the rock. "We'll give them something else to think about, then we'd best find a way outta here our own selves. I ain't waiting for them. I've heard men scream before."

He squinted down the cold blue barrel and set the trigger. Easing his finger back, he touched the now set trigger. The Sharps bolted in his hand and in a split second violently pitched one of the Indians below from the back of his pony and onto the desert floor.

There was a flurry of movement as the band took the team by the hand and began to ride away. They would seek out cover of the rocks in the distance and then decide what to do with the three captives. Then and only then would they plan their attack on the bluff and the big gun that never seemed to miss.

"Too small a group to be all of Mangus's bunch," Zac said, "but they know where to find him, no doubt."

Chupta nodded silently.

"I'd say good riddance to Hiatt." Zac replaced the rifle in its bag and tied the strings. "We best get the horses and put some distance between us and them. They'll be mighty careful coming up here and by then we'll be long gone."

The desert was wrapped in a blanket of darkness when Zac and Chupta rode to the floor of the Valley of the Sun. Overhead, stars twinkled and spread out a blanket of celestial lamps. A man could see well by the light of the stars. The narrow moon only added to the paint of light over the ground. A roadrunner darted across their path, suddenly stirred by the cantering horses.

To be alone on the desert at night was to be in a new creation all its own. The Indians called it being in the middle of the world and Zac could see why. All around him was nothing but the darkness painted in a glowing silver by the tiny brushes of the stars and moon. The dark, deep shapes in the distance, the mountains, appeared to soak up all light. They were pitch outlines of cobalt that emerged on the horizon as boundaries to the earth. Nothing could penetrate them, and no light could come from them.

Zac pulled up and walked the buckskin. Chupta stopped and waited for him.

"You reckon they'll follow us in the morning?" he asked.

"Not think so," Chupta responded. "They got wagon. They drink whiskey and think what they do with three white men tonight. Big gun keep them from following. They go find Mangus."

"It's a dangerous thing to have the Apache joining up with Mangus."

"Soldier man killed today. Apache hear. Apache want victory. No more want to live on white man's meat. Better to die a man than live a child."

"Julian's got himself quite a start on us, but he is heading north."

"He leave Arizona while Mangus ride loose. Too dangerous here for white man to steal."

"You got a point there. Where would he go?"

"San Carlos reservation east. He not go there. Army patrol New Mexico. He not go there. He go north to Utah."

"Well, I guess that's the place he's heading, all right. Where's the best spot to meet up with him?"

"He go to Lee's Ferry. He cross big river there."

"Good, then, that's where we'll go. We'll make as much distance as we can tonight and try to pick up his trail in that direction. The sooner we can say good-bye to all the hostiles riding around in these parts, the better I'll feel."

"We stop for water when sun come up. Chupta know a place."

"Sounds fine," Zac grinned. "Only problem I got with the places you know is that Mangus knows them too. We have to be plenty careful when we ride up. I don't exactly hanker to have my scalp hanging on the point of that fella's lance."

* * * * *

Julian, Raincloud, and Drago made good time. The extra horses were more of a problem than they first might have imagined, however. None of the ponies had been used to a saddle. After Drago failed in his attempt to get one of the horses to take to it, they all decided to ride bareback after they rested the saddled horses. Drago continued to cuss and talk to the animal that had thrown him, even if his behavior was a might comical.

Drago towed the string of extra horses, and Raincloud brought up the mules. Julian rode on ahead to scout out where they were going. They didn't need unpleasant surprises. Mangus was behind them now, but Julian knew full well they might run into an army patrol.

They rode through the darkness, each seemingly unable to suggest quitting. There was something about a band of renegade warriors on their tails that made each of them continue to push when they might otherwise have quit.

From up ahead, Julian heard the baby begin to cry. He jerked the reins on the Indian pony he was riding and kicked at its sides. Within minutes, he rode up to Drago and Raincloud.

"I'm sorry she is crying," Raincloud said. "I think she is hungry."

"No need to be sorry. I think we're all tired and hungry. We'll stop here for a spell and you can feed her. I got some pemmican in my bags. I'll break it out and pass it around."

Julian considered the pemmican—venison and fat, mixed with a few berries—quite tasty. Often, Indian women with no teeth prepared it by chewing the meat into a pliable texture and then mixing it with tallow and pounded berries. Julian had purchased the cakes from a store, but he knew enough not to ask any questions about its origin. Besides, he wasn't that picky and it tasted good.

They hadn't taken a drink since earlier in the day, by the spring. The desert had a way of drying out a man's throat. Julian took a bite of the composted meat, but the dryness of his mouth made chewing difficult. He held it on his tongue and uncorked the canteen. Taking a sip, he wet the substance and allowed the water to slowly trickle down his throat.

He surveyed Drago and Raincloud. Drago was biting off large chunks of the meat and grinding his teeth on it, releasing a singsong murmur as he ate. Occasionally, he would pause to take a drink of water and wipe his scraggly beard with the back of his hand. Raincloud was not eating. She contented herself with feeding Sunflower, giving the child her full attention.

Picking up two pieces of the meat mixture and his canteen, Julian sauntered over to where the woman sat. Squatting down next to her, he gave out what, for him, passed as a slight smile. "You best have something to eat and drink." He held out the canteen. "Take the water first. It'll prepare your throat for the meat."

"Thank you." She took the canteen and sipped slowly. "I get so busy with the baby, I forget."

"Guess that makes you a pretty typical mother, then. My own mother gave herself to us children. Sometimes I wasn't sure she had her own life. The only time I saw her spend time for herself was when she took the time to read or play music."

"Did your mother laugh?"

"Laugh?" He paused, a quizzical look on his face. "Sure, she laughed a lot, mostly at us children. Why would you ask that?"

"Because my mother laughed. My father was plain and simple, but it was the laughter of my mother that made me believe there was joy to be found on the earth. Among the Apache, it is the women who laugh."

"I reckon a man's place is to fight to survive. My daddy used to laugh. He would run through the house and tickle me and laugh so loud it hurt. When he got back from the Mexican War, though, I seldom heard him laugh."

"I just wondered," she said. She took a small bite of the pemmican. "You do not laugh."

"What I do doesn't lend itself to laughing."

"Why must you steal and kill?"

"There just ain't much use in this world for a man with one arm and one eye. The war taught me how to kill without feeling, and now it's the thing I do best."

"You want to kill, run, and hide for the rest of your life?"

"No, just till I've done enough to get by without being an old cripple in need of a handout. I won't beg, and I won't ever be beholding to another man."

"The Apache beg. Some are like you. Beaten men always beg for bread."

"Well, I ain't beaten, not just yet. The Confederacy may be done for, but Julian Cobb ain't."

"Is this why you kill the Yankee soldier man?"

Julian nodded. "That and more. Them and the scalawags that ran with them took our farm and drove us out. It wasn't enough that we were beaten; they had to make sure they took all the spoils their filthy hands could grab along with the victory. A man that beats me fair and square can be my friend the day after, but not one that steals my property when I can't defend it. I won't forgive them for that."

Raincloud took another bite of the meat cake. "Your war is through. The Apache's war is through. I remember the laughter of my mother. I think you should remember your mother, too. There is joy somewhere in the earth. To be a human being is to find the joy."

Julian got to his feet. "Right now, all I'm gonna do is find the gold. I'll look for the joy later."

Ambling away from her and toward the animals they had ground-hitched, he took the bandana from around his neck and soaked it with water from the canteen. One by one, he smeared the cloth around the horses' nostrils and matted it against their dry mouths. He knew it would buck up their spirits and keep them cool, even if they couldn't drink just yet.

Drago wiped his hand on his shirt and, walking over to where Julian stood with the horses, pulled the picket pin on the pony that had bucked him off earlier in the day. "Guess it's time I learned this here critter a lesson," he said. "I ain't no injun, but I'm gonna ride this here jughead."

"That stallion's green broke," Julian said, "and he ain't about to change the way he feels about the way you sit him. If you ask me, he'd as soon stomp you to death as look at you."

Drago looped the horse's reins around his neck. "I don't rightly care what he thinks." With that, he hoisted himself onto the back of the spotted horse. Drago sat high for a moment and smiled. "Guess we got him wore down."

All at once, the horse moved from side to side and began to buck. Drago crouched low and hung on. The big horse jumped, spinning in the air and crashing back to the ground with a sudden shock, only to once again bolt skyward.

Separated from the stallion, Drago landed with a stab of pain and a snap that all three of them heard.

Stepping in between the big horse and the suddenly prone Drago, Julian grabbed the reins. Turning back, he could see the hatred and agony all over Drago's face, and a gun in his hand poised at the horse. Julian stepped forward and kicked the gun from his hand. "I won't have you shooting that horse."

"He broke my leg. Snapped like a twig."

"You pull the trigger on that shooter of yours and it will be heard for miles around. Get ahold of yourself."

Jerking the horse to a standstill, Julian once again planted his picket pin into the ground. He then walked back to Drago and drew his knife.

"What you gonna do with that thing?"

Julian stooped down next to him. "Gonna cut your pants leg and have a look."

With several strokes, Julian sliced a clean cut up the front of Drago's pants leg. He peeled back the denim. "You got yourself a break, sure enough. We're gonna have to set it."

Cutting a low mesquite bush nearby, Julian produced a number of stout limbs. Raincloud tore strips of long cloth from her supply of clothing and silently handed them to him.

Julian took a short stub of the wood and gave it to Drago. "Here, clamp your jaws around this. I got to set that leg, and it's gonna hurt like the devil."

Julian sat down in the sand next to the man and placed his foot under Drago's arm for leverage. Grabbing the man's boot, he slowly pulled, listening to the bone slide into place.

The stub of wood had fallen from Drago's mouth. He lay passed out on the sand.

Turning to Raincloud, he signaled her to bring the bindings over. "We're gonna have to find us a spot to lay over through tomorrow, a place where Mangus will find it hard to follow."

"The houses of the ancient ones are east of here," she said.

"Yes, that would be perfect."

CHAPTER 29

+ + + + + + +

The canyon of the ancient ones
Monday, around midnight

It took the men the better part of an hour to pile enough large rocks beside the coach to make a spot that could support a lever. Gray had cut a large oak branch, and together the men pushed it into place. They lowered the limb to the ground, hoisting the coach onto its front wheels. "Pile some of them rocks under it," Peters grunted.

Gray and Philip Carol slid under the coach and scooted a large rock in the sand. They positioned the boulder under the coach. Scampering back out, they lent their backs to settle the coach onto its new cradle.

"All righty," Peters said, "let's get this axle out and do our best to salvage what we can."

Taking a number of rawhide thongs, the men carefully wrapped the cracked axle. Peters slapped on grease, and they slid the jury-rigged piece back into place.

Peters looked up at the stars. "Dagnab it. We ought to have been clear outta here hours and hours ago. We got to make us some distance before daylight. We'll have to lighten our load a might, too."

"The men and me can ride on the horses," Ruggles said. "That ought to help some."

"I can ride too," Tommy exclaimed.

Ruggles patted the boy's shoulder. "You can ride in front of me," he said.

Within minutes, each of the men had mounted the horses in their traces. Peters took a new place astride one of the lead animals. "All right, let's try 'er out." With that, he kicked the animal's sides and the team pulled the coach down the long canyon.

In another hour, they had managed to ride the team pulling the coach to a point near the mouth of the canyon. The entrance to the canyon was rough and rocky, and all of them were looking forward to the relatively even nature of the desert floor. The starlight gave them enough vision to see the best places to guide the team away from rocks and ruts that would have caused stress on the patched-together axle.

Peters pulled up on the lead horse and raised his hand. "We'll stretch our legs here," he said, "before we get out on the desert. Don't go far. We won't be 'round here for long."

Ruggles climbed down and then pulled Tommy off the back of the big horse. He took the boy over to the coach and opened the door. "You riding in there okay all by yourself?"

"Yes, I'm managing nicely, even though it is a bit lonely," Amy said.

Philip Carol walked to where Ruggles stood beside the open door to the coach. "Excuse me," he said to Ruggles. "May I talk with you in private?"

"Of course."

Carol gestured to a flat area that was studded with mesquite. "Let's just walk over there."

Ruggles relented. "You managing all right, Carol?" he asked.

"I'll do just fine. I may not have done this type of thing before, but I can ride."

"I don't doubt that a bit. That daddy of yours may have wanted to spare you from any suffering, but boys have a habit of finding their own way."

"I'm not a boy."

"No, I suppose you aren't. When I was your age, I was on my own. Never had anything to fall back on, even if I had a mind to."

"And I don't plan on falling back on anything. I plan on making my own way in life, and I certainly have no thoughts of taking advantage of anyone."

"Now, just what do you mean by that?" Ruggles asked.

"You know what I mean."

"No, I'm afraid I don't."

Carol looked over at the coach, to where Amy was watching Tommy run. "Amy is much too young for you. You're near thirty and she's only seventeen."

"I'm just doing for her and Tommy here what I promised their grandfather."

Carol smirked. "I don't believe that for a minute. You, a gambler, leaving a city full of money to go on some wild-goose chase for people you don't even know. That's a laugh. You may fool some people with that line of yours, but anybody with half a brain can see right through it."

Ruggles bit his lip. "I've been puzzled about that, too, ever since we came upon the leavings of that stage stop." He pulled off his hat and scratched his head. "I guess when a man says he's going to do something, he never knows where it might lead."

"I've been watching the way Amy's been looking at you today. I think you know exactly where it might lead."

Ruggles frowned. "Kid, you are a handsome man to look on; big dark eyes, strong chin, the best clothes money can buy, and with that family of yours and the education you're pursuing, you've got a lot to recommend you. But I wouldn't give an Indian-head penny for your instincts about people. It might be best that you not rely on them for your future."

"I trust my instincts. Usually I can read men pretty well. I get that from my father."

Ruggles laughed. "There you are, then. I took your daddy for over seven hundred dollars last week. He couldn't read me then, and you can't read me now."

"I don't believe you."

"Believe what you want, it's the truth all the same." He paused and looked questioningly at the young man. "Boy, take some advice from me. It won't cost you a dime, but it will save you grief. Don't ever try to judge a man's motives. Most of us never know the real reasons for what we're doing, at least not the depth of them. Men are a puzzlement and I must confess, you may be right about me. I can tell you this, if you know my motives, you're the only one between the two of us that does."

"If you don't trust yourself, how can anyone else?"

"Well, you can believe what you choose. I might judge you for being too proud of your daddy's money to know what it means to earn your own. I might say that you were so young and inexperienced that you needed that young woman's admiration to build your confidence. I might say that you wanted to feel like a man and needed to show you could protect her, just to clear up doubts about your manhood. I could say any of those things, but I won't. I'm not sure a man your age could even know those things. How can I judge a man about something he can't even see himself?"

Carol reached over and slapped his face. "You insult me, sir, and I want satisfaction."

Carol reached for his revolver, but before he could lay a firm grip on it, Ruggles had pressed his elbow to his side, springing the derringer he carried into the palm of his hand.

Carol blinked as Ruggles pointed the little gun directly between his eyes.

"There's only one thing more foolish than judging another man's motives," Ruggles commented as he cocked the hammers on the weapon, "and that's acting on that notion."

"Uh," Carol stammered, his mouth dropping open.

"Now, you may be used to slapping men at Yale, but around here you'd be better advised to close your fist and deliver a good punch. I've shot men along the Mississippi for far less than that."

Carol blinked. "Are you going to shoot me?"

Ruggles lifted the gun upright and set the hammers back down. "No. I kill men for maliciousness, but seldom for ignorance. However, if you keep on judging men the way you do, you'll soon find yourself an adversary without my scruples, and that daddy of yours won't be able to help you when you're dead. Am I making myself understood?"

Silently, Carol nodded his head and began to shake.

"Boy, you and I just might need each other before we're through with this thing. Now, if I'm not going to carry around any hard feelings about that slap of yours, then I'd suggest you get the thought of how close to dying you came out of your head."

"All right."

"One thing, though," Ruggles went on, "for the sake of politeness, I figure I'm due an apology. Those folks of yours raised you better than this and that college is trying to make you a gentleman."

Carol continued shaking. He tried to control himself. "I . . . I apologize."

"Is that all?"

"I was wrong. I apologize."

"That's more like it." Ruggles lowered his hand to his side. "Now, why don't you go and make yourself useful with the horses."

Carol promptly turned on his heels and scampered off to the

team. Ruggles slowly walked back to where Amy was now talking with the Reverend Black.

"What was that all about?" Amy asked.

"It seems your young friend there was worried about your honor."

Amy put her hand on his arm. "Should he have been?"

Black struck a match and lit his cigar. "Right now, I'd say the thing we ought to fret about is living," Black said as he puffed the long black cigar to life. "Honor can come later."

"Hello!"

At the sound of the distant shout, the men picked up their heads and looked to the west, near the head of the canyon. Peters and Gray drew their revolvers.

The people who approached them through the darkness were walking slowly. "Don't shoot," the man called out. "We got us a man here with a broken leg."

"Come ahead," Peters waved them forward.

The newcomers stepped forward. "Name's Cobb and this is my woman, Raincloud. My partner back here broke his leg; horse threw him. We'd sure appreciate it if you'd let us travel with you some. We're headed north to Lee's Ferry."

"That's where we're bound for too," Peters said. He turned to Ruggles and the other men, as if looking for an answer in their faces. "You sure are welcome to come along, mister. What with all them injuns runnin' around, having some more guns about would be pretty comfortin'. We're up here riding the traces 'cause we cracked an axle back yonder way."

"Well, you folks are welcome to ride our extra horses," Julian said.

Drago grimaced in pain. "Old Julian here stole 'em offa Mangus last night."

"He'll be on your trail," Ruggles shot back.

Drago blustered. "Maybe, but it'll be a while. Julian here sent the rest of his ponies runnin' cross the desert." His face blanched in obvious pain. "And I don't mind tellin' you none, laying down in that coach would 'bout be next to heaven for me right about now."

"We'd sure appreciate that," Julian joined in.

"Sure," Peters said. "If it goes and busts down on us, we'll just make out best we can. Those extra mounts of yours will save us some worriation."

"I can ride one of the horses," Amy added. "It wouldn't be that much difference."

They helped the distressed Drago down from his horse and carried him to the coach. "We won't be going very fast, but I'd watch myself and lay on the floor anyway. No sense in aggravating that leg by fallin' offa one of them seats."

+ + + + +

On the desert floor
Tuesday morning, not long after midnight

The band of Apaches rode around the wagon as it jolted its way into Mangus's camp. Mangus had been watching the stars, refusing to sleep. The Yavapai war chief rose from his bedroll near the smoldering coals.

His mind had been on the dream. He feared nothing, yet the dream was something he could not control. It came upon him in the midst of sleep and held him, powerless with horror. The idea of thrashing about in the deep water, where his feet could not touch the earth, left him with a deep, rootless feeling. A man was made to walk and ride upon the earth, not grope about in the water. It was the most fearful part of the dream. He always wrestled with the spirits of the silent night. He would resist them and refuse to sleep, until exhaustion took him away. He got to his feet and walked toward the wagon with Gandara by his side.

"Mangus," Campbell called out, "we sure is powerful glad to see you out here. We was afeared these 'paches wuz gonna skin us, and they might have if they hadn't found our whiskey. Lucky thing for us this feller Hiatt here could speak their lingo better than us, or they might have yet."

Gandara talked with the Apache, pointing out the stock of newly captured rifles. The young renegades shouted and raised their fists in the air. They ran to the new weapons and, one by one, pointed them to the sky and handled their actions.

Mangus watched them toy with their good fortune. There was no thought about defeat, no hint of caution, only the feeling of manhood in these men. They were like children deprived of the taste of sweetness for a very long time suddenly exposed to a find of honey, as much as their stomachs could hold. They had heard the news of the pony soldiers' defeat and now they saw with their own eyes.

Mangus turned and walked back to his bedroll. He listened to the laughter and the shouts of the new men. Their enthusiasm was intoxicating. He sat down cross-legged and watched as the three white men gathered around him.

"I'da thought you'd be a lot farther on by now," Campbell spoke out. "Kinda expected to see you and that stagecoach by now. What happened?"

Gandara joined them. He knew Mangus would never lower himself to speak to the white men directly. "A white man drove off horses last night," Gandara said. "It take us all day to find them."

Hiatt elbowed his way to the front of the group. "This man have one eye and one arm?" he asked.

Mangus looked up at the dirty miner. His eyes sharpened, but he seemed curious about how this stranger knew the man that had killed the sentry and driven away the horses. Reaching for a stick, he stirred the coals, then he gathered up a fresh bunch of mesquite branches and dropped them on the now breathing red coals. The blaze flared up, allowing him to see the man better.

"Yes," Gandara said. "That was the man. A long man with one eye, the eye of a hawk."

"He's plenty dangerous, a killer and a thief," Hiatt went on. "Him and that other feller attacked an army patrol and made off with their gold, lots of it."

"You know this man?" Gandara asked.

"He just about killed me. Then he hauled off and took my 'pache woman. He's being followed though, being followed by his brother and an Apache scout called Chupta."

Gandara suddenly looked at Mangus. Thoughts seemed to pass between them, thoughts spoken by their minds alone. Gandara turned back and queried, "Followed by his brother?"

"Yep, jest about as ornery and mean as he is, I'd say. Not a man to be trifled with. Can't say there's much love lost 'tween them two."

Gandara spoke to Mangus in Yavapai. The two exchanged words. He then looked back at Hiatt. "Apache say this man carries big gun, big gun that shoot far."

"That's fer durn sure," Campbell spoke up. "He's got him a Sharps buffalo rifle, but one like I ain't never seen before. He can shoot about as far as a man can see."

It was obvious that Mangus had been deeply disturbed by the

news. He frowned and again spoke in Yavapai to Gandara.

"What did he say?" Hiatt asked. Campbell put his hand on Hiatt's arm, as if to stop him from saying anything out of turn.

Mangus looked him directly in the eye. "I know this Chupta," he grunted. "He is an enemy. I will kill him and the others."

Campbell jumped at the sound of Mangus's voice. It was like the sound of low, rolling thunder from far away.

"We find them when the sun comes up," Gandara interjected. "We find them and we kill them all."

Silence settled over the camp. Mangus stared at the darkness through the licking flames of the small fire. He turned his back on the group and stirred the fire.

The three white men walked back toward the wagon. They talked in low, hush tones, seemingly unaware that Gandara was walking behind them. Each of them had his own set of fears, fears that were somewhat abated by years of dealing with the Indian.

To be here in this camp was to be a dead man for anyone else, but it was a risk each was willing to take. Greed had overridden the fear for the two of them, but for Hiatt, it was the need for revenge that pushed every other thought from his mind.

"Don't that beat all," Campbell muttered. "I've known that man for two years now and ain't heard him say more than three or four words all together. 'Spite the fact that we talked about them Cobb boys and how dangerous they were, the mention of that injun's name makes him talk. Now, how do you figger that?"

They were startled when Gandara spoke up behind them. "Mangus know Chupta well. The scout Chupta killed Mangus's only brother four years ago."

CHAPTER 30

+ + + + + + +

The two men watched the wagon roll into the camp. They had trailed the group of Apache that surrounded it for hours. Zac passed a canteen to Chupta. From the camp below, they could hear the shouts and screams of the Apache. "Looks like those boys have found their compadres," he said. "Wonder if the white men down there think they've found friends too."

Chupta tipped the canteen to his lips and swallowed. He wiped his mouth. "Mangus use them till they no good to him. When they give him all he wants, he kill them. Mangus hate all white men."

Zac shook his head slightly, then glanced down at the camp. "Poor dumb idiots. Like lambs being led to the slaughter. I guess when a man plays with fire, he's bound to get burned sooner or later."

"Chupta think sooner," Chupta said.

"Well, I think that woman of Hiatt's won't have much to worry about where he's concerned anymore."

Zac laid on his side and, taking the canteen back from Chupta, took a long drink. "I'm curious," he said. "Why is it you don't hate the white man?"

The scout rolled over onto his side, looking at Zac directly. "Chupta not say he does not hate white man. I only will not fight you anymore."

Zac paused. The man was a puzzle. "Then, you do hate us?"

Chupta nodded. "I hate all of you. I hate what you do to my land, my nation, and my people."

"Then why are you helping me?"

215

"The Indian is yesterday. The white man is today. It is a today of many tears, but Chupta is soldier. Chupta earn white man's money to buy food for family. He not stand in line for handout. You are too many to fight, but you are never too many to hate."

"Hatred is a waste of time and energy. My brother Julian has never learned that. He will go on hating as long as he has breath, and in the end, it will kill him. He may go on killing until somebody finally kills him, but it will be the hatred that does it, not another man's bullet."

"You will kill your brother?"

Zac paused and took another drink. It was a question he had been thinking about for some time. "I will do my job. I've dispatched many men, and since the war, few killings have bothered me. I don't worry about ghosts, and I sleep with my light off. The men I kill need killing, and I do it like a man would shoot a mad dog."

"Then, you will kill him. He is mad dog."

Zac gulped. "I'm honestly not sure what I will do, face-to-face. I can tell you one thing, though; even though you're a man who despises me and my kind, I will stop him any way I have to if he's getting ready to kill you."

"Umm," Chupta grunted.

"I'd do that for any man that rode with me, even ones I don't like, and I do like you."

"You do not hate the men that you kill?"

"No, I have no feeling for them at all. I try to never allow that. When what I do becomes personal, it'll be time to take up another line of work. Hatred clouds a man's thinking. On the inside, it makes him like the people he chases."

"You very strange man."

"No different than you. Both you and I are trapped by these jobs of ours. We do the thing we hate, with people we wouldn't have over to supper. I hope though, before we're through out here, that you and I can become friends. All white men are not alike. I wouldn't want to think that you hate me after you've gotten to know me. Besides, when we're done, I'd kinda like to have supper at your place."

"We see," Chupta grunted. "Man with much hatred in his heart, face-to-face with man who does not know what to think, usually wins a fight. Chupta think hatred is powerful medicine."

216

Zac got to his feet. "We better light a shuck out of here. If we give these folks a wide circle, we can make up for time before the sun comes up and they commence to looking for us. 'Course, we do have one thing in our favor."

Chupta stared at him with a quizzical expression on his face.

"It's not us they are looking for."

"Mangus will search for us now."

"Why is that?"

"Mangus and Chupta have spilled blood between us. If he know I am here, he will want me. Like I said, hatred is powerful medicine. It makes a man go where he should not go."

Zac gazed off at the camp. He could see the three white men talking to the Indians in the distance. "I'd say he knows by now."

Zac walked over to the big buckskin and swung himself into the saddle. "I've hunted many a man before, but this will be a first."

"How?"

"It will be the first time I've ridden with a man that's being hunted."

They slowly moved their horses across the rocky hills, craning their necks as they picked their way around the brush, their eyes darting back and forth to keep the camp below them in sight. Zac had donned his shotgun chaps. The tough, tight-fitting, fringed leather scraped the mesquite as they rode down the hillside. Each briar seemed like a claw in the night, pulling at him as if giving warning. Chupta's knee-length moccasins brushed softly against the sage. The desert below unfolded in the darkness like a fan spread out over the earth, and the sparkling stars bathed the ground in a silver hue.

A sheet of rock before them glistened with mica. The soft light bounced off the rocky surface, giving the appearance of thousands of rat's teeth, broken and scattered on the ground. They plodded slowly over it, their horses' hooves clicking sharply.

To their left, a bighorn sheep picked his head up and cocked it in their direction. With sudden swiftness, it bolted on all fours, scattering rocks. They watched its twitching white tail bouncing in the gathering darkness. It seemed to move from side to side before disappearing into the shadows.

The two men reached the desert floor and began a gentle lope. They would keep the North Star over their left shoulder. It shone like a beacon in the night sky, summoning them ahead. There would be no more tracking until they cut the trail of Julian and the mules. They would push on until morning. Every mile they made tonight Mangus would have to make up tomorrow. He would find their trail, of that Zac was certain. There was no concealing it until the sun was up, and then they could only hope to confuse Indian trackers. Even with their combined skills, they knew their success would be limited.

Perhaps an army patrol could come to their aid, but now that seemed out of the question. The army would have its hands full keeping the Apache on the reservation. It had already been hit hard, and it might take some time before reserves could be brought in to make up the difference.

A coyote cried plaintively in the distance, followed shortly by another. It would be a good night for hunting. The moon hung low in the sky, its light bathing the desert. Rabbits would have to look over their shoulders before this night was through. Zac only hoped that Mangus didn't have scouts this far north of the camp. Otherwise, he and Chupta would be two more desert rabbits running for their lives—running for their lives on played-out horses.

An hour later, both Zac and Chupta were walking. The horses needed the break, but it was one they couldn't afford. They would walk for a while and let the animals rest while moving.

"You suppose the army will know where Mangus is heading?" Zac asked.

Chupta shook his head. "It might be two days, maybe three, before army patrol is overdue. It take another day or two before they find where we bury them. That is too long."

"Too long to be of much help to us," Zac said. "Our best bet is to find the people we're chasing and light out before Mangus catches up to us. I don't see any other way."

"We could find trail, then hold up someplace I know. Let Mangus go and get people we chase."

"I'll think on that," Zac said. "It might be the smart thing to do, but our job is to find those people and bring them to justice."

"White man justice."

"It's the best we have."

"It best you have."

Zac mounted the buckskin. He stretched himself in the saddle. Every bone seemed to ache. Sleep had come only snatches at a time. He could get by like this, but only for a few days. There would have to come a time when he laid himself out and slept unconditionally. To be short on sleep and food would mean that he would be raw when he met up with Julian. He couldn't stand the thought of saying something he might regret, but what disturbed him was the notion of doing something that a clear head would prevent.

The two of them rode north. The horses kept a steady gait, no doubt thankful for the walking time with their backs clear of riders. With each steady mile, there was more distance between them and Mangus, distance that would eventually allow them to sleep. The lack of food presented little problem. Zac had always found that hunger made his senses more alert. The slightest noise would get him poised, the faintest aroma would rouse his senses, and the remotest sound would bring his sensibilities to full attention.

Hours later, the rose-colored dawn had begun to paint the tops of the mountains. The light had what seemed to be a gray hue to it, neither darkness nor light, the netherworld of the desert before dawn. Behind them, to the south, Mangus's camp would be stirring. Perhaps some of his scouts would already be searching for their tracks. It wouldn't take long to find them.

Chupta pointed to the slope of a rocky outcropping up ahead. "We go up there, on foot."

"Good idea. Let's try to stick to the rocks, if we can."

Dismounting, the two men tugged on their reins, pulling the horses up after them. The horses kicked at the rocks as they mounted the steep hill. All around them, rocks were scattered, jutted with low-slung brush.

Zac turned south, followed by the scout. They left a faint trail behind them, one a man would have to look carefully for, but one that could be found, nonetheless. The trail looked as if an attempt had been made to conceal their tracks, but it led in the wrong direction.

Breaking out on the rocky face, they walked the horses carefully. Moving between the rocky shelves, Zac led the way over the next one and broke off a branch of sage. The fresh break would tell their followers which way they had gone.

Zac stopped at the top of the rocks. He carefully led the buckskin down the rocks to the south and onto the soil. Climbing up another shelf of rock, he backed the horse up and turned north. He handed the reins of the buckskin to Chupta and motioned for him to move ahead. Following along behind, he turned over every rock disturbed by the horse's hooves and used the sage to brush any tracks that were left that the rock did not cover. It took time to lay down the false trail, but it was time well spent. For every minute they took, Mangus would have to take five to uncover their true path.

An hour later, they came to the shade of several scrub oaks. "You stay here and sleep," Chupta said. "I ride west. Maybe I find place where we can stay."

"Don't take too long," Zac said. "If I get to sleep, I just might not wake up till that Mangus fella sticks a lance in me. I figure we got about four or five hours on those people if they choose to look for us."

Chupta nodded. He walked his horse off toward the western hills, and Zac lay down. In moments, he was sound asleep.

He didn't know how much time had passed when he felt the gentle nudge of the scout on his shoulder. Blinking his eyes open, he could see the sun directly overhead.

"I find a place, a place where Mangus will not go, the place of the old ones. We can stay there and let Mangus pass. Indian not go near place of old people. It like walking over the grave of one's father."

Zac sat up.

"Stagecoach and horses there. They leave last night."

"No sign of Julian?"

Chupta shook his head.

"Then we'd better move north. It's him we're looking for, not a hideout."

+ + + + +

The desert floor
Early Tuesday afternoon

Ruggles cranked open the door to the coach. "You all right?"

Drago sat on the floor, his leg resting on several wadded-up blankets. Cradled in his arm was a large bottle of rye. He slapped it and grinned. "This tarantula juice'd draw blood blisters on a rawhide boot. Right now, I ain't feeling anything, nothing a-tall."

Ruggles looked back at Julian, who sat his horse beside Raincloud as she cared for the baby. He turned back and studied Drago, then felt the splints on his leg. "Your partner seemed to set this leg of yours pretty good, but it could do with better splints. We come up on a stand of timber, and I'll see you get some new ones cut."

He glanced up slightly at Drago while the man downed another swallow. "You say you found some gold on this trip of yours?"

Drago pulled the bottle down and wiped his mouth. "We got us some gold, all right." He grinned. "Twuz jest like takin' candy from a sleepin' baby."

Julian stepped out of his saddle. "What we do is our own business," he said.

Ruggles stood up straight, his lips creased delicately. His mustache turned with the smile and his eyes flashed. He dipped his chin slightly. "My apologies, sir. You are most correct. You'll have to forgive the habits of a gambler. Finding men who have been successful is often the key to my own good fortune."

Julian walked around Ruggles and closed the door to the stage. Keeping his back to it, he stood in front of Ruggles, glaring at him. "Curiosity about men and their money isn't the most healthy habit to be afflicted by. Prospectors don't usually talk about their work until it's been filed."

Ruggles stroked his chin. "I make it my business to know men, and I'd never have taken the two of you for prospectors. Both of you have the cut of men who live in the saddle, not on the ground."

"Then, it seems you still have a bit to learn about knowing men, mister gambler man. We have to ride hard to get to where we're going."

Ruggles studied the expression on Julian's face. The hardness of the man and the lean look about him made him someone to be reckoned with, and Lawrence Ruggles well knew it. "That's mighty strange, then."

"What's strange?"

"It's strange that you've been that successful."

"How's that?"

"Oh, I don't know. I don't dig in the ground for a living, but I make my way by knowing a lot of men who do. Most would say that a man finds what he's looking for by slowly walking over the dirt he's going to dig in, not by riding hard over it."

Peters walked over to the two men. "Did you say you wuz carrying some grub on them mules of yours? We ain't had more'n a bite or two in quite a while."

"We have more than enough. Why don't you get everyone together and we can pass some of it out."

"Sounds good to me," Peters said.

"Here, let me help you pass it out," Ruggles said.

"That won't be necessary," Julian quickly responded. "My woman can take care of that."

"Your woman?"

"His wife," Raincloud spoke up.

"Well, excuse me again. It isn't often a prospector travels with his wife."

"It isn't often he has one he can't bear to leave," Julian responded.

Raincloud handed Sunflower to Julian and then climbed down from her horse.

"No, I guess you're right, at that," Ruggles said. "You certainly have a fine-looking woman, Mr. Cobb. A man would be hesitant to say good-bye to someone like that."

The group sat down as Raincloud rifled through one of the mule's packs. She produced two large rawhide bags and began to distribute the contents to the entire group. They ate the mixture of fruit and pecans with great eagerness and carefully nursed their canteens. The dried beef along with the fruit and nuts made their mouths dry, but it was a price each of them was more than willing to pay.

"How far are we from Lee's Ferry?" Amy asked.

"If we don't break that axle again, a few days."

The Reverend Black had finished his handful of food. He produced another one of his long cigars and, rolling it over in his fingers, offered it to Julian. "I think we all appreciate you sharing your stores with us. Please take one of these. I don't carry much, but I do make sure I have enough of the venerable vegetable of Virginia to make do."

Julian took the cigar and bit off a piece of one end. "Thank you. I don't mind if I do."

He placed it in his mouth and Black lit a match with his thumbnail, leaned forward, and touched the end of the cigar with the flame. Taking out another cigar, he then rolled the end into the dying match and puffed it to life.

"Mighty kind of you and mighty strange for a preacher," Julian said.

"I'll tell you something, Cobb, most people 'round these parts see preachers as good for very little. They have no use for them. I make sure I can meet a man's needs first. Then and only then can I get him to listen to what I have to say."

Julian took the smoldering cigar from his mouth and studied its glowing tip. "For a man who hasn't had a smoke in over two weeks, you've got me all ears, Preacher."

Black sat back and smiled. "That's just the way I like my congregation."

Butch Gray pointed to Julian's .44. "Speaking for myself, I feel whole lots better with a man who can shoot straight, right about now. We may have to kill a passel of injuns before we're through."

Ruggles got up and dug his hand into the bag. Cupping his fingers, he looked back at the stage. "That partner of yours doesn't know he's hungry, but he'll need something nonetheless."

"You just set yourself down," Julian replied. "I'll take what needs to be taken to him. That curiosity of yours might make it hard for Drago to chew."

Ruggles narrowed his eyes. He dropped the fistful of food into Julian's outstretched hand. "I'll bet you can use that gun of yours pretty good too," he said, "for a prospector."

"You can rely on that," Julian said.

CHAPTER 31

+ + + + + + +

Near the foothills of the mountains
The following Friday, late afternoon

The stage had moved steadily uphill for several days, the desert fast disappearing behind the pine trees and oak. The going was hard on the axle, but everybody knew that the horses had taken the brunt of the uphill pull. Strung out on either side of the coach, the people who were riding towed the mules.

"There it is!" Peters called out. "Hot food and a fresh team of horses."

Nestled in the pines, a log cabin stood, a plume of smoke rising from the rock chimney. A corral and barn spread out to the north of the house, and a large stack of firewood had already been laid between the corral and the house. It was plain to see the people inside were expecting a hard winter; eight to ten cords of the stuff lay scattered on the ground like playthings tossed about by the hand of some giant. Animal skins were stretched tight over what a person could only guess to be rifle slits cut into the logs.

Peters pulled up on the reins, bringing the stage to a halt in front of the house. "Hello the house!"

A large man with checkered shirt and knee-high boots stomped out onto the porch. He lifted his suspenders to the tops of his shoulders, like a man just leaving the comfort of a heavy meal.

"Bernie, it's sure 'nuff good to see you with your hair still on," Peters called out, tying the traces to the brake handle. "Thought we'd never get here."

"Who you got with you?" The man barked out the question in a deep, gravely voice. He ran his hand through his heavy beard and stared at the group on horseback with black eyes that seemed to dart with fire.

"Just folks heading up to Lee's Ferry. Got my passengers and some prospectors. One of 'em has got himself a wife."

"Come on in, then. Better put them animals away and help yerself to some feed back there. Sarai's had some possum stew cooking fer days. Ought to be plenty ripe by now. We got a pot of coffee on, too."

Julian handed the reins of his horse to Ruggles. "If you'll get them over there, I'll be out when Raincloud gets situated. I'll bring you out some of that coffee, too." He looked at both Ruggles and Carol. "I'm gonna have to have some help getting Drago inside." Taking Raincloud by the arm, he steered her toward the open door as the big man stepped aside.

Inside the darkened cabin, lamps were lit, casting dancing shadows on the roughhewn walls. The cock of a revolver brought Julian to full attention. He stiffened his back, ramrod straight.

"Hello, Julian, remember me?"

Julian studied the lean face and the soft glow that lit up the barrel of the man's six-gun. "Zachary? Is that you?"

Zac nodded. "It is."

"What you doing here, boy, and why the gun?"

"I work for Wells Fargo now, and I'm here for you."

To the side of the room, Chupta cocked his rifle and gazed into Julian's eyes. "White man make a fine target in that door," he said. Chupta spoke to Raincloud in Apache, telling her to move away. Instead, she inched closer to Julian's side.

"You one of them people's bounty chasers, then? Somehow, I never would have figured you for that."

"And I wouldn't have guessed you'd turn out to be a thief."

Julian moved toward him. "And why the blazes not? They stole everything we ever worked for; why shouldn't I try and get some of it back? Way I figure it, we got it coming to us."

"What's past is past. Now, you just make this easy and unbuckle that gunbelt. Don't make the mistake of letting this blood thing go too far. Besides, even if I was to ponder a might and flinch, my Apache friend over there won't think twice about putting you down, and he shoots real good. Fact is, I think he'd kind of enjoy legally killing a white man."

On Raincloud's back, Sunflower began to cry. The woman unstrapped the carrier and took the baby in her arms. "She is hungry."

"You just step aside, ma'am, and you can feed the child on the chair over yonder."

Julian looked Raincloud in the eye and nodded. She slowly moved away, bouncing the crying baby in her arms.

The large man in the checkered shirt had stopped the others from coming through the door. He stood beside the coach and made small talk without explaining what was happening inside.

Julian slowly slid his hand to his side and unbuckled the bullet-studded belt. It fell to the floor. "Okay, little brother, satisfied?"

"For now."

"You just might be needing me and that gun if those injuns catch up with us."

"They seldom come this far north. Got no reason to."

"Don't you go to betting on that, little brother. That stage we come in with is carrying ammunition, ammunition for an army patrol that we never met up with. Them folks chasing us need that stuff to fight their own war with the Yankees."

"We buried that patrol last week."

"Then everything's gonna bust loose 'round here, sure 'nuff. You are gonna need me and Drago."

"Just kick that shooter over here and you can go and join that woman over there."

As Julian moved to the bed where Raincloud sat, Zac picked up the revolver on the floor and stepped toward the open door. "Mr. Suthers," he called through the open door.

The big man turned and walked back to the house.

"You know where this man's partner is?"

"They say he's got a broke leg. He's laying down in the bottom of the stage."

A short time later, the horses having been put away, the people were scattered around the room. Sarai had ladled the stew onto metal plates, and all of them were hungrily eating whatever was in the mess of brown meaty porridge. They were simply grateful to have something hot in their stomachs. They weren't about to question the contents of the dish. Zac silently watched Julian balance the plate on his lap and spoon the meal into his mouth.

Julian finished the meal and set the plate down. "So, boy, how long you been working for them Wells Fargo shysters?"

"A little over six years now."

"I reckon I've heard about you amidst all those tales of Wells Fargo 'hereos' since I got back in the States, but never heard tell any specific names. You like this life of chasing folks down and cutting them up?"

Zac ignored the question. He took out his pipe and stuffed it with tobacco. Striking a match, he lit the mixture.

"Well, you must like it. Looks like the work agrees with you. You've grown up all straight and tall like. You're all filled out, and you got sharp, clear eyes and a manly jaw. I'm sure Momma would have been proud."

"I don't think I could say the same about you."

The silence of the room engulfed everyone but the two brothers. Each member of the group seemed fascinated by what the brothers would say next, and yet nervousness had them all on the edge of their chairs. Reverend Black produced two long cigars. He got up and walked over to Julian, holding one out. "A hot meal deserves a fine cigar to finish it off, I'd say. Can I offer you one, Mr. Cobb?"

"Don't mind if I do, Parson."

"You boys remind me of a Bible story I know about, Jacob and Esau. There wasn't a whole lot of love lost between those two boys either, and when they finally met up, whew-eee. I can tell you, no one was sure what would happen."

Julian grinned. "No one can tell what will happen here, either."

Zac puffed on his pipe. "There's no mystery here. I'm taking you both to the nearest army post in St. George, Utah. And when the army tries you there, what will happen to you won't be a mystery either."

"You must want to see me hang real bad, little brother."

"I just want to get my job done, return that payroll, and let the law take its course. I'd want as much with any man I was after—that man being you doesn't make one iota of difference to me."

"You've gotten cold as you've aged, little brother."

"I've gotten a lot smarter, smart enough to know you can't trust a man's upbringing to make him turn out right."

Julian smiled. "You always were the idealist of the bunch, all the time reading and thinking, thinking and reading. There were times I thought you'd go and bust up your brain with all them books of yourn. Made a man wonder what a body ever got out of all them stories and jawing on paper."

"They taught me the difference between right and wrong."

"But I can see they didn't teach you not to kill. And from everything I've heard about you and your type, you got that down real good."

"I hold my own."

Ruggles had prepared a pallet in the corner for Amy. He silently pointed it out to her.

Sarai moved around the room with a coffeepot. She was a large woman, broad at the shoulders and large of hip. She walked over to Zac with the pot. "Here, you best have some of this. It'll quiet your nerves a might. You boys remind me of a couple of bad dogs we had 'round this place last year. They tore at each other till there weren't much left of either one of them. By the time they got through with one another, a jack rabbit could have took them on."

Hec Peters stood up and dropped his coat to the floor. "I'ma gonna take this here spot. I'd say we'd best all get some sleep. We'll be lightin' outta here afore the sun comes up."

"You and your wife should think about joining us, Mr. Suthers," Ruggles said. "Mangus has been making war on all white men, and he won't spare you just because you don't know him."

"We ain't got no truck with the injuns 'round here. In the years we been here we seen one or two of the white mountain 'pache. Mostly, what we get is the Navajo pokin' around. We don't give out no handouts, and we don't humor 'em none. Sarai and me ain't got no reason to leave our stock. If'n we was to leave, them Navajo would steal our place blind. We'd come back in a week and have to start from scratch."

"Suit yourselves," Zac joined in, "but you'd still have your hair."

"Man with hair and without two sticks to rub together ain't much of a man in my book. No, you folks get your rest. Me and Sarai will still be here when you come back our way. It's good to have you, though. All we gets is Mormon honeymooners as the usual passersby. T'ain't often we get ourselves some feller gentiles."

Zac looked over at Chupta. "You can sleep first."

+   +   +   +   +

The stage had been traveling for more than an hour before the sky was light enough to see Humphrey's Peak. The pines stretched up the foothills and two kit foxes ran for cover, their pinkish tails flagging at the passing stage. Zac had insisted that Julian and Drago ride inside the stage while he and the others rode the horses. Chupta had gone on ahead to look over the terrain they would travel.

Several hours later, Chupta rode back to join the group. "You have to go around to the west," he said.

"How come?" Zac asked.

Hec Peters watched the two men from his seat on the rolling coach. "He's found them there lava beds up ahead. We'll have to go 'round them, sure 'nuff. I doubt you'd want to even take them horses across them, to say nothing 'bout this here Concord coach."

A short time later, they came up on the shattered field of black lava. The grizzled mass of sharp rock had been buckled and stood out in dwarfish spires of jagged rock. The shattered ground spread out in all directions like a room full of playing cards casually tossed about. Some pieces were flat and others were stacked on end, jutting up into the air. At various locations, twisted bantam pines had pushed their way to the surface and fought for the sunlight. Fresh greenery dotted the black, sharp surface, like fresh-cut hair on the edge of a gigantic razor.

"We may as well rest the horses here a bit," Peters said.

Zac spoke softly to Chupta. "You'd better go back behind us a ways. I'd feel better if I knew Mangus wasn't breathing down our necks. What do you suppose is keeping him?"

"White man see Apache and Yavapai as just Indians. To him we are all the same. That not so. We speak two different tongues and have always been enemies. If the Apache that join up with Mangus are to ride with him, they had to wait to make medicine together."

"The ghost dance?"

"Yes, ghost dance. It take them maybe one, two days to come together in spirit, but they not far behind. They have plenty rifles, but need bullets we carry. They dance at the camp we saw them at, maybe for a night and a day. When they see the visions, then they come give us chase."

"Well, that was days ago. It won't take them very long to make up the distance, given how slow we've been going."

"If they come this way, they stop first to kill man and woman we with last night. They not like to leave whites behind them."

"I hope you're wrong about that."

"Chupta not wrong about much. Not wrong about that."

Ruggles and Amy rode over to where the men were talking. "If you two want to scout, you can trust me to guard that brother of yours. I shoot straight, and I won't hesitate to do it."

"Fine," Zac said. "You'll do. We'll let everybody stretch their legs a mite, then when the stage gets out moving again, Chupta and

I can fan out and look things over."

Zac stepped down from the buckskin and cranked open the door. "You want to get out for a spell, you can," he said. "We won't be stopping again anytime soon."

Julian stepped down from the coach. "Mighty chivalrous of you, little brother. Raincloud and me was getting a little stir crazy in there, all cooped up and the like. Nice to see the years haven't changed your decency. Drago ain't quite fit to move about yet, but I'd sure like to."

"Just stay close by, so I can see you."

Julian looked over the black field of lava and the imposing bluffs that surrounded them, their dark brown faces pouting at the sunlight. "Now, where we gonna go to get away from that long gun of yours?"

"Nowhere."

"That's what I figured. No, we'll stay right close. I got my little brother Zac to protect us here. Besides, when those renegades do catch up to us, you're gonna see that I'm here to protect you as well."

Zac ignored the comment and watched Julian help Raincloud over the sharp rocks. "Anybody didn't know any better, you'd take him for a family man."

"That you would," Ruggles joined in. "They make quite the domestic picture, don't they?"

"Just don't you forget," Zac said, "that brother of mine would just as soon gun you down as he would step on a bug. He has no conscience, none at all."

Julian held on to Raincloud's elbow as he helped her across the rocks.

"Why are you helping me?" she asked. "They all know we are not married."

Julian turned his head back toward the coach and the group that was watching them. "Ever seen a snake capture a bird?" he asked. "It always does it real sly-like, never seeming to move or change. It slides up near that bird so slowly that the bird barely notices the change. The snake keeps his eyes fixed to that bird, every second. He stares it down, never doubting for a moment that it will be supper. Then when the bird moves his head to look away or eat, it is."

He reached out with his hand and lightly touched her face, brushing away several strands of hair.

She tightened up inside.

"You just go along with me," he said. "Nothing is more disarming and nothing more innocent than a man in love."

"You do this for show?"

Leaning over, he kissed her. "I guess I'm not rightly sure. I've never had anyone to love before, don't know full well what it would feel like." He glanced slightly back at the group. "It is having quite the effect on them, though."

"I think," she said, "that it is an even longer time since you thought about anyone but yourself."

He stared blankly into her eyes.

It was near sunset when the group approached the ruins on the hill. They swung the coach and horses to the north side of the point and dismounted. There beside them, low stacks of stones formed the remains of long-ago lived-in hovels. The stones were flat, all carefully selected to give stability in the wind, and laid carefully, one upon another, tightly wedged to make the place windproof and waterproof. The walls had been torn down to the height of a man's chest.

Above them, on the summit of the hill, the citadel of an archaic fortress loomed. Prominent features of stone surrounded the ancient walls. The wind whistled around the stones, and the growing darkness shrouded its shape. The tall grass swayed back and forth in the rippling wind, obscuring a path that was now seldom walked.

"We can't stay down here," Ruggles said. "Rain or no, if they get that high ground, we'll pay for it."

"All right," Zac said, "we'll take that high ground and carry along whatever cover we can find with us. If it does rain tonight though, we'll all be soaked to the skin."

Gray looked up at the citadel. "Any fire we light up there is gonna be seen for miles away."

"Then we have to be plenty careful," Zac said. He pointed to Julian. "You can help that man of yours up the hill."

A short time later, they gathered in the open space between the old walls of the fortress. The rocks were the same smooth, flat mixture of stones they had seen in the houses below. The wall circled the top of the hill, breaking apart at various intervals to reveal the hollow to the south of them. Carved out from the earth, a rocky valley was studded with grass and sage. Sheer bluffs of red rock formed three sides of the small valley and, beyond it, a man could look forever to the south of them. The grassy, sage-spotted plain stretched out to the spot where the clouds gave themselves birth. Overhead, gray clouds streaked with white cottony pillows bloomed and hung heavy with rain. They seemed to move before them, darkening with the sky.

CHAPTER 32

+ + + + + + +

"Hello the cabin!" Zac yelled the words out over the azure water flowing slowly over rounded rocks. On the north side of the river, areas of thick brush dotted a sandy bank that lengthened along the foot of a series of small hills. Behind the hills, massive bluffs crested to the clear blue sky, giving off the appearance of timeless fortifications. Each bluff's parapet was flat on top and rings were cut deeply into the sandstone. The canyon itself was surrounded by bluffs that gave off a pinkish gray color.

It had taken them the better part of the morning to negotiate the bluffs that were cut into an opening near the river. Behind him, Zac could still hear the slow groaning of the wheels as the coach laboriously ground down the rocky surface. Across the river, several sturdy rock houses were studded along the flat, next to an incoming tributary.

A tall, angular man with a black frock coat and trousers emerged from one of the buildings. His pointed black hat was pressed down over his ears. He walked toward one of the small hills behind the beach. "You can bring your horses on across," he said. "I'll bring the ferry on over for the coach. It'll cost you twenty dollars, cash money."

A taut cable line stretched over the river. The ferry was flat-bottomed with barrels surrounding the sides. Sturdy logs were strapped together, and a platform was fastened to them with poles that held pulleys connected to the cable. On either side of the ferry, large sweeps were propped out of the water and tied off.

Zac waved the group forward. "Let's keep it moving," he said. "We can rest on the other side."

Peters and Gray walked beside the lead horses, each holding a harness and guiding the coach down the rocky slope. Julian, Drago, Raincloud, and the baby were all inside. The rest either rode or were walking the horses and mules.

Minutes later, the man had pulled the ferry to their side of the river and secured it to a small landing. "You can leave that there team hitched," he said. "We got ourselves plenty of room. Now, about my twenty dollars."

Hec Peters fumbled in his jeans pocket and produced a shiny double eagle gold piece. He handed it to the man, who promptly bit down on it and smiled. "That ought to do it," he said. Sticking out his hand to Peters, he said, "Name's Hiram Johnson. River's getting lower this month. You're plenty lucky 'bout that."

After loading the stage and horses onto the ferry, the men began the pull to the other side. Peters took off his hat and ran his handkerchief over his head. "I'll tell you somethin', we're plenty lucky 'bout lots. We been chased to kingdom come by the worst group of renegades you ever did see. We got us some rifle ammunition them folks wants real bad-like."

"Navajos?"

"Nope, Yavapai mostly, along with some Apache by now. They is sure kicking up a ruckus down in Arizona."

"They wouldn't dare come up here to Navajo land."

Ruggles hoisted on the line. "Don't you bet on it. That ghost dance has those people so full of visions about an Indian empire, they just might do anything."

When the ferryboat reached the north shore, Zac pulled the man aside. "You have a place over here we can lock somebody up?"

"Sure, we got ourselves a storehouse over yonder ways. Why?"

"I'm an agent for Wells Fargo. I have two prisoners I'm taking to St. George. Neither man can be trusted."

"Well, you go ahead on and lock up whoever you want. It don't make no nevermind to me."

Zac drew his revolver and cranked open the door to the coach. He pointed the weapon inside. "All right, this is where you get out for now. We'll be pulling out in the morning, and we'll all need a good night's sleep."

Julian stepped out of the coach. "You're the boss, little brother." He helped Raincloud down and then turned to Zac. "You really think you're going to see me to St. George?"

"I'm going to see you into the hands of the law and a hanging judge."

"And you really think you could pull that trigger?"

"I do my job. I've killed men before."

"Not your own brother, you haven't."

"I'd shoot you down just the same as you would me, if you were the one that had the gun."

"Now, what makes you think I'd do a thing like that?"

Zac looked Julian straight in the eye. "Julian, you and I both know you wouldn't hesitate for a minute to kill anybody who stood in the way of something you wanted. I figure anything you learned as a child you've already put aside to do what you do. You've drifted so far afield, you've forgotten every sense of right and wrong you were ever taught."

"But I remember what I learned about loyalty. I wouldn't work for the Yankees. I'd never think about being one of their Wells Fargo lap dogs."

Zac motioned toward the dugout cellar that the ferryman had pointed out to him. He followed Julian up the riverbank. "I work for myself," Zac said, "always have, always will."

Julian slowed up. "Little brother, if you work for Wells Fargo, then out here you're working for the Yankee in the White House. You might just as well carry about a secret service badge and wear a blue coat at fancy balls."

"You don't know what you're talking about."

"Oh, don't I?"

"No, you don't. I know you. You just want to do what you can to get me to thinking about anything other than the murders you've committed and the money you've stolen."

"I've just never given my hand to the Yankees, that's all. I won't be stolen from, I won't be sweet-talked into being a collaborator, and I won't be reconstructed."

"That war is long gone."

"Not while I'm breathing, it isn't."

"The judge in St. George will see to that, I suppose."

Julian swung around to face him, raising himself to his full height. "You can do what you want, but I'll never hang. I'd just as soon be shot down by you as I would let the trapdoor be sprung on me by some Yankee. You best remember that. You'd better think twice about that outfit you're working for, too. I've spent enough time soldiering for foreign governments these past ten years to know what they are. They don't get those high-paying government contracts for nothing. They do the dirty work those stuffed shirts in Washington send them to do, and they'd just as soon let somebody like you do the dying for it."

Zac waggled his revolver in the direction of the cellar door. "I just do my job—do my job and keep the law. Now, you just rest that mind of yours in there, and let me do the thinking for the both of us for a while."

When Zac had seen to it that both Julian and Drago were safely locked away, he joined the group on the beach as they readied the stage for the trip northward. He kept a wary eye on Raincloud. The last thing he needed now was for her to turn Julian loose.

Peters, Ruggles, and the ferryman had found another serviceable axle and were sliding it into position. A fire was burning with a bed of coals being prepared for cooking. Tommy ran around the fire, waving his arms, as the Reverend Black stirred the coals. Nearby, Philip Carol sat beside Amy and watched the fire burn brightly. They would get their cooking done in the daylight. By now, it had become too much of a habit to break; besides, cooking when a body could actually see was much preferable to fumbling around the fire in the darkness.

Butch Gray had stripped off his shirt and had a makeshift fishing pole in the water. "I seen some mighty pretty trout in here when we crossed."

Johnson grinned. "I'll tell you something right now; there's more of them things in this stretch of water than a body can shake a stick at. 'Round here we gets plumb tired of cleanin' and eatin' 'em.

"My momma didn't raise no such fool," Gray said. "Fish that's fresh caught is the bestest eating of all, to my thinking." He grinned and threw out his line.

With sudden impact, an arrow flew from across the river, spiraling through the air and landing directly in Gray's bare chest. He fell backward, giving out a soft grunt. The arrow was followed by gunfire and an eruption of arrows from across the river.

Zac drew his revolver and began to shoot. Ruggles dropped the part of the wheel he was trying to lift and made a dash for the fire. He watched as Black ran for the boy, scooped him up in his arms, then drove for a nearby log. Carol rolled off the log that he and Amy had been sitting on; Amy had begun to run toward Tommy, but Ruggles overtook her and sent her crashing to the ground with him. Peters and the ferryman lay underneath the stage. Peters grabbed the rifle he had propped nearby and was doing his best to return fire.

Zac drew out a second revolver. "Get up the bluffs," he yelled. "Keep up the shooting, but you had better get to running fast." He fired nonstop as he backed up the hill. One by one, the group began a dead run to the top of the bluffs.

Ruggles pulled Amy to her feet and pushed her along, keeping himself between the line of fire and the girl. As they neared the top of the bluff, he collapsed, pushing her forward. His right calf began to spurt blood, the bright crimson bloom covering his lower pants leg.

Zac rushed over and he and Amy reached down, dragging him up to the top of the sandy bluff.

Turning around to the huddled Raincloud, Zac called out, "You'd better get those two out of there. I want them here with us."

Raincloud laid down the crying Sunflower and, lifting her skirt, ran for the dugout.

"Them folk ain't no Navajo," the boatman shouted.

"No," Ruggles grunted. "It's Mangus, and he's come for that ammunition and our scalps."

Zac carefully loaded his revolver. "Can they cross there?" he asked Johnson.

"No way. They'd have to swim it. But about a quarter mile or so upriver, they could cross without too much trouble."

"Then, let's hope we've got some time before they find that spot."

"What do you aim to do, boy?" Black asked.

Zac motioned toward the stage. "The boot of that Concord has my rifle and ammo belt in it, along with two or three others. If we're going to stand a chance, we have to shoot something we can't miss with."

Ruggles groaned. "You going to get those?"

"You bet I am, or die trying." He closed the door to the cylinder on the revolver. "I am going to need some fire laid down for me, something to distract them a mite."

Ruggles tightened down a scarf on his lower-right leg. "We'll do what we can."

Moments later, Raincloud and Julian helped Drago hobble to the top of the bluffs. Zac spun his .45 and handed it butt first to Julian.

"Well, for now, you got what you wanted. Those may not be Yankees over there, but they're out to kill us, all the same." He spun the action on his short Shopkeeper Special. "I'm heading down for the rest of the guns—try to aim over me."

"Not even I would shoot you in the back, little brother."

Peters lay in the sand, gun poised. "You just do what you got to do. We'll keep 'em off you best we can."

Julian looked Zac in the eye. "You always were the hero, little brother. Cowards live longer."

"Maybe so, but heroes sleep better."

Julian aimed down the barrel of the Colt and squeezed off a round at an Indian who had ventured near the river. The man buckled and pitched headfirst into the blue water.

The shot signaled another round from the renegades, and Zac scrambled down the hill in the direction of the stranded coach. He ran low, in a zigzagging motion, dirt spitting at his feet from stray bullets. Arriving at the coach, he crouched low under the front seat. Reaching up, he pulled down the first rifle. Waving his hand over his head, he felt for the second, latching on to a shotgun instead. He pulled it down. Moments later, he had found the second Winchester and two boxes of ammunition.

The bullets around him clipped large chunks of wood from the face of the coach. Indians had never been known for their accurate aim with a rifle, and the scarcity of ammunition rarely enabled them to practice. But given enough time, any man could walk into a lucky shot, and Zac knew his time so close to the river was limited.

The Sharps lay propped up against the back wheel of the coach, his bandoleer of special ammunition wrapped around it. In the sudden shooting, he had instinctively reached for his revolver, never giving a thought to grabbing the long rifle, a mistake he now regretted. He took a blanket from the box of the coach and spread it on the ground. Laying the rifles and shotgun on it, he dropped to his belly.

With the little Shopkeeper in hand, he began to crawl the length of the coach, bullets spraying in the dirt on either side of him. As he reached the spot near where the Sharps was stationed, he looked up to see a warrior plunging into the river with his horse. The man had obviously become impatient with the near misses and wanted to take matters into his own hands.

Zac held out the snub nose .45 and cocked the hammer. He sent a well-placed round directly into the man's chest, spinning him off his horse and into the meandering stream.

He reached toward the rifle and grabbed it, pulling it under the stage with him. Drawing it closer to him, he began to inch his way backward. Moments later he was bundling the blanket around the dangerous hardware. He tied the ends of the blanket tight with leather thongs and, taking off his belt, fashioned a sling to carry it. Swinging it onto his back, he crouched low and looked off at the seemingly faraway bluffs. The revolvers had minimum effectiveness at this range and he knew it. But he also knew Julian could make good use of his, and he suspected Drago and Ruggles could do the same. He would need good cover fire for the long run. He hadn't seen Chupta, but the scout was somewhere with the only other rifle.

The Indians on or near the opposite bank were much closer to him than the friendly fire, and they would be poised and waiting for him to run. He had surprised them when he came down the hill toward the coach, but they wouldn't need any more warning for his sprint back up the hill. To run directly up the bluffs would be suicide. Each shooter on the opposite bank would be aiming directly at his retreating backside, and the heavy load and deep sand would slow him down.

A small stand of scrub oak stood along the banks of the river. If he could run parallel to the river, he just might take them by surprise. Once he had put the trees between him and the Indians, the branches might deflect some of the incoming rounds. He could keep moving slightly up the hills, keeping his movement quick and making them hit him on the fly, if they could. The bundle he carried on his back would offer him little protection, but it seemed to be his best chance.

He crouched low and signaled up the hill. Now, if he could just keep his own cover fire from hitting him as he ran.

All at once he scrambled directly along the shoreline in the direction of the low-slung scrub oak. He kept his head low and ran for all he was worth.

The gunfire exploded on both sides of the river and smatters of sand and dirt flew up into his path. The buzz of flying rounds whizzed past his head like the sound of angry bees zeroing in for a sting of death.

He dived headfirst for the protection of the trees. Up above, branches broke, showering him with debris.

On his elbows, he crawled forward. He was going to get up and run again, but he wanted to make sure he got to his feet at a spot some distance from where they had seen him go down. Edging forward on his arms and scooting his knees one at a time, he made some headway.

The singing of the bullets seemed to follow him, branches flying into the air and then onto the ground all around him. Several arrows were launched, landing in the ground nearby. Perhaps several of the renegades had the notion of lobbing death over the trees and into him, where the rifles had seemed to be, so far, ineffective.

He got up and crouched low. Once more, he'd have to make a run for it, to some nearby rocks. At least behind them, he could expect some shelter. He holstered his revolver. There would be no chance of stopping to return fire.

Digging his feet into the sand, he raced for the boulders. The sand gave way beneath his feet, which now seemed like lead. One of the shots ripped into the blanket wound around the rifles. The jerking of the material told him all too well what it would be like to catch one of those slugs himself. Panic made his feet dig in to the sand more furiously.

Rounding the rock, he turned to go directly up the bluff. The boulder would offer his backside some protection.

There ahead of him, Julian stood with the outstretched revolver pointing directly at him.

Zac stood up straight. His heart beat fast.

Julian took careful aim and fired.

CHAPTER 33

✦ ✦ ✦ ✦ ✦ ✦ ✦

Lee's Ferry on the Colorado River
Late Sunday afternoon

The careful shot sailed past Zac's right shoulder like a hummingbird intent on its target. He heard the soft grunt before he saw anything. Turning around, he saw an Indian collapse. The man had evidently crossed the river downstream, just where Johnson had said the water was shallow. He pitched forward, spilling the rifle that moments before had been carefully aimed at Zac.

Scrambling back to the rock, Zac picked up the gun and clasped it in his hand. He looked at the dead Indian very carefully and took something from the man's belt. Cramming it down his shirt, he turned and headed up the sandy slope. Julian continued to fire across the river as Zac pitched headlong at his feet.

Pulling himself up with the grass on top of the bluff, Zac hugged the ground and panted. "I'm sure thankful it was our army that taught you how to shoot that way," he gasped.

"You'd better be, little brother."

The little group gathered behind the bluff, and Zac passed out the rifles and ammunition he had managed to carry.

"You get a good look at Butch?" Peters asked.

"He didn't make it," Zac said. "I saw him lying there, but he wasn't breathing."

Zac had left Drago and Julian with two of the rifles near the edge of the bluffs, and the two of them were still managing to take occasional shots across the river.

Peters took the rifle and opened the action. "We'll have to go on back fer some more ammo after sunset," he said.

"That's reckoning we're still alive up here by the time the sun scts," Zac replied. "It won't take them too long to find that spot down there where they can all cross. Then they'll be behind us."

Ruggles looked at Johnson. "You got any help here?"

The ferryman shook his head. "Nah, they all left to go north for supplies three days ago. They ain't gonna even start back for a week or so." He continued to shake his head. "I just don't understand how them Indians could come this far north. Normally the Navajos would never even allow other redskins to come close. It just don't make sense. You sure this is the same bunch that chased you?"

Zac reached down the front of his shirt and pulled out a fresh scalp. The hair was reddish. "You recognize this?"

"That's Sarai's hair," Peters said.

"I took it from the Yavapai that was laying in wait for me down there. It's the same bunch, all right, and they won't go without that ammunition we got on the coach."

"Why don't we just give it to them, then?" Carol asked.

Ruggles and Zac both stared the young man straight in the eye. Their silence said all that needed to be said.

Ruggles had cut his pants leg from the calf wound down. Zac looked at the fresh wound. "You still got some lead in that thing that needs to come out."

Ruggles nodded.

Zac looked at Raincloud and Amy. "We're going to need us a fire and some boiling water if we're going to clean that out. We'll have to do it while we have some daylight to see." He looked over at Ruggles. "I've got a whetstone. I'm gonna let you sharpen that knife of yours your ownself. Been my experience that a man that's gonna be cut on tends to make himself a sharper edge than anybody else could." He took the stone from his pocket and tossed it to Ruggles.

"If those Indians have the numbers you say they have," Johnson said, "we ain't gonna last too long, and we can't outrun them."

"What's downstream of us?" Zac asked.

"Whew-ee," Johnson blew a burst of breath into his beard. "You ain't seen nothing like what's downstream. Them rapids are the meanest thing this side of perdition itself. I went down it first time with John Wesley Powell in 1869. He called it 'The Great Unknown' back then, but I sure know about it, and I wouldn't give none of us a chance."

"But you did make it?" Zac asked.

"Oh, we made it, all right, but we had us some tight boats we could portage, not some ferryboat full of women and kids. I still got one of them dories, but it could never fit the bunch of us."

"That ferryboat might be our only chance, then," Ruggles added.

"Like I said, it ain't no chance at all."

"If we can hold them back till nightfall, then we can put what we need on the ferry. Before dawn hits, we can cut it loose and float down as far as we can go. Any distance we make would be better than staying here and having all our scalps on their lances."

"I'm for that," Ruggles said.

Amy sat up from the fire she was preparing. "Anything we can do that puts our fate in our own hands would be preferable to staying here," she said.

Raincloud nodded. "Sunflower and I will go with you. We will go wherever Julian goes."

"Julian goes with me," Zac said.

"Well, we won't have to worry 'bout packin' no water," Peters added.

Ruggles sharpened the knife carefully. "I'd suggest we just make off with the clothes on our backs, the guns we can carry, and all the food we can pack."

"And the ammunition," Zac added.

"Yes, the ammunition."

"I can't believe I'm even here," Carol said, "and that those are our only choices."

"Well, we are," Ruggles said, "and they are. A man always has to go with the hand he's dealt and make the best of it. There just are no other cards, and we don't have the choice of folding in favor of another shuffle. What's your take on this, Reverend?"

Black had removed his coat and rolled up his sleeves. Taking out a cigar, he used a flaming branch to light it. "I'd say if we're all gonna get wet, I'd better enjoy this while I can. God puts man on this earth to make the best of where he is and who he is, and things like mountains and rivers are made for us to rise above."

Zac grinned. "An optimist. I like that. I suppose there's a time and a place for blind faith."

"No," Black said, "I'm a believer. There's a difference. A man's faith is only as good as what he puts it in. You can have a bundle of faith in yourself, sir, and you'll be disappointed. You can have a speck of faith in God, and it pays off every time." He held up both hands and smiled broadly, the lit cigar clamped between his teeth. "No sermon, just fact."

"May we take that to mean that you and your faith are going down the river with us, then?"

"You may indeed, sir."

"What about you, Johnson?"

"I suppose it's just a choice of when and how I want to die. We go down that river on that flatboat of mine, and we won't come out. I'm doubting we can even make it past Horse Rock rapids. You leave me here, though, to tend to them Indians you brought along with you, and I won't last more'n ten minutes. I guess if I gotta die, I'd just as soon put it off a bit longer. 'Sides, sounds like you're making off with my boat, and where she goes, I go too."

"I think I have the knife pretty sharp," Ruggles interrupted.

"Then, you men turn him over and hold him down. I don't want to chance a quick move that might jar my hand."

"You done this before?" Ruggles asked.

"Never," Zac said. "I've seen it done, though, and I haven't been queasy about anything in more than a coon's age."

"Good then, you're my man. I think I'd rather have a careful amateur than a drunk sawbones any day."

With that, he turned over onto his stomach and dug his fingers into the ground. The men carefully held down his arms and legs, and Zac dipped the knife into the boiling water. He turned to the women. "One of you find me some relatively clean cloth, if you can."

Amy lifted her skirt and tore off another section of petticoat. She handed it to Zac. He picked it up with the point of the knife and lowered it into the now boiling water. As he laid it over the wound and rubbed it, Ruggles jumped with silent pain.

Removing the hot cloth, he placed it back in the hot water. He swished the blade in the water and held it up. "I'm gonna tell you exactly the opposite of what my daddy used to tell me. This is going to hurt you far worse than it does me."

"Thanks," Ruggles grunted.

Placing the blade slightly above the wound, he cut the flesh deeply. Ruggles jumped, but the men held him down. In a matter of moments, fresh blood was streaming down Ruggles's leg. Zac heard the click of the knife and felt the pebblelike slug in the meaty calf. "Good thing it's not near the bone," he said, "or we'd have to take the leg off."

"Good thing," Ruggles growled.

Wedging the point of the knife around the bullet, Zac pried it upward. Moments later, he lifted it to the surface. Dropping the slug to the ground, he stuck the knife back into the water and once again removed the hot cloth. Placing it onto the bleeding wound, he stuck the knife into the licking flames. He held it there until the blade glowed red hot. He lifted it from the fire and held it over the wound momentarily, then laid it flat on the spliced muscle tissue. The smoke, along with the smell of burning flesh, turned several heads and sent Ruggles into contortions. "All right, wrap that leg with the hot cloth," Zac said, "then tear another bandage to wrap around it. I think that leg's gonna come outta this just fine, but we'll have to check it real careful-like tomorrow."

Amy tended to the leg and tore another bandage from her dwindling petticoat supply, wrapping the cloth around the wound. She sat up and wiped her forehead, then nervously looked around for Tommy. "Have you seen my brother?" she asked.

Ruggles started to get up, but then painfully grabbed his leg and fell back.

"He was here just a minute ago," Black said. "He couldn't have gotten very far."

The entire group spread out and began to search. Minutes later, the firing stopped. Julian called out to Zac and signaled him to come.

Crouching low, Zac moved toward the prone outlaws. There below, near the river, Tommy was running and spreading his arms, flapping them from side to side like a bird in flight. He watched two large herons as they flew along the surface of the river. They were undoubtedly the biggest birds he had ever seen, and the impression they were making on him was unmistakable.

Amy ran and sank to the ground beside Zac. He had to hold her down when she spotted Tommy. "I've got to get him," she yelled.

"No, you don't. You call him."

"Tommy, come up here, Tommy!"

The boy ignored her, continuing to imitate the birds, even though they had flown away.

"Tommy, please come up here."

From across the river, she could hear laughter. Then all at once, several voices sounded out from behind rocks across the river. "Tommy, come here. No, Tommy, come over here." A voice that sounded like the voice of Ed Hiatt laughed and joined in the chorus. "Hey, Tommy, come over here. I want to show you something."

"Why are they doing this?" Amy asked. "Why are they deliberately tormenting us?"

"Because they hate us," Zac said. "They're making a point before they kill us."

"What point?"

"They're driving home the point that they can kill us anytime. It's a form of torture before they even have us. We are their captives now."

Amy continued to watch Tommy's reaction to the strange voices across the river. She had never known from one minute to another what the boy would do in any given situation. He stood still as a statue now, hands clasped to his side, listening to every call from the strange, invisible voices that all knew his name. "Why don't they just ride over here and get it over with? Why drag this thing out?"

"Julian and Drago here have been keeping them from trying that shallow spot. They could cross it all right; they have enough men to do it, but they'd lose a few in the process."

Julian squinted down the barrel of the Winchester and squeezed off a round, dropping a renegade into the water who had ventured too close to view from around a rock. He smiled. "Indian lives are precious. There's just so many of them, and they figure there's an endless supply of our kind. If we can make the cost too high for what they're gonna get, they may just get a mite anxious to find more defenseless farms and leave us be."

"You may have a point there," Zac said. He turned back to Amy. "Try calling him again."

"Tommy, this is Amy. I have something for you, honey. Why don't you come to us and get it."

Amy's strategy was quickly repeated by the voices from across the river. "I have something for you, Tommy," one called out. "I have something for you, Tommy," called out another.

"If we blew up the ammunition, we could go a long way to making them wonder if we were worth the trouble and dying," Zac said.

"It might work," Julian replied.

Raincloud scampered up behind them. She flattened herself on the ground beside Julian. "I can hear my husband's voice," she said. "He is alive. He is over there with them on the other side of the river."

"He's over there, all right," Julian replied.

"We cannot leave the little boy down there." She started to get up. "I will go get him."

Julian reached up and grabbed her, pulling her down. "Use your common sense, girl," he snapped. "Just what makes you think that even if those Yavapai let you walk on down there that man you call your husband won't just up and shoot you?"

"I know my husband. He hates me too much to just shoot me. He needs to put his hands on me and give me pain."

"Tommy's my brother," Amy said. "I will go get him. They won't shoot a woman."

"They will do just that to a white woman," Zac said. "You saw Sarai's scalp, didn't you?"

"I will go with Sunflower," Raincloud said. "If I carry her and she cries, the Apache on the other side will not shoot me. The Yavapai will not, for fear of angering the Apache that ride with them. I will sing my death song and walk down to the river."

"You have no call to do that," Julian said. "He ain't your brother."

Raincloud put her hand on his arm. "You were kind to me and you had no call to do that either."

Julian stared blankly into her eyes.

He started to speak, but Raincloud put her hand to his lips. "You must know that even though I just pretended to be your wife, I have feelings for you."

"I know," he said.

"Do you have tender feeling for Raincloud?" she asked. Before he could answer, she spoke for him. "There is no need for you to say. I can see it in your polished eye. It is enough."

Julian twisted his fingers into her sleeve. "I don't want to lose you." Glancing down at the riverbank, he pointed to some rocks. "Get close to those rocks," he said. "If shooting starts, you take that kid and hunker down behind them. I don't want you standing down there by the river if the fur starts to fly."

She nodded. Getting to her feet, she held Sunflower in her arms and began a loud, melodious chant. The sound of the sacred song of her heart brought Tommy's head around. He watched as she walked carefully down the bluff, singing her song.

The river was still and the noise of the men on the other side stopped as she approached the blue stream. It was as if they each knew that something very special was happening, something that they couldn't have planned for, something they didn't know how to respond to.

Tommy stood stone-still as the singing Raincloud and crying baby walked up to him. His hands were down by his side and then, all at once, he began to dance to the music. The boy reached out his hands to her, and Raincloud took one with her right hand. She continued to sing her song as he swayed back and forth to the music.

Across the river, Ed Hiatt stepped out from around a rock. He carried his rifle in his hands. "Come here, woman."

Raincloud ignored him and, still singing, edged Tommy closer to the rocks.

"I said, come here, woman. You obey me now, or you'll suffer for it, you and that breed of yourn."

Raincloud continued to sing, raising the pitch of her voice to a higher level.

"That injun gibberish ain't gonna help you none here, girl. Them people you're with are dead anyway. The only chance you got is to do jest exactly what I say." He raised the rifle to his shoulder. "If'n you don't do what I say, woman, I'ma gonna shoot that there little boy. Now, you wouldn't want that on that missionary-educated conscience of yours, would you?" ·

As he raised the rifle to his cheek, a shot rang out from the bluff behind her. The blast ripped the rifle out from Ed's hands.

All at once, Raincloud scooped up Tommy in her arms and dove for the rocks. The three of them hit the ground as general shooting commenced. A number of slugs broke off pieces of rock over Raincloud, and she held the crying baby and boy close to her.

Julian lowered his rifle and looked over at Zac, who was extracting the spent shell from the Sharps. "I gotta say, little brother, you're a cussedly poor shot with that big gun of yours."

"I always hit exactly what I aim at."

Julian watched Ed scramble around some rocks. "You should have killed him."

"What I did do worked just as well, maybe not for your purposes, but it did for me. I didn't turn that woman you care about into a widow, but that suits me just fine. One less person to pine about you after you're hung."

"You really think you're gonna hang me?"

"I always do what I set out to do. I didn't come to Arizona to meet up with you, but I did come to stop the payroll robberies and see the men who did them hang. Right now, dear brother, that appears to be you."

CHAPTER 34

+ + + + + + +

On the bluffs overlooking Lee's Ferry
Sunday night

Mangus sat beside the coals of the dying fire listening to Gandara and several others explain the plans for the morning attack. Occasionally he would glance at the Apache squaw man who sat brooding close by. The man was like a pup that had been kicked, too timid to bite back, too hurt to forgive. He was weak inside like all the white-eyes. No man needed to think more than once about any woman.

"The Apache will cross the river tonight," Gandara said. "We find a place upstream where water not deep. If we can shoot arrows with fire across the river here, we can make the white-eyes come to us and not watch place where Apache cross. We will shoot fire arrows at flat boat. It is the white-eyes' only escape."

Mangus grunted without speaking. The next day would be a day he needed to have all his wits about him and he knew it, but he dreaded sleep. To sleep would be to dream the dream again, and he had now seen the river. It was the place of his dream that he had never imagined existed before. The fear of the dream was more intense to him than the actual event. He could control what happened to him while he was awake—what he could never control was the dream.

"When the first rays of the sun strike the water below, the Apache will attack," Gandara went on. "When they attack, we will cross the river and go to the flat boat."

The sound of falling rocks brought every head in the war council around. Moving down the slope were the two white traders who had been with them for most of the day. They were leading a small In-

248

dian, a man with black, stringy hair tied with a broad bandana and stooped shoulders.

"'Scuse us, but we got ourselves here somebody you need to meet. He's Navajo, but he's bought and paid for, all the same." The two men separated, allowing the old man to step forward. "He calls himself 'Man With No Teeth.' He's said to know all about this here river and the canyons along it, and he's agreed to be our guide, if we need him."

Gandara stood up. "We not need Man With No Teeth. The white-eyes all die in the morning."

Campbell stroked his chin. "You can't never tell 'bout folks down there. They got a coupla boys with 'em smarter than coons and that Apache scout to boot. That one feller I was with, the one with the long gun, looked to be about as deadly as a graveyard."

"We sell you his scalp in the morning," Gandara said.

Mangus got to his feet and walked away, looking once again at the river and then at the night sky that twinkled through the surrounding cliffs. Gandara quickly followed him.

"This is not our place to die," Mangus said. "It belong to the people of the mountains. It is my place to die, but it is not the place for our people to die."

The sight of the river had brought an unsettled feeling over Mangus; Gandara could see that. "The Apache is with us. They come for the fight," Gandara said.

Mangus asked, "And what if the white man Campbell is right? What if the white-eyes not stay here to fight?"

Gandara fell silent. He looked back at the men around the dying embers.

"If the white-eyes leave on the river tonight," Mangus said, "we will go south with empty hands and broken promises. What will the Apache think then?"

Gandara hung his head slightly. He knew of no answers to Mangus's questions and would not betray his ignorance by giving out words that made no sense.

Mangus reached out and took Gandara's arm, squeezing it slightly. "You must be ready to lead the people. These are questions you must have answers to. A man must lead by the way he thinks." Mangus motioned back to the camp with his hand. "We have many men who can fight. These are all brave warriors or they would not be here with us. But we do not have many who can think for all the people."

Gandara raised his head. "We must not go south with the smell of defeat in our nostrils. To do that would mean to go to the white man's jailhouse."

Mangus nodded in agreement. They both walked back to the group and Gandara spoke for them. "Man With No Teeth can stay with us tonight. We attack in the morning. If the white-eyes get away, we may need him to guide us."

Campbell smiled. "Fine thinkin'. That Apache scout Chupta is more than likely already finding a way for them to get out of that place down there."

Mangus's head jerked up. His eyes blazed.

"Oh, I forgot, you know this White Mountain Apache scout." Campbell's face beamed. To get Mangus's recognition about anything was far more than he had ever hoped for, and now he had the man's undivided attention.

Mangus stiffened, a hard look in his eyes. It was as if he were looking into the past, staring into the face of an enemy, a hated enemy. He turned and walked away into the darkness without responding. Gandara watched his retreating back. He knew they would not go south again until Chupta was dead.

+ + + + +

Zac stirred what was left of the coals with a stick, igniting the campfire into a small blaze. He pushed back the hat on his head and stared at Julian, seated across the fire. "That money belt you got on, part of that payroll?"

"What if it is?"

Zac poked at the flame. "It can't buy you anything but a rope out here, and I'd hate for you to be all heavied up if you fell in that river."

"You let me worry about that, and you needn't concern yourself about my hanging."

"I never concern myself with a sure thing," Zac said.

Ruggles was sipping some hot broth that Amy had prepared. "Where's that scout of yours?" he asked.

"He's not mine," Zac said. "He's his own man, and he goes where he chooses. He was just brought on to help me find these two, and now that his job is finished, he might have lit out."

"You sure don't keep track of your people, do you?" Julian added.

"Like I said, he's not my people. If I was you, I'd just as well ponder that he might be out there in the dark with his rifle sight trained on your backside right now."

Drago shifted nervously. "I hope he knows which one of us to shoot."

"I reckon he could kill you both quicker than a cat could wink his eye."

"Who's watching the ford upstream?" Ruggles asked.

"The preacher and that kid are up there," Zac said. "We'd hear them if something was up."

"He didn't take his cigars with him, did he?" Ruggles asked.

"No, I made sure of that. A lit cigar makes a mighty fine target in the dark." Reaching into a bag, Zac took out the Russian .44 that Julian preferred. Zac tossed it to Julian along with his gunbelt and ammunition. "I figure you'll do better with this."

Julian stood up and strapped on the gunbelt. Spinning the chamber on the revolver, he planted it in the leather. "You got that right, little brother. I shoot it like it's part of me."

"You may need to before we get out of here."

"Do we have all the guns?" Ruggles asked.

"We do now," Zac said. "I went down with Peters after dark and saw to that."

Ruggles turned to Johnson. "Is the ferry ready?"

"It will never be ready for what you want to do to it, but it's as ready as it'll ever be. We just have to throw off the mooring lines and we're gone."

"How long before we hit the first set of rough water?" Zac asked.

"When we leave here, it's about five miles till we go through Marble Canyon. The Badger Creek rapids are about three miles farther on. We may not make it past that one. I do have one of Powell's dories he left behind when he went down that river, but we can't rightly all fit into that. I figured we'd tow it along behind us, just in case."

"Good, we'll pack an extra case of ammo in it and all the food we can carry."

"We won't be floating on that river long enough to digest the food we done ate," Johnson shot back.

Ruggles watched the river moving slowly below and reached down to massage his wounded leg. "Sounds like we have a good hour before we hit those first rapids, then," he said. "I'll feel more like sleeping when we get out of here."

Johnson chuckled slightly. "We'll all sleep sound enough after we is all drownded."

"I don't find your pessimism the least bit amusing," Amy said.

"Ma'am, I ain't trying to amuse you. I know that river. I'm just telling you the truth. There's parts of it I ain't never seen and never wanted to, parts of it that only some of Powell's men told me about. I can tell you, just the hearing of the thing made me turn white as a new set of sheets."

Hours later, Zac roused those who were able to get some sleep. He shook Johnson. "You go upstream and get the preacher and young Carol. Peters and I unloaded most of the ammunition and coated the pile with pitch. When we set the torch to it, I want to be underway."

Johnson scrambled to his feet and hitched up his trousers. Strapping on his gunbelt, he scampered off into the darkness.

Raincloud gently nursed Sunflower and watched the men break camp. She knew full well that the last thing they needed now was a crying baby.

Amy unwound Ruggles's bandage. She inspected the fresh, bright red wound. "It looks bad," she said, "but I don't think there's any infection." Carefully, she applied a fresh compress.

"Thanks, baby sister."

"I thought we were done with that."

His lips creased into a smile, and he wiped them with the back of his hand. "I guess you thought right. I hadn't figured on you taking care of me on this trip, though."

She busily wrapped the new bandage around his leg. "Few things turn out the way a person plans."

Ruggles removed the small bag from his pocket. Taking out a leather strap, he strung it through the drawstring. Bending toward her, he slung it around her neck. "I'd feel a whole lot better if you carried your grandfather's diamond. I wouldn't know just what to do with it anyway, and rightfully, it belongs to you."

She clutched the bag and sat back slightly. "Thank you. My grandfather did know what he was doing in trusting you."

"Just so you trust me."

"I more than trust you, Lawrence. I'm in love with you, something I never thought was possible for me to feel for any man."

"You mean, for a gambling man."

She smiled. "Yes, for a gambling man. But there's something about you, Lawrence Ruggles, something I can't explain. I've never felt quite this way before. You make me feel safe. With you, for the first time in my life, I can relax. I can be exactly who I was meant to be on the inside and not worry about what you think."

"What I think?"

"Yes, when I'm with you, there need be no pretenses. I don't have to wear something to turn your head, although I do enjoy that. I don't have to sound a certain way. There is no playacting."

Ruggles leaned forward and, reaching out, lightly touched her cheek. "Sweet Amy, when I see you, I see a young woman who is innocent and pure."

"If you only knew."

"I know all there is to know. We have so much in common that I could actually believe that we grew up together, that we took long walks in the summertime, that we shared all of our dreams as children. I love everything there is about you." Leaning over, he gently kissed her.

A short time later, Johnson came back with the other two.

Zac looked over the group. "All right," he said, "let's get everybody down to the ferry. We'll go in small bunches. I don't want a mob stumbling through the dark. I'll go last with Raincloud and Julian here. I'll bring a torch and fire that pile of ammunition on my way."

"What about your Apache scout?"

"He's done his job," Zac said. "He's gone and so is his horse. Can't say as I blame him, either."

Ruggles got to his feet and leaned against Peters. "Guess we'll go first. I'm not much of one for a foot race just about now—kinda looking forward to the ride." Ruggles looked over at Johnson. "You'd better come with us. That way you can make sure we've got everything."

"When we get to the ferry, stow your arms away in the crate that Johnson and I rigged up last night," Zac said. "We have it tied secure to the raft with some floats on it. I want to make sure we don't get disarmed by this river."

Ruggles drew his revolver and hobbled off in the darkness next to Peters, followed by Amy, Johnson, and Tommy.

Zac looked at the Reverend Black. "Okay, Preacher, you and

young Carol here tote Drago down and get yourselves settled in."

Black nodded and slung the bandit's arm around his neck. "Don't you wait too long now, ya hear?" Black said. "There's nobody watching out for that ford up yonder."

"My mother would say the Lord takes over where people leave off," Zac said.

"I stand corrected by your mother. Don't take too long."

Zac stooped down next to the glowing coals and picked up a stick. Wrapping some used bandages around it, he quickly fashioned a torch.

"We may never come out of this you know, little brother," Julian said.

"Oh, we will. I got too much living and you got too much dying left to do."

Julian crouched down next to him. "You sure are a hard head, aren't you?"

"I have to be. It's what I'm paid for."

"And just what makes you think you can take that hard head of yours and go back to live with decent folk?"

"I do what I have to do, but I refuse to turn out like you, a man filled with bitter hatred he can't let go of."

"I don't pretend to be anything," Julian said, "but I'll wager you do. You got anybody waiting back there for you to come out of this?"

"I have a woman I intend to marry and a boy that ain't mine, but looks to me to be his pa. I got them and a ranch I own free and clear. They're all waiting for me. You, all you got is a rope waiting for you at St. George."

"Then, you're just foolin' them and yourself too. You're a gunny same as me, only difference is I know what I am, and you're still too blamed muley to own up to it."

"The only thing that's the same about us is the name Cobb. Everything you were ever taught you laid aside, except for the skill of how to shoot straight." Zac shook his head slowly. "No, I grew up admiring you and now all I feel for you is pity and shame."

"Then, you'd be best advised to conjure up some fear of me, little brother, because I ain't about to let you take me to hang."

The sudden rustle in the brush behind them brought both men spinning around. Julian drew the .44 with blazing speed and cut the first running warrior down with a snap shot. Zac drew his knife and met the second head on, pulling the painted renegade over and tossing him to the ground. Zac jumped to his feet and went at the man, who was also armed with a knife.

Julian sent Raincloud down the bluff and continued to fire in the direction of the brush.

Zac wrestled with the second warrior, throwing him to the ground and spinning around on top of the man. Each man grabbed the other's wrist and both flexed their muscles, frozen in a moment of death and brute strength. With knives slowly pressing toward each other and their faces contorted, the Indian launched Zac backward, onto the ground.

Both men were up in a flash, flicking their blades back and forth. The warrior lowered his head and launched himself directly at Zac's midsection. The wind seemed to rush out of Zac as he fell to the ground. Unable at first to find the hand that held the knife, Zac hung on tight and rolled over and over to the edge of the fire circle.

When the warrior raised his arm, Zac spotted the knife and quickly grabbed the man's wrist. Suddenly shifting his weight, Zac spun the man to the ground and thrust himself on top. Each one again holding the other's wrist, Zac pushed hard on the man's arm, pressing it close to the glowing coals. With a sudden heave, he lowered the man's arm onto the glowing embers. The man shrieked in pain and dropped the knife, loosening his grip on Zac with the other hand. Zac suddenly rammed his knife into the man's ribs. He watched the breath run out of the man and turned him over. He looked up and growled at Julian, "Let's get!"

Backing away, Julian reloaded his revolver as Zac lit the torch. They both ran down the bluff, and Zac stopped momentarily to light the pile of ammunition. Julian began to lay down cover fire at the top of the bluff. "You reckon Ruggles has already cut them loose?" he asked.

"If he has any sense, he has," Zac said.

With the pile ablaze, they both began to sprint down the riverbank to the place where they had left the ferryboat. Overhead, flaming arrows streaked across the still-dark sky. The boat was there, tethered by a single line to the dock. Julian jumped aboard, followed by Zac. Reaching down, he cut the rope.

CHAPTER 35

+ + + + + + +

On the Colorado River at Lee's Ferry
Monday before dawn

Johnson swept the large oar back and forth, working hard to keep the ferry near the north shore of the river. The black water moved the flat boat steadily forward. Zac and Julian watched the pile of ammunition ignite beyond the trees. Even from where they were, they could see the first of the rounds begin to burst. Sparks flew up and then a ground swell of land-launched meteors erupted into the dark sky, sending shards of fire across the black river.

Philip Carol nudged up next to Zac. "You think that will stop them from coming after us? It is what they wanted, isn't it?"

The Reverend Black struck a match and held it to the end of a cold cigar. "What they want is more than guns and ammunition. They want most what guns can never give them back, their manhood." He blew out the match and tossed it into the river. "I reckon, in the end, it's the same as most men want. We all want what God gave us when He made us."

"You can never tell what gets into the mind of an Indian," Julian replied. "They're already a long way from home."

"That's right," Philip said, "and they don't know this area, do they? Maybe without that ammo to chase, they'll just go back to where they came from."

"This man Mangus doesn't give up very easy," Zac said. "If he'd been the type to be a quitter, he wouldn't have come north of the mountains."

"Don't let that little brother of mine scare you none. He always was the type to look on the worst—comes from reading all them scary stories as a boy."

256

"I'm alive because I always prepare for the worst."

"You're just lucky," Julian said.

"Humph, I always found that the man who was the best prepared seemed to have all the luck."

Philip stared off at the exploding ammunition. "I still don't know why they would bother to follow us. It just wouldn't make any sense."

"Those Indians that attacked us weren't Yavapai," Zac said. "They were Apache. If Mangus has himself a war going on, he may just need to provide those people with a victory or two before they turn around and go home."

"I hope you're wrong," Philip said.

"I hope so too, but I'm not."

It was some time before the explosions died down and then finally stopped. Johnson swept the stern sweep back and forth, and with the gathering dawn, the blackness of the river turned an indigo blue. The dory they towed bobbed behind them, its paddles strapped to the hatches. They had passed the Paria River almost as soon as they left Lee's Ferry, and the noise up ahead told them that they would hit the first group of rapids before the sun was fully up.

"That's the Paria Riffle," Johnson called out. "When we get past that, we're gonna be in Marble Canyon. We best hope them injuns ain't followin' us this far, elsewise we'ze apt to see some arrows and rocks droppin' down on us. Not a thing we can do about it, though. We'ze down here now and there ain't no stoppin', ain't no speedin' up, and there sure ain't no slowin' down. Nah, sir, we'ze down here like bugs on a piece of sticky paper."

The Reverend Black flicked ash into the river and held out his hand. "Every one of us is in the hand of God. There ain't a safer or a more fearful place to be found in all the world."

A railing ran around the ferry, but one that would never hold up to people clinging to it. Beneath it and over the top, Johnson had strung heavy cable to tie down the wheels of wagons he ferried. Ruggles had spotted it at once and begun to pass out lengths of rope. "Here," he said. "You folks had better use some of this to tie yourselves down to that cable. Loop it through your belts or around your waists. We don't want to lose anybody."

Julian called out over the growing noise of the water, "If there are Indians on that canyon wall, what are we going to use to shoot back with?"

The box Zac had placed the firearms in was bolted to the ferry. He scampered toward it and opened the hasp. Taking out his bandoleer, he slung it over his shoulder.

He picked up a Winchester and tossed it to Julian. "Just keep your sights high," he said. "I'm watching you same as I'm watching Mangus's men." Picking up his Sharps, he slid it from the buckskin bag and closed the box, securing it once again.

When he got to his feet, Julian shot him a hard glance. "Little brother, if I'd wanted to kill you, I'da done it back there on that bluff. I'da shot you instead of the Apache that wanted to take your scalp."

Zac returned the hard look. "I guess you would have, at that, but it don't change my job and it don't change who you are."

The riffle churned in front of them, sheets of whitewater that stretched across the river followed by a blanket of snarled current and bubbling foam.

"Try to tuck your feet under the cable," Ruggles called out. He crouched down beside Amy and Tommy, holding his hand on the boy's shoulder.

Drago and Peters hung on near the front of the boat, each clutching to the boards that covered the log bottom.

The ferry bucked violently with the first of the shining water, then lifted on the surging current and shot forward over the waves. Behind them, the dory swung wildly. The wake of the ferry helped to break the worst of the current for the empty boat. Johnson had taken the time to weigh it down with rocks, and that and the weighted hull helped to hold it in the river.

"We're gonna have to carry that dory up here with us," Johnson yelled. "It'll make it through this, but we can't tow it past this one, and I'm having a hard time with this here sweep with that tow rope back there."

Zac had crouched down next to the man, and as close as he was, he heard the warning. He nodded to him. "You just get us through this one and find us a place to pull up on shore. I guess there's still enough of us to get that dory on. 'Sides, it just might pay off to have something else on top here to keep our heads behind."

"If'n them injuns foller us down this here river, we'll be durn thankful fer that there boat up here. I knows a pretty spot up here in Marble Canyon, a place that ain't too hard on the eyes."

Zac let out a slight smile. "Good, we'll just trust you to find the pretty places, and I'll worry about the rest."

"Suits me just fine," Johnson roared.

There was no holding back with the river. The best they could hope for was for Johnson to keep the big boat pointed reasonably straight with the sweep. With each bucking drop into the water, spray cracked the air with a wet chill. The loud thump of the ferry's bottom as it hit the water sent shivers up each spine.

With each cloud of water, Tommy raised his hands and laughed. His giggles of delight were a sharp contrast to the look of panic on Amy's face. Ruggles bent low next to the boy's ear. "This is fun, isn't it?"

"Yes!" Tommy yelled. "The most fun in the world."

Amy tried to hold his arms down, but Ruggles reached up and grabbed her arm. He leaned next to her ear to be heard. "They'll be plenty of time for fear before this is all over. You might just as well let the boy enjoy it while he can. Some people see reasons for difficulty in every joy, and some see reasons for joy in every difficulty. Right now, I'd rather see things Tommy's way."

Amy nodded silently.

Raincloud scooted closer to Julian and tried to shield Sunflower's face from the flying water. With the baby in her arms, she clung to Julian. He lowered himself and braced her between his legs. The roar of the water made sure that no one but Raincloud could hear him. "We'll come out of this all right," he said. "I'll see to it that nothing happens to the baby. I've got a plan. You'll just have to trust me on this one."

The chute intensified as the canyon narrowed. On either side of the river, sloping bare ground climbed to the feet of sheer cliffs. Rocky outcroppings dotted the surface and the flattened tops of the cliffs sparkled with the first light of dawn.

The rush of the water steadily pushed the ferry forward. "We got us a drop up here!" Peters yelled. "Y'all better hang on."

The sudden drop was a small one, but it jarred the ferry, and Raincloud gasped in sudden panic. Tommy swung his arms into the air and yelled loudly. "Yippee!" he screamed. Spinning his hands in the air, he cranked his head backward and gazed up at the morning sky.

Ruggles met Amy's look of concern with a smile. "We're having a good time here," he said.

"You're having a good time, you mean. Personally, I'd much

rather be on dry land. This is like a hurricane that doesn't quit."

The bend in the river filled all of them with a sense of dread. There was no way anyone could tell just what lay around the slanting rocks. The ferryboat kept to midstream, thanks to Johnson's skill at swinging the sweep and maintaining a steady course.

Around the bend, a small stand of bright green trees and brush stood in stark contrast to the rusty rocks. The walls of the canyon behind and through the trees looked like sparkling diamonds blazing in the new sun. Several plumes of falling water cascaded down the pockmarked rocky face of the cliff, splashing the rocks and giving off the appearance of jewels dancing in the light.

Johnson pointed up ahead. "That there's Vassey's Paradise—lots of fresh water to drink and bathe with. It'd be a good spot to put in and dry off for a bit. We can lash this dory up on the ferry there. It's gonna be lots worse on down. That last little ripple was just a sample."

"All right," Zac said. "We're far enough away to be able to take a little breather. We'll get that little boat tied down and give the women a rest before we move on."

Johnson pushed the sweep over and edged the boat toward the stand of greenery. Minutes later, they scraped the sand and Zac jumped down to tie the ferry to one of the trees. "All right, folks, we're gonna get ourselves situated here."

Julian jumped into the knee-high water and helped Raincloud down. "Do you mind if we start a fire and cook some breakfast?"

"Not at all, as long as it's that woman you got there that does the cooking. From your looks, I'd say folks wouldn't fare too well on any grub you might rustle up."

Julian smiled and slapped his thin waist. "You got yourself a point there, little brother."

Moments later, the group assembled themselves on the rocky beach. Drago lowered himself to the ground and rubbed his leg. "Thing is tightening up on me."

Tommy started to run to the trees and Amy followed him, taking his arm. The boy pranced like a horse and waggled his head as he tried to run. Carol watched them and walked off toward the hill to where the two of them had disappeared.

"The ladies can wash their faces and such," Johnson said. "The water is cool and clean. There's firewood here and I speck the cliffs are so high up there that we won't have to worry 'bout that bunch comin' down on us. There jest might be snakes in there though, so I wouldn't go thrashing about if'n I was you."

Ruggles picked up two wooden canteens and walked up toward where Amy and Tommy had gone.

"I might as well stay here with these folks," the Reverend Black said. "We just might get ourselves into a good discussion."

"You all go ahead," Julian said. "I'm afraid what you've got to discuss, Preacher, is something we're beyond hearing. I'll stay right here with Raincloud and gather up some firewood for her. Drago won't be hiking around much, either."

"All right," Zac said.

Peters picked up two more of the canteens and a strip of beef. "Let's get on with it," he said. "Sooner we get ourselves out of this here canyon, the better I'll like it."

Johnson laughed. "You flatland folks have got a bunch to learn. It's gonna be more'n a week afore we get outta this canyon, if we get out at all. I'll show you boys around. This here's a mighty pretty place."

Amy found a spot where Tommy could play. She took off her shoes and, sitting down, waved her feet in the pool of clear water that splashed in front of her. Overhead, the waterfalls tumbled down the sides of the orange and red bluffs, spraying a steady stream of white plume and creating a rainbow in the morning air. She leaned back. It was the first peaceful sight she had seen in a long time. She heard steps behind her and turned to see who it was.

"Mind if I join you?"

Amy looked up and squinted into the filtered sunlight. "Philip, please do." She looked back at the waterfall and splashed her bare feet in the pool. Taking a deep sigh, she reclined once again. "It's so beautiful here."

"I'd say it's much more beautiful with you here."

She snapped her head around and looked at him as he took his seat on the rocks beside her. "Thank you. What a nice thing to say."

"Well, I mean it, mean every word of it."

Amy stared down into the cool water. "I can't say spending a week in that stagecoach has made me feel very pretty."

"There's some girls that just can't hide their natural beauty. Lots of women back East try to cover their faces with powder and things, but a washcloth does yours just fine."

Amy ignored the comment and moved her feet back and forth in the water.

"Are you really serious about that man?"

"Lawrence?"

"Yeah, the gambler."

"He's not like other gamblers I've known. Lawrence Ruggles is one of a kind."

"No one's one of a kind. Trouble is, you won't find that out until it's too late." He picked up a pebble and dropped it into the pool, sending out ripples. "You must know how I feel about you, Amy."

"How you feel about me?"

Taking up another small stone, he flung it, skimming it over the surface. "Yes, I think you're kinda special."

"Well, thank you, Philip. That's nice of you to say."

"And you and I are about the same age. Ruggles is much too old for you. I guess I don't know how to put this quite right. I'm not sure exactly what I have to do to get your attention."

Amy looked at him. "You have my attention."

"Then, what could you possibly see in an undependable man, when it's obvious the way I feel about you. My father owns a lot of Arizona and some day it will all belong to me, me and the woman I choose to share it with."

"Lawrence is a *very* dependable man. I've know many gamblers in my life and few I would trust with more than a nickel, but he's different. I've trusted him with my life."

Carol gently fingered the edge of her sleeve. "But you could do so much better. You're not only pretty, but you can think."

Amy frowned. "And most women can't?"

"You know what I mean. Girls I know giggle a lot. They never think about serious things, just dresses and babies."

Amy pulled her sleeve away. "Well, it's plain to see I haven't been thinking much about dresses in a while, and I've been tending to a baby since I was eight."

"And I could help you with that too. My father could find a place for him where you wouldn't have to worry about him."

"I don't worry about Tommy. I love him."

Carol dropped his chin and stared into the pool. "For somebody studying the law, I guess I need to learn to speak my mind more clearly."

"Listen, Philip, you're a nice boy, but you still have a lot of growing up to do. I know what you're asking, and I'm flattered that you think well of me. A week or so ago, I might have jumped at the opportunity."

"But not now?"

"No, I'm afraid, not now."

"Then, it's Ruggles?"

"Yes, it's him—and it's me, too. I've changed. He makes me think that there's more to life than a safe big house and a carriage. With him, I feel as though I want to see things and know what it means to be alive. I've been to lots of places, but before I never thought I could be with someone who could take care of me, someone I totally trusted."

The noise on the trail behind them caused them to fall silent. They turned to see Johnson twisting some tree branches away from the path, followed by Zac, Ruggles, and Hec Peters. Peters blew hard at the top of the rise and bent over, holding his hands to his knees. "Normally, I'm paid to drive, n-n-not to climb hills," he stammered. Sitting down beside the stream that ran down the hill from the pool, Peters pulled off his boots and began to rub his feet.

Zac walked to where Amy and Carol sat and unslung the big rifle from his shoulder. He spotted Tommy at play. The boy ran from tree to tree, hiding from some invisible intruder. "Nice place," he said to Amy and Philip.

"Yes, it is," she replied.

Ruggles limped up to the pool and stooped down. Taking off his black hat, he splashed water on his face. Using both hands, he gently scrubbed a beard that had been allowed to grow unchecked for several days. Quietly, he took from his pocket a straight razor and a small piece of soap.

Zac caught the flash of the blade as Ruggles opened it. "Going to the ball?" he asked.

Ruggles dipped his hands in the water and lathered up his face. "I always find that when a man looks his best, he feels his best." He flashed a smile at Amy. "What do you think, Amy girl?"

She laughed. "I'm all for what will make you feel the best."

Zac looked behind them. "The parson turned off the trail back there with his Bible. Guess he was thinking to keep his soul clean." He rubbed his stubble. "Maybe I can take a turn at that razor before we head back. Unlike you, though"—he shot a sly glance in Amy's direction—"I've got nobody to impress around here."

Ruggles began to rake the beard from his cheek. He looked up at the all-too-uncomfortable-looking Philip Carol and paused. A broad smile creased his lips. "Son, you think you got enough of a beard to merit a razor?"

Carol shot to his feet, his hands clinched to his side. "I'm going back to the river," he murmured to Amy. With that, he stormed deliberately down the hill and past the trees.

Ruggles continued to smoothly run the razor over his face, swishing it clean in the pool. "Now, just what do you think got into that boy?"

Amy slipped her shoes back on. "I think that's just his problem right now. He doesn't want to think of himself as a boy anymore."

"He may not have to worry about that by the time we get out of here," Zac said. "That daddy of his may have sent him off to school to become a man, but life and death have a way of smoothing out the wrinkles of the mind faster than most chalkboards—not that I'm adverse to book learning."

"You seem to be quite educated, Mr. Cobb," Amy said.

"Enough to know, I guess, that a man's education really begins on the day he leaves school. School may tell you where to go for the answers, but it's life that tells you what the real questions are."

They heard the shouting below before they saw Philip running back up the hill through the trees. He bounded up the hill breathlessly. "They're gone! They're all gone."

Ruggles got to his feet. "What are you talking about?"

Philip pointed to Zac. "That brother of yours, he's gone. So is the Indian woman and that Drago fella. They're all gone and they took the little boat, too."

CHAPTER 36

+ + + + + + +

Vassey's Paradise
Monday afternoon

The crackling fire lapped at the air and the ferryboat tugged steadily at its moorings. The river ran deep and quiet. Zac was the first to arrive at the beach. He waded out and climbed aboard the flat boat, opening the box on top. Peters helped Ruggles hobble down the hill, Amy close behind with Tommy and Philip.

"Did they take everything?" Peters called out.

Zac continued to sift through what had been left to them. He stood up and held out two of the bags of food they had packed. "They took half the food and both of the rifles. Lucky thing we had our six-guns on us." He held up the Sharps. "If I'd left this, they'd more than likely have taken it too."

"Nice of that brother of yours to leave us anything at all," Ruggles barked. "He could just as well have taken it all."

Zac murmured. "Maybe he has a little bit of conscience left in him and decided not to starve his own brother and a woman."

Johnson pulled his suspenders to the top of his shoulders. "Food ain't gonna be much of a problem 'round here. There's lots of fish in the river and every kinda critter a man's been known to eat."

Zac climbed down from the boat and waded ashore. "It's the fact that he left us to the Indians that bothers me most. Staked us out like a goat for the lions."

"I wouldn't worry about that until we know Mangus is still following us," Ruggles said. "He doesn't have much of a reason to anymore. It's not his country, and we don't have the ammunition. But I'll admit I don't like being around here for very long. It won't take him long to regroup and head our way and, Lord knows, he won't

265

have to go to any bother to find us. He'll just have to find a way to get down to us."

Zac surveyed the surrounding cliffs. "That would be a rough thing for him to do about now," he said. "I'd suspect it would take a man half the day to make it down to this river, even if he knew the way."

Removing his hat, Johnson scratched his forehead as he shook his head. "We ain't gonna make it in that big boat of mine." He pointed at the moving current. "That Badger Creek rapid up ahead is gonna be too much fer it to handle, I'm afeared. It's about four or five miles farther down and it's got a twelve- to fifteen-foot drop. That water's more trouble than a sack fulla bobcats."

Ruggles took his arm off Peters' shoulder. "Maybe we should just abandon the ferry, then, and climb out of this canyon."

"Look who's talking about climbing," Zac said, "and you with that bum leg of yours."

"What I lack in ability right now, I make up for in stubbornness."

"Well, you can just forget it," Johnson said. "This here is Marble Canyon. The rest of this place farther on is bad enough, but there just ain't no way outta here. 'Sides, if'n them injuns is close by, they're sure to get to us if we climb out now."

"The short guns we still have left won't hold off Mangus and his bunch should we chance on them," Zac said. "This Sharps of mine will do a fine job, but it's not going to keep all their heads down." He looked down. "I never should have let him out of my sight. He always was the type to lull you into thinking the wrong thing about him. He kept his real thoughts out of sight. It was a mistake to trust him, even a little bit."

"We all live and learn," Ruggles said.

Zac shook his head. "A few of us just live, I guess."

"Well, no sense worrying about that now," Ruggles said. "That brother you want and the supplies and boat we all need is getting farther downriver with each breath we take."

"I doubt they get too far," Johnson joined in. "They don't know that river and they sure don't know what to do in them rapids. I'll reckon they won't make it past Badger Creek. 'Sides, that one-eyed gent ain't gonna paddle too well with only one arm, and they got themselves a baby to worry about. I surely do fear what will happen to that little one when they capsize."

"The man's a fool," Zac said. "Always thinking just about himself and saving his own hide, no matter who he hurts doing it. Well, this time, he's in the wrong place, doing the wrong thing, and he's got the wrong man chasing after him. I can tell you one thing; when I do catch up to him, I'm gonna hog-tie him and drag him all the way to the hangman, if I have to."

Johnson scratched his black head of hair violently and squashed down his hat on top of it. "We'd best get to moving if we're gonna go at all. That dory runs faster than we can muster, and with a cripple sportin' a broke leg, a one-armed man, and a woman with a baby, we're gonna find us some bodies afore long."

+ + + + +

Drago pulled his paddle through the water to try to keep the dory straight. It fishtailed back and forth through the foam. "You hear that?" he yelled.

Julian sat in the middle, holding on to Sunflower, while Raincloud paddled in front. "Sounds like some rough water up ahead," he said.

"I ain't too sure about this here idea of yourn," Drago replied. "I can handle myself on a horse pretty well, but I don't know nothin' about no boats."

"Face it," Julian said, "right now, you'd have trouble handling a stretcher with that leg of yours, but you do have two good arms. I'd say this was just about our best chance. We can get on ahead and leave them to the Indians. Besides, I'm not about to go to the gallows."

The water churned ahead of them and turned a light brown color in the bright sunlight. Rocks stood out prominently in the stream bed, jutting like giant teeth ready to tear the bottom out of the boat and send it crashing down the rapids in splinters. The creek that flowed into the river was a dark brown and carried a silty mixture, bubbling with the foaming churn of the rocky rapids.

Drago swung his paddle to the right, dragging it in the water and shooting the dory to the left of the river. It scraped the large rock with a shudder, and then the bed of the river seemed to drop beneath them. Sunflower screamed and Raincloud stretched forward, parrying the rocks below away from the bow of the little boat.

The dory shot down the swelling river, launched by an unseen hand. It swerved in the eddy beneath the rock, swinging the boat around and taking them backward into the next set of wicked waves, spinning them once again completely around.

The paddles Drago and Raincloud hung on to moved furiously, more from nervousness than from any knowledge of what to do. There was no talking among them, only the continued screams of the baby and the furious splashing of the paddles.

Julian watched Raincloud. Only once did she try to look back at the baby in his arm. This woman was all business at whatever it was she was doing at the moment. He liked that in anybody, and it was especially attractive in a woman. It made him feel trusted, even if he didn't know what to do. He clutched the child tightly in his arm, banging from side to side. He never tried to shield himself from the blows of the sides of the boat. He had only to worry about staying inside it and holding on to the baby for dear life.

The nose of the dory rose high in the water and slammed back to the water below. Several times, it followed the same pattern, bucking underneath them and crashing back to the bottom of the waves. They were helpless against the fury of the river and they knew it. There would be no control, only the fight to stay afloat, the struggle to survive. Julian knew better than anyone that should they lose the boat beneath them, none of them would ever make it to shore alive. Even that, however—the feeling of being helpless against the mighty waters beneath them—was better than the thought of walking up a hangman's gallows. At least here, they had a chance—a slim one, but still a chance.

Even before they saw the drop, they knew it was coming. Raincloud screamed at the top of her lungs and froze in the boat, staring straight ahead at the edge of what seemed like a flood of water pouring onto the rocks below.

Julian grasped a tighter grip on the baby and dug his feet beneath the wooded staves of the boat. If they were going to die, this would be it.

+ + + + +

Zac and Peters loaded the canteens onto the ferryboat while Johnson tied the sweep tighter, wrapping the large paddle to the beam that held it with a fresh cord. "I don't know if'n any of youse kin handle one of these very well, but one of you is gonna have to try." He pointed to the sweep tied above the front of the flat-bottomed boat. "These things don't stay in one direction in the river.

They swing 'round and 'round," he explained as he circled his hand in a sweeping motion. "A body might not be able to tell front from back. If'n we do swing around, somebody's gonna have to handle that rudder up front and keep us away from them rocks."

"What if we hit one of the rocks?" Amy asked.

"It'll more'n' likely shake our teeth, but that might not be the worst of it." Johnson made a fist with his left hand and held it out for all to see. "Let's say this is the rock."

Flattening his right hand, he pushed it up against the simulated rock. "If this here is the boat and it gets pinned up next to a rock, the water will push the upriver side of the boat down." He looked up from the simulated demonstration and frowned. "That would sure enough be bad, could flip the boat."

"What do we do if that happens?" questioned Amy.

"I'm comin' to that, girl." He paused, making sure he had everybody's attention. "If that happens, I'll yell out 'high side,' and that means everybody's got to move to the high side of the boat, next to the rock. That'll force that side of the boat down and the water will come underneath us and carry us on around." He paused. "At least that's how it's s'pose to work."

"And what if it doesn't work that way?" Carol asked.

"Then, sonny boy, that water's gonna continue to pour over the upriver side of the boat and flip us over and you and me is gonna be in the river, along with everybody else."

"If everything you say about this river is true," Ruggles joined in, "I'd say the chances of that happening are pretty good anyway."

"That's fer sure." Johnson stooped low and looked them all in the eye, one by one. "And I'ma gonna tell you what, if you do fall in that water, don't do what comes naturally. You make sure you don't go down that river headfirst. You swing around and let the water carry you feetfirst, if you can. Them rocks and deadheads will split yer skull clean open. You go down with yer toes pointed forward and push off of anything you come in contact with. I got some cork floats on board—not near enough, but you try and grab one if we throw it to ya."

"I'd say we've got our work cut out for us," Zac said.

"That we have. Main thing, though, is to keep that boat off the rocks. We slam that thing into something sharp and it'll split clean open. You think you can handle the forward boom?"

"I'll do my best," Zac affirmed.

"Good. Just keep it outta the water, unless we spin around. Then you just try and maintain us midstream or anyplace else I yell fer you to go."

"All right."

Peters sat on the lockbox and shook his head. "I hates the water my ownself, never did like it none. Plain fact be told, I even shy away from a bathtub."

Zac smiled. "I don't think that bit of news surprises us in the least." The whole group laughed.

The Reverend Black walked down the hill, putting his small Bible in his inside pocket. "I can see they up and skipped out on us," he said. "I wondered if that might happen when they didn't want me to stay with them."

"Then, why didn't you say something?" Zac asked.

"My boy, I've learned one thing in dealing with people the many years I've had to put up with them; you never stand in the way of what a man really wants to do. He's got to change his wants first before you can be any use at all."

Ruggles picked Tommy up from the shore and hobbled through the thigh-deep water, lifting him to the deck. He turned back to get Amy, only to see that Philip Carol had picked her up and was wading to the ferry. He started to speak, but Amy shook her head.

Johnson untied the ferry from the tree that secured it. Throwing the line onto the boat, he splashed through the water and jumped on board.

The current moved steadily and once again Ruggles passed among the group, tying them securely to the cable that held the logs and ferry deck together. He secured the lines with a slip knot, making sure each person knew how to yank free should it be necessary.

Zac opened the lockbox to look for further supplies. He stood up straight and gazed upriver. "That man's a fool," he said.

"How's that?" Peters asked.

"He took the gold before he left. That little boat they're in will have enough trouble on this river without being weighted down even more." He shook his head and closed the box, securing the hasp.

The sides of the canyon rose majestically in the air, bluffs of red and pale limestone that seemed to be directly overhead. Two big-horn sheep stood on a cliff above them and watched the curious sight, their heads cocked to see the river and the odd-looking craft.

Bathed in the morning light, the cusp of the moon stood as a dim lamp hanging in the sky. "The river looks so peaceful here," Amy said. "I don't know how anyone could think about trouble."

"There's plenty to be found, little girl," Johnson retorted. "We'll get the first piece of it up ahead, just around that next bend."

The ferry slid over the surface, silently, the gentle pull of the Colorado dragging them ever forward, onward to the chaos beyond.

"When we get past that next bend, I'ma gonna show you a few things to watch out for," Johnson said. "The rapid ain't so bad at first, and it'll let me teach you a few things about running a river like this. You'll probably forget most of what I tell you, but then again, you just might remember it at just the right time."

The canyon walls stood as a silent witness to the little group. Each person appeared to be lost in thought—all but Tommy. He dragged his hand in the river beside the boat, splashing the still water and laughing at the noise of the water and the spray he was creating.

Everyone knew that the peaceful bend up ahead of them held a dark secret behind it. They could hear the fast waters on the other side, a boiling sound that carried down the canyon. Several birds flew low past them and, rounding the bend, suddenly darted up into the air, as if spooked by the ferocity of the noise and the spray from the foaming water.

Johnson pointed to the rock ahead and spoke loudly enough for Zac to hear at the front of the ferry. "There's a big eddy behind that one," he said. "The water curls up behind them things and afore you know it, you're being swung 'round upstream. We'll go over to the far left to stay away from it. We get ourselves swung 'round before we hit them big rapids, and you just might not know what to do."

Johnson pushed the boom forward, swinging the ferry to the left. "We'll just slip into the tongue here. That's what we call the flat water that snakes on into the rapids." He pointed to the smooth pillow of water off to their right. The river bulged up and formed a wave like the swell of the sea. "That's a sleeper," he said. "River's sliding over a rock just underneath. Some would see that and try to roll over it. The thing would pretty near tear the average boat's bottom clean out."

Zac looked downstream. His eyes scanned the rocks and foaming water ahead. Anyone could see that he was more than just angry over losing a prisoner. He was silent, his jaw set like a rock.

"That's why I tell you," Johnson went on, "no one-armed man that ain't used to the river, along with a cripple and a woman and child, could ever make it far on this thing. I don't care what boat he was trying to do it in, and that there dory is one of the best. Them folks just don't know enough. If'n they got past Beaver Creek up there, it would have to be blind luck."

The sun bathed the red rocks in a warm morning light. A shadow knifed down the side of the bluff, cutting a dark line across the limestone. The feel of the cold water on their faces braced them. Underneath the ferryboat, the river lapped gently at the supporting logs.

+ + + + +

Drago pulled with his paddle for the shore. The worst of the rapids were now behind them, and even with the hatches that covered most of the small boat, the entire dory sloshed with six to eight inches of water. There would be no way to go any farther if they didn't stop to bail the water out. "That there gold's weighing us down," he said.

Julian brushed water from the crying child's face. "That may be, but I ain't about to bury it here. You think either of us would want to come back to dig it up, even if we could find it again?"

"No, I reckon not. Right now, though, I just got myself a deeper hankerin' to go on breathing, that's all."

Beaching the boat at a bend in the stream, Raincloud turned and took the crying baby. She hugged the child close to her and spoke gently.

Julian and Drago climbed out and pulled the craft to a more secure position on the sand. Drago hobbled as he tried to hoist the boat. His splint was holding and his leg was healing, but it was still very tender and weak. Drago motioned him aside. "You think we can make it much farther with that baby and all?"

Julian looked back at the boat and watched as Raincloud tried to quiet the child.

"I'm thinking we just ought to up and leave her right here. I wouldn't want to be near that woman if'n something happened and we lost that little girl. 'Sides, them folks will pick her up. You don't have to worry."

"You're forgetting," Julian held out the stump of his left arm, "I ain't much use when it comes to paddling."

"Is that the only reason you insisted on taking her?"

"What other reason would there be?"

Drago shook his head. "Sometimes you is plumb hard to figger. Most things you do got a reason, but sometimes I wonder."

Julian stared at him. "You've known me long enough to know that there's only one hide I ever worry about and that's mine. When we get to somewhere that's safe to take off and she begins to slow us down, we'll leave her to whatever's there. Until then, you just let me do the thinking. That's what I do best."

"All right," Drago held up his hands, "if'n you say so. You've just got me a mite concerned, that's all."

"I know what I'm doing."

It took the three of them some time to bail out the boat enough that they could turn it upside down. The water drained out in a puddle on the sand. Raincloud fed the baby while the men checked the guns and supplies.

The sound of several pebbles skittering down the face of the cliff brought all three of them to quick attention. Julian cupped his hand over his eyes and scanned the top of the high limestone bluff.

Drago pointed. "Up there. I seen them. There's a group on horses."

CHAPTER 37

+ + + + + + +

The bluffs overlooking Marble Canyon on the Colorado River
Monday noon

Man With No Teeth crouched low over the side of the sandstone cliff and pointed out the position of the small boat below. Gandara looked over the man's shoulder with several of the warriors. "Not all the whites there," Gandara said.

Ed nervously paced up and down the side of the cliff. He squinted with excitement at the small group far below. "That's my wife down there, my wife and the baby."

Gandara eyed the man with suspicion. A man might be willing to say anything if he was afraid enough. He had been watching this white man ever since they had found him. When the man spoke of his wife, there was never any love in his face. The woman he spoke of was someone he hated, not someone he shared his life with.

Campbell squatted cautiously next to Gandara. "Where's the big ferryboat, then? That gold and most of them supplies will be on that thing."

The old Navajo looked up at him and pointed back up the river. "Cannot see all the river from here. Big boat will come."

"That's the one we want. Is there any way to get down to the river from up here?"

The old man shook his head. "We go on ahead. Canyon too steep here. Horse or man, be too dangerous to go down. I know place ahead, but it take us rest of day to get there. Two places are near there." The old man crossed his hands and grimaced. "You shoot white men from two places close together."

Campbell looked quizzically at Gandara. "Will Mangus go on? Does he want them folks bad enough?"

"He want Apache scout. Mangus not care about your gold."

"I don't rightly care about what he wants, just so he gets us to what we're after. Now, don't get me wrong, though. With all that gold, we could buy plenty of guns and ammunition. What we could get with that would make you a plenty powerful war."

Gandara got to his feet. He mumbled. "All white men alike. You want gold to make life easy. Indian just want the land like it used to be."

Campbell walked after him, trying hard to once again get his attention. "You got us wrong. Sure we want the gold, but we want the war too, want it bad, just like you do. You just tell that to Mangus. We come this far. He'd look like a fool sure 'nuff, if'n we quit now."

+ + + + +

Mangus sat his horse well away from the bluffs. He made sure that he was able to study each of the men as they scouted the river. Most of what he knew about leading men came from making careful observations of the men he led, and he could tell the white men were getting nervous.

Gandara stood next to him and made his report in Yavapai. "Boats are separated. The small boat is below us on the river. Man With No Teeth say the big boat will follow. He say there is a way to get down to the river farther ahead. Man With No Teeth say there are two places to shoot at the river."

"Is Apache scout with them?"

"I could not see to tell. I think he not on the small boat below. He with the big boat that comes."

"Should we go with the old man?" Mangus asked.

The fact that Mangus asked his advice made Gandara swell with pride. He knew he was being trained to lead and that Mangus was more than likely testing his ability to read a situation—that fact alone made him slightly hesitant to answer. Gandara looked over the men and the horses gathered around them. He tried to read their faces, faces that were frustrated over the loss of ammunition, faces that wanted to rejoin their families, and yet faces that itched for some sort of victory they could again shout about.

That Gandara paused before speaking satisfied Mangus. Mangus was cautious about sending men into battle. But once the decision had been made, he attacked without mercy and never with a second thought to the decision. If Gandara could be taught to think this way, he could be a good leader.

"I think we should follow the old man some more," Gandara said. "The people in the boats will be too busy to shoot back. We could separate the Apache and us in the two places." He motioned with his hands, flattening them and driving them at angles toward one another. "We will shoot and kill them easily, if old man shows us this good place."

"Good," Mangus said. "We go, then."

Gandara turned at once and reported the decision to the men. The discussion seemed to make all three of the white men relieved. Gandara spoke to them in English. "We will follow the old man a little longer."

Ed and Paco both nodded their heads eagerly.

Mangus motioned Gandara back over to him. He spoke in Yavapai so that the white men could not understand. "The white-eyes are of little use to us here. Kill the two traders, but save the white squaw man."

"I not think he married to Indian woman," Gandara said. "I see anger in his eyes when he speaks of her."

Mangus watched Hiatt as he walked back over to the edge of the cliff. "We will see," he said. "If this man knows them, any of them, he may bring them into open." He nodded as he watched Hiatt. "We may need him later."

+ + + + +

The Colorado River
Monday afternoon

It didn't take Julian and Drago long to right the boat and throw the supplies back in. The sight of the horses and riders on the bluff answered some nagging questions for them. "Them injuns is still coming," Drago said. "That's a sheer puzzlement. Without that ammunition, they ain't got much reason to, outsida sheer cussedness."

Julian climbed in and took the baby while Raincloud stepped into the front hatch and picked up her paddle. She looked back at Julian. "I am very scared," she said. "I fear for myself, but mostly I fear for Sunflower. She cannot fight whatever happens to her."

"I understand. This water doesn't look too friendly to any of us."

Drago shoved the boat deeper and jumped in.

Raincloud dipped her paddle into the water and pulled toward the middle of the river. "I would feel better in the desert," she said.

"So would I," Julian replied.

"Then, why do we have to do this? I don't understand."

"We didn't have much choice."

"We could have waited and all gone together. It would be better, being together."

"Not for me and Drago, it wouldn't. If we'd stayed with them, we'd be outnumbered and outgunned. Besides, I might have been forced to kill that bullheaded brother of mine."

Raincloud put down her paddle and once again turned around toward him. "Many women would find it hard that a man would risk her and her baby to only think of himself."

Julian grew silent.

She looked him straight in the eye. "But I think I know who you are, maybe better than you do. You have had only yourself to think about for many years now; no one to love you, no one to love. You are like a wounded lion in the hills. To fight and to kill is all that fills your heart. You have no home and no mother lion to care for your cubs. You have no one else to think of that you must feed."

"I reckon, I've had quite a bit of practice in being a taker. The notion of being a giver slips by me."

Raincloud looked at the baby in his arms. "Maybe holding Sunflower will teach you what it feels like to be this giver you speak of."

Julian's mind raced. Raincloud's talk reminded him of things his mother had told him as a boy, and right now he felt like one—a boy on his mother's knee, too proud to admit wrong and too ashamed to argue. "Maybe so," he said.

Raincloud turned back to paddle.

"We might just get the hang of this thing afore long," Drago called out. "That ferryboat man said this here thing had made this trip twice before. That was sure a far sight more than he could say about that big flat boat they're all swimming in."

"Then, maybe us taking this thing was the best chance we had," Julian grunted, more to be heard by Raincloud than to agree with Drago. "There ain't room in this dory for more than a few."

The water seemed to rise before them and then they felt the rock underneath. The water caught the bow of the boat and spun it around, lifting it off the rock and sending it stern first down the chute of whitewater. Drago tried to turn the boat, swinging his paddle around and digging at the chuin. They dropped a few feet into the swirling torrent and Raincloud screamed.

Rushing past the rocks that jutted on either side, the river flattened into a mass of murky swells, waves bouncing the little boat, jarring all of them. Drago continued to dig with his paddle, finally positioning the boat into place for the next drop.

The canyon seemed to cover them, with water flying into the air. The roar of the river deafened the screams of the child as Julian clutched her. He held her tightly, bracing himself with his boots tucked under the staves of the boat. Nervously, Raincloud glanced back, a look of panic on her face.

"She's all right," Julian yelled. "I got her tight. She ain't about to go anywhere."

The trough of water spat the boat suddenly to the right and down a powerful pull of rushing foam. There was no stopping it, even if they tried. Shooting out from the rocks, a whirl of water caught them and twisted them around. Raincloud pulled with her paddle, and Drago raked his violently in the water. Once again, they were righted and speeding forward.

Drago cursed in the back of the boat and, swinging his paddle from side to side, continued to make the boat go forward. "I don't know how much more of this we can take," he yelled. "Does this go on forever?"

No sooner had he yelled than another drop came. It stood before them, five feet at least and all at once. The water poured over the sides of the rocks, boiling at the bottom. The boat seemed to hang in the air for a moment, as if daring itself to go over. Raincloud gasped and held on to the paddle as the boat dropped into the watery sinkhole.

Falling almost straight down, the dory hit the hole, sending water flying and slamming all of them back into their seats underneath the deck. The rear of the craft spun in midair, tailing in the sky like the hand of a drowning man. It swung around and landed in the river, shooting backward down the raging deluge.

* * * * *

Johnson swung the boom on the ferry from side to side, pushing the big boat midstream. "These here sweep booms weren't ever made for this rough water," he yelled at Zac. "You be plenty careful!"

The cable wrapped around the log girders strained, making a moaning sound that drew the boatman's immediate attention. The sound and strain of the logs were directly under Philip Carol's feet. He jumped to the side of the boat as if he'd been bitten by a snake. Clutching the side of the lockbox, he watched the logs grind at each other.

Rushing headlong into the ripping current, the ferryboat dropped and seemed to stand still in the swift water, the backwash of the current holding it still. Pinned in the mighty river by the force of the sweeping current, the big boat was like a beached whale dying in the place it was designed to rule.

Zac reached a foot out, pushing off from a rock to their left and once again sending the big boat hurtling down the river. Amy moved to the front to try to help Zac stabilize the forward boom. Tommy leaned over the side of the boat, keeping his face pointed into the flume of spraying water. As he leaned farther, he began to lose his grip.

Watching the boy, Carol seemed frozen with fear, unable to move across the logs that only a moment before seemed destined to tear apart. Paralyzed, he didn't even cry out. Scampering immediately toward the boy, Ruggles grabbed him by the waist and hauled him back into the middle of the ferry. Both he and the boy tumbled backward, sliding along the slick deck. Ruggles held him tightly as Amy screamed.

Johnson hurriedly reached out to steady the two of them and prevent a further slide. As he let go of the boom, the ferry swung to the side. Hurriedly rushing back to the big paddle, he began to swing it violently in the water. The crack of the big boom was audible to all, a nauseating sound that spelled trouble.

The boat continued down the raging water, wide side forward, and it was plain for everyone to see that it was out of control. Johnson began to scream orders as Zac manned the other boom. "Whip that thing," he yelled. "Hold 'er back against that water or we'ze gonna wind up on a rock."

A large boulder loomed ahead of them in midstream, water pouring around it. The ferry was heading straight for it, and there seemed to be little anyone could do to stop it.

Amy scrambled back across the deck and took hold of Tommy,

burying him in her arms beside the lockbox.

As Zac continued to swing his big paddle, the ferry slammed against the rock, its side seemingly stuck by the force of the water pouring around it. The big boat rose higher, climbing onto the obstruction, and rushing water poured over the upstream portion of the deck.

Johnson screamed at the top of his lungs, "Everybody get to the high side. Do it now!"

Zac abandoned the boom and climbed up the highest portion of the ferry as it stood beside the rock. Peters and Black scrambled up the slick timbers, positioning themselves beside Zac. As Johnson climbed the turned-up boat with Amy and Tommy, the craft, under their combined weight, began to edge down the rock. Ruggles reached back and pulled Carol to his feet. He tried to steady him, then pulled him with all his might onto the edge of the floundering but suspended craft.

Once again in the stream, the ferry swung to the left and shot down the ripping current. It slowly spun from side to side, revolving and turning as it ran with the raging tide.

Johnson took control of the remaining oar. "We're heading for that small beach over yonder. If'n any of you folks is the praying kind, you better do it now, 'cause if we miss that we ain't got no mercy for quite a ways."

✦   ✦   ✦   ✦   ✦

Julian rolled in his seat in the dory with the crying baby. It was small and helpless; he knew that. Right now, though, he was more afraid of hurting the child himself than worrying about whatever damage the river could do. There was a new determination in him, however, a sheer grit to prove that everything that had been said about him was wrong. He could think about someone else, even if he died doing it. For him, there would be no tomorrow, not if he let anything happen to Raincloud or her baby.

The rapids kept up a steady pull on the boat, much of the extreme violence all at once behind them. He sat up, bouncing the crying child and holding her close to his face. The baby's tears were mixed with the water that covered him, but Sunflower's face was soft, softer than anything he'd ever felt before. There was a tenderness to the child that caught him off guard. He'd never been much for children; they were a nuisance. Right now, though, this was a nuisance he was determined would make it, with or without him.

Raincloud nervously continued to paddle, constantly swinging her head around to see Sunflower as she cried. A mother's devotion to a crying child was something Julian could only barely understand. There was a bond between mothers and children that no one could explain, one that went on through the years. His mind raced back to his own mother, to the times that she would hold him close and kiss his forehead. It seemed so long ago—another time and him a different person. Yet he knew one thing for sure, if his mother were here with him right now, she'd love him just like before. Zac had been right about him. Her heart would be broken over how he'd turned out, but she'd have loved him, all the same.

Drago called out behind them. "How long you reckon this is gonna go on? I don't speck we can take a whole lot of that stuff behind us."

"It'll go on till we're through it," Julian shot back. "Right now we couldn't stop if we had a mind to."

Suddenly, the river's brutality seemed to subside, the rapids becoming lower and the water getting deeper. He spoke in a low tone to Raincloud in front of him. "You got some power in you, little lady, some power I ain't never seen before."

Raincloud looked back at him, her face shining with water.

Julian nodded at her and bounced the child. "You were right about me, too. It's been a long time since I seen the kind of love you got. I'd forgotten what it was all about."

"I do what I have to do."

"No, you do more than that, much more than that. Anybody does what they have to do. What you do is something only a woman with a child could do, a woman who knows how to love."

Turning a bend in the river, the water ran deep. It smoothed the dory out, and there was a sudden unexpected peace all around them. It was like being in another world. Rock walls climbed to the sun overhead and shadows flowed into the water, giving it the appearance of a dark and mysterious inland sea.

Raincloud put down her paddle and, reaching back, took the crying baby.

Drago picked his paddle out of the water, allowing the dory to glide on the smooth surface. The beauty of the place held all of them speechless. Sheer red walls rose straight up and touched the sky. Birds cut the silence with their screeching, their nests rutted into a series of crevices in the crimson walls.

"You see what I see?" Julian asked.

Drago put his paddle in and began to push the water behind them. "I sure do."

There, to their left, a low crack in the red wall blossomed into a massive cavern. The edge of the river flowed into it, carving out a beach and piling sand onto the sloping rock.

"Let's make for it," Julian said. "We could build us a fire and dry these clothes off a mite."

"You got that right. I could stand to cram some vittles down this gullet of mine, too."

Minutes later, they beached the dory inside the cavern. What had appeared to be a crack at the water level upstream was much more than that. A massive cavern spread itself before them, stretching out into the darkness. An entire city could have been built in the constant shade of the red rock structure. They stood at the entrance in awe.

Julian walked along the beach and began to gather dried driftwood while Raincloud sat down to feed the baby. In just a short time, a small fire burned, a coffeepot nestled on top.

Drago called out to them from the darkness of the cavern. "Here, you two better come over here and look at this."

Julian and Raincloud got to their feet and walked into the shadows. Not forty feet from them was a human skeleton, its bleached bones spread-eagle, half buried in the sand.

CHAPTER 38

+ + + + + + +

Near Tiger Wash, south of Marble Canyon
Late Monday afternoon

Johnson angled the big boat toward the small beach. The current swept it along the shore at a rate that seemed much too fast for them to be able to land. Zac took the tow rope in hand and signaled to Peters. "It's gonna take a bunch of us to pull it in." He looked over at Ruggles. "And I'm gonna need men with two good legs."

Ruggles nodded. Carol still clung to the lockbox on the far side of the ferry. He had hunkered down beside it as the only stable thing he could hold on to. "We don't know how deep it is here," he said.

"Come on, boy," Peters said. "We ain't got much time to lose if we want to get to some dry land."

Carol only gripped the box more tightly. Amy and Ruggles exchanged a quick glance.

"Philip is very strong," Amy said. "I'm sure he would be of great help."

The word from Amy seemed to bolster his confidence—or shamed him into attempting to get to his feet. He scooted over the deck toward the approaching shore and stared down at the dark, swirling water. Peters jumped in first, followed by Zac and the reverend. Chest deep and swept along by the raging current, the three men held on to the line and strove toward the shore.

"They need you, Philip," Amy said softly.

Swallowing hard, he jumped into the water and grabbed for the tightening rope.

The four men tugged at the line, swinging the ferry's glide toward the small beach. Johnson kept up his attempt to steer the vessel on a course toward the struggling men.

In a matter of moments, the men stood waist-deep in the shallow water and heaved. As the ferry edged into the beach, they kept the line taut and backed up onto the wet sand. Zac found a nearby tree and quickly secured the line. "There," he said, "that ought to do it."

Minutes later, the entire party stood dripping on the shore. Zac proceeded to hack at the branches of some scrub oak with his knife. He spoke over his shoulder. "I don't know what it will take to shore up that cracked boom, but these ought to help. We can lash them down around the spot and see if they make do."

Ruggles had gathered a batch of dry driftwood and was attempting to shave kindling into a small pile. Black searched his pockets trying to find a dry match, but Zac produced a piece of flint from his pocket and tossed it to Ruggles. "Always have a little something to use in an emergency."

Ruggles chuckled. "From what I've seen so far, I wouldn't be surprised if you had a plan for stampeding buffalo in the desert."

Zac smiled. "In my line of work, there's those that's ready and there's those that's dead. I'd just as soon be one of those that's ready."

"I'd drink to that," the Reverend Black said, "if I were a drinking man."

Before long, Ruggles had managed to start a stream of sparks with the flint and the blunt end of his knife handle. He continued, the crisp sound of the metal end knocking off sparks from the flint, until a small flame was kindled. Bending down, he blew gently on the flame, coaxing it to life. "That ought to do it," he said.

Amy had seated herself in one of the few patches of sunlight to try to dry off her dress. She pulled the small bag up from around her neck and, opening it, dropped the diamond into the palm of her hand.

Ruggles leaned several sticks of wood into the growing fire, stood to his feet, and limped over to her. "You should keep that thing out of sight," he said. "These folks all seem harmless enough, but I wouldn't want any of them to get strange ideas."

"Why would they?"

"The best way to avoid temptation is to never see it in the first place," he said.

"You were man enough to not be drawn into having something that didn't belong to you. Why would they be any different?"

"I've lived my whole life watching other people be tempted by quick money. It's how I make my living. There's very little in the way of temptation I haven't seen, and nothing I haven't watched better men than I give in to."

Amy clutched the diamond in her hand. "This thing has always seemed to comfort me. It makes me think of future possibilities, of a life I might be able to lead someday."

"That's the difference between you and most. You see the future in that thing, and most people would see only the here and now."

"I see a future for us," she said.

He lowered himself and squatted down beside her. Reaching out to her wet hair, he pushed it aside. "I'm having a hard time seeing a future for any of us, I'm afraid. Of course, most of my life has been lived for what I could see right in front of me."

"And do you like what you see in front of you?"

"I like it very much. I only wish any of us had any promise of it on this river."

"You don't think we can make it, then?"

"Johnson says this thing will get much worse. I just don't know how that ferryboat will hold up to much more of this, to say nothing about the part that he describes."

"Then, there's no hope?"

"There's always hope. Only trouble is, that's about all we got right now."

She tightened her grip on the diamond. "Then that's enough for me. I have to see what could be, especially since what is seems so disturbing."

"It's the kind of fix a man uses to get his accounts squared up with God and anybody else he's ever wronged. Makes a body pause on his regrets."

"And do you have any?"

He looked down into her eyes and, holding her chin, ran his thumb across her cheek. "You've done something to me, Amy, something I thought would never happen to me. You've given me something to believe in, something that's right and proper. I'm in love with you, girl." He blew a stream of air from his mouth and shook his head. "There, I said it. Never thought I ever could. I feel it and I've said it. I just can't do anything about it."

"Why can't you? You've made a good start."

Black had continued the process of building up the fire. He stood next to it and opened his coat, trying hard to get dry. Amy noticed him eyeing them and smiled. Leaving the comfort of the fire, he walked over to them. "You two young people seem to be making plans. Anything I might be of help in?"

"I'm not sure, Reverend. For a man who believes in the present, Lawrence here hasn't asked me anything."

The parson put his hands on his hips and stared down at Ruggles. "What's wrong with you, son? It's plain to see the two of you love each other. Why don't you just get on with it?"

"Get on with what?" Ruggles asked.

"Ask her to marry you, man."

"We might not make it through another day," Ruggles said. "That kind of talk would be foolish."

The Reverend Black smiled. "Quite the contrary. If we ain't got long, it's all the more reason to make the best of the time we've got. If today's all you've got, then I'd just make sure you packed as much living into it as you could." He looked around at the group, now huddled up next to the fire. "You got lots of witnesses here and even a preacher. What more could you want?"

Amy and Ruggles quickly got to their feet. "This is sort of sudden, isn't it?" Ruggles asked.

The preacher rubbed his chin. "I wouldn't say so. Those feelings you're carrying around for each other are ones generally followed up with marriage, don't you think?"

"I suppose so," Ruggles said, "but, here and now?"

"Why not? You're here and we're all here. If we won't see tomorrow, then I'd say you've got a lot of living to do today."

"Not exactly my idea of a honeymoon," Ruggles responded.

"This ain't exactly my notion of a stagecoach ride, either," Black laughed. "But first things first. You got to ask her. She might just say no, but I wouldn't count on that."

Ruggles turned to Amy. He looked the part of a lost puppy—wet, hungry, and confused.

Amy smiled slyly. It was the first time she'd ever seen Lawrence Ruggles at a loss for words and without an inkling of what to do next. The man had always been the height of competence, a stalwart of the strong masculine type who only acted acquiescent when he knew it would bring about the best results. He never went off at the mouth without thinking, even when he was wrong. If he was going to be proven wrong, he wanted it to be about something he'd given a lot of thought to. "You're much more lovable when you don't know what you're doing," she said.

"Well, then, I ought to be downright adorable right about now, 'cause I don't know the first thing about what I'm doing."

She laughed. "I wouldn't worry about it. If Johnson's right, nobody will be left alive to tell anyone what a fool Lawrence Ruggles made out of himself."

The Reverend Black held up both of his hands. "I'll sure never tell, and the Lord himself will keep your secret safe." He looked back at the fire and cleared his throat. "I think I'll just make my way back to that warmth over there and leave you two young people here to work this out your ownselves. Like I said, though, today is the only day you've got. If it was me, I wouldn't want to leave anything unsaid."

Ruggles took her by both hands and pulled her closer. "You know how I feel about you, Amy. I've already told you that much."

"I know. I'd just like to hear it again."

Ruggles gulped. "I love you, Amy Franklin, and if you could ever think about marrying a gambler, I'd like to be the one."

"There, now that wasn't so bad, was it?"

"It was worse than bad. Makes me feel clumsy inside."

"You've just never needed anyone. Do you need me?"

He dropped his chin slightly and looked into her eyes. "Yes, I need you. I never thought I could need anyone, let alone need them to love me, but I do you. I've lived almost thirty years and most of it by myself. I can't say as I'll ever change." He looked back at the preacher. "Although, what that man's been talking to me about when we've managed to get alone might just make me different. I never could understand faith and all. I only trusted myself, and then only sometimes."

"He is a godsend."

"That's what he claims to be. I guess it's his job."

He stood and stared at her silently while she watched him, trying to surmise what he was on the inside. It was a moment in time she didn't want to pass by. "I love you, Lawrence Ruggles, and yes, I'll marry you, here or any place you choose."

Ruggles heaved a big sigh and tightened his grip on her hands.

✦ ✦ ✦ ✦ ✦

Six miles south of Tiger Wash
Late Monday afternoon

Raincloud held the baby close, and Julian and Drago huddled by the fire. "I don't like this place," she said. "It is a place of much death and suffering."

Julian watched the dark water ebb by them. He nodded toward the river. "I'd say that is the place of death, out yonder. Whoever that was back there probably took kindly to crawling up here and dying on dry land."

"I'm with the lady," Drago snapped. "This place gives me the heebie-jeebies."

"I'm not talking about those bones," Raincloud said. "This whole place has ghosts that talk."

"If the ghosts talk here," Julian said, "then they'd more than likely be telling us to stay for a while, eat and dry off."

"Don't you believe in ghosts?" Drago asked.

"If I did, then, they'd probably be following me around by now. I've made myself a few ghosts in my day."

Raincloud watched him. There was seldom any fear on Julian Cobb's face—he feared no man, and had even less fear of what he couldn't see.

"What do you believe in, then?" Drago asked.

"I believe in a God that judges the living and the dead, just like my ma and pa taught me. I believe in His wrath and I been used a time or two to show it on others."

"Then, you think you're going to be judged?"

"The more a man knows, the more he has to answer for, and I know plenty."

Raincloud rocked the baby back and forth. "He is a merciful God, too."

"I ain't never seen much of that."

"Maybe you do not look for it. He showed mercy when the soldiers did not find you out. They would have taken us with them, and we would have all been with them when they died."

Julian paused and looked down. "I guess you've got me there. I suppose, too, I could have met up with a bounty hunter that would have shot me down on the spot when he had a chance to, instead of running into that brother of mine. That was a mercy too, I suppose."

"Yes, it was. Your brother loves you very much. I can see the old memories of you in his eyes when he looks at you."

"The memories he has of me *are* old. I'm not the man he once knew."

"Yes, you are. Deep inside, you are still that man and still the little boy that ran and played with him."

"That was another world, another world and another life for both him and me. When I knew him, he wouldn't have stepped on a bug. Now he's a hard killer, same as me. He may be working for the law, but he's a killer, just the same."

"Only God is just the same. He never changes."

"We'll have to see about that. The gentle Jesus meek and mild has been giving me the back of His hand since the war." He held up the stub of his left arm. "He's been taking me down one piece at a time and now He wants to come for the rest."

"When He comes for you, He wants to find a man who has turned his back on what is wrong and tries to do the good."

"I'm afraid that's gonna take a powerful lot of changing."

"He can change anyone. He need not bother with the good people on this earth."

"Maybe so, but I have to let Him, and just right now, I'm not ready to do that. Besides, if that brother of mine has his way, I ain't gonna have much time. He won't be satisfied until he watches me climb up those gallows."

A sudden breeze created a moan in the cavern, turning all their heads around.

"I don't like this," Drago said. "This place reminds me of death."

"Let's go," Raincloud joined in.

Julian stood up and stirred the coals. "All right, you two don't know how well off you got it in here. I'll give you one thing, though, the farther ahead of them we can stay, the better I'll like it."

Within minutes they had shoved the dory off the beach. The sun was lower on the horizon, putting the entire river in dark shadow.

The water seemed relatively calm as Raincloud and Drago dipped their paddles in the water. It was like a dark sheet of glass, sparkling with an occasional glimpse of sunlight, but still not allowing them to see through it. The dory glided, the only sound the swish of the paddles.

"We do need to stop for the night," Drago said. "Can't rightly tell what time of day it is in this here canyon, but we'd better keep a look for a likely spot. Just so I'm not shut into some cave. I ain't no mole, you know. I'd sure hanker to have stars overhead when we stop, if I had my druthers."

The canyon seemed to dip its feet in the river, plummeting straight down and into the dark water. All around them was silence. They continued to paddle for some time before they heard the rapids up ahead. It was somewhere around the next bend and they knew it—not too close, but near enough to be heard. Sound carried well across the water, so there was no telling how long the smooth paddling and the sleeping baby would last.

"I do not like going down this river," Raincloud said. "If we spill over, Sunflower will die. We might all die, but she will die first."

"We've made it so far," Julian said.

"Even more reason that I should walk with her. God has smiled on us so far, but we are not listening to Him."

CHAPTER 39

+ + + + + + +

South Canyon
Late Monday afternoon

The river raged, tossing the ferry mile after mile; then it ran deep and quiet. The sudden silence of the calm water hushed the entire group. It was as if they were entering a tomb, a place of the long-ago dead. The ridges of the rocks formed layer after layer of colors, as far up as they could see. The entire river was in shadow, and it was plain to see that if they were going to rest for the night, they'd best do it right away. There were stretches of the river where no one could expect to pull the big ferry to the side, and the idea of being trapped in the swirling currents during darkness was too horrible to consider.

"I got us a place to put in for the night," Johnson said. "Stopped there twice with Powell. The place will make the hair on the back of your head stand up, but you'll get dry there and it won't be a-rainin' on you."

"How far away is it?" Ruggles asked.

"It's just a few miles ahead of us on our left, Redwall Cavern. It's plenty big. Major Powell thought it would seat over 50,000 people, if'n you could get that many people sitting still in one place long enough. There's a nice place to put in, a sandy beach."

"Sounds fine," Peters grunted. "I'm hungrier than a bear."

"Yeah, it's a fine place to stop for a meal, but most folks wouldn't want to sleep there."

"Why not?" Ruggles asked.

"Nothing wrong with the place. Rain can't hit you none, but I guess there's many folks that says it has its drawbacks. You won't have to worry 'bout no injuns in there, though. The ancient ones used to use the place to sacrifice people to their gods—leastwise that was what the rumor was."

He continued to swing the big paddle from side to side, keeping the ferry midstream. "Anyways, ain't no injun gonna come close to it. They're mighty peculiar 'bout things like that. Got some kinda sense inside them that knows 'bout spooks and such."

"We won't bother them," Zac added, "and they won't bother us."

"That might be," Johnson said, "but there's one thing you ought to consider—Redwall Cavern would be the best place for that brother of yours to be holding up. It's got cover and he's got the rifles."

Zac studied the river and the dying sunlight. "That may be, but I'd suspect him to be making all the miles on us he can, while he can. He doesn't want a shoot-out; he wants distance."

Johnson grunted loudly. "The man's a fool. He doesn't know this river. If he keeps going much farther, he's gonna be up to his neck in whitewater in the dark." He shook his head. "Fool."

Tommy had taken off his shoes and tied the laces together, hanging them around his neck. Sitting on the side of the ferry, he dragged his bare feet in the black water. Philip Carol clung to the side of the boat, near the lockbox. He seemed lost in his own thoughts, watching the river ahead of them.

The Reverend Black had salvaged a cigar that wasn't thoroughly wet and, biting off the end, lit it with a match. He puffed it to life, put his head back, and smiled. "Ah, God gives us so much to enjoy. I'd say most of us are just spoiled children."

"We have been very lucky so far," Amy added.

"Luck has nothing to do with it," Black responded. "One of the problems we have with God is the regularity in which He performs His miracles. He does them in our lives with such dailiness that we view them as a normal thing."

Peters removed his hat and scratched his head. "Hard to sell that notion to all of us, Preacher. With what we've been through, I've seen cattle in a slaughterhouse more comfortable."

Black grinned, the cigar perched between his teeth. "Friend, if you knew what might have happened, you'd be plenty thankful for what did."

Peters crushed the hat back on his head. "Preacher, I been in the territory for 'bout twenty years now. I been stepped on by cattle, nearly scalped by the 'pache, rolled on by a horse a time or two, shot at, spit on, and punched by drunks. I liked to died of thirst more times than I can count and nearly drowned today. But I'd run to all them smiling if'n I could swap for this simple little stagecoach job I've been on this past week or so. I'm long past trying to keep the customer happy. I just want to get through it or, barring that, die in one piece where they can pick all of me up without a shovel."

"You don't want much, then," Black responded.

"Nah, sir. Right now, I'm a man of simple ambition." He pulled off his hat again and scratched at his head furiously. " 'Course, I'd be plumb pleased to get myself rid of these here head lice. I surely would now."

Zac smiled. "When we camp tonight, I can help you there. There are scissors in the lockbox and the gambler over there carries a straight razor. I can just take all that hair clean off you and then you can scrub down. It would cure that problem and it wouldn't make scalping you worth the trouble if we meet up with that Mangus again."

Peters replaced his hat. "I guess that would just about do it, sure 'nuff."

The late afternoon had brought out a few bugs, and nearby a fish broke the surface to retrieve one. Tommy squealed and pointed.

Ruggles patted the boy's head. "I think we can rig up some fishing gear when we make camp. Would that please you?"

The boy nodded his head. "Yes! Yes, I like to fish."

"I think we could all use some fresh meat," Zac added.

A short time later, the bend in the river showed the dark shadow that was Redwall Cavern. Johnson swung the big paddle toward the right, moving the barge toward the beach. As they edged onto the sand, the men jumped onto the shore, pulling the tow lines. Looping the ropes around standing rocks, they made the craft secure.

"Come on over here," Ruggles yelled out to Zac. "You'd better take a look at this."

Zac spotted the dying coals of a fire at once. Moving toward it, he lowered his hand to the coals. "They were here," he said, "just hours ago."

"They don't have much of a lead on us, then, in spite of a faster boat."

"Maybe not, but with darkness coming on, we're not going anywhere till morning. We'll rest here and cook up some hot food. Johnson says this is the best place to stop." Zac looked out at the flowing river. "That's one big advantage on our part; we have someone who knows this river. They're out there on this thing blind."

+ + + + +

Lower Marble Canyon
Monday, early evening

The dory swung wildly in the water. In the bow, Raincloud paddled furiously as the craft pitched headlong up and down the raging swells of foam. Drago worked hard with his paddle to keep it centered in the river. "I don't want to be in this thing when it's dark!" he yelled.

Julian held the now crying baby. "We better start looking for a place to put in. Sooner we get some hot grub in us, the better we'll all be."

The canyon had begun to break with its usual high walls. They had passed a canyon with a small stream running down it, and Julian regretted that they had not stopped there. Now, the rapids made it impossible to stop anywhere, safe or not. It swept them forward and down the rocky canyon. To their right, a series of high arches formed, its streaked limestone bowing up and allowing the faint remainder of daylight to creep through. They raced by the arches and back into the dark canyon.

When the river smoothed out, it took an abrupt turn to the left, high walls of rock making it impossible to find any shelter. Around the bend, they could clearly hear the next set of rapids. It was like being blind and groping around one of those dangerous New York City factories; noises they could not see or understand promised calamity ahead.

Making a sudden right turn, they could see the rapids. These were smaller than the ones they had already negotiated, but darkness would make them and others like them far more dangerous.

The dory shot through the boiling water, spewing down the raging river. They rounded large rocks and could see still more ahead. The boat moved rapidly down the middle of the river, lunging forward with each belch of the stream.

Up ahead was a drop of some four feet. The water poured through the trough and boiled at the bottom. There was no escaping it. It would be on them in a matter of moments.

Raincloud looked back at the baby, and Julian could see the

worry written all over her face. He understood. "Don't worry," he said. "I got her real tight. Ain't nothing gonna happen to her."

Raincloud turned to face the fall through space. She would be the first to see the drop as it came on them. She pulled with the paddle to steady the boat.

The current seemed to shoot them into the falls, the bow of the dory hanging momentarily and then the drop down, down, down; down the slide they went, crashing into the surging pool beneath. The dory spun, with Drago pulling to correct the front end. The wild activity of Drago and Raincloud made little sense to either. It was a way of doing something, a way of not giving in to the feelings of helpless abandonment.

Moments later, the set of rapids was behind them and the river took a hairpin turn to their right. The water seemed to run calmly, as if to give them a moment to recover, a time to gather their thoughts.

Outcroppings of rocky shale winked at them, magic in the walls of the canyon. They were the glances of a thousand angels, each of their eyes shining in the dwindling light. Two smaller sets of rapids lay ahead of them, the noise rising with each passing moment.

Drago pointed. "Over there! Them small canyons. There ought to be a place in there."

They pulled toward the break in the walls. Trees choked the off-shooting canyons—their first sight of the muted greenery of vegetation in what seemed like hours.

"Pull hard, girl!" Drago shouted. "We got to make it into one of them canyons."

+ + + + +

Redwall Cavern
Tuesday morning, an hour before sunrise

The string of fish caught the night before lay smoldering in the coals of the fire. Their aroma was hard to resist. There would be enough to supplement the diet of dried food they had packed. Julian hadn't taken everything. Zac was thankful for that.

"Do you think we'll catch up to them folks today?" Peters asked.

"I don't reckon we will," Johnson responded. "I ain't too sure they made it past the night. There ain't too many places they could put in before Saddle Canyon, and they'd have to be plenty lucky to get there." He fingered a piece of the hot fish in his hand and stuck it in his mouth. "No, I speck they're clean gone, and I don't exactly mean skeedaddled."

Philip Carol had been quiet since they'd gotten to Lee's Ferry. He fidgeted on the log he was sitting on. "Frankly speaking, I hope they get away."

Ruggles lifted his head. "Now, why would you say that? That just might be some of your daddy's money they stole."

Carol swung his head around the group slyly, trying to judge the reaction. He was looking to get attention and perhaps being outrageous was his only way. "When I agreed to come aboard the stage, my objective was to get to a destination, not to chase bandits. No one deputized me. Whether they are caught or get away is of no concern to me. This Wells Fargo man is paid to do this. I don't know why I should put my life in jeopardy in order for him to earn a paycheck."

"That man put us in great difficulty by leaving us without those rifles," Amy piped in.

"The kid's right," Zac said. "This is my show. I was sent to bring those people in, not to drag innocent people along with me and put them in harm's way."

"We haven't gone one inch out of our way," Ruggles said. "What we're doing is sheer survival, nothing more."

✦ ✦ ✦ ✦ ✦

Saddle Canyon
Tuesday morning, sunrise

Raincloud had gone to bathe in the creek just before dawn, and Drago stirred the coals of a new fire flaming up underneath the coffeepot. Sunflower lay curled up sleeping in a blanket near the fire. "Now, what we gonna do if that there baby starts to cry?" Drago asked.

"Womenfolk always hear their babies first." Julian got to his feet and strapped on his gunbelt. "I think I'll go check on her."

"And leave me with that baby?"

"You'll be all right."

"No, I won't, either. And you shouldn't walk up on a woman that's trying to take a bath, either," Drago smiled. "Not unless you take me with you."

"You just sit tight and finish stowing things away. We're leaving here soon as I get back with her."

"Now, just when might that be?"

"Shortly."

Julian pulled his hat tight and started up the creek bed that flowed into the river. He danced from rock to rock. Keeping dry was something he'd given up on for a while. The river would make sure of that.

Walking upstream, he noticed the light from the morning sun ahead. He'd been so used to the sheer walls of the canyon that the opening took him by surprise. Pulling in at night hadn't given him time to look the place over, and now he wished he had. There just might be a way out of the canyon, a way that would take them off the river. They'd be on foot, but they'd be alive. He could bury the gold and take what was needed to survive. The thought made him pick up the pace and scour the walls above for a trail that might lead up them.

As he rounded the rocks ahead, he heard laughter and voices. He pulled out his .44. Crouching low, he edged his way around the large boulder in his path. There below, in the shallow pool, two Indians teased Raincloud, pulling on the dress she clutched in her hands.

He cocked and leveled the revolver, then fired, spinning one of the braves with the impact. As the man hit the ground, the second man dropped his hold on Raincloud's dress and ran for the rocks.

Julian bounded down the hill and took her by the hand. Without waiting for her to dress, he pushed her up the hill and backed up after her, keeping his eyes on the rocks.

Moments later, he stood beside her as she hurriedly dressed.

"I didn't see them until they were next to me," she yelped.

Julian turned and motioned her down the trail. "We got to hit that river and fast."

Skipping down the rocks that dotted the creek, they heard gunfire from the camp below. As they came out from the trees surrounded by a group of rocks, they watched Drago fall.

There on the sides of the cliff, five warriors had taken cover and were pouring fire down into the campsite. Julian grabbed Raincloud's arm and twisted it as the baby let out a series of chilling screams. "You stay here!" he demanded.

"No!" she shouted. "She's my baby. You get the rifles, and I will get the baby."

He nodded and cocked his revolver. Running toward the boat, Julian fired up at the men above. His second shot sent one of the men falling down the face of the cliff, and the subsequent shots kept the aggressors' heads down.

Reaching the boat, he grabbed the rifle and slung an ammo belt over his shoulder. He then turned and fired the revolver once again as he watched Raincloud running back for the rocks, the baby in her arms.

Moments later, he crouched beside her and began reloading the .44. "Going down that river with only you able to paddle is gonna be a might difficult, but we ain't got much choice. Drago's done for."

"We could wait for the other boat."

Julian swung his head around, surveying the rocks. "If we float down a mite, we could put ashore farther down and try to climb out of here. There's got to be a way. If they got down, we could get up."

"We could wait for the other boat. It will come soon."

"If it does, they can draw their fire while we get away." He looked at her. Her eyes said it all. She had no desire to try the river again, not with just the two of them and him with one arm. "Look, Raincloud, we don't even know if they made it past the water we've done been over. They might all be dead for all we know. If we just sit here, those people will get a better position on us."

The sound of a familiar voice brought their heads around. "Raincloud, you down there? You down there with the baby?"

It was Ed Hiatt.

"You gotta help me, girl!" he yelled. "These injuns mean business. Is that Apache scout down there with you?"

"Don't tell him anything," Julian said.

Raincloud raised her voice. "I am here with Sunflower. I have friends."

"What about that Chupta fella? Is he there with you?"

The man's voice echoed through the canyon. He was not close, but he could be heard very well. Raincloud was silent.

"Girl, you got to help me. No telling what these people gonna do. They already killed the men I was with." His voice broke. He sounded plaintive, something she had never known from Ed Hiatt.

"Girl, they got me tied to a tree up here. You got to come and cut me loose. They ain't gonna let me go, and they don't believe no injun woman would have me for a husband. They won't kill you.

You're injun, same as them. They just want to know if you'd walk up here and cut me loose."

Raincloud started to get up, and Julian pulled her back down. "What in the blazes are you doing? That man wants to kill you. It's a trick, an Indian trick. They just want us out in the open so they can kill us like they did Drago."

"He is my husband. I can't just let him die."

"You don't love him, and it's for sure he hates you. You go up there and they'll latch on to you for all the world."

"Raincloud . . . please." Ed's voice was scratchy and full of pain. "You got to show them that I ain't no liar when I said you was my wife. I'm sorry 'bout them things I done."

Raincloud's expression showed her inner turmoil. She squinted her eyes and frowned. "You go up there and we're both dead. You don't think they're about to let you just sashay up there and free that man, do you? You know what those bucks had in mind for you. Well, you go up there and they're gonna finish it. It's best to just let Mangus have his way with the man."

Hiatt let out a loud scream. "Raincloud, you remember what they taught you in that mission school. Don't you forget it," he called in a hoarse voice.

+ + + + +

The pain of her short years with Ed Hiatt flooded her mind. For her, there had seemed to be no escape. Many times she had dreamed of killing the man, just killing him and being free. Now the death of her husband would be easy. All she had to do was do nothing, just sit where she was and listen to him die. It was something he deserved, something he had been born for.

CHAPTER 40

+ + + + + + +

Saddle Canyon
Tuesday morning

Raincloud stiffened. The woman was determined; Julian could see that. He watched her brace with every sound from her husband on the trail above them. Her warm, dark eyes danced with a fire from inside, a fire that blazed with deep feeling.

"That man is your past," Julian said. "I'm your future, me and that baby of yours."

"I have no past and no future," Raincloud said. "I only have now. This is what I must do to live with who I am now."

Julian stared into her black, shining eyes. This woman had a soul of flint. She always seemed to do just exactly what she set out to do. "You sound like me, woman, just like me. I've never thought of having a future, and I've tried my best to push the past away. Was doing pretty good at it, too, until that brother of mine showed up."

She rested her hand on his collar and her face softened. "Some of your past is the sweet part you need to remember. Much of what you've done are things you need to seek forgiveness for and forget, never bring back to mind again. When you can do that, you will have a future. Raincloud wants her future to be your future."

"I want that too, very much."

She turned her head at the sound of Ed's voice.

"Raincloud," he groaned, "come cut me down. You got to show these people that I ain't lyin'."

Looking back at Julian, she lowered her voice. "He is my past. I must face my own past, or I will never have a future."

"You pull that man's fat out of the fire, and you're still gonna have a husband."

300

"Then, it is God's will. God chooses what is best for me and I must believe Him."

"But you ran away. That wasn't trusting."

She hung her head. "I know, but I did not run away to have him die, and I did not run away to love another man."

"And now you're just expecting me to stay here and look after your baby, while you walk up there and get yourself killed?"

"No, I take Sunflower with me."

Julian got to his feet and held out his .44. "Do you know how to use this?"

She nodded. "I know."

"Good, then, I'm just going to stick it behind you, in your belt. I'll follow you with my rifle. You get into the first sign of any trouble, you pull that thing up shooting, you hear?"

"I hear."

He shook his head and forced a smile. "Girl, what you don't know might just get you through. I can't convince you how much the odds are stacked against you, then, can I?"

"No," she shook her head, "you can't."

"You remind me of two boys I saw one time when I was a kid. They had two broomsticks and were trying to catch the big one in what was only a muddy puddle. I argued with them for quite a spell trying to convince them there just weren't no fish in there. The more I talked, the faster they fished. Finally I just walked on. When I looked back, they still hadn't caught a fish, but they were happy. You see, the way I figure it, they weren't fishing with broomsticks, they were fishing with hope. You can't fight that and a body shouldn't even try."

"I have hope in God, not in the puddle."

"We'll see."

Raincloud strapped Sunflower into her carrier and slung it onto her back. She took the revolver and placed it under her belt, behind her back. Julian watched her crouch low as she walked carefully up the creek. He jacked a round into the Winchester and walked softly behind her, stopping to watch the rocks overhead.

Moving to the edge of a large boulder, he watched Raincloud as she picked her way over the rocks, toward the sound of the plaintive cries up ahead. This was quite a woman, he knew that. She was willing to brave a river she knew nothing about, all on his say-so, risking herself and all that she loved for him. She was also willing

to look her past square in the face, even if it meant her own life. H
shook his head in disbelief.

+ + + + +

Johnson swung the big sweep back and forth, working it to keep
the ferry midstream. The riffles in the water had smoothed out
since they'd gone past the last set of dangerous currents. The walls
of the canyon climbed straight up into the morning sun, touching
the robin's-egg blue sky. "We got us a big drop just beyond this,"
Johnson called out. "You folks better get yerselves tied down. We
already come lots farther with this thing than I ever thought possible."

The Reverend Black smiled. "We've all come further in this life
than any of us thought possible."

The river took a swing to their left, following the drop of the
canyon. Its current moved steadily onward. The blackness of the
water showed no bottom. Stretching out before them, it snaked its
way around the towering, silent cliffs. Overhead, several birds
swung silently in the currents of the air, their wings outstretched
and motionless.

As the river bent back toward the right, they could hear the rapids ahead. The sudden noise, where there had once only been a
muted sound, made knuckles turn white. With each minute the
noise grew louder, until finally, they could see the boiling white
water ahead.

"There she is, folks," Johnson roared. "About a four- to six-foot
drop. Get yerselves a grip now. I'ma gonna try to take us straight
down the middle of this here thing. If we go up on one of them
rocks, be ready to climb this thing again. We'll have to move fast,
too. The way this river's running, it wouldn't take us long to flip
clean over. Then we'd all be in the water."

+ + + + +

Raincloud moved cautiously over the rocks. Many of them were
high and dry, and she tried to stay on them. To fall now would mean
a crying baby and a howling husband. She stepped around the curve
of the small stream, toward the cut of the steep canyon. Ahead, she
could see Ed.

He was tied to a tree, twisting at the bindings that held him secure. He bucked against the ropes harder when he spotted her, call-

ing out her name. "Raincloud, come quick, woman, come quick."

She spotted several shapes moving behind the rocks overhead. Disregarding them, she drew her knife and stepped quickly over the rocks toward Ed.

"Quick, woman, cut me loose."

Moving behind him, she glanced around and began to saw on the ropes. In moments, she had his wrists cut free.

As he rubbed his wrists hard, he spotted the revolver behind her and jerked it from her belt.

"Don't," she said. "Give me that."

He sent the back of his hand hard to her face, knocking her suddenly to the ground.

Sunflower began to scream, and movement in the brush made Ed whirl around to face whoever was coming down the trail.

Raincloud scooted away, backing up. She watched as three warriors ran through the brush down the trail.

Ed began to cock and fire the .44, too frightened to take careful aim. He missed his first three shots, but his fourth hit an attacking Indian in the shoulder, tossing the man to the ground.

From behind them, Julian's rifle boomed. A second Indian fell.

The third warrior stooped low and fired from the hip. The shot hit Ed like the kick of a mule, spilling him backward toward Raincloud and the still-screaming child.

Once again, Julian fired. The third warrior tumbled into the brush.

Julian ran to her side and picked up the revolver. He holstered it and, reaching down, pulled Raincloud to her feet. "Get going! Get back to the river! I'll be along. I'm gonna make sure they don't follow too closely." With that, he pulled out the .44 and shoved it into her hand. "Use this!"

Raincloud ran frantically down the rocky, watery trail that led back to the boat. Behind her, Julian began to fire at the cliffs and then back down the trail at anything he suspected of moving.

Minutes later, he ran to the rocks beside the river, where Raincloud had taken refuge. She held Sunflower close. "I am sorry. I almost got you killed. I should have just gone myself."

Julian swung the rifle's muzzle from side to side. His eye darted at the cliffs overhead, and he squeezed off a shot. He started to speak, but stopped himself.

She scooted close to him. "It was something I had to do. No matter what he was, he was my husband."

"Well, now you have no husband." He fired off a shot at the cliff beside them. "You just have yourself and that baby. If they decide to rush us, you won't have much to worry about."

"We should get in the boat and go," Raincloud said.

Julian kept his eye on the creek that flowed in front of them. "I wonder why they're not rushing us," he said.

Raincloud pulled hard on his shoulder. She shook it. Pointing up the river she said, "That is why they are not coming."

Julian looked and saw the ferry. It was a ways off, but coming on. "That little brother of mine! He shows up at the worst and the best times." Looking back at the cliffs overhead, he took another shot. "They want them in here so they can kill us all. Those people on that flat boat won't have anywhere to hide."

+ + + + +

Zac held the big rifle close to his shoulder.

"I'll try to edge us up a little," Johnson yelled.

Ruggles scooted back across the deck toward Zac. "We go gliding through there and we're gonna be meat on their table."

Zac nodded. "I'm sure that's what they want." He had already spotted a number of men crawling around the rocks above where the creek poured into the river. "They're up there, all right, up there and waiting for us."

Zac looked over the frightened group. "All right," he shouted, "we're gonna do the only thing we can. If we try to glide by there, they're gonna shoot some of us down. We're just too close. Everybody get in the water on the far side of the ferry. You'll have to tie a line to yourself and just hang on."

Peters growled, "Boy, I can't swim worth a lick. I don't mind dying, but I sure ain't got no hankerin' to be drowned."

Johnson smiled. "You won't drown, not here at least. There's plenty of places downriver where you can worry a-plenty about that."

Peters gulped. "Well, I thank you for that. You give a body plenty of cause to stay on dry ground."

The group scattered quickly around the deck and began to tie any amount of line they could find to themselves. They looped the rope underneath the cables that held the logs together.

Zac watched them as Ruggles made sure the knots were adequate. Zac turned to Johnson. "You got to go over the side too. You're the only one that knows this river. We lose you and we're all in trouble."

"*You're* in trouble?"

"Just go over the side when I tell you."

"You just betcha I will."

One by one, each member of the group slid into the cold water. They hung on tight to the lines and the slippery side of the ferry's deck. Zac crouched next to the lockbox and took careful aim. Setting the trigger on the Sharps, he held his breath and let it out slowly. The gentle squeeze on the trigger brought an explosion of the muzzle and sent an Indian falling down the face of the cliff. He turned to Johnson. "That ought to keep their heads down."

"Maybe so. But there's so many of them up there, that one gun of yours is gonna be kinda outnumbered when we put in."

"We just don't have many choices here."

"No, I reckon not."

Several minutes later, the ferry neared the place where the dory was on shore. The ferry glided toward the shore. Zac had fired several more shots, at least one of which had found its mark. He turned to Johnson. "Okay, you better tie that tiller off now and get over the side. They might not shoot too good, but as many of them as there appear to be, they might not have to."

Johnson tied the sweep into place, lashing it into position. He tipped the edge of his hat to Zac and jumped over the side.

Zac watched as Julian fired at the rocks overhead and then fired up the canyon at an unseen target.

Several shots bit into the surface of the raft, gouging chunks of wet wood. Zac took careful aim, scoring one more hit. He held the rifle and slipped over the side.

Moments later, the ferry hit the soft sand near where the creek came in. Zac looked at the men in the water by the ferry. "We got to get that dory and put it on top. Julian's got our rifles. Ruggles, you and Peters lay down some fire. The rest of you lift that dory and get it on top here. Now, untie yourselves and get ready to go."

He looked at Johnson. "You stay put right where you are."

"Okay by me."

Carol waved his hands frantically. "I'm not going there. I'm staying right here."

"You do what I say," Zac said. "You either do what I say, or I swear I'll leave you right here."

"You wouldn't!"

"Boy, you ain't never seen the things I wouldn't do. Now, you just go on out there with the rest of us and do what I say." He looked at the frightened group. The shots were flying overhead. "Now, let's go!"

As one, the group of men rounded the ferry and ran for the cover of the rocks where Julian and Raincloud were. They collapsed on the sand next to the beleaguered pair. Zac rolled over and faced Julian. "Where's the rifles?"

"Only got this one. Drago had one more in the boat." He paused and looked at Zac. "Little brother, you got a way of always turning up at either just the wrong or right time."

"At least I turn up. I ain't about to leave you like you did us."

Julian aimed and fired once again. "Got places to go, boy, and the gallows ain't one of them. I done told you that."

"Before we're finished with this mess you got us in, you may not see more than fifty yards down that river."

Julian aimed and fired again. "Boy, you just get to shooting. You're gonna talk me to death."

Zac looked back at the gathered men. "Ruggles, you grab that rifle when you get there. Me and this brother of mine will try to give you men cover. You all grab that dory there and put it on the ferry. When we get it on, it can give us some cover. We'll be needing it before we get too much farther downriver."

Reverend Black grinned. "Let's get on with it, then."

Zac looked at Julian. "You better load up. We'll be needing all the cartridges you can cram in there."

Moments later, when the two brothers had shouldered their weapons, Zac nodded and the two started shooting. The men ran for the dory and began to wrestle it into the water.

Julian looked over at Raincloud. "Run for it, girl. Get behind that ferryboat. I'll be along directly."

She ran for the vessel as the men heaved the dory onto the deck. The shots from above peppered the water near her. As the men hoisted the boat onto the ferry, one shot slammed squarely into Hec Peters' back. The man groaned and slipped into the river.

"Okay," Zac said, "it's our turn now."

The two of them backed slowly into the water and continued to

306

fire at the hills around them. When they reached the raft, they scooted around it and hung on. Ruggles had begun firing with the rifle from the dory.

"All right," Zac shouted, "push off! Let's get this thing off the shore."

Digging their heels into the soft sand, the group edged the big ferry into the current. It began to pick up speed. Minutes later, it was midstream. The shooting from the shore had stopped. One by one, each of the group began to cautiously crawl back on deck. They lay still, behind the dory.

"I would never have believed them to still be trailing us," Amy said. "That was very dangerous."

Johnson smiled. "Little lady, them rapids ahead are gonna make them injuns seem like child's play."

In front of them, they could see the first of the riffles in the water, and the body of Hec Peters drifting with the current. The group watched it bob through the rapids.

"He didn't drown," Zac said.

The tongue of deep water fanned into the first set of rapids. Beyond that, spanning the entire river, a drop of several feet allowed the water to flow into a series of foaming falls. Each seemed like the rest—high rocks that shouldered the pouring water and rushing currents that spilled onto the level below.

To the untrained eye, there was no difference between the channels, but Johnson pulled back hard on the sweep, edging the ferry to the left. Hitting the current that sped the boat into position, Johnson centered the sweep and tied it down. "You all better grab hold of something," he yelled.

Nearing the edge of the drop, they could see to the right of the river. Along all the other locations, drops of six to eight feet fell straight down to the river below. Any of these routes could have flipped them over. Below them, a three-foot spill poured into a pool of boiling water and then down once again the remaining three to four feet.

They grabbed the cables on the deck as the boat suddenly dropped beneath them.

CHAPTER 41

+ + + + + + +

South of Clear Creek Canyon
Tuesday, late afternoon

"Welcome to the Grand Canyon," Johnson shouted, "the place Major Powell called the great unknown."

The gorge was black and narrow. Near the bottom, red and gray rocks flared up into crags and angular peaks dotted the walls. The ferry silently glided over the water, its deep blue moving steadily onward. On their right, a clear creek poured down a series of red rocks, the shine of the afternoon sun glancing off the sparkling stream.

Johnson pointed to it. "Powell named that the Bright Angel Canyon."

Some distance below the creek, another series of rapids boiled, sending a mist into the air.

Black stared at the beautiful creek running down the distant rocks. "I can see why," he said. "It is like the footsteps of the angels leading straight up to heaven itself."

"It's beautiful," Amy exclaimed. "I never thought such a place existed on this earth."

Ruggles slipped his arm around her waist. "It's a fitting place for you, darling. One angel comes to meet the rest."

The calm water had given Raincloud a chance to feed the baby. She looked up at the beauty of the canyon. Beyond it, distant bluffs and a mistiness that showed the airborne haze of rapids to come riveted her eyes. "Sunflower and I will stop here. We will go no farther."

"There's a ways to go yet," Johnson said. "We got us some bad ones up ahead."

Raincloud looked around at the man and then at Julian, whose attention rested on her. "That is why we go no farther. The baby cannot continue through these bad waters."

"Where will you go?" Ruggles asked.

"We will stay here, then we will walk up the canyon. Indians can walk. We can walk."

Amy looked concerned. "What if that band of renegades followed us? They haven't stopped so far."

Raincloud was matter-of-fact. "It is better to be alone with the baby than with a group. If they did follow us, they will look for your boat, not for a woman alone with a child."

"Woman's got a point there," Johnson said. "I'da never thunk it possible fer them desert types to come all the way down here with us. Guess a man never knows. When we shove off from here, she just might be the safest one of us."

Carol spoke up. "Then, why don't we all stay right here? If it's dangerous up ahead, why not just stay?"

Zac busied himself with looping the lines into coils that were easy to reach. He spoke up, "Just like the lady said, alone she might have a chance. If we bunched ourselves together and they are following us, we'd be just exactly where they want us to be, on foot and outgunned."

"We'd better just move on come morning," Ruggles added.

Julian looked at Raincloud. "I think I should stay with the lady and her child and offer her some protection." His eye twinkled as he looked over at Zac. "After all, that would be the way of a Southern gentleman. Mother would want us to be chivalrous, now, wouldn't she, little brother?"

"I think we've had just about enough of you taking off on your own," Zac replied. "You're staying with me. If the lady wants off, that's her call. You don't have a call."

Julian dropped his hand next to his Russian .44. "You know, little brother, you're gonna press me too far. I've done my best to fight shy of a showdown with you direct-like, but I'm not sure you're gonna be satisfied with anything less."

Ruggles pushed his coat back, exposing his revolver. "The agent here has my backing. You try that, and you're gonna have to be mighty good to bring us both down."

"Now, boys," the preacher spoke up. "Brothers should be brothers. What you do when we get to safety will be up to the both of you, but for the sake of us all, we can't afford to lose either of you, let alone both."

"The man's right," Ruggles added.

The Reverend Black looked off at the bright stream cascading down the red rocks. "Now, why don't you boys just relax and enjoy the beauty of God's world. He placed this all here for us to enjoy, not just to be buried in."

As evening fell, they had finished a hot meal of fresh fish. Tommy had kept back a large one he couldn't bear to part with, just yet. The stream that tumbled down the rocks made a noise of bright laughter, its music echoing in the dark. The boy began to climb up the canyon wall barefoot, testing his footing with each step.

Amy got up and watched him anxiously. She stepped forward, out of the firelight and into the darkness. "Don't fall and hurt yourself," she called out.

Ruggles walked up behind her and placed his hands on her waist. "You've got to let the boy be a boy. No matter what you tell him, the way God made him is telling him something else on the inside. Now, just who do you think he's going to listen to?"

"I suppose you're right."

He grinned. "I make my living by being right. I was right about you, wasn't I?" He turned her around gently to face him.

"Yes, and I was wrong about you."

"Oh, I don't know. You may have been right about some things."

Leaning forward, he kissed her softly, lingering with his arms pulling her close. "Now, why don't we just follow him and make sure we're both there to pick up the pieces?"

She reeled for a moment, the touch of his lips on hers sending shivers up her spine. "Th-that sounds good," she stammered.

"Besides, it might be the only chance we get to be alone."

The boy climbed higher up the glittering creek as it tumbled noisily down the rocks. The moonlight bathed the redness of the stone with a soft, warm-looking hue. The spilling fresh water glowed with life in the semidarkness, a million diamonds of light winking at the nighttime sky.

Above them, a trail moved off to the left. It skirted the river's edge and offered a view of the Colorado at night that took their breath away. They watched as Tommy ran on ahead, darting behind boulders, trying to keep himself unseen.

"He's been so restless on that boat all day," Amy said.

Ruggles smiled. "I've been restless, too, so close to you and nothing I could do about it."

"Well, you did have your chance."

Ruggles took Amy by the wrist and turned her around. "I'm sorry," he said.

"Sorry about what?"

"I'm sorry I didn't do what the parson advised me to do—marry you, marry you right then and there. I just didn't think it was the right time or the right place, but now . . ."

"Now, what?"

He looked off at the river below them. "I can't think of a more beautiful place nor a better time."

"I'll still be here for you when we get down the river."

"Maybe so, but still."

"You were probably right," she said. "There seems to be so much to do just to survive that a honeymoon would be too distracting."

He put his hand to her cheek and ran his thumb over it. "You and me in many ways are the most chancey of pairs. I know we have so much in common—maybe that's why we're so unlikely. You know me and my kind all too well."

"Lawrence, you have no kind. You are in a place all by yourself. I am coming to know you and I love everything I know."

He hung his head slightly. "I guess I've just lived so much of this life, and yours seems to be all ahead of you."

"Thirteen years doesn't seem to be all that much difference," she said.

"I know. It's just that those are years I wish I'd spent growing up with you, years I'd rather not look back on."

"We can grow together the rest of our lives."

"None of us know how long that will be. I just want to spend what's left of mine with you, doing whatever it takes to make you happy."

"You make me happy right now, Lawrence."

"I suppose there have been times these last few days when I suspected that in years to come all I am going to be is just some sweet memory that visits you with a smile from time to time. Perhaps then when you think on me, you can feel warm inside and know that I loved you and that, wherever I am, I'm loving you still."

"Don't talk foolish."

Leaning over, he pressed his lips onto her forehead. "Darling, I hope I am being just foolish. Somehow though, foolishness and Lawrence Ruggles seem to be words that don't quite fit together. I've lived my life carefully watching and counting the odds." He looked down below at the dark, silent waters of the Colorado. "I suppose with what I've seen of this river, I don't think ours are none too promising."

She reached up and put her arms around his neck. "With you I feel protected. I've never felt safer and more secure in my life. There is no river and no danger that could make me feel insecure when I'm with you, Lawrence. You make me feel that way, just by watching you."

"You have so much life in you, Amy. I just hope that I'm not a passing shadow that touches and loves you and is gone with the morning sun. But if I am"—he glanced up at the night sky—"I want to enjoy these dark hours with you, a time when I can be the loving shadow in your memory."

"You're more than my memory, you're my future."

He smiled. "You've come a long way in a short time, girl."

"When I first saw you, I hated you. You were everything I had hated about men from my early memory: undependable, self-seeking, and without compromise. Still, I couldn't get you out of my mind. Even my mistrust of you kept you constantly in my thoughts, every second, every minute, every hour of the day. In the last few days my thinking has completely changed, but you're still filling my mind"—she shook her head from side to side—"filling it with beautiful thoughts of what it means to be a woman who is loved. I know I'm loved when I'm with you. Whenever I look at you, no matter what you're doing or saying, I know that in your heart you're saying all the while, 'Amy, I love you, Amy.' Those thoughts fill my heart, and I won't be without them, not ever."

"I'm just being myself, Amy."

"Yes, and isn't it strange? Last week when you were being yourself, I despised you. Now, all I can see is you telling me that you love me. All you have to do is stand there and the words come out silently."

He held her tightly and kissed her, pressing their lips together. Pulling back, he looked down the trail. "As much as I'd like to keep this up, we'd better find that brother of yours."

"Yes, I suppose we should."

The two of them moved down the moonlit trail, Ruggles walking ahead, his eyes peering through the darkness. The wound in his leg was healing well; still, it slowed him down and ached. Rounding a rock, he saw Tommy dancing in the moonlight. The boy spun like a top and laughed. Then, standing straight up, he waved his arms in the air, as if summoning the angels.

Ruggles stopped and held his hand back to Amy to stop her. There was something about the scene he didn't like. Tommy hadn't seen them, but he was performing as if he were being watched, being watched by someone Ruggles couldn't see. Ruggles reached under his coat and drew his revolver. He stepped forward.

Suddenly, a swift kick out of the night sent the six-gun spinning out of his hand and into the darkness.

"Ohhh, " Ruggles exclaimed.

"What's wrong?" Amy asked.

A man was on him in a moment, sending him sprawling to the ground.

"Run, Amy, run!" he yelled.

The big Indian rolled on the ground with him. Ruggles could smell the medicine in the bag tied around the man's neck—a big powerful man. It was a strong, pungent aroma, spices mixed with the smell of death. As they wrestled, Ruggles could see Tommy watching, unable or unwilling to move. "Run, boy," he yelled. "Run!"

The big Indian drew a knife and Ruggles grabbed his arm. "Who are you?" Ruggles shouted.

The big Indian was on top of him, pressing the knife down. "Mangus," the Indian growled, continuing to press the knife ever downward.

Ruggles strained with all his might. The man was strong, very strong. Rocking from side to side with the Indian on top of him, Ruggles turned over, throwing the man to the side.

Both of them were on their feet in a flash, Mangus circling him with the large, gleaming blade still in hand. Ruggles moved his bare hands in the air, ready to catch the man's blade if need be.

With the rapidity of a striking snake, Mangus flicked the knife at him, the first stab leaving a ribbon of blood down Ruggles's wrist. The gambler jumped back, grabbing his wounded limb.

Ruggles now circled, putting his back to the cliff. If Amy was going to run to the camp below, he wanted them to have a clear shot at the man when they arrived. The blood ran down his hand, warm between his fingers, warm and slippery. "Why are you here?" Ruggles asked. He was hoping to buy any time he could.

Mangus grunted. "A chief always scouts where his men should attack. I come to look for your people. We will not go home until you all are dead and your scalps are on our belt. We will kill you all, or I will die here."

Ruggles backed up to the cliff. "Look, we have nothing here that you want. The guns we have are few."

Mangus launched himself at Ruggles, head down, driving him into the cliff wall and sending his breath rushing out of him.

Ruggles could feel the life ebbing from him. He gasped for air.

With a swift strike, the blade rammed into his midsection. His eyes dulled. The night sky overhead spun around. It was a dull, numb feeling. He lay helpless, arms now limp by his side.

Mangus grabbed his hair and screamed into the night. It was a bone-chilling scream of a man's revenge, revenge not for anything Lawrence Ruggles had done, but for a thousand others just like him—for what they had done.

Suddenly, out of the night sky, a man clothed in white dropped on top of Mangus. The explosion of the impact sent the war chief tumbling over the ground. With fierce rage, the avenging angel drew his own blade and attacked the suddenly prone Mangus.

The two men wrestled, arm in arm. Kicking the man over, Mangus got to his feet. They ran at each other, clashing body against body, like two rams bent on proving their masculinity. Their bared knives flashed at their sides as they wrestled upright.

Ruggles's mind drifted with the loss of blood. He watched the struggle, blinking back the tears that until now had refused to fall. On the trail, he heard the men coming, heard the metallic sound of rounds being shoved into chambers.

The two men struggled next to the cliff. Mangus roared out words in a language only he could understand. With a powerful push, the man sent Mangus over the side of the cliff. He stood quietly and watched him fall into the river below.

Ruggles could make out the sound of Zac's voice. "Don't shoot, it's Chupta."

Ruggles closed his eyes. He felt himself being lifted and carried down the slippery slope.

Amy was at his side. "Lawrence, we're going to get you to camp. Don't die on me now, don't die. I need you."

The next thing he knew, he was by the fire. His shirt was being removed, and Zac pressed his stomach hard with a dry cloth. Amy held his hand.

Zac got to his feet and looked at Chupta. "I didn't think I'd see you again. Your job was finished."

"My work is finished now," he said. "I no good on boat. I take my horse and follow. My horse back up water canyon. I go now. They not follow you again. They choose new chief and go home."

"You did something that was neither required or expected. I respect you for that. I'd ride with you anywhere, anytime." Zac extended his hand to the man, but Chupta ignored it and walked off into the darkness.

The stars were fuzzy overhead as Ruggles struggled to see. Amy's face was close to him. "I love you," she said.

"I know you do," he whispered. "Is Tommy all right?"

"He's fine."

"You remember what I said."

She nodded.

"No matter where I am, I will always love you."

"You're going to be right here with me," she stammered.

"I'm going to be with you. I'll always be with you. I'm going to be a memory in your life darling, a memory that loves you."

CHAPTER 42

✦ ✦ ✦ ✦ ✦ ✦ ✦

Bright Angel Canyon
Wednesday morning, before dawn

The sound of the water as it lapped on the beach was like a thousand thirsty dogs gathered at a pool. It was the only sound that could be heard. The small group stood silently around the fresh mound that covered Lawrence Ruggles. This was a special man and all of them knew it. The Reverend Black had just concluded a recitation of the twenty-third Psalm. He clutched his small Bible tightly.

"This man touched all our lives. He was a man willing to sacrifice all that he was for those he loved. I came to know him these last few days. We had some quiet talks and even prayer together, and I for one would not bring him back from where he really is right now. Selfishly, we want him here. But he was selfless, and we should be too."

Amy stood next to him, quietly stifling the tears. Black put his arm around her. "Lawrence Ruggles will always be with us," he said. "It's fitting that we leave him here at the stairsteps of the angels."

Each of them stood staring at one another. They couldn't stay, they knew that. They had gotten up early in order to leave before the Indians that were trailing them could take revenge for their fallen leader, but now, each of them seemed hesitant to go. It was as if the next word spoken would break the spell of the moment, a spell that made them remember Lawrence Ruggles.

"I speck we better get movin', then," Johnson said.

Raincloud backed up to the dying coals of the fire. She dropped several branches into them. "Sunflower and I will stay."

Zac jerked the Russian .44 from Julian's holster and tossed the

316

revolver to Johnson. "The rest of us will be moving on now."

Julian backed up slightly and stared at him, hatred in his eye.

"We're going to leave the dory with the woman," Zac said. "I won't just abandon her here without her being able to change her mind."

"Boy, we're gonna need that there boat," Johnson said. "Like I done told you, I don't speck that ferry can make it all the way. It's hard enough on them little boats, and them cables that's holding us together has some give in 'em. I'm kinda wonderin' if we can make it down many more sets of them rapids, and the worst is still ahead of us."

"There's seven of us," Zac said, "and that dory can take only four. Now which three do you propose we throw in the river?"

Johnson shook his head and slipped the revolver behind his belt. "I dunno. I just reckoned that by the time we was really needin' that thing, there might just be only four of us left."

"Not if I can help it," Zac said. "I'm depending on you to help it, too. Now, let's unload that dory and leave it ready to go so the woman can use it in a hurry, if she has a mind to."

The men spent the next few minutes preparing the small boat. Julian took supplies and some dried food and carried them to Raincloud. He pulled her to her feet and then brought her close to him. He spoke in a low tone. "Good-bye for now, Princess. Don't worry about me. I'm gonna make it, and when I do, I'll come looking for you and the baby. No matter where you are, here or elsewhere, I'm gonna find you."

He kissed her softly and, turning, walked back to the group. "That's decent of you to leave her the boat," he said in an aside to Zac. "More gentlemanly and respectable than I gave you credit for." He locked his eye on Zac. "I think she ought to have a weapon, too."

Zac ignored the verbal jab. The idea of Julian setting himself up to judge another man's respectability seemed absurd on the surface. "She can have Ruggles's revolver," he said.

"Fine, I'll take it to her."

"No, I'll take it to her. You just get on the boat."

Minutes later, the ferry was once again sliding down the river and into the dark canyon. The faint light of approaching day would be a long time coming over the walls of the gorge. The light of the moon danced on the water, showing what little they could see of the rivulets of the swift current.

Black stood next to Amy. "Don't have any regrets, girl—he wouldn't have wanted that."

"I only wish we'd done just what you said the other day."

He put his arm around her. "I know you do, but, as usual, the man was thinking about you, not about himself. He wanted to marry you, Amy. Told me so himself. I don't think he saw himself as good enough for you, though. The man was a bachelor in his mind, always was. His independence was what he valued most, but you changed all that. I think for the first time in his life, he started to see himself as just a half of the whole."

Philip Carol watched the two of them talk. He'd said very little. Amy caught his eye, and he looked away. She knew there'd never been any love lost between the boy and Ruggles. Lawrence was like that. Someone who compared himself to the man always came out on the short end. The notion had galled Carol. What made her proud of Lawrence made Philip Carol ashamed.

Julian busied himself with twisting rope and inventorying supplies. Zac watched him closely. He thought he had seen him drop some dried beef and fruit down his shirt, but he couldn't be sure. One thing Zac knew, however—Julian needed watching closely. The man was like a caged tiger, seemingly passive, but very deadly.

When they had been small, there had always been a darkness about Julian before he struck, one that had tipped Zac off to an explosion in the works. As Julian got older, however, that all changed. It was as if his conscience had given up on all internal arguments. One minute he could be whistling a merry tune and making easy banter with a grin, and the next, a body might find himself reeling from a blow to the head.

Occasionally, Julian would glance up, as if keeping careful track of Zac's position on the boat. The farther downriver they got, the safer Zac would feel. From where they were now, Zac knew they were still much too close to where they had left Raincloud, a woman with a boat and a gun. Thinking back on it from the perspective of temptation for Julian, that had been a bad idea. It was the only thing he could have done, however. Abandoning a woman and child would have given him sleepless nights like nothing else would have.

Johnson pointed ahead to the dark, foaming water. "We got us a seven-foot drop up ahead," he called out. "It's gonna be a bad one. You folks get yerselves tied on."

+ + + + +

Raincloud rested for a while beside the river. She had laid two fish on the coals and now prepared to eat them. What she had could last her for some time, she knew that. Still, the freshness of the fish revived her. She pulled the gleaming white flesh from the small bones and crammed it into her mouth.

The noise of the stream running down the rocks behind her would mask all but the loudest of sounds. She knew if the men who had trailed them were to come, it would be at dawn. There were a few places where she might hide, but they would find her. To walk in the darkness now, up the trail they would be taking, would be foolish.

She looked at the still-sleeping baby. Sunflower was so very fragile. What would happen to her? Men in a war party would never stop to care for her. If they came, they would make sport of her and finally kill her. The baby would be left to die alone. It filled her heart with sadness. Perhaps to have stayed unloved in the desert was indeed better than to die in this place, alone and apart from the man she knew loved her. Why had she ever wanted a better life? God had put her where she had been. Was running away a sin? She didn't know. All she knew was that fighting the hand of God was wrong. God loved her and wanted her best. She should have trusted Him.

She lay down beside Sunflower but couldn't sleep. Her sin weighed heavy on her soul, making her restless as she wondered why she couldn't have just been content.

The night would be over very soon. Already, she saw the light in the valley beyond kiss the edges of the cliffs overhead. She hoped the Apache scout had been right. If these men had lost their chief, they would need to return home. Only if there were another man among them, one they respected, would they stay and fight on? Even then, they might go no farther, but they would at least come down the cliff to find out if they could kill the white-eyes at dawn.

She had been foolish to stay here. She knew that now. The river filled her heart with much fear. There would be no way for little Sunflower to survive in the midst of it. Several times they had almost been in the water, and if the things the man called Johnson had said were true, what chance would they have?

Reluctantly, she got to her feet. She would leave Sunflower sleeping here for the moment and go to keep watch. If she saw them, she could take the little boat.

Quietly, she waited beside the large rock that met the tumbling creek. This was a lonely place to be and a lonely place to die. Up ahead, she could see two birds dart between the trees. They flew from branch to branch, together. How she envied them, being together in the sky. Suddenly, they flew away. It was a sign, the sign she had been looking for. Men were coming. They were coming for her and little Sunflower.

Turning on her heels, she ran back to the beach.

Quickly, she scooped up the supplies the group had left her and placed them in the little boat. She would go a little farther down the river. It frightened her to be on the water alone, but to stay here now would be to kill both her and her daughter. She would go down the river, out of sight. If she could leave this place before the warriors came, they might go home.

As she gently picked up Sunflower, she hushed the baby. "Do not cry, little one. Mother will not let you die."

She pushed the boat out into the water and climbed in with the child. Nestling Sunflower between her legs, she paddled furiously into the darkness.

+ + + + +

The cables held fast, but their groaning through the vicious rapids had been apparent to everyone. After clearing the white-water surge, Johnson swung the big sweep, sending the craft into the slow-moving water near the shore's northern edge. "You see what I told you," he said. "There was something I didn't tell you, though."

"What?" Zac asked.

"When we went down this thing in them little boats that was cut out for it, we had to portage them things around some spots; otherwise, I wouldn't be here."

The entire group looked at him in silence.

"W-w-why didn't you t-t-t-tell us this b-b-b-b-before?" Carol asked, the nervous hitch in his voice growing more pronounced as he spoke.

"I did warn you. I warned you all. 'Sides, there just t'weren't much of a choice back at the ferry landing. It was the river or the scalpin' knife, fer as I could see."

"I didn't come down here to drown," Carol exclaimed.

Johnson went on. "So you can see, we ain't gonna finish up on this river in one piece. There just ain't no way we can heave this here ferryboat up on the dry land and carry it past them bad ones. Down below us, there's rapids that look like mountains, and drops that go ten to twelve feet or more. The woman back there was smart. I wouldn't have stayed where she did, what with them injuns and all, but she was smart, all the same."

"Then, we'll have to go as far as we can and walk out," Zac answered. He watched Julian carefully, knowing full well that with the prospects of leaving the river, Julian would be wanting to make his play as soon as possible. With Raincloud so close, he'd jump ship all the sooner. What Zac couldn't tell was what he himself would do if Julian took flight. It was one thing to take his own brother back to be tried and hung, but it was quite another to shoot him while he tried to escape. Would he do that? Was he even capable? He didn't know anymore.

The whirlpools and eddies twisted the ferry in circles, spinning it like a top suspended on a string. On either side of the boat, violent waves crashed, showering them with a constant spray of cold water. They shook in the emerging morning light, quivering and with teeth chattering. It was a miserable feeling. To have the beauty of the silent canyon all around and to be wet and petrified by fear showed the difference between what God could do and how tiny man was in comparison. The cliffs and towers God created were stable and calm, each seeming to look down on the helpless boat with quiet detachment. While they fought for their lives, the cliffs stood by, their shoulders holding up the sky overhead.

The sun shone brightly when they decided to pull into the nearest spot to eat. Shaking in their wet clothes, they tore off strips of dried beef and chewed with eagerness.

Julian edged up close to Zac. He seemed untouched by their circumstances, not shaking like the rest of the group. The man was hard. It was as if the blood that ran inside of him was colder than the chilly river water. "You figured out what you're gonna do?" he asked.

"About what?"

"About me."

"I figured that out back in the desert when I found out it was you I was chasing."

"Somehow, I don't think so. What would you do if I was to just walk off right now?"

321

"Watch you die." He lied about how he really felt but tried to make it sound convincing.

Julian's face hardened, then calmed—a cool, collected look at the brother he'd spent his early years with. "Somehow, I don't think you would. You may think all that toughness on the outside will serve you here like it has with everybody else you've gone up against, but I know better."

Zac remained calm while, on the inside, doubt raged. This was someone he'd admired growing up, someone he'd always wanted to be like. In many ways he was like him, hard and determined. The only thing he couldn't do that Julian seemed to practice with ease was to put on the show of a smile and then calmly do just the opposite. He knew, however, he couldn't let the shadow of a doubt come to the surface. To tell people his mind was something he'd never been known to do, and to do so now, with a potential adversary, would have been pure foolishness. Doubt was on his side and he wanted to keep it just that way. He pulled out his pipe and stuffed it with the whiskey tobacco mixture he carried. Unwrapping an oilcloth that protected his matches, he lit the mixture. "You used to know better, but not anymore," he said.

"Oh, you think so?" Julian smiled.

"You used to be different. You had things down deep inside that mattered. You had a sense of what was right and what was wrong. You're different now. You don't know up from down, and you shouldn't guess to think that you know me."

"I know Ma and Pa didn't raise their boys to kill each other."

"Don't be too sure about that." He puffed his pipe to life. "I knew men in the war that went up against their brothers wearing different-colored uniforms, and that didn't stop them from shooting. You knew stories like that too, and don't tell me otherwise."

"Maybe so, but it's one thing to shoot at a bunch of men in different clothes, and it's a horse of another color to shoot a man down at close range you grew up with, an unarmed man at that."

Zac smiled. "Now there's a picture, big brother, you helpless and unarmed! I wouldn't believe that for a gnat's heartbeat. If you don't have a weapon, it's only a matter of time until you get one. If you'd lost both arms, you'd just as soon kick and stomp a man to death as look at him."

"You ain't quite the innocent you used to be, are you?"

"No, I'm not. I've grown up quite a mite since I've been chasing scoundrels for a living. None of them can be trusted, except to stab you in the back when you turn it on them, especially you."

Julian put his hand on Zac's shoulder. "You got me pegged, don't you? Now, whatever happened to all that brotherly love and forgiveness you used to read about in the good book? You getting scarce on that?"

"You think this is easy for me? It's not. I loved you and I still do. The problem isn't my lack of love, it's your lack of conscience. That God of love you want to hide behind is a God of justice, too."

"And you've just gone and appointed yourself His servant in that regard, I take it?"

"No, I won't do that. I work for Wells Fargo. I'll let Him part out His justice when you see Him face-to-face, and you will."

"I suppose I will. 'Course, you want to make sure it's sooner rather than later."

"Sooner would be a whole lot easier on the good people that earn the money you steal and the men you kill in the taking of it."

"And just what makes you think I won't change?"

Zac paused. He looked down and then straight into Julian's eye. "Real change, big brother, is something you do when you want to, not when it suits you to say it."

"Well, I ain't never had no reason to change, but I think I got one now."

"And what would that be, going to your hanging?"

Julian motioned upstream. "No, it's that woman and baby back up that there river. I ain't never had a woman that cared enough about me to risk what she did for me. She's as true blue as I ever seen, and she loves me, I know she does."

"And you think the love of a woman can change somebody?"

"Yes, Ma always said it could. That gospel of hers and Pa's they'd always spout off with was about God's love changing the world one person at a time."

"All the change in the world won't bring the men you killed back to their wives and children, now, will it?"

Julian hung his head. "No, I suppose you're right there and I do feel a mite bad about that. I didn't before, but I'm starting to understand how important family really is, and right now, you're all of it I got left."

Zac shook his head. "I wish you'd thought about that before. Like I said, this is the hardest thing I've ever had to do."

"Maybe you'll think better about that. Love's a powerful thing, little brother, or ain't you found out about that yet?"

"I got a woman that loves me, one I'd be with now, if it weren't for you."

"Well then, little brother, I'd just get on back to her then. You got that payroll with you. You've done gone and done your job. All you got to do is leave it somewhere on the river and come back and pack it out. I won't stop you. You could just leave the rest of this business alone. The company would be plenty happy and you could sleep nights."

"I could?"

"Yes, you could. You wouldn't have to worry about what Ma would say if she were alive—you going ahead and spilling blood with your own brother."

"I wish it were that simple. If I did what you say, I'd have to turn a blind eye to what I believe about justice, just because you're my brother."

"You're a hardheaded rascal, just like Pa."

"You're more like him than me. Only thing is, he was honest."

"Well, you better be ready to shoot me, then, 'cause I'm gonna walk away."

Zac took Julian's hand off his shoulder. "I wouldn't have to shoot you. I'd take you down and hog-tie you to that boat of ours."

"Don't let this stub of mine fool you none, little brother. I'm a sack full of bobcats when I need to be."

CHAPTER 43

+ + + + + + +

Elves Chasm
Wednesday afternoon

The bright water cascaded down the black basalt, tumbling from pool to pool. The green haven of clear basins and sparkling water seemed like a series of wading pools for the angels. Just looking at them made the group on the ferry feel soothed and refreshed. Green ferns grew at the sides of the pools, and the sun bounced off their clear surface.

"Kinda pretty, ain't it?" Johnson asked.

All the while, Zac watched Julian carefully. With each mile covered, they were getting more distant from Raincloud. Zac could see his brother's impatience with each new stretch of river. The canyon walls were a prison for the man and Zac knew it.

Johnson went on. "Better enjoy the view whilst you can. About five miles on down, near as I recollect, we got us some ugly water and about a six- or seven-foot drop. It's gonna be peaceful fer a ways, though. This here river's like that, nice and calm one minute and sheer purgatory the next."

"Major Powell called this the great unknown?" Amy asked.

"Yessum, he sure 'nuff did—and it was, then. That was back in '69, though. Most folk these days just call it the river of no return."

"Why is that?" she asked.

"Guess 'cause few people ever make it through. 'Course, maybe it's 'cause those who do manage to get down it never want to return." He laughed. "'Course, here I is. I ain't no innocent, but I sure is a blame fool."

"We're still alive," Carol added.

"That we are, boy, leastwise fer a little bit yet."

"Life is a gift," Black said, "a gift from God." The preacher stared at the mossy backdrop behind the tumbling waterfalls. "And I'd say everything we see here is evidence that He makes His gift beautiful if we will just open our eyes and see."

Johnson began swinging the boom from side to side. "That it is, Parson, that it is."

"We don't have too much farther to go," Johnson said. "Maybe two days or better. We'll stop at Separation Canyon, that's where a group split off from Powell and us back in '69. The Howell brothers and Will Dunn just couldn't go no farther. They thought Powell was crazy to even try, and we thought they was touched to go off on their own. We give 'em two rifles and a shotgun, but they wouldn't take any of our rations."

He paused and looked at the cliffs. The ghosts of the man's memory were powerful and vivid. " 'Course, the cook left 'em some fresh biscuits. Lordy, I tell you, when we waved good-bye to them fellers, we thought they was fools and they thought the same about us."

Amy listened with interest. "Whatever happened to them?"

"Well, fact is, I'm here and they ain't."

A little more than an hour later, the water began to pick up speed. The cool, calm river was pulling them through the high walls of the canyon. Then with a sudden rush, waves of surging water took the craft—which until that point they had felt some control over—into a wild rush down the canyon and into the foaming waters ahead. Wave after wave rose up the smooth rocks on either side. The landlocked river had every appearance of a wild storm at sea, its dark water rising some five to six feet and then submerging into the dark water ahead. This raging sea, however, had blue skies overhead—blue skies and a rocky coastline on either side abruptly lifting to the sky. Death and destruction was unforgivingly only feet away from them.

The bow of the ferry rose in the water, sending the group sliding across its surface, only to fall again and scoot them along the deck. Underneath, the logs that held the deck in place groaned with the strain of the cables that bound them together.

Each of the group fought furiously to tie themselves to the cable. They might end up a group of corpses tied to debris, but it was the only chance they had to stay on the deck of the wildly racing vessel.

Julian worked at the knot. Watching Zac, he tied a slip knot that was easy to free himself from, and held on to the lines that ran along the length of the ferry.

"I'm throwing out a drown line," Johnson yelled. He tied several knots of white canvas onto several locations on a length of rope. "This might be something you can see." He looped the rope around the post that held the sweep secure and threw out the line. "If you go over, grabbin' on might be your only chance. This stretch is plenty dangerous. We're like children hangin' on to a wild mustang."

The curve of the canyon was sudden. It bent to the south, sending the water sweeping up the north side of the sheer, black walls. The whirlpool of black and white water spun the ferry into a series of wicked turns. The group watched as the canyon walls flashed before their eyes.

Johnson had pushed the sweep up out of the water. There would be no controlling this vessel, at least not now. To leave the sweep in the water was to risk snapping it off. They were completely in the grasp of the merciless river.

Up ahead, a series of boulders dotted the river. Water rushed around each immovable object. The largest of the boulders stood dead center in the river. Water rose up its face and over each side. Johnson quickly dipped the sweep back into the river and heaved back on it. Zac scrambled to his side. He held a grip on the big boom and launched himself backward, bringing his full weight to bear.

Slowly, the ferry edged its way into the stream of wild water to the south of the big rock. They hit the sudden surge of current and shot forward, passing only inches away from the obstruction. Down a two-foot drop, the craft was spat out on the other end into a wild eddy that once again sent the boat into a slow spin.

"We got us a seven- or eight-foot drop somewhere up ahead," Johnson yelled directly into Zac's ear. "The river drops and pours over that ledge like nothing you ever seed before."

Zac nodded.

The wild, raging torrent sent echoes up and down the steep canyon. There would be no holding back now. There would be no place to stop. This was a place of deep, dark water, a place to die.

Rolling over the mounds of watery blackness, the ferry slammed up and down, jarring every member of the group. The water-borne roller coaster ride sent them rising with each swell and cascading down the backside of each watery hill. There was no letup in the speed of the river. It surged as it pulled the boat, directing it like a wet missile.

Suddenly, a small canyon cut its way into the steeper canyon. A small creek sparkled as it dropped to the river below. Ferns and enamel-coated shoots gleamed in the sun.

Julian jerked his knot loose and Zac lunged at him, wrestling him to the deck of the ferry. "You're not leaving us again, not here, not now!"

Julian wrestled his legs underneath Zac, tumbling back to the rear of the boat. In an instant, they wobbled toward each other and grappled.

Zac grabbed for the man's good arm and hung on. Julian was like a tiger, a grimace on his face. He groaned and strained with all his might, shaking Zac to the deck.

Zac kicked violently, cutting Julian's legs out from under him.

Dancing to their feet, they braced themselves as the ferry rolled over a large wave. The boat slammed down on the river, sending them once again sprawling.

On hands and knees, they went at each other. The group fought to keep their distance from the brothers, watching as these two men struggled to get an upper hand. Wrestling to the deck, they rolled to the side. Julian pressed Zac's head over the side of the boat, the spray rooster-tailing a plume into the men's faces.

Zac heaved, holding the man away from him. He strained and braced his arms as Julian continued to press down on him. "Don't make me kill you, little brother!"

With a rush of strength, Zac turned Julian over to his side and pulled himself on top.

Julian rolled, sending Zac onto the lockbox on the other side of the deck.

Getting to their feet, the two men rushed each other and grappled in the middle of the deck. They held each other fast, moving their feet over the slippery surface. Straining against each other, they held on in a wet and cold embrace, their feet gliding and struggling for position, for any crack in the deck that might provide them with leverage.

Suddenly the boat dropped beneath them. The ferry went cascading down the sheer wall of falling water. Amy screamed as they plummeted over the waterfall.

In the water, Zac held Julian tight. Underneath the surface, the two of them fought for control, each struggling to gain mastery over the other, refusing to let go, spurning all notion of surrender. Zac felt his brother suddenly go limp and then released his grip.

Beneath the falling water, Zac felt the force of the cold torrent press him to the floor of the sudden shallowness. Bouncing against the rocky bottom, he struggled to surface. The force of the water held him underneath, refusing to let him come up. His lungs ached, straining for air; he was pinned underneath the falls, suspended by the force of the raging river.

He strained and kicked to move beyond the falls, pulling himself along the rocky bottom, his lungs feeling as though they were going to burst.

The mind was a funny thing. He knew that all too well. Many times he had wondered what thoughts would fill his mind if he knew he was going to die. He had faced death many times before, but never like this. Always before, he had been consumed with fighting an opponent. Death was something that was so swift in those situations, there would be no struggling against it. There would be no time to consider his thoughts. Now, as he fought it, his mind wandered.

He saw himself smiling now as a boy on his mother's lap, safe in her arms. He heard her say to him over and over, "Zachary, Jesus will help you, if you ask Him."

In his heart he prayed, "Jesus, help me, help me now."

Reaching his hand to the surface, it broke the water. The line Johnson had thrown was snaking along the surface, switching itself back and forth in the water. Zac felt it and latched on, pulling himself up. His head broke the crest of the whirlpool, and he held fast to the line. He gulped precious air, sending it roaring down into his lungs.

As suddenly as he had found the lifeline amidst the swirling water, he lost it. The line jerked itself from his grip, pulling him forward and then losing him in the watery confusion. He caught a glimpse of the big ferry and then was flattened by the fresh waves from the mountain of falling water behind him.

The group's screams sounded faint to him, their cries drowned out by wave after wave of surging river that carried him along its surface, bouncing him like a doll up and down and then sending him shooting ahead at great speed.

He swung around, remembering the warning about going down

the river headfirst. The rocks were upon him without warning. He pressed his feet into them and shoved out to free himself. Moving out into the main current, he raced forward, struggling with each breath to take in air. There was no control. To be in the river was to be abandoned.

He saw the ferry ahead. Amy and the Reverend Black were stooped over the side, working to manipulate the lifeline that waved along the top of the water. Grabbing for it, he held on.

They both pulled, joined by Carol and Johnson. Zac grappled with the rope and pulled hand over hand.

Moments later, he was at the edge of the ferry. The group wrestled him to the deck, and for what seemed like a spinning eternity, he lay there panting, unable to move. He spat water and gasped. "Where's Julian? Did he make it?"

Amy held his head. "I don't know. We thought we saw him for a moment, but then he disappeared."

"He was under that waterfall where you was," Johnson yelled, "but then we lost sight of him. There ain't no lookin' fer him now. If he's still in the water, he's long past caring. We might just be a-pickin' up his body when we stop farther on down. I wouldn't give a one-armed man much of a chance."

Zac sat up. "You don't know him like I do. He's as strong as a bear and he's got the will to live."

"You are too, boy, and you like to not have made it yer ownself."

"Man, you could have drowned," Carol said. "Why'd you do such a thing?" The young man was animated. Zac merely looked up at him.

"I've seen people dedicated to their work before, but nothing like that. My father is like that, but I don't think I'd ever want to be."

"You never do anything in life," Zac said, "unless you want it bad enough. That's my job and he's my brother."

In a matter of minutes, the ferry had rounded another bend in the river, a place where the swells subsided. The rapids had disappeared behind them and along with it, the small beach they had seen. In front of them, a strange sight greeted them. A formidable tower of stone rose in the middle of the river, its massive black, craggy surface rising over five hundred feet out of the water. "That there's Vulcan's Anvil," he said. "We got another three days of good river afore we hit the stuff we can't be getting around."

The monolith was unclimbable. It shadowed the river and

loomed like a misplaced mansion of rock. Birds swooped above its black, flattened top, and sparse vegetation dotted the surface.

"I think we've just about had enough for one day," Zac said. "Is there a place to put in?"

"Hell's Hollow is just about four miles farther on. We could stop there if you've a mind to."

Reverend Black stooped down next to Zac. "You worried about that brother of yours?"

Zac nodded.

"And you're blaming yourself, I take it."

"I should have just let him walk off."

"Son, forgiveness has a price to it. A body doesn't just throw it around all that freely. Most forgiveness that I've ever seen has been bought at a dear price. It cost our Lord His life, and it'll cost you something, too."

"I should have just let him walk off."

"Don't hold yourself to blame. What that man did with his life was never your making. It was his and his alone."

"I should have told him how much I loved him. I was just afraid to, afraid he'd try to take advantage."

"And he would have, too."

"Still, I owed that much to my ma and pa. He was their firstborn. There was a time when the sun rose and set on that brother of mine."

Black put his hand on Zac's shoulder. "You don't have to answer for him, he does. You did the best you could."

Zac turned his head back upriver, watching the water as it curled around the bend of sheer rock wall.

"You just expect to see him floating down behind us, don't you?"

"I'm not so sure of that."

"Well, chances are he'll be along directly. Then we'll have the sad task of burying him."

"Somehow I don't think we're going to see him. Maybe that's for the best."

"You don't think he drowned?"

"I'm not sure what to think. I do know this, the man's tougher than nails. If there was a way to make it out of there, Julian Cobb found it."

"Well, then, you can rest easy."

Zac looked up at the preacher. "Not hardly. Knowing him like I do, if he did make it, I'll more than likely be trying to chase him down next year this time. I just don't think the man can ever change. He is what he is."

+ + + + +

Several miles upstream, Raincloud held the baby between her legs and continued to paddle. Sunflower's crying had subsided into a shaking squall; the child had received little or no rest from the constant spray of water and the violent bouncing of the boat. What was left of the Yavapai were now safely behind her, but there seemed to be no place to stop and enjoy what little rest she might be able to find. She continued to stroke her paddle in the water, hoping against hope that she could catch the big boat up ahead of her. The dory was far more stable than the cumbersome ferry, but there was no rest from the furious white water.

The sun that had been overhead dipped behind the high canyon walls, chilling both her and the baby. Long shadows crossed the dark water up ahead. The dress she wore clung to her skin, and even the soft breeze seemed to knife through it and pierce straight through to her bones. The fierce paddling helped stave off the effects of the cold water, but she knew full well that there would be little hope for either of them if the rapids had their way.

She watched the foam gather on the water up ahead, water slapping itself with rugged violence and sending plumes of spray high into the air. She thought of Julian. He had wanted to stay with her. She knew his desire was genuine. He had wanted to protect her and Sunflower.

The man was hard, but she had been with hard men before. The Apache were hard. And they, too, had been betrayed and left with no hope. The taste of defeat was something that always coated their tongue. She could understand this white man with the hatred in his heart for the Yankee soldier, understand him better than most. She had seen something else in him, though; she had seen what she thought was the light of love break through the hardness of his heart, a love for her. It had been so very long since she had felt anything like it that she hadn't known what to make of it at first. Now, though, she had to find that feeling again. She had to find Julian, even if it meant following him to the white man's gallows.

CHAPTER 44

✦ ✦ ✦ ✦ ✦ ✦ ✦

The Colorado River
Saturday morning

Johnson pointed off to the south wall of the canyon. "That there's the Travertine Canyon. Don't let it fool you none, though. There ain't no climbing out of there; I've tried."

Dark shadows cut through the walls of the canyon and sweeping shapes of rocks looked like waves of granite, darkly multicolored and mixed with sunlight.

Tommy sat quietly on the deck. The peace of the river in contrast to what they'd all been through was a feeling to be savored, even for Tommy. The Reverend Black watched him closely. "Never seen that brother of yours so calm," he said.

"I know," Amy replied. "He just sits and watches the river. It's almost as if his soul has found some sort of rest that he never knew before."

"What about yours?" Black asked.

"I guess mine has, too. Lawrence Ruggles did that for me. I never really believed, you know. I didn't believe in God, and I didn't believe in people. I guess over the years I learned to trust in only the things I could see. Lawrence taught me to believe in what I could feel, too."

"And in God?"

"Yes, He's been with us every mile. I still haven't seen Him yet, but I've felt His presence."

Black smiled. He looked back at Tommy. "Perhaps that's what your brother feels in this place, the presence of God. I know I do."

The ferry gently bounced over a small set of rapids, and a brightly colored waterfall cascaded down the side of the cliffs and into the river. "That's Travertine Falls," Johnson said.

The erosion of the water on their soft sandstone surface had formed them into a forest of rock castles standing at the base of the waterfall. Their peaks were sharp and pointed, like blades of grass on the lawn of God.

"Separation Canyon's coming up," Johnson said. "That's about as far as we can go." He paused and looked up at the cliffs. He stared off as if by looking he might once again see his missing comrades, eyes staring back into time, searching for the faces of friends gone long ago.

Amy watched his faraway look. "How did they die?" she asked.

His eyes blinked, bringing him back into the present. "Who?" he asked.

"Your friends. I just thought that when you talked about that canyon, you were thinking of them. How did they die?"

"Injuns, we reckoned. We were sure we were being watched from time to time. Guess them boys just met up with them." Once again, he looked up at the cliffs. "It'll take us two days to climb outta here and maybe three days more to reach Needles. The railroad's there in Needles, a hotel too, and a mighty fine restaurant."

"That sounds like heaven," Amy responded.

Johnson laughed. "Far from it, little girl. It's about the closest thing to hell on this earth. There are times it gets to be a hundred and ten degrees."

✦ ✦ ✦ ✦ ✦

Needles, California
Late Thursday afternoon

It had taken the group the better part of an hour to clean up and meet at the Harvey House. Fred Harvey's restaurant sat near the tracks, next to the meandering Colorado River. Zac walked along the very hot, dusty street and into the large, savory-smelling dining room. He spotted the group at once, sitting next to the window, watching the river roll past them.

He walked up to their table. "Missing that river, are you?" He smiled.

"Not by a long shot," Carol blurted out.

Johnson sat back and poked at his steak. "I'll be back at Lee's Ferry in a little over a week, so there ain't no need to miss it very much. That old Colorado's been running through my veins since '69 with Powell. It sort of never leaves me alone, never far away."

"I do have some employment for you," Zac said.

The man blinked and then smiled. "You'll be wanting to go back for that payroll we buried in the canyon, won't you?"

"Yes, just wired Wells Fargo. They authorized me to hire you and three others, along with whatever it takes to bring the money in."

"Why three more?"

Reverend Black slouched forward, putting his elbows on the table. "You're going back for him, too, aren't you?"

Zac didn't answer. He looked through the window at the river. "That river's beautiful, but you can never tell about it."

"You are going back after him," Black said.

"He's dead," Amy said. "It won't do you any good to look for him now."

"I won't look hard," Zac replied. "I've seen all of that water I care to see. If that brother of mine is crazy enough to be along my path when I go get that payroll, then I'll bring him in. If he's gone, then I'll hear about how much or how little he really changes. If he did drown, then he has his judgment. I couldn't possibly add any more to that."

✦ ✦ ✦ ✦ ✦

The train platform at San Luis Obisbo, California
Ten days later

Jenny stood beside the platform as Zac threw his poncho over his arm and shouldered the Sharps. He smiled at her as he stepped down. A soft breeze blew in from the coast, carrying with it the aroma of the sea. The blue dress she wore was the color of a robin's egg; she casually brushed the strands of blond hair away from her face.

"I was sorry to hear about your brother," she said.

"Don't be," he frowned. "I'm afraid he got just what he deserved."

There were times when it was best not to ask questions, Jenny knew. If there was something he wanted her to know, he would come around to telling her. Waiting had never been a difficult thing for Jenny Hays to do. Her father had always told her that waiting for something was one of the best things a body could do in life. It placed value on a thing. She walked beside Zac and watched his face change from the frown at the thought of his brother to the kind of expression a man gave off when he was glad to be home.

"Skip's in school, I take it."

She nodded. "Just where he thought you'd want him."

His gait down the boardwalk was stiff from the long train ride. "I reckon he'd want to please me that way, but right now, I'd just as soon see him. The innocence in the boy's face might go a ways to taking the sting out of this trip."

She casually slipped her arm in his and patted it. "I know it was hard on you."

He nodded and kept his head down, as if staring off at a faraway place. "The bad thing about little boys, I reckon, is that they grow up to be men."

"Skip will never grow up to be someone like that brother of yours. There's too much kindness in him, and he wants to do the right thing."

Zac stared straight at her. There was an expression of pain in his eyes that she hadn't seen before. He looked like a little boy who had lost something precious, something that he could never find again. "Julian was just that way, at times. I remember him as someone I admired and wanted to grow up to be like. We both had the same Christian parents, people who prayed their hearts out for the both of us. That blasted war changed the both of us, but what it did to him was something I can't explain."

"A man still has to decide. Prayer won't force a man to do the right thing."

Zac's expression softened. He brushed her hair back. "And I reckon you've been praying a whole bunch for me, haven't you?"

"Yes, I have. I always do."

"And it hasn't forced me to do the right thing either, has it?"

She smiled softly. "It's done more than you can imagine. It's made you into a man who can talk to me about what you're feeling, and that was something I never expected. It also brought Skip into your life and gave you somebody to care about, somebody you had to protect and look after. You've come a long ways, Zachary Cobb."

"I guess I have, at that."

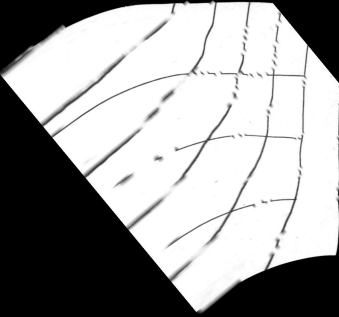

*In memory of Richard, Edward and the countless
others whose lives were a struggle with
addiction, and who never discovered
a spiritual path to recovery.*

*This book is especially dedicated
to those family members and
friends who have found the
courage to seek recovery.*

*In appreciation of the many individuals who
participated in researching and preparing the
materials used in this text. Their willingness
to participate and provide feedback was
a vital contribution to this book.*

NOTICE

This book is designed to provide information regarding the subject matter covered. It is provided with the understanding that the publisher and author are not engaged in rendering individualized professional services.

NOTE FROM THE PUBLISHER

Those who participated in the writing and review of this material are recovering Christian lay people and clergy. Their intention is to carry the message of the Twelve Steps and Christ's love to all hurting people. Central to the theme of this work is that healing is possible for those individuals whose childhood has been impacted by addictive or emotionally repressive parents or responsible adults. The talent and insight they brought to this book were founded in the belief that, through Scripture and the Twelve Steps, God's love and wisdom could restore hurting Christians to wholeness.

Their intention is to offer a workable tool for discovering one's own personal story of recovery. This has been achieved by incorporating the proven wisdom of Bible truths and the Twelve Steps as adapted from Alcoholics Anonymous. The material emphasizes self-understanding and the unchanging love of God for all humanity.

The philosophical foundation for this book is based on the Twelve Step concept that has helped hundreds of thousands of individuals recover from many forms of addictive, compulsive or obsessive behavior. The Twelve Traditions of Alcoholics Anonymous stress personal anonymity as a vital element in personal recovery. "Friends in Recovery" have chosen to remain anonymous to pursue their personal recovery.

As "Friends in Recovery," we place our confidence in the person of Jesus Christ, rather than in principles. We offer these materials, not as an end in themselves, but as a means to developing a healthy relationship with God and with others.

Table of Contents

IMPORTANT INFORMATION

Appendix One contains a suggested
meeting format for group study
and includes review questions
for each Step.

Appendix Two contains an overview
of *The Living Free Program,*
a Christ-centered recovery
ministry which includes
the use of this book.

THE TWELVE STEPS AND
YOUR SPIRITUAL PILGRIMAGE

The Twelve Steps is not a program sponsored by any particular religious group or entity. Though people using this program find it harmonious with their own personal theology and spiritual beliefs, it has no official religious affiliation. It is, however, a program that helps us to rediscover and deepen the spiritual part of ourselves and recognize its importance in our lives. We learn to live our lives according to the guidance of our Higher Power, God. We realize that the void or despair we have felt is caused by ignoring or rejecting our relationship with our Lord, Jesus Christ.

With God's power, The Twelve Step Program becomes an empowering tool to relieve our suffering, fill our emptiness, and help us extend God's presence in our lives. This will release great quantities of energy, love and joy, which we have never before known. It is a program that we follow at our own pace, in our own way, with God's help and the support of others who are in the Program. All we need is an open mind and a willingness to try. Much of the work will be done by God working through us. We will suddenly notice improvements in ourselves: our awareness, our sensitivity, our ability to love, to be free. We will often be surprised by our own spiritual and emotional growth.

The purpose of this book is to illustrate the Twelve Steps as a recovery tool, fully integrated as an ongoing part of our spiritual pilgrimage. The book uses Biblical insight to help us identify and deal with issues that are interfering with our lives. As we work through the problems, relying on the dynamics of the Twelve Steps, we will experience recovery that initiates physical, emotional and spiritual well-being.

Trust in God's guidance is necessary when reading the material. In this Program, it is important to realize that it is God's desire that we be returned to wholeness. He will give us the courage to work and struggle in order to succeed. Keeping a positive attitude will be very helpful in our recovery process. Negative thoughts can be damaging and will slow your progress. As we surrender to the process of working each Step, we realize we are in God's presence and our negative feelings are minimized. There is no right or wrong way to work the material. Timing will vary among individuals; however, each person will experience growth and change.

Reading this book can be used as a way out of self-destructive behavior, as well as an opportunity to learn new behavior. It provides an opportunity to experience feelings, enjoy new life one day at a time, and develop healthy relationships. Using this material with a group of people can be a powerful and transforming process. Loneliness will lessen as friendships develop. Individuals can learn to be close to others, by giving as well as receiving comfort and support.

The Twelve Step material used in this book is meant to be a framework upon which our own life experiences can be reviewed with love and courage. We realize we have reached this point knowing very little about ourselves. As we develop a deeper relationship with God, more will be disclosed to us. Slowly we will be given the strength to put the past behind us and build a new life. The depth of our relationship with God will be increased as our lives become less and less compromised. A commitment to work the Steps as a daily routine for the rest of our lives will provide us with the ongoing gift of peace and serenity.

Give freely of yourself and join us. We shall be with you in the Fellowship of God's Holy Spirit.

GOD BLESS YOU.

INTRODUCTION

The Twelve Steps for Christians is a comprehensive book that enables the user to gain an understanding of the spiritual power of the Twelve Steps when worked within a Christian perspective. This material is intended to reach those individuals who experienced trauma or some type of deprivation in childhood. The focus of this material is directed primarily to adults whose childhoods where traumatically affected by chemically dependent, violent, or other dysfunctional behaviors from the responsible adults. Since the founding of Alcoholics Anonymous in 1935, the Twelve Steps have become a way for many millions of people to change the course of their lives.

This book contains scriptural passages that illustrate the compatibility between the practice of Christianity and the working of the Twelve Steps. The material is not based on a creed or specific statements of faith from any particular denomination. Its goal is to provide an understanding of the Twelve Steps within a Biblical context. When used as intended, the Steps are profoundly powerful tools for allowing God to heal damaged emotions. This book constitutes a spiritual program that helps us regain balance and order, and leads us to full restoration of health and happiness through a renewed relationship with God.

The fact that God's plan for us is revealed in the Holy Scriptures is easily accepted by those of us who are Christians. Both mature Christians and those who are just being awakened to a personal relationship with God can find tremendous value in the Twelve Steps. By applying them to the events of one's life on a daily basis, they become an effective means for enriching one's relationship with God and allowing His plan for us to unfold. The Steps are especially powerful when used in conjunction with the regular Christian practices of prayer and Bible study. We will discover the unique ways in which the Holy Scriptures support and expand our understanding of the Steps.

The twelve-step process of recovery is a spiritual journey. It takes us from a life where we experience confusion and grief to one of peace and serenity. Many changes can and will come over us, but they won't necessarily happen all at once. The process takes time, and patience. God will, in His time, instill in us the strength of character that only comes from a healthy relationship with Him.

Commitment to recovery will be strengthened by our growing trust in ourselves and others. An important sign of recovery occurs when we become more open and communicative, and begin to value the counsel of others who are sharing this program of recovery. People who are participating in this program with us will become an important part of our lives. We will learn what open sharing can do for us when we become willing to reveal ourselves to others.

We may have many self-defeating habits or behaviors that need correcting. When looking at our methods of relating, it is important to remember the way in which these patterns began. Because of the chaotic conditions in which we were raised, we developed behaviors that now sabotage and assault the successful management of our lives as adults. Having grown up in emotionally repressive families, we became accustomed to denying our pain and discomfort. During our early years, most of us found it necessary to shut down our feelings and "keep everything locked inside." We learned in childhood that expressing our own wants and needs caused rejection. This rejection stimulated the growth of intense feelings of inadequacy. It seemed to us that, no matter how hard we tried, things always got worse.

As adults, we sometimes find it difficult to accept the reality of our pasts. This has kept us from seeing the disabling behaviors we have developed. In our present environments, we may experience pain, fear and rage that cannot be expressed freely. Repressing our true feelings is a result of our continuing to view our environment as we did in childhood. When we express our needs openly, we risk being rejected. Rather than risking rejection, many of us compensate for our repressed feelings by doing things to extremes.

Our behavior may range from being overly involved in work, over-eating or using mood-altering substances such as drugs and alcohol.

For many of us, denial has been a major tool for survival. Denial is a learned pattern of behavior and, as such, is incredibly cunning. We can consciously deny reality by telling a blatant lie to hide some truth about ourself or someone else. Conversely, we can be unaware of our denial by the secrets we keep from ourselves. Denial can block any and all reality from our minds. It cleverly protects us from realizing the consequences of our actions, because we simply do not acknowledge any responsibility for them. The power of denial is represented Biblically by Peter in his denial of Christ. It was less painful for Peter to deny that he was a follower of Christ than to face the consequences of admitting his relationship with Him. Peter's fear of recrimination and rebuke was stronger than his love for Jesus. In a similar way, we prefer to continue behavior that "saves face," rather than to acknowledge reality and accept the consequences of our actions. We find it easier to hide from our true feelings by being seemingly over-attentive to our families, our churches and our jobs. Staying busy allows us to ignore our true feelings, thereby denying them.

As we enter this program of recovery and begin to look honestly at ourselves, we see the damage that has resulted from our personal history of dysfunction. God has given us free will, which makes it possible for us to choose alternative ways of relating to the events in our lives and to those around us. It is important to set aside some of our childhood messages and begin the work of learning new behaviors that will better serve our highest good. Rather than filling our lives to overflowing with activities, we need time to be with our Lord in prayer and quietness. Through prayer and the competent exercise of our free will, we will learn to make healthier choices.

Our lives to this point are comprised of all of our experiences. We do not always know the extent of the damage that has been done to us or to others in our lives. The pain of remembering is simply too great. No matter how hard we try to forget their presence, these memories continue to be driving forces in our lives. Inappropriate behavior continues to surface, and we must learn that, in order to change it, we must accept the past and deal with it honestly.

Some of us have been taught to believe that, if we are Christians, our lives will "automatically" be in order, and we will experience peace and serenity. As reassuring as this may seem, it is rarely possible to find someone raised in a dysfunctional situation who does not experience some form of disabling behavior. For some, intense devotion to religion makes them feel guilty, because they know their lives are in turmoil.

For Christians who suffer from an addictive disease, or who are the product of a family with addictive traits, the Church's judgmental messages can be especially troublesome. They can keep a person from seeking recovery. To admit to imperfection might mean that we are not good Christians. However, as true recovery begins and the Twelve Steps are worked, we see that all of us need help, comfort and courage to face our problems.

As we become willing to admit our dysfunction to ourselves and others in recovery, we will see that this process is healing and rewarding. Our Christian walk will be enhanced by the fact that we stop the denial and become honest with ourselves and others. This alone will start an important phase of healing.

As we begin to acknowledge and even befriend our negative or repressed nature, we see, even as we stand in the sunlight, that we cast a "shadow." Standing before the Lord and seeking His guidance does not automatically relieve us of the burdens cast by our "shadow." However, we will find that by facing it squarely, with God's help, the darkness slowly diminishes as our strength and health return.

By diligently applying the material in this book, we will be able to reexamine our relationship with God and discover new ways in which He can empower our daily lives. We will learn to look fearlessly at our "shadow," and to accept our unwanted tendencies such as anger, inappropriate sexual behavior, hostility, or aggression.

Remember, this process includes inviting Jesus to help us redefine the limits we set for ourselves as we discover that "all things are possible for those who love the Lord."

This Twelve Step Program enables us to reclaim our birthright as children of God. We are created in God's image and have unlimited gifts available to us. The journey we are about to begin will awaken us to God's creation and give us an opportunity to experience peaceful and productive living. He will help us heal our damaged emotions. Feelings of unworthiness, anxiety and inferiority will disappear. Focusing on our new relationship with God will eliminate our obsessive need for other people's approval. Our attention will be captivated by the promise of the wonderful adventure calling us to a new life in Jesus Christ.

GOD BLESS YOU

THE TWELVE STEPS OF ALCOHOLICS ANONYMOUS

1. We admitted we were powerless over alcohol—that our lives had become unmanageable.

2. Came to believe that a Power greater than ourselves could restore us to sanity.

3. Made a decision to turn our will and our lives over to the care of God *as we understood Him.*

4. Made a searching and fearless moral inventory of ourselves.

5. Admitted to God, to ourselves, and to another human being the exact nature of our wrongs.

6. Were entirely ready to have God remove all these defects of character.

7. Humbly asked Him to remove our shortcomings.

8. Made a list of all persons we had harmed, and became willing to make amends to them all.

9. Made direct amends to such people wherever possible, except when to do so would injure them or others.

10. Continued to take personal inventory and when we were wrong promptly admitted it.

11. Sought through prayer and meditation to improve our conscious contact with God *as we understood Him,* praying only for knowledge of His will for us and the power to carry that out.

12. Having had a spiritual awakening as the result of these steps, we tried to carry this message to alcoholics, and to practice these principles in all our affairs.

THE TWELVE STEPS
AND RELATED SCRIPTURE

STEP ONE

We admitted we were powerless over the effects of our separation from God—that our lives had become unmanageable.

I know nothing good lives in me, that is, in my sinful nature. For I have the desire to do what is good, but I cannot carry it out. (ROMANS 7:18)

STEP TWO

Came to believe that a power greater than ourselves could restore us to sanity.

For it is God who works in you to will and to act according to his good purpose. (PHILIPPIANS 2:13)

STEP THREE

Made a decision to turn our will and our lives over to the care of God as we understood Him.

Therefore, I urge you, brothers, in view of God's mercy, to offer your bodies as living sacrifices, holy and pleasing to God—which is your spiritual worship. (ROMANS 12:1)

STEP FOUR

Made a searching and fearless moral inventory of ourselves.

Let us examine our ways and test them, and let us return to the Lord. (LAMENTATIONS 3:40)

STEP FIVE

Admitted to God, to ourselves, and to another human being the exact nature of our wrongs.

Therefore confess your sins to each other and pray for each other so that you may be healed. (JAMES 5:16A)

STEP SIX

Were entirely ready to have God remove all these defects of character.

Humble yourselves before the Lord, and he will lift you up. (JAMES 4:10)

STEP SEVEN

Humbly asked Him to remove our shortcomings.

If we confess our sins, he is faithful and just and will forgive us our sins and purify us from all unrighteousness. (1 JOHN 1:9)

STEP EIGHT

Made a list of all persons we had harmed and became willing to make amends to them all.

Do to others as you would have them do to you. (LUKE 6:31)

STEP NINE

Made direct amends to such people wherever possible, except when to do so would injure them or others.

Therefore, if you are offering your gift at the altar and there remember that your brother has something against you, leave your gift there in front of the altar. First go and be reconciled to your brother; then come and offer your gift. (MATTHEW 5:23-24)

STEP TEN

Continued to take personal inventory and, when we were wrong, promptly admitted it.

So, if you think you are standing firm, be careful that you don't fall. (1 CORINTHIANS 10:12)

STEP ELEVEN

Sought through prayer and meditation to improve our conscious contact with God as we understood Him, praying only for knowledge of His will for us and the power to carry that out.

Let the word of Christ dwell in you richly. (COLOSSIANS 3:16A)

STEP TWELVE

Having had a spiritual awakening as the result of these steps, we tried to carry this message to others, and to practice these principles in all our affairs.

Brothers, if someone is caught in a sin, you who are spiritual should restore him gently. But watch yourself, or you also may be tempted. (GALATIANS 6:1)

COMMON BEHAVIOR CHARACTERISTICS
OF ADULT CHILDREN

Research involving chemically dependent or emotionally repressed individuals and their families has determined that certain behavior characteristics are common in adult children from these homes. The behaviors reveal an underlying structure of disorder which is damaging to those involved. Although the general population demonstrates many of the behaviors, individuals from dysfunctional families tend to have a higher incidence of these characteristics. The following are intended to help you identify whether or not these are areas of your life in which dysfunctional behavior characteristics are evident.

■ We have feelings of low self-esteem that cause us to judge ourselves and others without mercy. We try to cover up or compensate by being perfectionistic, caretaking, controlling, contemptuous and gossipy.

■ We tend to isolate ourselves and to feel uneasy around other people, especially authority figures.

■ We are approval seekers and will do anything to make people like us. We are extremely loyal even in the face of evidence that indicates loyalty is undeserved.

■ We are intimidated by angry people and personal criticism. This causes us to feel anxious and overly sensitive.

■ We habitually choose to have relationships with emotionally unavailable people with addictive personalities. We are usually less attracted to healthy, caring people.

■ We live life as victims and are attracted to other victims in our love and friendship relationships. We confuse love with pity and tend to "love" people we can pity and rescue.

■ We are either super-responsible or super-irresponsible. We try to solve others' problems or expect others to be responsible for us. This enables us to avoid looking closely at our own behavior.

- We feel guilty when we stand up for ourselves or act assertively. We give in to others instead of taking care of ourselves.

- We deny, minimize, or repress our feelings from our traumatic childhoods. We lose the ability to express our feelings and are unaware of the impact this has on our lives.

- We are dependent personalities who are terrified of rejection or abandonment. We tend to stay in jobs or relationships that are harmful to us. Our fears can either stop us from ending hurtful relationships or prevent us from entering into healthy, rewarding ones.

- Denial, isolation, control and misplaced guilt are symptoms of family dysfunction. As a result of these behaviors, we feel hopeless and helpless.

- We have difficulty with intimate relationships. We feel insecure and lack trust in others. We don't have clearly defined boundaries and become enmeshed with our partner's needs and emotions.

- We have difficulty following projects through from beginning to end.

- We have a strong need to be in control. We over-react to change over which we have no control.

STEP ONE

We admitted we were powerless over the effects of our separation
from God—that our lives had become unmanageable.

I know that nothing good lives in me, that is,
in my sinful nature. For I have the desire to
do what is good, but I cannot carry it out.

(Romans 7:18)

❖ ❖ ❖

The ideas presented in Step One are overwhelming to most of us until we begin to see our lives as they really are. It is threatening to imagine that we could be powerless, and that our lives could be unmanageable. Our life experiences, however, remind us that our behavior does not always produce peace and serenity. Our background, if affected by alcohol or other types of family dysfunction, subverts our highest intentions, motivations and ambitions. In many cases, it has caused a separation from God. Although it is often not our intention, frequently our behavior is not what we want it to be.

We may have been taught to believe that all we have to do is accept Christ as our Lord and Savior for our lives to be complete and satisfying. This may have been the magic we relied upon to prepare us for the here and hereafter. Our proclamation that "I am born anew; the past is washed clean; I am a new creature; Christ has totally changed me" may be helping us to deny the actual condition of our lives. Grace in God's sight is achieved the moment we accept Christ into our lives. Achieving the condition of reconciliation, however, is an ongoing life-long process.

The fact that we still feel pain from our past is not a sign of a failed relationship with God, nor does it lessen the impact of salvation in our lives. This is simply a signal we need to continue the process of working the Steps and praying, looking to God to make the necessary changes. This acknowledgment may seem to be a contradiction of our strong claim to salvation, but it is not. The Bible is full of accounts of men and women who struggled continually to overcome past mistakes, the weaknesses of their human nature and life's many temptations.

The idea that there are areas of our lives over which we are powerless is a new concept for us. It is much easier for us to feel that we have power and are in control of our lives. Paul the Apostle, in his letter to the Church of Rome, describes his desperate powerlessness and the unmanageability of his life. He writes of his continued sinful behavior as a manifestation of his separation from God. (Romans 7:14) His acknowledgment of this does not interfere with his commitment to do God's will. Without knowing the details of Paul's background, we can only assume that his self-will was a detriment to his functioning effectively in his life. Because of our background, we function in much the same way as Paul did, allowing our self-will to work against us. We do have the power to choose to look to God, and exercising this choice will be enabled by our work in Step Two.

We live in a culture that places a high value on individual accomplishment. Most of us, from the time we were small children, were bombarded by the ideal of high achievement. Competition for grades, high achievement in sports and competitiveness in business are all viewed as the norm in our society. They are considered to be measures of success. We are taught that if we compete hard enough we will be "winners" and, therefore, good people. If, however, we fail to measure up to what is expected of us and are "losers," we will be bad people. Due to the absence of appropriate role models in childhood, many of us are confused as to where we fit in. We continue to allow our worth and self-esteem to be determined by what we do and what others think of us, and not by who we are in Christ. Looking back at our past, we may continue to classify ourselves as "losers," and to condition ourselves to fail. Our low self-esteem keeps us from becoming "winners." Living in this environment creates extreme stress and anxiety.

As we mature, matters get worse. The stressful lives we lead give us no satisfaction and compound the problems. Our fears and insecurities increase, creating a sense of panic. Some of us revert to abusing mood-altering substances such as drugs, alcohol, or food in order to relieve the tension resulting from our condition. In more subtle ways, we may bury ourselves in church activities, work, relationships, or other addictive/compulsive behaviors to try to combat the anxieties that exist in our lives. When we come to grips with ourselves and realize that our lives are just one big roller-coaster ride, we are ready for Step One. We have no alternative but to admit that we are powerless and that our lives have become unmanageable. When we begin to recognize the seriousness of our condition, it is important that we seek help.

Step One forms the foundation for working the other Steps. In this vital encounter with the circumstances of our lives, we admit our powerlessness and accept the unmanageability of our lives. Surrendering to this idea is not an easy thing to do. Although our behavior has caused us nothing but stress and pain, it is difficult to let go and trust that things will work out well. We may experience confusion, drowsiness, sadness, sleeplessness, or turmoil. These are normal responses to the severe inner struggles we are experiencing. It is important to remember that surrender requires great mental and emotional energy and determination.

❖ *Looking to Scripture* ❖

In Step One, we come to grips with the reality of our lives and ourselves. Perhaps for the first time, we finally admit defeat and recognize that we need help. In looking at Step One, we see it has two distinct parts: (1) the admission that we have obsessive traits and try to manipulate the affairs of our lives in order to ease the inner pain of separateness from God; that we are in the grip of an addictive process that has rendered us powerless over our behavior; and (2) the admission that our lives have been, and will continue to be, unmanageable if we insist on living by our own will.

> *I am worn out from groaning; all night long I flood my bed with weeping and drench my couch with tears. My eyes grow weak with sorrow; they fail because of all my foes.* (PSALM 6:6-7)
>
> *When we fall away from the plan God has for us, our despair, chaos and disorder can cause us to feel physically sick and may result in serious illness.*

Our instinct cries out against the idea of personal powerlessness and the fact that we are not in control. We have been accustomed to accepting full responsibility for all that happens in our lives as well as in the lives of others. Having been raised in a dysfunctional environment, it is natural for us to have some reaction. Some of us take on the role of being super-responsible while others of us withdraw and become super-irresponsible. Until we reach an intolerable threshold of pain, we will be unable to take the first step toward liberation and renewed strength. The fact that we are powerless is a truth we must realize before we can totally surrender.

> *This day I call heaven and earth as witnesses against you that I have set before you life and death, blessings and curses. Now choose life, so that you and your children may live and that you may love the LORD your God, listen to his voice, and hold fast to him.* (DEUTERONOMY 30:19-20)
>
> *We choose life when we become willing to look at ourselves and our lives honestly, and to seek the help we need for our healing to begin.*

As we begin to accept the reality of our condition, we naturally look to others for answers. We feel like timid spiritual beginners and wonder why the quality of life we were seeking has escaped us. Friends may tell us to read our Bible or "pray about it." Some may suggest we talk with our minister. No matter how many outside sources we seek, there will be no relief for us until we, by ourselves, in our own minds and hearts, acknowledge our powerlessness. Then, and only then, will we begin to see that Step One is the beginning of a way out.

The man who thinks he knows something does not yet know as he ought to know. (1 CORINTHIANS 8:2)

Convincing ourselves that our lives are working successfully is a form of denial that prevents us from seeing our condition as it really is.

Step One is not a once-and-for-all commitment. We must remember that our old traits, habits and behavior patterns are still with us. They are unconscious reactions to the common stresses of life. We must continually monitor our behavior and watch for the appearance of destructive tendencies. If we then admit our powerlessness and seek God's help, new courses of action will open up for us.

That day when evening came, he said to his disciples, "Let us go over to the other side." Leaving the crowd behind, they took him along, just as he was, in the boat... A furious squall came up, and the waves broke over the boat, so that it was nearly swamped. Jesus was in the stern, sleeping on a cushion. The disciples woke him and said to him, "Teacher, don't you care if we drown?"

He got up, rebuked the wind and said to the waves, "Quiet! Be still!" Then the wind died down and it was completely calm. He said to his disciples, "Why are you so afraid? Do you still have no faith?" They were terrified and asked each other, "Who is this? Even the wind and the waves obey him!" (MARK 4:35-41)

Lack of trust and fear of the unknown contribute to our feeling of powerlessness.

The second part of Step One, admitting that our lives are unmanageable, is equally as difficult as admitting that we are powerless. We can come to terms with this by continually observing all the things we have used in the past to hide the truth about ourselves. We need to be totally honest in order to drop the disguises and see things as they really are. When we stop finding excuses for our behavior, we will have taken the first step toward achieving the humility we need to accept spiritual guidance. It is through this spiritual guidance that we can begin to rebuild ourselves and our lives.

> *"I am the true vine and my Father is the gardener. He cuts off every branch in me that bears no fruit, while every branch that does bear fruit he trims clean so that it will be even more fruitful. You are already clean because of the word I have spoken to you. Remain in me, and I will remain in you. No branch can bear fruit by itself; it must remain in the vine. Neither can you bear fruit unless you remain in me.*
>
> *"I am the vine; you are the branches. If a man remains in me and I in him, he will bear much fruit; apart from me you can do nothing. If anyone does not remain in me, he is like a branch that is thrown away and withers; such branches are picked up, thrown into the fire and burned. If you remain in me and my words remain in you, ask whatever you wish, and it will be given you. This is to my Father's glory, that you bear much fruit, showing yourselves to be my disciples."* (JOHN 15:1-8)
>
> *Realizing that we have non-productive behaviors which damage our health helps us understand why and how our lives have become unmanageable.*

Just as the healing of a physical disease can only begin when we acknowledge the disease, so the spiritual healing of our obsessive/compulsive behavior begins when we acknowledge the existence of the problem. In Mark 10:51, it was obvious to others that Bartimaeus was blind. However, he had to openly ask Christ to heal his blindness. Until we realize this truth, our progress toward recovery will be blocked. Our healing begins when we are willing to acknowledge our problems.

> *When he came to his senses, he said, "How many of my father's hired men have food to spare, and here I am starving to death!"* (LUKE 15:17)

When we truly see the reality of our lives and acknowledge our need for help, we invite our Lord into our lives; then the healing process begins.

As we progress through the Steps, we will discover that true and lasting change does not happen by trying to alter our life conditions. Although it is tempting to think so, exterior adjustments cannot correct the problem that exists within us. Deep and profound healing requires surrendering the belief that we can heal our lives by manipulating our environment. Our willingness to work the Steps will enable us to begin our true healing, which must begin on the inside.

"I know that nothing good lives in me, that is, in my sinful nature. For I have the desire to do what is good, but I cannot carry it out. For what I do is not the good I want to do; no, the evil I do not want to do—this I keep on doing. Now if I do what I do not want to do, it is no longer I who do it, but it is sin living in me that does it." (ROMANS 7:18-20)

No matter how sincere our intentions, we are often powerless to change our behaviors.

As we work toward complete and ongoing recovery, we become aware that we are not alone. Our Lord has said He will not leave us comfortless. As we grow in faith, we will come to know His constant presence. To the degree that we desire to increase our spiritual strength, it will grow. Eternal vigilance is necessary so that we do not slip back into our old behaviors. Each day is a new opportunity to admit our powerlessness and our unmanageability.

But he said to me, "My grace is sufficient for you, for my power is made perfect in weakness." Therefore I will boast all the more gladly about my weaknesses, so that Christ's power may rest on me. That is why, for Christ's sake, I delight in weaknesses, in insults, in hardships, in persecutions, in difficulties. For when I am weak, then I am strong. (2 CORINTHIANS 12:9-10)

When we give up our struggle for control and put our lives into God's hands, we find His strength sufficient for every need.

As we begin our journey toward recovery by working the Twelve Steps, old truths will have new meaning for us. We will know what it means when we say we can never be separated from the love of God. Our faith in God, and our renewed emerging faith in ourselves and others, will sustain us as we experience the inevitable pain and suffering that our rigorous self-examination will cause. It is the only way out for us; the only way to a new life in Christ.

He who trusts in himself is a fool, but he who walks in wisdom is kept safe. (PROVERBS 28:26)

We cannot rely on our will alone; we also must rely on the strength of God working through us.

STEP TWO

*Came to believe that a power greater than ourselves
could restore us to sanity.*

*For it is God who works in you to will and
to act according to his good purpose.*

(Philippians 2:13)

❖ ❖ ❖

Having come to grips with the fact that we are powerless
and our lives are unmanageable, our next step is to acknowledge the existence of a Power greater than ourselves. Believing
in God does not always mean that we accept His Power. As Christians, we know God, but do not necessarily invite His Power into
our lives. In Step Two, we have an opportunity to experience
God in a different light. As Jesus asserted in John 14:26, the
Holy Spirit will be sent in His name, to teach us and remind us
of all He has taught. Here we begin to re-establish our relationship,
or, establish a relationship with God for the first time. The purpose
of this Step is to show us that He is a Power greater than ourselves
and a vital part of our daily lives.

For many of us, this Step presents major problems. The aloneness
of our present condition demands that we depend on our own
resources. We do not trust ourselves or others. We may even
doubt that God can heal us or, indeed, even be interested in doing
so. Unless we let go of our distrust and begin to lean on God,
we will continue to operate in an insane manner. The chaos and
confusion of our lives will only increase.

Depending on our religious background, some of us may have
been taught that God is an authority to be feared. We have never
come to know Him as a loving God. As children, we were very
anxious and fearful of doing something wrong. The threat of being
punished by God was used by adults to control our childish behavior.
Our fear of displeasing God magnified our growing sense of guilt

11

and shame. As adults, we continue to fear people in authority and are often overcome by guilt and shame for simple misdeeds.

We still may be harboring childhood anger at God because He disappointed us many times. Due to the severity of our experiences, some of us have rejected God because He did not give us relief from our pain. Despite our conviction that God is with us, in moments of fear we doubt His presence. Even those who are coming to terms with their problems, and are in contact with their Higher Power, experience moments of doubt. In Step Two, our goal is to fully accept the presence and guidance of God, in order to begin the journey to peace and serenity.

For some of us, belief in self-will and our ability to manage our own lives is all we have. We perceive God as a crutch for children and weak-willed individuals who are incapable of managing their own lives. As we begin to see the true nature of God, a weight is lifted from our shoulders, and we begin to view life from a different perspective.

One of the great paradoxes of Christianity is that man is never completely free until he has become totally submissive. In John 8:32, Jesus made a promise when he said, *"You shall know the truth and the truth shall make you free."* In this Step, we begin to recognize that God does, in fact, have the power and intention to alter the course of our lives. In the scriptures, we are assured of God's presence within us. We are shown beyond all doubt that through Him all things are possible. If we have accepted the truth regarding our condition and are ready to surrender to our Higher Power, we are well on our way to ultimate submission and true spiritual freedom.

Step Two is referred to as the Hope Step. It gives us new hope as we begin to see that help is available to us if we simply reach out and accept what Jesus Christ, our Higher Power, has to offer. It is here that we form the foundation for growth of our spiritual life, which will help us become the person we want to be. All that is required of us is a willingness to believe that a Power greater than ourselves is waiting to be our personal savior. What follows as we proceed through the Steps is a process that will bring this Power into our lives and enable us to grow in love, health and grace.

❖ *Looking to Scripture* ❖

Coming to believe in a Power greater than ourselves requires faith. In the past, we have placed our faith in our own abilities to run our lives, and that faith has proven worthless. It was misplaced and could never have done for us what we thought it would. Now we need to actively place our faith in Jesus Christ. (Romans 10:8-10) At first, it may seem unrealistic to place our faith in a Power we cannot see or touch. Yet the very existence of our universe in all its glory gives ample evidence of the true power, love and majesty of the God we seek.

Immediately Jesus made the disciples get into the boat and go on ahead of him to the other side, while he dismissed the crowd. After he had dismissed them, he went up into the hills by himself to pray. When evening came, he was there alone, but the boat was already a considerable distance from land, buffeted by the waves because the wind was against it. During the fourth watch of the night Jesus went out to them, walking on the lake. When the disciples saw him walking on the lake, they were terrified. "It's a ghost," they said, and cried out in fear. But Jesus immediately said to them: "Take courage! It is I. Don't be afraid." "Lord, if it's you," Peter replied, "tell me to come to you on the water." "Come," he said. Then Peter got down out of the boat and walked on the water to Jesus. But when he saw the wind, he was afraid and, beginning to sink, cried out, "Lord, save me!" Immediately Jesus reached out his hand and caught him. "You of little faith," he said, "why did you doubt?" And when they climbed into the boat, the wind died down. Then those who were in the boat worshiped him, saying, "Truly you are the Son of God." (MATTHEW 14:22-34)

Relying on a Power greater than ourselves will give us confidence and hope.

Faith grows through practice. Each time we state a conviction and prove it by our actions, our faith becomes stronger. Every time we ask Christ, our Higher Power, for help, we will receive it, and our faith will be strengthened. We will finally accept the fact that He is dependable and will never leave us. All we need to do is ask for help and trust in His Power.

He replied, "Because you have so little faith. I tell you the truth, if you have faith as small as a mustard seed, you can say to this mountain, 'Move from here to there' and it will move. Nothing will be impossible for you."
(MATTHEW 17:20)

With our smallest first step to God, we will experience the comfort He has promised us.

"'If you can'?" said Jesus. "Everything is possible for him who believes." Immediately the boy's father exclaimed, "I do believe; help me overcome my unbelief!"
(MARK 9:23-24)

Regardless of our past struggles, we must realize that God's power, not our own, ensures our success.

One of the greatest secrets of learning to have faith is found in the joyful revelation that the Spirit of God is always available. His greatest desire is that He might share that kind of relationship with us. He can and will be as close to us as we allow Him to be.

The LORD is close to the brokenhearted and saves those who are crushed in spirit. A righteous man may have many troubles, but the LORD delivers him from them all; he protects all his bones, not one of them will be broken. Evil will slay the wicked; the foe of the righteous will be condemned. The LORD redeems his servants; no one who takes refuge in him will be condemned. (PSALM 34:18-22)

Even though we have rejected Him in the past, God will always be close to us and mend our broken spirit.

As we develop a relationship with Jesus Christ as our Higher Power, we begin to rely on Him to help us become aware of the extent of our disabling condition. Step Two implies that we are insane. The dictionary defines insanity as "inability to manage one's own affairs and perform one's social duties . . . without recognition of one's own illness." In this sense, we can see our behavior as insane. We still may be blaming everyone and everything for our condition instead of taking responsibility for our own behavior.

Indeed, in our hearts we felt the sentence of death. But this happened that we might not rely on ourselves but on God, who raises the dead. (2 CORINTHIANS 1:9)

However desperate we may be, God's power will relieve our depression and lead us to a new life.

Because of our traumatic childhood experiences, we have become defiant, indifferent, resentful, self-deluded and self-centered. These conditions indicate that our lives need to be restored to a more balanced state. We can do this if we are willing to believe that a Power greater than ourselves can restore us to sanity. If we attempt to do it alone, we easily can deceive ourselves by looking to outside sources for the causes of our disability. With the help of Christ, we will heal these deceitful behaviors.

For it is God who works in you to will and to act according to his good purpose. (PHILIPPIANS 2:13)

God can restore us to wholeness and free us from the hurt and pain of our past.

One of the ways in which Christ helps us see our condition clearly is by bringing us into contact with others who have had experiences similar to ours. It becomes evident, when sharing our stories, that each of us can maintain "emotional sobriety" only one day at a time. We soon see that all worry, depression, compulsions and obsessions are unhealthy. The fact that we ever believed we could control ourselves without help from our Higher Power was insane. He helps us realize that actions which are destructive to ourselves or to others are not acceptable. As we become more dependent on our Higher Power, the quality of our lives will improve.

Not that we are competent...to claim anything for ourselves, but our competence comes from God.
(2 CORINTHIANS 3:5)

If we trust Him, our Lord will lead us out of the despair we feel when we recognize the dysfunction in our lives.

When we started this program, we may have been expecting instant results. From our childhood, we remember feeling anger or confusion when things didn't happen "right now." In this program, sudden change is the exception, not the rule. It requires patience and perseverance to achieve the recovery we seek. Each of us is unique, and recovery begins for each of us at different stages in the Steps. Some of us may experience instant relief, whereas others may not begin to feel stronger until later in the Program. There is no rule or guideline. Your progress will occur at the appropriate time for you.

Do you not know? Have you not heard? The LORD is the everlasting God, the Creator of the ends of the earth. He will not grow tired or weary, and his understanding no one can fathom. He gives strength to the weary and increases the power of the weak. Even youths grow tired and weary, and young men stumble and fall; but those who hope in the LORD will renew their strength. They will soar on wings like eagles; they will run and not grow weary, they will walk and not be faint. (ISAIAH 40:28-31)

16

We must work to set aside our impatience and frustration, believing that God will give us sufficient strength to meet our needs.

Step Two promises a restoration to sanity. Allowing this state of mind to unfold requires humility. Humility grows within a gentle and nurturing character, without pride and aggressiveness. For most of us, lack of humility contributed to our present situation. Developing humility is a recurrent theme of the Program. We become humble as we are slowly able to relinquish our pride. In Philippians 2:5 we are told, *"Your attitude should be the same as that of Christ Jesus."*

For I am convinced that neither death nor life, neither angels nor demons, ... neither height nor depth, nor anything else in all creation, will be able to separate us from the love of God that is in Christ Jesus our Lord.
(ROMANS 8:38-39)

Neither our pride nor any evil can put us beyond the reach of God's love for us.

When we become ready to accept fully our powerlessness and unmanageability (Step One), when we accept Jesus Christ, our Higher Power, and our insanity (Step Two), we will be ready to take action and turn our lives over to the care of God (Step Three). There is no need to rush the process of working the Steps. The important thing is to heed the Bible's admonition *"the hour has come for you to wake up from your slumber."* (ROMANS 13:11) Move forward in faith so you will be able to proceed with the remaining Steps.

So do not fear, for I am with you; do not be dismayed, for I am your God. I will strengthen and help you; I will uphold you with my righteous right hand. (ISAIAH 41:10)

Our deepening spiritual strength reminds us of God's constant presence in our lives.

For God so loved the world that he gave his one and only Son, that whoever believes in him shall not perish but have eternal life. For God did not send his Son into the world to condemn the world, but to save the world through him. (JOHN 3:16-17)

Seen in the light of God's love, the Twelve Steps are a pathway to our salvation.

STEP THREE

Made a decision to turn our will and our lives over to the care of God as we understood Him.

Therefore, I urge you, brothers, in view of God's mercy, to offer your bodies as living sacrifices, holy and pleasing to God—this is your spiritual act of worship.

(Romans 12:1)

❖ ❖ ❖

Step Three is the central theme of all the Steps. It is the point at which we make a decision to turn our will and our lives over to the care of God. Step Three is an important cornerstone for building an effective and peaceful life. In Steps One and Two we established the basis for turning our lives over to the care of God. The commitment we now make in Step Three must be repeated more than once, for actually we are just beginning to turn things over to God. Repeated working of the first three Steps helps to build a solid foundation for working the total program.

Many of us come to this program with strong negative perceptions about the world in which we live. They may be based on hurtful childhood experiences, unprincipled academic training, or simply the accumulated lessons of our lives. As a result of other experiences from our past, we may have understood God to be unloving and judgmental. Whatever the source, our recovery is hindered if our beliefs make it difficult to let go of our fear and surrender our lives to God. If we have experienced extreme violence as children, we may be resistant to risk trusting anyone or anything—even God. In Step Three, we decide to take the leap of faith and put our lives in His hands.

Biblical figures often resisted following God's will. The Bible illustrates some examples of doing God's will when it didn't make any sense. Yet, the end result demonstrated it was wise to follow God's guidance. Acts of faith are exemplified by Moses leading the Jewish people out of the wilderness; by Abraham's willingness to sacrifice his son Isaac. Also, despite criticism of his contemporaries, Noah built the ark. The essence of these actions is summarized in HEBREWS 11:6; *"And without faith it is impossible to please God, because anyone who comes to Him must believe that He exists and that He rewards those who earnestly seek Him."*

Until now, our inaccurate perceptions of reality have led us into many compulsive/obsessive behaviors. Admitting our responsibility for these dysfunctions is too difficult. It implies that we have not been "good people." Denial is our only recourse. Our denial acts as a shield against confronting ourselves as we really are. When denial is at work, it is like a shuttered window, closing out the sunlight. In Step Three, we begin the process of opening the shutters and allowing the light to enter. Our trust in God is a source of light with which we can examine our behavior.

Step Three is an affirmative step. It is time to make a decision. In the first two Steps, we became aware of our condition and accepted the idea of a Power greater than ourselves. Although we began to know and trust Him, we may find it difficult to think of allowing God to be totally in charge of our lives. However, if the alternative is facing the loss of something critical to our existence, such as family, job, health, or sanity, God's guidance might be easier to accept. Right now our lives may have many beautiful and rewarding relationships which are being ruined by our addictive/compulsive behavior. We must not be discouraged by these discoveries. Our healing work continues in Step Four where we identify our dysfunctions. Remember, it takes relentless courage to search out our weaknesses and turn everything over to God for healing.

As we begin to allow God's will to act in our lives, our self-destructive tendencies become weaker and much less distracting. Often, the confusion and grief we cause ourselves and others prevent us from successfully working and practicing the Steps. Making the decision to begin this journey to health is an act of great importance and should not be made in a time of emotional upheaval. Turning our lives over means consciously relinquishing our destructive self-will and our compulsive behaviors, as well as our talents, potentialities, skills and ambitions. The key elements here are making the decision with a clear and rational mind, being committed to that decision and, finally, trusting the outcome to God.

As we surrender our lives and stop carrying the burdens of our past, we will begin to feel better about ourselves. The more we learn to trust in the Lord, the more we will trust ourselves and extend that trust to others. Our decision to choose God's way will restore us to fullness of life. As we free ourselves from our negative behaviors, we will deal more effectively with the daily routine of our lives. Our impatience and irritability disappear as we come to know His love and yearn to share it with others. Our lives transform into a lived-out relationship with God, and we will become the persons He meant for us to be—workers in His kingdom.

❖ *Looking to Scripture* ❖

In Step Three, we make an important decision. It is time to acknowledge our need for God's presence in our lives, and to give ourselves to Him. We make the decision to surrender our lives to God. He becomes our new manager, and we accept life on His terms. He offers us a way to live that is free from the emotional pollution of our past, thereby allowing us to enjoy new and wonderful experiences. Step Three provides us with an opportunity to turn away from behavior that fosters addiction, discouragement, sickness and fear.

Trust in the LORD with all your heart and lean not on your own understanding; in all your ways acknowledge him, and he will make your paths straight. (PROVERBS 3:5-6)

When we trust in the Lord and not in ourselves, His guidance will straighten our path.

> *Teach me to do your will, for you are my God; may your good Spirit lead me on level ground.* (PSALM 143:10-11)
>
> *The guidance of the Holy Spirit will bring us peace.*

Many of us begin this Step Three process by deciding to turn over only certain parts of our lives. We are willing to surrender the most difficult problems when we see they are making our lives unmanageable. We cling to other areas of our lives because we think we can manage them. We eventually realize that we cannot barter with God. We must be prepared to surrender our entire will and every part of our lives to His care in order to recover. When we are truly able to accept this fact, our journey to wholeness has begun.

> *Therefore, I urge you, brothers, in view of God's mercy, to offer your bodies as living sacrifices, holy and pleasing to God—this is your spiritual act of worship.* (ROMANS 12:1)
>
> *Surrendering our will and turning our lives over to God's care will relieve our stress and anxiety.*

Step Three may make us feel we are losing our identity. We may feel we are going to lose everything. Not knowing what is going to happen is frightening. Most of us have tried desperately to control our environment. Many of these behavior traits were developed during childhood and came about as a direct result of the atmosphere in which we were raised. Deep within us may be a fearful and trembling child, anxious about someone's anger, criticism, threats, or violence. As children, we tried to fix or take care of the people around us so they would not abandon us, leaving only broken promises and shattered dreams.

> *Yet to all who received him, to those who believed in his name, he gave the right to become children of God— children born not of natural descent, nor of human decision or a husband's will, but born of God.* (JOHN 1:12-13)

Our childhood relationship with God is still an influence we must deal with in learning to trust that our true Father is God.

The conditions in which we were raised often kept us from ever having trust in God. Our prayers may have been unanswered, and we could not imagine how a loving God could be so cruel to us. Step Three is an opportunity to start over. As we work the Steps and get in touch with the forgotten child within us, we see that God's healing love will repair the damage that has been done. Jesus told us that we must become like children to enter the Kingdom of God. This statement helps us recognize that a childlike state will enable us to regain our capacity to give and receive unconditonal love. With this in mind, we can look forward to getting in touch with the child within us, who so desperately wants to give and receive love and nurturing.

"Come to me, all you who are weary and burdened, and I will give you rest. Take my yoke upon you and learn from me, for I am gentle and humble in heart, and you will find rest for your souls. For my yoke is easy and my burden is light." (MATTHEW 11:28-30)

The Lord wants us to give Him the burdens of guilt and shame we have carried with us since childhood.

Learning to trust in God and accept His support will enhance greatly the quality of our lives. We will no longer feel the need to carry our burdens by ourselves. Much of the pain of our past is a result of feeling totally alone. With His presence, our sense of self-esteem will improve, and we will begin to recognize that we are worthwhile human beings. Our capacity to receive and give love will increase, and we will come to place great value on fellowship and sharing.

It is better to take refuge in the LORD than to trust in man. It is better to take refuge in the LORD than to trust in princes. (PSALM 118:8-9)

> *Our growing trust in God will give us courage to extend love to ourselves and others.*

Christ exemplifies "turning it over" by acceptance of the will of His Father, which led to the Cross and the victory of resurrection. During His life on earth, Jesus' love for us led him into constant confrontations with the forces of evil. He was strong and steadfast because He placed His trust in His Heavenly Father. We, too, will be strong in the face of trial and temptation because we know that God, our Heavenly Father, will never abandon us.

> *Going a little farther, he fell with his face to the ground and prayed, "My Father, if it is possible, may this cup be taken from me. Yet not as I will, but as you will."*
> (MATTHEW 26:39)
>
> *Whatever trials we face, we are not alone; we are one with God, whose love always triumphs over evil.*

In this life, we also have crosses to bear. Some of us still may be experiencing the powerful impact of our history of disabling behavior. Whatever our addiction may be—drugs, destructive relationships, sex, alcohol, money, or food—we face the possibility of spiritual as well as physical death. As we turn away from these temptations, we accept God's offer to cast our burdens upon Him.

> *I have been crucified with Christ and I no longer live, but Christ lives in me. The life I live in the body, I live by faith in the Son of God, who loved me and gave himself for me.*
> (GALATIANS 2:20)
>
> *When Christ lives in us, we can acknowledge and defeat temptation.*

It is important to remember that, as we practice Step Three on a daily basis, we will see a change come over us. We will be calmer, and will no longer feel responsible for everything and everybody. Peace and serenity will come to us in measures never before experienced. Our eyes will be opened, and we will have a fresh start in life. We will become increasingly aware that God is guiding us. People around us may notice that we have become more confident and trustworthy.

Commit to the LORD whatever you do, and your plans will succeed. (PROVERBS 16:3)

God leads us to victory over the trials of this life, so that we may be perfect in His sight.

No matter how far we progress in recovery, we must continually turn our lives over to the care of God and be vigilant. It is foolish for us not to anticipate relapses. We need only to recognize this, and to be willing to work the Program on a daily basis. It is especially important to continue to practice Step Three. Our willingness to trust in God ensures our victory.

I tell you the truth, anyone who has faith in me will do what I have been doing. He will do even greater things than these, because I am going to the Father. And I will do whatever you ask in my name, so that the Son may bring glory to the Father. (JOHN 14:12-13)

The improvements we begin to see in our lives are the first fruits of the goodness God has in store for us.

"For I know the plans I have for you," declares the LORD, "plans to prosper you and not to harm you, plans to give you hope and a future. Then you will call upon me and come and pray to me, and I will listen to you. You will seek me and find me when you seek me with all your heart. I will be found by you," declares the LORD.
(JEREMIAH 29:11-14)

When working Step Three, we discover the depth of God's love for us and understand that through Him all things are possible.

The path you are about to take has been walked by countless thousands of people seeking to experience peace, serenity and companionship with the Lord. Our daily task is to continually ask God for guidance. We receive Christ by personal invitation. "Here I am! I stand at the door and knock. If anyone hears my voice and opens the door, I will come in and eat with him, and he with me." (REVELATIONS 3:20)

Reciting the following prayer can strengthen us in our daily walk.

STEP THREE PRAYER

Lord Jesus, I turn my life over to you,
to mold me and do with me as you will.
Trusting that you guide my steps,
I enter the world with hope;
that I may better do your will.
I welcome your Holy Spirit's Power, Love
and Guidance in everything I do."
Amen.

STEP FOUR

Made a searching and fearless moral inventory of ourselves.

*Let us examine our ways and test
them, and let us return to the Lord.*
(Lamentations 3:40)

❖ ❖ ❖

Step Four begins the growth steps of our journey. Here, we examine our behavior and expand our understanding of ourselves. The adventure of self-discovery begins with Step Four and continues through Step Seven. During this time, we will prepare a personal inventory, discuss it with others in the Program and invite God to remove our shortcomings. Being totally honest in preparing our inventory is vital to the self-discovery that forms the foundation of our recovery. It allows us to remove the obstacles that have prevented us from knowing ourselves and truthfully acknowledging our deepest feelings about life.

Step Four helps us get in touch with our "shadow," that part of us which we have hidden away for so long—our repressed nature. In the process of making our inventory, we will develop and broaden our understanding of our behavior. We will see that our "shadow" is an integral part of our nature and must be accepted by us. This part of our nature hides our resentments, fears and other repressed feelings. As we reveal ourselves, our acceptance of our whole character will free us to discover that these behaviors, begun in childhood, provided us with the means of survival. In the context of our turbulent early years, these behaviors were life-saving; but their continuation into our adulthood renders us dysfunctional.

Denial is a key survival skill that we learned early in childhood. It stunted our emotional growth by keeping us in a make-believe world. We often fantasized that our situation was better than it really was. Denial protected us from our feelings and helped us repress the pain of our family environment. Our shame and guilt caused us to be silent, rather than be honest and face the fear of being ridiculed by others. This withdrawal hindered us from developing into mature, emotionally healthy adults. As our self-discovery unfolds, we begin to recognize the role that denial has played in our lives. This realization is the basis for our acceptance of the truth of our personal history.

Resentment and fear are two issues that need to be dealt with before we begin the process of preparing our inventory. Our resentment toward people, places and things that have injured us keeps us preoccupied and limits our ability to live in the present moment. Resentment results from hiding the bitter hurts that have tarnished our lives. It evokes anger, frustration and depression. When our resentments are unresolved, we risk developing severe physical and mental illnesses.

Fear limits our ability to be rational. When fear is present, it is difficult to see situations in their true perspective. Fear is the root of other repressive and painful feelings. It prevents us from expressing ourselves honestly and stops us from responding in appropriate ways to threatening situations. In order to change our behavior, we must first face and accept our fears. By acknowledging our fearful nature, we can expect a temporary loss of self-esteem, which will return as we become more willing to rely on God.

Preparing our inventory requires that we look to God for guidance. Having renewed our relationship in Steps Two and Three, we now ask God for help. We will be looking closely at our personal histories and acknowledge what we see there. Remembering that God is with us will make this task much easier. With God's help, we can courageously review our strengths and our weaknesses. As the process unfolds, we will begin to recognize the need for change.

Step Four gives us the opportunity to recognize that certain skills, acquired in childhood, may be inappropriate in our adult lives. Blaming others for our misfortunes, disclaiming responsibility for hurtful behavior and resisting the truth are behavior patterns we must discard. These certain learned behaviors were developed early in life and have become character defects. Looking at them now can be extremely troublesome. Painful memories may return, and we will remember things that we had thought were forgotten. Our willingness to be honest about what we uncover will give us the clarity of mind that is vital for our complete recovery.

Putting our thoughts on paper is valuable and necessary when completing Step Four. The process of writing focuses our wandering thoughts and allows us to concentrate on what is really happening. It often causes repressed feelings to surface and gives us a deeper understanding of ourselves and our behavior. Making our fearless moral inventory provides insights regarding our strengths and weaknesses. Rather than judge ourselves, we need to accept whatever we discover, knowing that this discovery is merely another step toward a healthy life. Successful completion of Step Four requires us to be honest and thorough. With God's help, and our personal courage, we can expect to receive limitless benefits.

❖ *Looking to Scripture* ❖

Denial stems from our childhood environment, which we were unable to control. This was our reaction to the confusion, instability and violence of the care-taking adults around us. We rationalized what was happening and invented acceptable reasons for their unacceptable behavior. By doing this, we ignored the chaos and denied the insurmountable problems. As we matured, our denial continued to protect us from the need to face reality and helped us hide behind our delusions and fantasies.

"The heart is deceitful above all things and beyond cure. Who can understand it? " "I the Lord search the heart and examine the mind, to reward a man according to his conduct, according to what his deeds deserve."
(JEREMIAH 17:9-10)

Attempting to survive the chaos by denying its existence fosters deceit and illusion.

The power of denial is illustrated in the Bible when Peter denies Christ. Because of his great love for Him, Peter thought it inconceivable that he could deny Christ. However, when Peter was confronted with the situation, it was easier for him to deny Christ than it was to admit being a follower and face the consequences. When Peter realized what he had done, he was devastated. In much the same way, when we realize what denial has done to us, we will experience feelings of self-hatred, which need to be acknowledged and resolved.

While Peter was below in the courtyard, one of the servant girls of the high priest came by. When she saw Peter warming himself, she looked closely at him. "You also were with that Nazarene, Jesus," she said. But he denied it. "I don't know or understand what you're talking about," he said, and went out into the entryway. When the servant girl saw him there, she said again to those standing around, "this fellow is one of them." Again he denied it. After a little while, those standing near said to Peter, "Surely you are one of them, for you are a Galilean." He began to call down curses on himself, and swore to them, "I don't know this man you're talking about." Immediately the rooster crowed the second time. Then Peter remembered the word Jesus had spoken to him: "Before the rooster crows twice you will disown me three times." And he broke down and wept. (MARK 14:66-72)

When we fear the consequences of telling the truth, we are inclined to tell lies.

Denial has many faces and can be easily masked. It appears in different ways and operates in various fashions. Some recognizable forms are:

- **Simple Denial:** Pretending that something does not exist when it really does (e.g., ignoring physical symptoms that may indicate the presence of problems).

- **Minimizing:** Being willing to acknowledge a problem, but unwilling to see its severity (e.g., admitting to estrangement in a relationship when in fact there is overt infidelity).

- **Blaming:** Placing blame on someone else for causing the problem; the behavior is not denied, but its cause is someone else's fault (e.g., blaming your parents for your current inappropriate behavior).

- **Excusing:** Offering excuses, alibis, justifications and other explanations for our own or others' behavior (e.g., calling in sick for a partner when the actual cause of the absence is drunkenness).

- **Generalizing:** Dealing with problems on a general level, but avoiding personal and emotional awareness of the situation or conditions (e.g., sympathizing with a friend's flu symptoms when you know chemical dependency is the underlying cause of the problem).

- **Dodging:** Changing the subject to avoid threatening topics (e.g., becoming adept at "small talk").

- **Attacking:** Becoming angry and irritable when reference is made to the existing condition, thus avoiding the issue (e.g., being unwilling to share your feelings).

If anyone thinks he is something when he is nothing, he deceives himself. Each one should test his own actions. Then he can take pride in himself, without comparing himself to somebody else, for each one should carry his own load. (GALATIANS 6:3-5)

Our pride can limit our capacity to be honest and is a critical element in making our searching and fearless moral inventory.

Taking a personal inventory is similar to cleaning a closet. We take stock of what we have, examine what we want to save and discard what is no longer useful or appropriate. It doesn't have to be done all at once, but it will have to be done eventually. If we take small sections at a time, the cleaning is more thorough and the long-term results are better. In the same way that clothes can trigger memories of the past, our inventory may provoke both good and bad memories. We must remember that the past is only history. It is not the purpose of our inventory to dwell on the past. This reflection is only a tool to help us understand our current behavior patterns. Our main concern now is for our future. Approaching the inventory in this manner can lessen our fears surrounding this task.

Let us examine our ways and test them, and let us return to the LORD. (LAMENTATIONS 3:40)

Personal examination of our lives will give us insight into the ways in which we have turned away from God and become self-destructive.

In Step Four, we will get in touch with many of the behaviors and attitudes that have been with us since childhood. Our emerging awareness about the way we were raised will help us understand that our present behaviors are natural outgrowths of our early need to survive. As adults, we are now in a position to choose a different lifestyle for ourselves. We can learn to conduct ourselves in a manner that is nurturing to us. As we look at our strengths and weaknesses, we will become aware of the areas of our lives that need to be strengthened. We will also see those areas in which we exhibit strength through our wise choices. We can use the inventory to decide which areas of our lives need changing, and which areas seem to be the way we want them to be.

Search me, O God, and know my heart; test me and know my anxious thoughts. See if there is any offensive way in me, and lead me in the way everlasting. (PSALM 139:23-24)

We extend our trust in God by asking Him to be part of our process of self-discovery.

Our next task is to look at resentment and recognize how damaging it is to us. It is the "number-one" offender and often the major cause of spiritual disease. As we list our resentments, we see how they have affected our self-esteem, our well-being and our personal relationships. Holding on to resentment causes stress, anxiety and uncontrollable feelings of anger. If these are unresolved, serious emotional and physical consequences will develop. If we allow our resentments to prevail, serious depression can develop and ultimately destroy us.

My dear brothers, take note of this: Everyone should be quick to listen, slow to speak and slow to become angry, for man's anger does not bring about the righteous life that God desires. Therefore, get rid of all moral filth and the evil that is so prevalent, and humbly accept the word planted in you, which can save you. (JAMES 1:19-21)

Resentment and anger keep us focused on the person or situation precipitating the negative feelings and prevent our accepting God's promise of healing.

The second most destructive offender is fear. It is the emotion we most strongly feel when we begin to look at ourselves. When fear is present, our need to deny, ignore and avoid reality is increased. Our unrealistic perspective becomes greatly exaggerated and intensifies our emotional responses. Fear can cause us a great deal of pain. It attacks us physically and causes feelings that range from apprehension to panic. When fear is present, we may become nervous, nauseated or disoriented. As we inventory our fears, we may discover that they are a direct result of our inability to make decisions. Or we may believe that, if we could make the right decisions, things would be different.

There is no fear in love. But perfect love drives out fear, because fear has to do with punishment. The one who fears is not made perfect in love. (1 JOHN 4:18)

The guilt and shame we feel about our past behaviors may inhibit our ability to conduct a thorough inventory. God's love for us will remove our fear.

Facing our resentments and fears requires a great deal of courage. Our past tendency has been to shut down our feelings. Now we begin to look at areas of our lives that we have never seen before. It is important to realize that God is with us and will help us every step of our way. As Christians, we have the added support of knowing that the Lord understands and shares our struggle. With God's help and understanding, the pain will diminish.

> *Examine yourselves to see whether you are in the faith; test yourselves. Do you not realize that Christ Jesus is in you —unless, of course, you fail the test? And I trust that you will discover that we have not failed the test.*
> (2 CORINTHIANS 13:5-6)
>
> *Our faith grows as we examine ourselves and see how Jesus Christ is present in our lives.*

As part of the Step Four inventory, we will look at our character traits and see our strengths and weaknesses. Our strengths appear in behavior that has positive effects on us as well as on others. Our weaknesses are manifested in behavior that is destructive to ourselves and others. Before we can correct our problem areas, we need to acknowledge and examine both. Understanding begins when we discover how we became the people we are— how we formulated the ideas, beliefs and attitudes that govern how we act.

> *Get rid of all bitterness, rage and anger, brawling and slander, along with every form of malice.*
> (EPHESIANS 4:31)
>
> *Unexpressed feelings will contaminate the peace and serenity for which we strive.*

When preparing your inventory, you may encounter some difficulties. If you appear to be blocked at some point, denial may be operating. Stop for a moment and reflect on what you are attempting to do. Take time to analyze your feelings. Ask God for help. In times like this, God's presence means a great deal to us, and we must be willing to look to God for support.

I remember my affliction and my wandering, the bitterness and the gall. I well remember them, and my soul is downcast within me. Yet this I call to mind and therefore I have hope: Because of the LORD'S great love we are not consumed, for his compassions never fail.
(LAMENTATIONS 3:19-22)

God's love will lead us through the darkness of the past and into the light of a new life.

Blessed is the man who perseveres under trial, because when he has stood the test, he will receive the crown of life that God has promised to those who love him.
(JAMES 1:12)

Our courage grows as we complete our personal inventory and triumph over the temptation to avoid facing the truth of our past.

The inventory we are preparing is for our own benefit. It will help us make a major breakthrough in our self-acceptance and lead us further along the road to recovery. As we proceed to Steps Five, Six and Seven, we will see the process continue to unfold. We will acknowledge the truth about ourselves, discuss it with others and, finally, ask God to remove our shortcomings.

Put to death, therefore, whatever belongs to your earthly nature: sexual immorality, impurity, lust, evil desires and greed, which is idolatry. Because of these, the wrath of God is coming. You used to walk in these ways, in the life you once lived. But now you must rid yourselves of all such things as these: anger, rage, malice, slander, and filthy language from your lips. (COLOSSIANS 3:5-8)

Our Fourth Step inventory will help us realize how far we have strayed from God's way. It is our first step toward putting the past to rest.

IMPORTANT GUIDELINES IN PREPARING YOUR INVENTORY

The material offered in this Step Four Inventory Guide is somewhat different from the inventory guides used in other Twelve Step Programs. Emphasis is on those feelings and behaviors most commonly found in Adult Children from homes where alcohol-related or other damage-inducing behavior was prevalent. When preparing your inventory, choose the traits that specifically apply to you. Don't tackle them all at once. Use recent events and record words and actions as accurately as possible. Take your time. It's better to be thorough with some than incomplete with all.

The inventory begins with exercises on resentment and fears, followed by a series of feelings and behaviors to be examined. This process enables you to prepare yourself for Step Five. You are the primary beneficiary of your honesty and thoroughness in this inventory.

It is important to refrain from generalizing. As you will note in the example provided for "Isolation," being specific helps identify active traits. When you list specific examples, include who, when, where, what. To the best of your ability, give the names of all persons involved in the situation with you (who); record the date the behavior took place (when); indicate the place where this behavior occurred (where); and, finally, describe the feeling or behavior.

RESENTMENT AND FEAR EXERCISE

Resentment and fear are underlying causes of many forms of spiritual disease. Our mental and physical ills are frequently the direct result of this unhealthy condition. Learning to deal with resentment and fear in a healthy way is an important part of our recovery process.

Examine situations in which resentment or fear is a problem for you. The following questions can be helpful.

■ What or whom do you resent or fear (e.g., people, institutions, principles)?

■ Why are you resentful or fearful (e.g., what happened to cause this resentment)?

■ How has this resentment or fear affected you (e.g., lowered self-esteem, loss of employment, difficulty in relationships, physical harm or threats)?

■ Which character defect is active (e.g., approval seeking, control, fear of abandonment)?

EXAMPLE:

I resent my boss because he doesn't care to hear my explanation of why I am depressed. This affects my self-esteem. This activates unexpressed anger.

I fear my spouse because I feel that I can never please him/her. This affects my self-esteem and sexuality. This activates my fear of abandonment.

CHARACTER TRAITS

The example below will assist you in completing your Fourth Step Inventory. Follow the suggested guidelines and be as thorough as possible. Refer to Isolation in the inventory section for definitions.

ISOLATION

- List specific examples of your behavior that indicate you are isolating yourself; e.g.,

  I declined an invitation to Sharon's party last Saturday, because I feared I would be unable to participate.

  I felt embarrased at work when my supervisor asked me why I did not actively participate in the management meeting.

- Identify and explain the underlying causes (such as fear, resentment, anger, guilt); e.g.,

  I am afraid that if I let myself go I will do something foolish. This inhibits my ability to have fun. I worry about not fitting in or being conspicuous.

  I fear personal criticism if I express myself freely. Instead, I isolate myself by not talking.

- Identify and explain what is being hurt and threatened (such as self-esteem, goals, security, personal or sexual relations); e.g.,

  My self-esteem is affected when I reveal myself to other people. I judge myself without mercy. This interferes with my desire to have a love relationship and to meet new people.

  I feel my job security is at risk.

RECOVERY FROM ISOLATION

■ List specific examples of your behavior that indicate you isolate less frequently than before; e.g.,

Today I went to lunch with Diane and Evelyn. I felt comfortable and at ease, and was able to share in the conversation. I risked sharing some special feelings about my desire to be in an intimate relationship. I did not feel threatened because I could see that they were sincerely listening and would respect my confidentiality.

During last Monday's management meeting, I expressed a concern relative to risking business expenses. Rather than being criticized, I was thanked for taking the time to provide the insight.

■ What do you hope to achieve as you become more confident about situations in which you would usually isolate yourself; e.g.,

I want to cultivate new, healthy relationships that will expand my confidence and help me be more comfortable in social settings. I hope to become more flexible so that I can learn to be spontaneous and have fun.

I want to become more assertive and participatory in business settings. I believe this will give me an opportunity to realize my full potential.

REPRESSED ANGER

Anger is a major source of many problems in the lives of Adult Children. It is a feeling that we often suppress, because admitting it makes us uncomfortable. In our chaotic homes, the turmoil was so intense that we either denied our anger or expressed it inappropriately. We felt it was safer to protect ourselves and simply hoped our feelings would go away. We were not aware that repressed anger can lead to serious resentment and depression. It causes physical complications that can lead to stress-related illnesses. Denying anger or expressing it inappropriately causes problems in relationships, because we cannot be truthful about our feelings and must always be pretending.

When we repress anger, we may experience:

Resentment	**Depression**
Self-Pity	**Sadness**
Jealousy	**Stress**
Anxiety	**Physical discomfort**

RECOVERY FROM REPRESSED ANGER

Learning to express anger is a major step in our recovery. It releases many hidden emotions and allows healing to take place. Expressing anger lets others know our limits and helps us to be honest with ourselves. As we learn to express anger more appropriately, we are better able to cope with our own hostility as well as the anger of others. Our relationships improve as we begin to feel comfortable expressing ourselves. Stress-related problems diminish, and we even feel better physically.

As we recover from repressed anger, we begin to:

Express Anger	**Set limits for ourselves**
Identify hurt feelings	**Enjoy inner peace**
Make reasonable requests	**Reduce stress and anxiety**

APPROVAL SEEKING

As a result of our dysfunctional upbringing, we fear disapproval and criticism. As children, we desperately wanted to receive approval from our parents, grandparents, siblings and significant others. This rarely occurred for most of us. As a result we were constantly seeking validation of our selves. This need for approval continued into adulthood and seriously affected the way we pattern our lives and thinking around the needs of others. Rather than look for approval in a positive way, we seek validation in order to feel better about ourselves, and get people to like us. This keeps us out of touch with our own feelings and desires and prevents us from discovering our own wants and needs. We look for reactions in others and attempt to manage their impression of us. We constantly strive to please everyone and often stay in relationships that are destructive to us.

When we have a need for approval from others, we may be:

People pleasing	**Feeling unworthy**
Fearing criticism	**Ignoring our own needs**
Fearing failure	**Lacking in confidence**

RECOVERY FROM APPROVAL SEEKING

As we begin to rely on our own approval and that of our Higher Power, we understand that wanting approval is okay, and we learn to ask for it rather than manipulate others to get it. We accept compliments from others and learn to simply say "thank you," believing that the compliment is sincere. We say "yes" when it is a comfortable answer. We are willing to say "no" when "no" is appropriate.

As we recover from inappropriate approval seeking, we begin to:

Recognize our own needs	**Be loyal to oneself**
Tell the truth about how we feel	**Build our confidence**

CARETAKING

As long as we took care of others, solved their problems and supplied their needs, we did not have time to look at ourselves. As this trait became more pronounced, we completely lost our own identity. As children, we assumed the responsibility for concerns and problems of others that were far beyond our capability to handle and, as a result, were deprived of a normal childhood. The unrealistic demands placed on us, and the praise we received for being "little adults," made us believe we had God-like powers. Taking care of others boosted our self-esteem and made us feel indispensable. It gave purpose to our lives. As caretakers, we are most comfortable with chaotic situations in which we are often assured that we are needed. Although we often resent others for taking and not giving, we are unable to allow others to care for us.

As caretakers we may:

Feel indispensable   **Lose our identity**
Rescue people   **Feel super-responsible**
Ignore our own needs   **Become co-dependent**

RECOVERY FROM CARETAKING

As we put aside the role of caretaker, we become less and less responsible for everyone and everything and allow individuals to find their own way. We give them over to the care of their Higher Power, which is the best source for their guidance, love and support. By dropping the burden of meeting everyone's needs, we find time to develop our own personalities. Our obsession with caring for others is replaced by an acceptance of the fact that ultimately we have no power over the lives of others. We realize that our main responsibility in life is for our own welfare, and we turn other people over to God's care.

When we stop being caretakers, we begin to:

Stop rescuing others   **Develop our own identify**
Take care of ourselves   **Recognize dependent**
Set limits   **relationships**

CONTROL

As children, we had little or no control over our environment or the events that took place in our lives. As adults, we have extraordinary needs to control our feelings and behavior, and we try to control the feelings and behavior of others. We become rigid and unable to have spontaneity in our lives. We trust only ourselves to complete a task or to handle a situation. We manipulate others in order to gain their approval and keep a balance of control that makes us feel safe. We fear that our lives will deteriorate if we give up our management position. We become stressed and anxious when our authority is threatened.

Due to our need to be in control, we may:

Overreact to change	**Be judgmental and rigid**
Lack trust	**Be intolerant**
Fear failure	**Manipulate others**

RECOVERY FROM CONTROL

As we become more aware of the way we have attempted to control people and things, we begin to realize that our efforts have in fact been useless—that we did not control anything or anyone except ourselves. We discover more effective ways to get our needs met when we start accepting God as the source of our security. As we begin to surrender our wills and our lives to His care, we will experience less stress and anxiety. We become more able to participate in activities without being primarily concerned with the outcome. Saying the Serenity Prayer is helpful whenever we begin to recognize the reappearance of our need for control.

As we learn to give up control, we begin to:

Accept change	**Reduce our stress levels**
Trust in ourselves	**Find ways to have fun**
Empower others	**Accept others as they are**

FEAR OF ABANDONMENT

Fear of abandonment is a reaction to stress that we developed in early childhood. As children, we observed unpredictable behavior from responsible adults. Never knowing from one day to the next whether or not our parents would be there for us, many of us were abandoned either physically or emotionally. As their addiction increased in severity, so did their inability to parent. As children we simply did not exist. As adults, we are inclined to choose partners with whom we can repeat this fear. We try to be perfect by meeting all our partner's needs in order to avoid experiencing the pain of abandonment. Reducing the possibility of abandonment takes precedence over dealing with issues or conflicts and causes poor communication.

When we fear abandonment, we may:

Feel insecure	**Worry excessively**
Be caretakers	**Feel guilty when standing**
Avoid being alone	**up for ourselves**
Become co-dependent	

RECOVERY FROM FEAR OF ABANDONMENT

As we learn to rely more upon the ever-present love of God, our confidence in our ability to manage our environment increases. Our fear of abandonment diminishes and is replaced by the feeling that we are worthy people in our own right. We seek out healthy relationships with people who love and take care of themselves. We feel more secure in revealing our feelings. We transfer our old dependence on others to trust in God. We learn to understand and accept a nurturing and loving fellowship within our community. Our self-confidence grows as we begin to realize that with God in our lives, we will never again be totally alone.

As fear of abandonment diminishes, we begin to:

Be honest about our feelings	**Consider our own needs**
Feel comfortable alone	**in a relationship**
Express confidence	**Reduce caretaking traits**

FEAR OF AUTHORITY FIGURES

Fear of people in roles of authority can be a result of our parents' unrealistic expectations of us—wanting us to be more than we were able to be. We see people in authority as having unrealistic expectations of us and fear we cannot meet their expectations. We are unable to deal with people whom we perceive as being in positions of power. Simple assertiveness displayed by others is often misinterpreted by us as anger. This can cause us to feel intimidated and to become oversensitive. No matter how competent we are, we compare ourselves to others and conclude that we are inadequate. As a result, we constantly compromise our integrity in order to avoid confrontation or criticism.

Fear of authority figures may cause us to:

Fear rejection
Take things personally
Be arrogant to cover up

Compare ourselves to others
React rather than act
Feel inadequate

RECOVERY FROM FEAR OF AUTHORITY FIGURES

As we begin to feel comfortable with people in roles of authority, we learn to put our focus on ourselves and discover that we have nothing to fear. We recognize others as being like us, with their own fears, defenses and insecurities. Others' behavior no longer dictates how we feel about ourselves. We start acting rather than reacting when responding to others. We recognize that our ultimate authority figure is God and that He is always with us.

As we become comfortable with authority figures, we begin to:

Act with increased self-esteem
Stand up for ourselves

Accept constructive criticism
Interact easily with people in authority

FROZEN FEELINGS

Many of us have difficulty expressing our feelings or even realizing that we have them. We harbor deep emotional pain and a sense of guilt and shame. As children, our feelings were met with disapproval, anger and rejection. As a means of survival, we learned to hide our feelings or repress them entirely. As adults, we are not in touch with our feelings. We can only allow ourselves to have "acceptable" feelings in order to stay "safe." Our true nature is distorted in order to protect ourselves from the reality of what is actually happening. Distorted and repressed feelings cause resentment, anger and depression, which often leads to physical illness.

When we have frozen feelings, we may:

Be unaware of our feelings	**Experience depression**
Have distorted feelings	**Develop physical illness**
Suppress our feelings	

RECOVERY FROM FROZEN FEELINGS

As we get in touch with our feelings and learn to express them, strange things begin to happen. Our stress levels decrease as we become able to express ourselves honestly, and we begin to see ourselves as worthy. We learn that expression of true feelings is the healthy way to communicate, and we find that more of our own needs are being met. All we have to do is ask. As we begin to release our feelings, we experience some levels of pain. But, as our courage increases the pain goes away, and we develop a sense of peace and serenity. The more willing we are to take risks in releasing our emotions, the more effective our recovery will be.

As we experience and express our feelings, we begin to:

Feel free to cry	**Experience our true self**
Openly express feelings	**Express our needs to others**

46

ISOLATION

We find it safe in many instances to withdraw from surroundings that are uncomfortable for us. By isolating ourselves, we prevent others from seeing us as we really are. We tell ourselves that we are not worthy and, therefore, do not deserve love, attention, or acceptance. We also tell ourselves that we cannot be punished or hurt if we don't express our feelings. Rather than take risks, we choose to hide, thereby eliminating the need to face an uncertain outcome.

When we isolate ourselves, we may be:

Fearing rejection	**Feeling defeated**
Experiencing loneliness	**Non-assertive**
Procrastinating	**Seeing ourselves as different from others**

RECOVERY FROM ISOLATION

As we begin to feel better about ourselves, we become more willing to take risks and expose ourselves to new surroundings. We seek friends and relationships that are nurturing, safe, and supportive. We learn to participate and to have fun in group activities. It becomes easier to express our feelings as we develop a stronger sense of self-esteem. We recognize that people will accept us for who we really are. Our self-acceptance allows us to experience the precious gift of living more comfortably and serenely.

As we isolate less often, we begin to:

Accept ourselves	**Complete projects**
Freely express our emotions	**Actively participate with others**
Cultivate supportive relationships	

47

LOW SELF-ESTEEM

Low self-esteem is rooted in our early childhood, during which we were never encouraged to believe that we were adequate. As a result of constant criticism, we believed that we were "bad" and the cause of many family problems. To feel accepted, we tried harder to please. The harder we tried, the more frustrated we became. Low self-esteem affects our ability to set and achieve goals. We are afraid to take risks. We feel responsible for things that go wrong, and when something goes right, we do not give ourselves credit. Instead, we feel undeserving and believe it is not going to last.

When we experience low self-esteem, we may:

Be non-assertive	**Isolate from others**
Fear failure	**Have a negative self-image**
Appear inadequate	**Need to be perfect**
Fear rejection	

RECOVERY FROM LOW SELF-ESTEEM

As we work with our Higher Power to build confidence in ourselves and our abilities, our self-esteem increases. We are able to interact with others and to accept ourselves as we really are. We see our strengths as well as our limitations and learn to accept ourselves at face value. We become more willing to take risks; we realize we can achieve many things that we had never dreamed would be possible. Sharing feelings with others becomes more comfortable—we feel safer as we come to know others and allow them to know us. Relationships become healthier, because we are able to trust and validate ourselves, and no longer need to look to others for validation.

As our self-esteem increases, we begin to:

Be more confident	**Love ourselves**
Act more assertively	**Openly express feelings**
Easily interact with others	**Take risks**

OVERDEVELOPED SENSE OF RESPONSIBILITY

As children in a dysfunctional home, we felt responsible for our parents' problems. We tried to be "model children" and make things be the way we thought others wanted them to be. We believed that we were responsible for the emotions and actions of others; even for the outcome of events. Today we remain supersensitive to the needs of others, and we try to assume responsibility for helping them get their needs met. It is important to us to be perfect. We volunteer to do things so people will appreciate us. Our sense of responsibility causes us to overcommit, and we have a tendency to take on more than we are capable of handling effectively.

When we are overly responsible, we may:

Take life too seriously	Be a high achiever
Appear rigid	Have false pride
Be perfectionists	Manipulate others
Assume responsibility for others	

RECOVERY FROM OVERDEVELOPED SENSE OF RESPONSIBILITY

Accepting the fact that we are not responsible for the actions and feelings of others forces us to focus on ourselves. We understand that we do not influence the lives of others and that people are responsible for themselves. As we assume responsibility for our own actions, we become aware that we must rely on God for guidance and take care of our own needs. Then we will find time and energy to support and nurture ourselves.

As we stop being overly responsible, we begin to:

Take care of ourselves	Accept our limitations
Enjoy leisure time	Delegate responsibility

REPRESSED SEXUALITY

We find ourselves confused and uncertain about our sexual feelings toward others, particularly those to whom we are close or those with whom we hope to be emotionally intimate. We have been trained to think of our sexual feelings as unnatural or abnormal. Because we do not share our feelings with others, we have no opportunity to develop a healthy attitude about our own sexuality. As small children, we may have explored our physical sexuality with peers and been severely punished. The message was "sex is dirty, is not talked about and is to be avoided." Some of us saw our parents as very disapproving or even as totally nonsexual beings. We may have been molested by a parent or close relative who was out of control. As a result, we are uncomfortable in our sexual roles. We do not freely discuss sex with our partners for fear of being misunderstood and abandoned. As parents, discussing sex with our children is difficult and sometimes avoided.

Due to repressed sexuality we may:

Lose our sense of morality	**Feel guilt and shame**
Be confused about our	**Be frigid or impotent**
sexual identity	**Manipulate others by**
Be lustful	**seductive behavior**

RECOVERY FROM REPRESSED SEXUALITY

Relying upon the constant love of our Lord, our self-worth increases and we see ourselves as worthy in His eyes and in the eyes of others. As we increase our self-love and our ability to take care of ourselves, we seek to be with other healthy people who love and take care of themselves. We are less fearful of commitment and are better prepared to enter into a healthy relationship—emotionally, intellectually, and sexually. We feel more secure in sharing our feelings, strengths, and weaknesses. We are honest about our own sexuality with our children. We accept their need for information as they develop their own sexual identity.

When we accept our sexuality, we begin to:

Discuss sex openly	**Express our own desires**
Accept our sexual self	**Share intimate feelings**

STEP FIVE

Admitted to God, to ourselves, and to another human being the exact nature of our wrongs.

Therefore confess your sins to each other and pray for each other so that you may be healed.

(James 5:16a)

❖ ❖ ❖

Step Four laid the foundation for identifying many of our shadowy deeds and thoughts, as well as for recording the strengths we have developed from childhood patterns of survival. Completing our Step Four inventory has made us aware of many truths about ourselves. This realization may have caused us pain. The natural reaction is to feel sadness or guilt or both. We have faced ourselves and our history honestly. We have courageously identified some behaviors we want to eliminate and others we want to develop in the future.

For those of us who have been honest and thorough, Step Four has provided the foundation upon which we will build our recovery. It identified the unresolved feelings, unhealed memories and personal defects that have produced resentment, depression and loss of self-worth. Asking God for help and acknowledging that God is light (JOHN 1:5-9) helped us commit our lives to walking in the light of His truth. Acknowledging our wrongs and moving toward restoration of our self-worth lifted a great burden from our hearts and minds. Now that we have identified some of our character traits, it is possible to relieve ourselves of the burden of guilt and shame associated with our wrong-doings. This step requires that we engage in honest confrontations with ourselves and others, by admitting our faults to God, to ourselves, and to another person. By doing so, we begin the important phase of setting aside our pride so that we can see ourselves in true perspective.

Admitting the exact nature of our wrongs to God is the first phase of Step Five. Here, we confess to God all that we have worked so hard to conceal. It is no longer necessary to blame God or others for what has happened to us, but rather to accept our history for exactly what it is. This brings us closer to God, and we begin to know that He is always there for us. Our confession helps us receive God's love and accept ourselves unconditionally. We must remember that we are all children of God and will never be rejected.

Admitting our wrongs to ourselves began in Step Four, as we wrote our inventory and had the opportunity to see our behaviors for what they really are. In Step Five, as we consciously admit our wrongs, we develop the desire and strength to release them. This builds our self-esteem and supports us as we move toward Step Seven, where we ask God to remove our shortcomings.

Telling our story to another person can be a frightening experience. Many of us have spent a major portion of our lives building defenses to keep others out. Living in isolation has been a way of protecting ourselves from further hurt. Step Five is our pathway out of isolation and loneliness. It is a move toward wholeness, happiness and a sense of peace. It is a humbling experience, as we are required to be totally honest. We can no longer pretend; it is time to reveal ourselves completely.

We will unveil parts of our nature that we have concealed from ourselves. We may fear the impact that our truthfulness will have on our lives. Telling our story to another person may cause us the additional fear of being rejected. However, it is essential that we take this important risk and confess our wrongs. With God's help, we will have the courage to disclose our true natures. The result will be worth all the agony of the unburdening process.

Ask for God's help in choosing the person to whom you will confess. Remember that the other believer should reflect the image of Christ and be a spokesman for Him. God intended us to speak to others, to share our sorrows and joys as members of His family. Look for qualities you admire in the other person which will inspire your confidence. Find someone on an equal spiritual level, with similar understanding. God's Holy Spirit works spiritually through all of His children. Sharing our personal experiences will help us come to know the depth of God's unconditional love for all His human family.

❖ *Looking to Scripture* ❖

As we prepare for Step Five, we see how our growing relationship with God has given us the courage to examine ourselves, accept who we are and reveal our true selves. Step Five helps us acknowledge and discard our old survival skills and move toward a new and healthier life. Being thorough and honest in completing our inventory places us in a position to face the facts and move forward.

Submit yourselves, then, to God. Resist the devil, and he will flee from you. Come near to God and He will come near to you. Wash your hands, you sinners, and purify your hearts, you double-minded. (JAMES 4:7-8)

Our personal inventory lets us acknowledge our past and turn with single-mindedness to the future.

Step Five consists of three distinct parts. We will confess our faults to God, to ourselves and to another human being. For some of us, it will involve telling our life story for the first time. As we do it, we will cleanse ourselves of the excess baggage we have been carrying. As we open our hearts and reveal ourselves, we will achieve a deeper level of spirituality.

O LORD, we acknowledge our wickedness and the guilt of our fathers; we have indeed sinned against you.
(JEREMIAH 14:20)

Focusing on God, we become aware of our desire to move away from the evil and toward the good.

Admitting our defects to God can be very frightening. If we believe that God is in charge of the universe, that all events are His will, then blaming God can be a way for us to deny our part in the problem. It is important to understand that God has given us free will. He wants what is best for us, but He allows us to make choices free of His manipulation. As we admit our wrongs to Him, we see that His love for us is unconditional and everlasting. It becomes clear that He will strengthen and guide us, as we fulfill His desire for us to lead a healthy and peaceful life.

So then, each of us will give an account of himself to God.
(ROMANS 14:12)

Admitting our wrongs to God initiates the restoration of our personal integrity by removing the masks behind which we have hidden.

Our admission to ourselves is the least-threatening part of Step Five and can be done at minimal risk. Sharing our wrongs with ourselves doesn't force us to be honest, for we can easily deceive ourselves. Through denial, we have fooled ourselves all of our lives; confessing to ourselves only allows this pattern to continue. However, as a first step in getting to know our true selves, we must begin at this point.

If we claim to be without sin, we deceive ourselves and the truth is not in us. If we confess our sins, he is faithful and just and will forgive us our sins and purify us from all unrighteousness. (1 JOHN 1:8-9)

Self-deception is human nature. In Step Five, we are challenged to be honest.

Admitting our wrongs to another human being is the most powerful part of Step Five. It is a true exercise in humility and will help us begin the break down of our defenses. Being rigorously honest with another human being may be frightening enough to cause us to procrastinate in completing this portion of Step Five. It is tempting to believe that telling God is all that is necessary, because He ultimately forgives all sins. While this is true, it comes after our sharing with another person, for this is where our sense of self-worth begins.

"When he came to his senses, he said, 'How many of my father's hired men have food to spare, and here I am starving to death! I will set out and go back to my father and say to Him: Father, I have sinned against heaven and against you. I am no longer worthy to be called your son; make me like one of your hired men." (LUKE 15:17-19)

When we realize how far we have fallen, we clearly see the extent of our sin, perhaps for the first time.

When choosing a person for Step Five, we will want to select a loving, caring person, one who will be there for us and who will provide unconditional acceptance. The person must be dependable, trustworthy and not be shocked or offended by what we reveal. It is wise to choose someone who is familiar with the Program. Sharing will flow easily if there is honesty and ample opportunity for feedback from the other person. Trusting the person with whom we share our story is vital to the success of Step Five and will provide a safe atmosphere.

When I kept silent, my bones wasted away through my groaning all day long. For day and night your hand was heavy upon me; my strength was sapped as in the heat of summer...Then I acknowledged my sin to you and did not cover up my iniquity. I said, "I will confess my transgressions to the LORD"—and you forgave the guilt of my sin... (PSALM 32:3-5)

Bearing the burden of our transgressions drains us of vital energy. Confession will enervate our existence.

In telling our story to another person, we can expect more than just being heard. We must be ready to listen to the other person's response. The interchange can be helpful and productive if we are willing to listen with an open mind to the other person's viewpoint. This broadens our awareness of ourselves and gives us an opportunity to change and grow. Feedback is vital to us as a means of completing the process of revelation. Questions asked in a caring and understanding manner can reveal insights and feelings of which we are unaware. Sharing our life story in this way can be the most important interaction of our lives.

Therefore confess your sins to each other and pray for each other so that you may be healed. The prayer of a righteous man is powerful and effective. (JAMES 5:16)

Prayerful sharing with a brother or sister in Christ prepares the way for healing to begin.

He who conceals his sins does not prosper, but whoever confesses and renounces them finds mercy.
(PROVERBS 28:13)

In Step Five, we must relentlessly expose the exact nature of our wrongs, being always certain of God's merciful pardon.

When Step Five is completed, some expectations may remain unfulfilled. We need to understand that God's timing is not always our timing. God works in each one of us according to our own capacity to respond to Him. We are not to submit to our anxiety, but rather to trust God. The real test of our Step Five admission is our willingness to trust that God will strengthen and develop our capacity to change our lives.

"If you have played the fool and exalted yourself, or if you have planned evil, clap your hand over your mouth!"
(PROVERBS 30:32)

Acknowledging our lustful, prideful nature can be our first exercise in experiencing humility. We begin to understand how much God must love us.

Upon completion of Step Five, we will realize that we are not always in control. It is not easy to change our old behavior patterns all at once. Admitting the exact nature of our wrongs does not stop us from acting in our old ways. We can expect to have moments of weakness, yet be strong in knowing that our relationship with God can help us overcome them. If we sincerely desire to change our ways, God will give us the strength and courage that we require.

For all have sinned and fall short of the glory of God.
(ROMANS 3:23)

Our Step Five admissions help us realize how we have fallen short of God's plan for us.

IMPORTANT GUIDELINES FOR PREPARING YOUR FIFTH STEP

Choose your Fifth Step listener carefully; one who is familiar with Twelve Step Programs. The individual can be:

- A clergyman ordained by an established religion. Ministers of many faiths often receive such requests.

- A trusted friend (preferably of the same sex), a doctor or psychologist.

- A family member with whom you can openly share. Be careful not to disclose information that might be harmful to spouses or other family members.

- A member of a Twelve-Step Program.

In preparing for the Fifth Step, either as communicator or listener, the following suggestions are helpful:

- Begin with prayer, calling upon Christ Jesus to be present as you prepare to go through your Fourth Step revelations and insights. Ask God to guide and support you in what you are about to experience.

- Allow ample time to complete each thought and stay focused on the subject. Discourage unnecessary explanations.

- Eliminate distractions. Telephone calls, children, visitors and extraneous noises should be eliminated.

- Remember that Step Five asks only that we admit the exact nature of our wrongs. It is not necessary to discuss how the wrongs came about or how changes will be made. You are not seeking counsel or advice.

- As the listener, be patient and accepting. You are God's spokesperson and are communicating God's unconditional acceptance.

- As the listener you are there to help the communicator express thoughts clearly. Ask questions when necessary so the information can be clearly understood by both of you.

- When Step Five is completed, both parties can share their feelings about the experience. It is now possible to extend to each other the love God extends to us through Christ Jesus.

- Observe confidentiality. What you have shared is personal. Nothing defeats honesty and damages relationships faster than a betrayed confidence.

The following information is helpful when completing your Fifth Step with God:
- Step Five is for your own benefit—God already knows you. You are beginning a process of living a life of humility, honesty and courage. The result is freedom, happiness and serenity.

- Start with prayer; e.g., "Lord, I understand that you already know me completely. I am now ready to openly and humbly reveal myself to you—my hurtful behaviors, self-centeredness and traits. I am grateful to you for the gifts and abilities that have brought me to this point in my life. Take away my fear of being known and rejected. I place myself and my life in your care and keeping."

- Speak out loud, sincerely and honestly sharing your understanding of the insights you gained from your Fourth Step inventory. Be aware that emotions may surface as part of the powerful cleansing experience taking place.

- The objective is balance. Remember that each of your character traits has a strength and a weakness. Begin with resentments and fears. Then proceed to those traits you have included in your Fourth Step Inventory.

The following information is helpful when completing your Fifth Step with yourself:

- Writing your Fourth Step inventory began the process of developing your self-awareness, the first step toward what will become genuine self-love.

- Solitary self-appraisal is the beginning of your confession, but it is insufficient in itself. The Fifth Step is where you turn that knowledge into enhanced self-acceptance.

- Sit in a chair with your imaginary double seated across from you in an empty chair. Or sit in front of a mirror that allows you to see yourself as you speak.

- Speak out loud. Allow yourself time to hear what you are saying, and to note any deeper understanding that occurs.

- Acknowledge your courage for proceeding to this point. This and every part of this process releases excess emotional baggage that you have carried around because of low self-worth.

The following information is helpful when completing your Fifth Step with another person:

- Simply stated, it takes considerable humility to bare ourselves to another person. We are about to reveal our self-defeating, damaging and harmful character traits, we will also disclose our positive and contributing traits. We must do this to remove the stage-character masks we present to the world. It is a bold step toward eliminating our need for pretense and hiding.

■ Review the guidelines for choosing your Fifth Step listener when selecting a person to assist you in completing your Fifth Step. Begin your sharing with the Resentment and Fear Exercises in your workbook and then proceed by disclosing the character traits you wrote about.

You may never see that person again, which is okay. It is your decision to continue the relationship in whatever direction you choose, from casual friendship to deeper spiritual companionship.

After completing your Fifth Step, take time for prayer and meditation to reflect on what you have done. Thank God for the tool you have been given to improve your relationship with Him. Spend time rereading the first five Steps and note anything you have omitted. Acknowledge that you are laying a new foundation for your life. The cornerstone is your relationship with God and your commitment to honesty and humility.

Congratulate yourself for having the courage to risk self-disclosure, and thank God for the peace of mind you have achieved.

STEP SIX

*Were entirely ready to have God remove
all these defects of character.*

*Humble yourselves before the
Lord, and he will lift you up.*
(James 4:10)

❖ ❖ ❖

Having completed Steps One through Five, some of us may
believe that we can stop here. The truth is, that much more
work lies ahead, and the best results are yet to come. In Steps
One and Two, we recognized our powerlessness and came to
believe in a Power greater than ourselves. In Step Three, we turned
our wills and our lives over to God's care. Steps Four and Five
created an atmosphere for developing self-awareness and humility
by admitting our wrongs to God, to ourselves, and to another
person. This foundation for recovery that we have built may create
the illusion that everything is okay and that the remaining Steps
may be marginally relevant. If we believe this, we will surely
undermine our spiritual growth, as many of us have.

Actually, Steps One through Five helped us to steer in the right
direction as we built our foundation for ultimate surrender. Approaching Step Six, we are confronted with the need to change
our attitudes and lifestyles. Here, we prepare to make these changes
and totally alter the course of our lives.

The changes that are about to take place in our lives will result
from a cooperative effort—God provides the direction while we
provide the desire and action. All we need is the willingness to
let God lead our journey. He never forces Himself on us. We
must invite Him into our lives, content in knowing that He will
never leave or forsake us.

We are not expected to remove our character defects alone; we are expected only to let go and let God. Step Six is not an action step that we actually take. It is a state of being that enables us to release our faults to God. As our willingness to surrender increases, we will reach the point where we are ready to let God take over and remove our defects as He sees fit. We do this by working the Program, one day at a time, whether or not we can see that we are making any progress.

We must remind ourselves that the character traits we want to eliminate are often deeply ingrained patterns of behavior, developed through many years of struggling to survive. They will not vanish overnight. We must be patient while God is shaping us into new people. Through this willingness to let God be in control, we learn to trust Him more completely.

Step Six is similar to Step Two. Both Steps deal with our willingness to allow God to work through us to change our lives. In Step Two, we are seeking our restoration to sanity by coming to believe in a Power greater than ourselves. In Step Six, we are seeking total readiness to let God remove our defects of character. Both Steps acknowledge the existence of problems and require that we seek God's help in being freed from them. The fact that we "came to believe" will strengthen our capacity to be "entirely ready."

❖ *Looking to Scripture* ❖

To be successful with Step Six, we must sincerely desire to change our disabling behaviors. Our past has been dominated by our self-will, through which we sought to control our environment. We victimized ourselves by our self-will, rarely calling on God for help. By recognizing our life condition and being honestly determined to eliminate our behavior flaws, we see that self-will has never been enough to help us. We must be ready to accept help and relinquish our self-destructive natures.

Therefore, prepare your minds for action; be self-controlled; set your hope fully on the grace to be given you when Jesus Christ is revealed. (1 PETER 1:13-14)

Focusing on preparation for change will encourage our faith by allowing us to gracefully detach from our past.

At this point in our Program, we see that change is necessary to live life to the fullest. Recognizing the need for change and being willing to change are two different matters. The space between recognition and willingness to change can be filled with fear. As we move toward willingness, we must let go of our fears and remain secure in the knowledge that with God's guidance everything will be restored to us. When we are "entirely ready," we begin to see the possibilities available to us once we change our behavior. The excitement of this revelation will help us do whatever may be necessary to achieve the results we want. From now on, there will be no turning back.

Delight yourself in the LORD and he will give you the desires of your heart. Commit your way to the LORD; trust in him and he will do this. (PSALM 37:4-5)

Learning to live in the light of God's love, we glimpse the new life that is possible for us.

Not that I have already obtained all this, or have already been made perfect, but I press on to take hold of that for which Christ Jesus took hold of me. Brothers, I do not consider myself yet to have taken hold of it. But one thing I do: Forgetting what is behind and straining toward what is ahead, I press on toward the goal to win the prize for which God has called me heavenward in Christ Jesus. (PHILIPPIANS 3:12-14)

Forgetting the past and putting it behind us is an important element in our recovery.

In preparing to have our character defects removed, we will see that they are familiar tools to us, and losing them threatens our capacity to control ourselves and others. We can trust that God won't remove anything we need. This creates in us a beginning sense of comfort. The smallest beginning is acceptable to God. Scripture tells us that if we have "faith as small as a mustard seed" nothing is impossible for us (MATTHEW 17:30). When we have planted our seed of willingness, we need to look for and protect the tiny sprouts of positive results. We do not want the weeds of self-will to overrun our new garden. These seedlings of "willingness" respond quickly to our nurturing.

Do not conform any longer to the pattern of this world, but be transformed by the renewing of your mind. Then you will be able to test and approve what God's will is—his good, pleasing and perfect will. (ROMANS 12:2)

As our minds turn from things "of this world" to things "of God," our transformation begins.

Our ability to talk to God is an important part of Step Six. We need to communicate with God in a way that shows our humility and invites His intervention. When we say, "Dear God, I want to be more patient," we are making a demand and telling God what we want. When we say "Dear God, I am impatient," we present the truth about ourselves. This allows God to manifest our behavior change based on our admission of error. When we pray in this manner, we exhibit humility, relinquish our pride and ask God to act on our behalf.

Humble yourselves before the LORD, and he will lift you up. (JAMES 4:10)

We demonstrate our humility by allowing God to lead us through our healing. Our guideline must be His way, not our way.

If any of you lacks wisdom, he should ask God, who gives generously to all without finding fault, and it will be given to him. But when he asks, he must believe and not doubt, because he who doubts is like a wave of the sea, blown and tossed by the wind. (JAMES 1:5-6)

Our doubts are overcome by our growing faith in what we know to be true—that God, our heavenly Father, will never forsake us.

This Step requires that we look at those defects of character we will ask to have removed. We may be unwilling to give up some of them. They may seem useful to us, so we respond, "I cannot give up...yet." We have a potential problem if we say "I will never be any different, and will never give up..." These attitudes shut our mind to God's saving grace and can precipitate our destruction. If we respond this way to any behavior, we need to renew our trust in God and recommit ourselves to doing His will.

But the Lord is faithful, and he will strengthen and protect you from the evil one. (2 THESSALONIANS 3:3)

Chaos and confusion can occur when we experience changes in our lives. As we begin to rely on God's presence within us, our feelings of comfort and safety will overcome our anxiety.

As we follow the principles of the Program in our daily lives, we gradually and unconsciously prepare to have our shortcomings removed. Sometimes, we are even unaware of our readiness to have our defects removed. At first, we realize that we are behaving differently—that we have changed. Sometimes, others note the changes before we become aware of them ourselves. Approval-seekers begin to function more independently; control addicts become more easygoing and more relaxed; caretakers become more sensitive to their own needs. People who diligently work the Program as an integral part of their lives become calmer, more serene, and genuinely happy.

In the same way, count yourselves dead to sin but alive to God in Christ Jesus. Therefore do not let sin reign in your mortal body so that you obey its evil desires.
(ROMANS 6:11-12)

Temptation's hold on us is shattered by our willingness to let Christ lead us to healthy behavior.

A radiant, confident person lives in each of us, hidden under a cloud of confusion and uncertainty, distracted by ineffective behavior. If someone asked us if we wanted to be freed from our character defects, we could give only one answer—we are entirely ready to have God remove them.

I seek you with all my heart; do not let me stray from your commands. I have hidden your word in my heart that I might not sin against you. Praise be to you, O LORD; teach me your decrees. (PSALM 119:10-12)

Centering our attention on the word of God enables us to receive His teaching and do His will.

This is the assurance we have in approaching God: that is if we ask anything according to his will, he hears us. And if we know that he hears us—whatever we ask—we know that we have what we asked of him. (1 JOHN 5:14-15)

As we come closer to God in our minds and in our lives, we soon trust that He will hear our prayers and heal us.

STEP SEVEN

Humbly asked Him to remove our shortcomings.

*If we confess our sins, he is faithful and
just and will forgive us our sins and
purify us from all unrighteousness.*

(1 John 1:9)

❖ ❖ ❖

Humility is a recurring theme in the Twelve Step Program and the central idea of Step Seven. By practicing humility we receive the strength necessary to work the Program and achieve satisfactory results. We recognize now, more than ever before, that a major portion of our lives has been devoted to fulfilling our self-centered desires. We must set aside these prideful, selfish behavior patterns, come to terms with our inadequacies and realize that humility alone will free our spirit. Step Seven requires surrendering our will to God so that we may receive the serenity necessary to achieve the happiness we seek.

We are growing in wisdom and understanding, not only as a result of our seeking it, but also from the insight we have gained by examining the pain of our past struggles. We gain greater courage by hearing how others have coped with their life challenges. As we work through the Steps, we begin to recognize the value of acknowledging the truth of our past. Although the pain of this reality may seem to be unbearable, the insights we achieve are the only means to our release.

Step Six prepared us to let go of our old defective behavior patterns and develop the powerful new ones that God intends for us to use. Asking God to remove our defects is a true measure of our willingness to surrender control. For those of us who have spent our lives thinking we were self-sufficient, it can be an extremely difficult task, but not an impossible one. If we are sincerely ready to abandon these deceptions, we can then ask God to be instrumental in letting go of our past and in the creation of our new life.

Step Seven is the first and most important part of the cleansing process and prepares us for the next stage of our journey. During the first six Steps, we became aware of our desperate situation, looked at our lives honestly, disclosed previously hidden aspects of ourselves and became ready to change our attitudes and behaviors. Step Seven presents us with the opportunity to turn to God and ask for removal of those parts of our character that cause us pain.

Prior to beginning this Program, we avoided ever looking at ourselves honestly and admitting the extent of our disabling behavior. Meditating on Christ's presence in our lives will focus our attention on living life according to His example and free us from this disabling burden of "self." Our partnership with Christ will increase our concern for the whole human family and put our obsession with "self" into its proper perspective. We will finally recognize the person we have been, understand who we are now and look forward with joy to the persons we are becoming.

Preparing to have our defects removed requires our willingness to work with God to revise and redirect our attention and activity. Our progress will be halted if we continue our destructive behavior patterns. We must be ever-vigilant and alert to the possible return of "old behaviors" and work diligently toward eliminating them from our frame of reference. It is wise to be gentle with ourselves and remember that it took us a lifetime to develop these habits. It is not realistic to expect them to disappear overnight.

When looking to God to remove our shortcomings, we must realize that God gives grace through other people as well as directly to us through prayer and meditation. God often uses outside forces to correct our defects. Ministers, teachers, medical doctors and therapists can all be instruments of God's grace. Our willingness to seek outside help can be a clear indication of our readiness to change. Compulsive worriers can pray to God to release their worries and, at the same time, seek help from a counselor to relieve their anxiety. Persons who over-indulge in food or drugs can seek professional help to gain control over their obsessive habits. We need to pray for God's help in removing our shortcomings, and have the courage to seek appropriate professional help when we know we need it.

❖ *Looking to Scripture* ❖

Through working the Steps, we are progressing toward a happier and healthier life. We see how the opportunities and blessings that God brings into our lives surpass anything we could ever have created on our own. Having completed the first six Steps, we are becoming aware of the multitude of benefits available to us. Through this awareness, we become grateful for God's presence and secure in the knowledge that our lives are improving.

Good and upright is the LORD; therefore he instructs sinners in his ways. He guides the humble in what is right and teaches them his way. All the ways of the LORD are loving and faithful for those who keep the demands of his covenant. For the sake of your name, O LORD, forgive my iniquity, though it is great. (PSALM 25:8-11)

As we work the Steps and learn from His work, we begin to see the gifts of God's grace being manifested in our lives.

Step Seven implies that we ask for removal of all our shortcomings. However, the process will be more manageable if we deal with them individually, working on the easiest ones first to build up our confidence and strength. If we are patient, God will see that we achieve our goal at a pace that is comfortable for us. Our willingness to accept God's help builds our trust and encourages the growth of confidence in ourselves and in God. If we ask God to relieve us of a burdensome behavior pattern and it doesn't seem to go away, we need to work harder on our willingness to release it. Becoming angry or discouraged is self-defeating. When things do not seem to be going according to our timetable, reciting the Serenity Prayer can work to our advantage.

Do not be anxious about anything, but in everything, by prayer and petition, with thanksgiving, present your requests to God. (PHILIPPIANS 4:6)

Through prayer and meditation, our anxieties are relieved and our faith is strengthened.

If we confess our sins, he is faithful and just and will forgive us our sins and purify us from all unrighteousness. (1 JOHN 1:9)

Confession and forgiveness free us from the bondage and burdens of our past; all things are made new.

Letting go of negative behavior patterns, however destructive they are, may create a sense of loss and require that we allow ourselves time to grieve. It is normal to grieve for the loss of something we no longer have. If, however, in our childhood we experienced "things" being taken from us abruptly or before we were ready to release them, we may now be overly sensitive and may cling to "things" to avoid the pain of loss. Rather than using our own ineffective strategies to avoid or deny the existence of our fear of giving up, we can turn to our Lord for courage and trust the outcome. Even though our childhood learning did not adequately prepare us for grieving the adult losses we must handle, our love and trust in God can heal our memories, repair the damage and restore us to wholeness.

For whoever exalts himself will be humbled, and whoever humbles himself will be exalted. (MATTHEW 23:12)

Our recovery will be encouraged if we set aside our prideful self-will, and humbly ask God for guidance. A daily time for prayer and reflection is especially helpful.

Changing our behavior can be temporarily alarming to our sense of self. Our fear of not knowing what is ahead may cause us to repeat past destructive actions. We may retreat into feeling isolated and lose our sense of belonging. Having faith and trusting in our relationship with God is an indication of our willingness to release the fear of being lost, frightened, or abandoned.

But he gives us more grace. That is why Scripture says: "God opposes the proud but gives grace to the humble." Submit yourselves, then, to God. Resist the devil, and he will flee from you. Come near to God and he will come near to you. Wash your hands, you sinners, and purify your hearts, you double-minded. (JAMES 4:6-8)

Being submissive to God means seeking His presence, knowing His word and doing His work.

As we begin to see our defects being removed and our lives becoming less complicated, we must proceed with caution and guard against the temptation to be prideful. Sudden changes in our behavior can and do happen, but we cannot anticipate them or direct them. God initiates change when we are ready, and we cannot claim that we alone removed our character defects. When we learn to ask humbly for God's help in our lives, change becomes God's responsibility, and we cannot accept the credit.

Create in me a pure heart, O God, and renew a steadfast spirit within me. Do not cast me from your presence or take your Holy Spirit from me. Restore to me the joy of your salvation and grant me a willing spirit, to sustain me. (PSALM 51:10-12)

In periods of despair and doubt, we may feel separated from God. Being quiet and praying for guidance can restore our spirit and renew our trust.

Destructive behavior patterns that remain with us after we complete Step Seven may never be eliminated, but may have to be transformed. We have an opportunity to transform these aspects of our character into positive traits and learn to use them in a healthy way. Leaders may be left with a quest for power but with no desire to misuse it. Lovers will be left with exquisite sensuality, but with enough sensitivity to refrain from causing pain to the person they love. Those who are materially wealthy may continue to be, but will set aside their greed and possessiveness. With the help of Our Lord, all aspects of our personal life can be rewarding. By continuing to practice humility and accept the tools God is giving us, we will eventually begin to aspire to a more Christ-like life, sharing with others the love we have received.

Humble yourselves, therefore, under God's mighty hand, that he may lift you up in due time. Cast all your anxiety on him because he cares for you. (1 PETER 5:6-7)

As our fear lessens and we accept God's care and control, we begin to experience love and joy in our lives.

In order for the Program to be successful, we must practice the Steps on a daily basis. When we have moments of inner struggle, we can simply say "This too will pass"; "I let go and let God"; "I fear no evil"; "I choose to see the good in this experience." Whatever affirmation we use, its power keeps us from reverting to our obsessive/compulsive behavior. Depression, guilt and anger can be acknowledged and understood to be temporary.

Have mercy on me, O God, according to your unfailing love; according to your great compassion blot out my transgressions. Wash away all my iniquity and cleanse me from my sin. (PSALM 51:1-2)

When temptation and trial threaten our peace of mind, we call upon the Holy Spirit for assistance.

We need to stop for a moment and acknowledge ourselves for our commitment to recovery. Note how our determination enables us to break the bonds of our unhealthy habits and behaviors. Accept the positive, spontaneous thoughts and feelings that occur and see that this results from our personal relationship with God. We learn that the guidance we receive from our Lord is always available; all we need to do is listen, receive and act without fear.

Repent, then, and turn to God, so that your sins may be wiped out, that times of refreshing may come from the Lord. (ACTS 3:19)

Step Seven has relieved us of the guilt and shame that shaped our lives for so long. Now our day of grace has come.

SEVENTH STEP PRAYER

My Creator, I am now willing
that you should have all of me,
good and bad.
I pray that you now remove from me
every single defect of character
which stands in the way of
my usefulness to you and my fellows.
Grant me the strength,
as I go out from here,
to do your bidding.

AMEN [1]

Big Book (A.A.)

1Alcoholics Anonymous, Alcoholics Anonymous World Services, Inc. (New York), p.76.

STEP EIGHT

Made a list of all persons we had harmed,
and became willing to make amends to them all.

Do to others as you would have them do to you.
(Luke 6:31)

❖ ❖ ❖

Prior to entering the Twelve Step Program, many of us blamed our parents, relatives and friends for the turmoil in our lives. We even held God responsible. In Step Eight, we begin the process of releasing the need to blame others for our misfortune and accepting full responsibility for our own lives. Our Fourth Step inventory revealed that our inappropriate behavior caused injury not only to us, but also to the significant others in our lives. Now we must prepare to accept full responsibility and make amends.

Steps One through Seven helped us to center ourselves in the healing power of Jesus Christ, and started the process of getting our lives in order. We were given the tools to examine our personal experiences and to see the importance of letting go of the past; thus becoming free to continue our personal growth. We must not be deterred by the pain of our past mistakes. Our personal progress is directly related to our success in facing our history and putting it behind us. Like barnacles on a ship's hull, our past wrongdoings prevent us from sailing smoothly to a life filled with peace.

Working Steps Eight and Nine will improve our relationships, both with ourselves and others, and lead us out of isolation and loneliness. The key factor here is our willingness to make amends to those whom we have harmed. As we continue to welcome Christ's presence into our hearts, we will develop a new openness with others that prepares us for the face-to-face admission of our past misconduct. In Step Eight, we examine each past misdeed and identify the persons involved. Our intention is to make amends in order to heal our past so that God can transform the present.

Reviewing our Fourth Step inventory will help us determine who belongs on our list. Preparing to make amends is a difficult task—one that we will execute with increasing skill, yet never really finish. Again, uncomfortable feelings may surface as we come to grips with our past behaviors. As we recognize the damage caused by our actions, we will glimpse the great relief that we will feel when we no longer cause injury to ourselves and others.

For many of us, admitting our misdeeds will be difficult. The pattern of our lives has been to blame others and to seek retribution for the wrongs done to us, rather than to admit we have initiated harm. As we become willing to look at ourselves, we see that, in many cases, the retribution we vainly sought just created more havoc. By insisting on our own measure of justice, we lost the ability to set and achieve positive goals. Cycles of hatred and hard feelings were created, and we kept our attention focused away from ourselves.

Forgiving ourselves and others helps us overcome our resentments. God has already forgiven us for the harmful actions that separated us from Him. Developing the ability to forgive ourselves is an important element in our ongoing recovery. To do so, we first must accept responsibility for the harm done and make amends with dignity and self-respect. Making amends without personally extending our forgiveness leads to dishonesty and further complicates our lives.

To repair our past wrongdoings, we must be willing to face them by recording the harm we think we have caused. When preparing the list of people whom we have harmed, we must sustain thoughts that enable us to initiate reconciliation, even though our intentions may be rebuffed. In some cases, people on our list feel bitter toward us and may resist our attempts at restitution. They may hold deep grudges and be unwilling to reconcile with us. Regardless of how we are received, we must be willing to forgive. We must remember that the list we make is principally for our own benefit, not the benefit of those whom we have harmed.

❖ *Looking to Scripture* ❖

Step Eight begins the process of healing damaged relationships through our willingness to make amends for past misdeeds. We can let go of our resentments and start to overcome the guilt, shame and low self-esteem we have acquired through our harmful actions. We can leave the gray, angry world of loneliness behind and move toward a bright future by exercising our newly developed relating skills. Through the gift of the Steps, we have the necessary tools to overcome these damaging conditions and mend our broken friendships.

> *But Zacchaeus stood up and said to the Lord, "Look, Lord! Here and now I give half of my possessions to the poor, and if I have cheated anybody out of anything, I will pay back four times the amount."* (LUKE 19:8)
>
> *As we identify those we have harmed, we also must prepare to make restitution.*

As Christians, we are taught the importance of having and maintaining deep, loving relationships. Through Christ's example, we see how He devoted His ministry to loving people and encouraging them to love one another. Jesus taught that being reconciled to God requires reconciliation with other human beings. In Step Eight, we prepare ourselves to carry out God's master plan for our lives by becoming willing to make amends. Once we have prepared our list of those whom we have harmed, we will be able to extend our love and acceptance not only to the injured persons, but also to all other members of God's family.

> *Dear friends, since God so loved us, we also ought to love one another. No one has ever seen God; but if we love one another, God lives in us and his love is made complete in us.* (1 JOHN 4:11-12)

Our willingness to make amends gives us an opportunity to love one another and experience how God lives in us.

For if you forgive men when they sin against you, your heavenly Father will also forgive you. But if you do not forgive men their sins, your Father will not forgive your sins. (MATTHEW 6:14-15)

Withholding our forgiveness inhibits our spiritual growth and perpetuates the continuance of guilt and shame.

You, therefore, have no excuse, you who pass judgment on someone else, for at whatever point you judge the other, you are condemning yourself, because you who pass judgment do the same things. (ROMANS 2:1)

Passing judgment on others removes us from God's grace and condemns us to repeat the pain of the past.

Forgiveness is a two-way street. As Christ declared in the Lord's Prayer: "Forgive us our trespasses, as we forgive those who trespass against us..."; we need to ask forgiveness of those whom we have harmed, as we forgive those who have harmed us. As we reflect on our Lord, we see how He encourages us to "turn the other cheek," to love our enemies and pray for our persecutors. Only in this manner can we break the cycle of hatred and violence.

"But I tell you who hear me: Love your enemies, do good to those who hate you, bless those who curse you, pray for those who mistreat you. If someone strikes you on one cheek, turn to him the other also. If someone takes your cloak, do not stop him from taking your tunic. Give to everyone who asks you, and if anyone takes what belongs to you, do not demand it back. Do to others as you would have them do to you." (LUKE 6:27-31)

Our healing will be noticeable to us when we are willing, even eager, to return good for evil.

78

When making our list, we need to examine our relationships with people at home, in our community and in the world at large. We must learn to forgive, and to accept the grace that comes as a part of such forgiveness. If we ask God to help us, our task will be much easier. We can ask Him for guidance in determining the names of the persons with whom we need to communicate. Setting aside our pride will help us see that all thoughts and feelings have worth and value. We do not have to agree with everyone, nor must they agree with us, but we can stop hating people for what they think and do—resenting them because their views are different from ours.

"Do not judge, and you will not be judged. Do not condemn, and you will not be condemned. Forgive, and you will be forgiven. Give, and it will be given to you. A good measure, pressed down, shaken together and running over, will be poured into your lap. For with the measure you use, it will be measured to you. (LUKE 6:37-38)

Receiving the gift of God's love and freely giving it to others assures an abundant life for us.

In some cases, we will be prevented from facing the people on our list directly. They may be deceased, separated from us or unwilling to meet with us. Whatever the situation, we still need to put them on our list. When we actually make the amends in Step Nine, we will see why amends are necessary, even if they cannot be face-to-face. Being willing to make the amend will release us from hard feelings and enable us to experience serenity and peace of mind.

Be kind and compassionate to one another, forgiving each other, just as in Christ God forgave you. (EPHESIANS 4:32)

Step Eight involves replacing bad feelings with compassion for ourselves and all of God's human family.

When looking at those persons whom we have harmed, we see how our character defects have played a major part in sabotaging our lives and our relationships. Examples of this behavior are:

- When we became angry, we often harmed ourselves more than others. This may have resulted in feelings of depression or self-pity.

- Persistent financial problems resulting from our irresponsible actions caused difficulty with our family and creditors.

- When confronted with an issue about which we felt guilty, we lashed out at others rather than looking honestly at ourselves.

- Frustrated by our lack of control, we behaved aggressively and intimidated those around us.

- Because of our indiscriminate sexual behavior, true intimacy was impossible to achieve or maintain.

- Our fear of abandonment sometimes destroyed our relationships, because we did not allow others to be themselves. We created dependency and tried to control their behavior in an effort to maintain the relationship as we wanted it to be.

We who are strong ought to bear with the failings of the weak and not to please ourselves. Each of us should please his neighbor for his good, to build him up. For even Christ did not please himself, but, as it is written: "The insults of those who insult you have fallen on me." (ROMANS 15:1-3)

As we grow in spiritual strength, we become willing servants of God, caring for our neighbors as He cares for us.

When making a list of people to whom making an amend is necessary, we need to remember to focus on ourselves. As adult children, many of us have been victims of self-inflicted pain because we did not have the skills to take care of ourselves appropriately. We spent time and energy trying to be available for everybody and sacrificed ourselves in the process. We may have become our own worst enemy and experienced excessive self-blame, guilt and shame. Taking time to look at the harm we have inflicted upon ourselves and being willing to forgive ourselves is essential to our continued growth.

> *"Why do you look at the speck of sawdust in your brother's eye and pay no attention to the plank in your own eye? How can you say to your brother, 'Let me take the speck out of your eye,' when all the time there is a plank in your own eye?"* (MATTHEW 7:3-4)
>
> *Honest self-appraisal is a daily necessity if we are to be restored to wholeness. Vigilant appraisal of our thoughts and habits must become routine.*

In Step Nine, we will seek out the people whom we have harmed, and make amends wherever necessary. For now, all we need to do is list them and describe the harmful behavior. The consequences of our actions may have produced emotional, financial or physical pain to others. We need to take as much time as necessary to reflect on our list and be as thorough as possible. Being totally honest with ourselves is a major factor in our ability to make restitution for our past destructive actions.

> *"And when you stand praying, if you hold anything against anyone, forgive him, so that your Father in heaven may forgive you your sins."* (MARK 11:25)
>
> *God's promise of healing cannot be fulfilled if we refuse to relinquish our anger and resentment. Our success in working Step Eight will depend directly on our ability to forgive.*

AMENDS LIST GUIDELINES

The following are three main categories in which we may have caused harm and for which we must be willing to make amends.

Material Wrongs: Actions which affected an individual in a tangible way, such as:

■ Borrowing or spending extravagance; stinginess; spending in an attempt to buy friendship or love; withholding money in order to gratify yourself.

■ Entering into agreements that are legally enforceable, then refusing to abide by the terms or simply cheating.

■ Injuring or damaging persons or property as a result of our actions.

Moral Wrongs: Inappropriate behavior in moral or ethical actions and conduct, including questions of rightness, fairness or equity. The principle issue is inovlving others in our wrongdoing:

■ Setting a bad example for children, friends, or anyone who looks to us for guidance.

■ Being preoccupied with selfish pursuits and totally unaware of the needs of others.

■ Forgetting birthdays, holidays and other special occasions.

■ Inflicting moral harm (e.g., sexual infidelity, broken promises, verbal abuse, lack of trust, lying).

Spiritual Wrongs: "Acts of omission" as a result of neglecting our obligations to God, to ourselves, to family and to community.

■ Making no effort to fulfill our obligations and showing no gratitude toward others who have helped us.

■ Avoiding self-development (e.g., health, education, recreation, creativity)

■ Being inattentive to others in our lives by showing a lack of encouragement to them.

AMENDS LIST

Person	Relationship	My Wrong-doing	Effect on Others	Effect On Me
Joan	Wife	angry insults	fear, anger	guilt, shame
John	Co-worker	sexual advances at party	distrust, shame	loss of self-respect

STEP NINE

*Made direct amends to such people wherever possible,
except when to do so would injure them or others.*

*Therefore, if you are offering your gift at the altar
and there remember that your brother has something against you, leave your gift there in front of
the altar. First go and be reconciled to your
brother; then come and offer your gift.*
(Matthew 5:23-24)

❖ ❖ ❖

Step Nine completes the forgiveness process that began in Step
Four and fulfills our requirement to reconcile with others. In
this Step, we clear our garden of the dead leaves and "rake up
and discard" the old habits. We are ready to face our faults, to
admit the degree of our wrongs, and to ask for and extend forgiveness. Accepting responsibility for the harm done can be an
awkward experience, as it forces us to admit the affect we have
had on others.

Since we began our recovery, we have come a long way toward
developing a new lifestyle. We have seen how the powerlessness
and unmanageability of our lives caused havoc. Our commitment
to face our character defects, to admit them to others and, finally,
to ask God for their removal has been a humbling experience.
In Steps Eight and Nine, we proceed with the final stage of rebuild-
ing our character.

Good judgment, a careful sense of timing, courage and stamina
are the qualities we need to develop when working Step Nine.
We will know we are ready to make amends when we are confident
of our new skills and when others begin to observe that we are
improving our lives. As we become more courageous, it will be
easier and safer to talk honestly about our past behavior and admit
to others that we have caused them harm.

Making amends will release us from many of the resentments of our past. It is a means of achieving serenity in our lives by seeking forgiveness from those whom we have harmed and making restitution where necessary. Without forgiveness, the resentments will continue to undermine our growth. Making amends releases us from guilt and promotes freedom and health in mind and body.

In preparing to make our amends, we realize that some people in our lives feel bitter toward us. They may feel threatened by us and resent our changed behavior. When considering the appropriateness of facing these people directly, we can pray about it and ask that Christ's wisdom be made known to us. If we are to forgive ourselves completely, we must first acknowledge the pain that others have endured as a result of our actions.

Some stumbling blocks appear in Step Nine. We may procrastinate by telling ourselves "the time is not yet right." We may delay by finding endless excuses to avoid facing those whom we have harmed. We must be honest with ourselves and not procrastinate because of fear. Fear is lack of courage, and courage is an important requirement for the successful completion of this Step, as well as the rest of the program. Our readiness to accept the consequences of our past and take responsibility for restoring the well-being of those whom we have harmed is the very spirit of Step Nine.

Another delaying tactic is the temptation to let bygones be bygones. We rationalize that our past is behind us, that there is no need to stir up more trouble. We fantasize that amends for past misdeeds are not necessary, that all we have to do is alter our current behavior. It is true that some of our past behaviors may be laid to rest without direct confrontation, but facing as many people and issues as possible is a good idea. The more situations we face, the more rapidly we will progress to our new life of peace and serenity.

❖ *Looking to Scripture* ❖

In order to successfully complete Step Nine, we need to review our list from Step Eight and determine the appropriate way to make each amend. Most situations will require direct contact, although some may be handled by simply changing our behavior. Whichever alternative we choose, it is important that the process of making amends be as complete as possible.

We love because he first loved us. If anyone says, "I love God," yet hates his brother, he is a liar. For anyone who does not love his brother, whom he has seen, cannot love God, whom he has not seen. (1 JOHN 4:19-21)

If we love God, we cannot hate any of His creation. A measure of our love for Him is visible when we give this love to others.

Step Nine has two distinct parts regarding making amends:

"MADE DIRECT AMENDS TO SUCH PEOPLE WHEREVER POSSIBLE,"

People who are readily accessible and who can be approached as soon as we are ready.

These people include family members, creditors, co-workers and others to whom we owe an amend. They can be friends or enemies. As part of making the amend, we must try to repair the damage that has been done to the best of our ability. The other person's response may be surprising to us, especially if our amend is accepted—we may wonder why we waited so long to resolve the conflict.

"You have heard that it was said, 'Love your neighbor and hate your enemy.' But I tell you: Love your enemies and pray for those who persecute you." (MATTHEW 5:43-44)

When we extend love to our enemies, we diminish their power over us and offer God's forgiveness, which He has so graciously given to us.

Situations that will not allow us to make direct personal contact.

This involves people who are no longer accessible or who are deceased. In these cases, indirect amends can satisfy our need for reconciliation and are accomplished through prayer or by writing a letter, as if we are actually communicating with the absent person. We can also make amends by performing a kindness for someone else we may not even know, but who is connected in some way to the person whom we have harmed.

Above all, love each other deeply, because love covers over a multitude of sins. Offer hospitality to one another without grumbling. Each one should use whatever gift he has received to serve others, faithfully administering God's grace in its various forms. (1 PETER 4:8-10)

The fellowship of persons in a program of recovery offers an excellent opportunity to more fully understand what it means to be God's willing servant.

"EXCEPT WHEN TO DO SO WOULD INJURE THEM OR OTHERS"

People to whom we can make only partial restitution because complete disclosure could cause harm to them or others.

These people may include spouses, ex-partners, former business associates or friends. We must analyze the harm they would suffer if complete disclosure was made. This is especially true in cases of infidelity. In such situations, irreparable damage could occur to all parties. Even if the matter must be discussed, we should avoid bringing harm to third parties. Amends for infidelity can be made by concentrating sincere affection and attention on persons to whom we have made loving commitments.

"Therefore, if you are offering your gift at the altar and there remember that your brother has something against you, leave your gift there in front of the altar. First go and be reconciled to your brother; then come and offer your gift. (MATTHEW 5:23-24)

Clearing our lives of the damage caused by our past actions may appear insurmountable in the beginning of our Program. Nevertheless, our commitment is to confront our resistance to doing God's will.

In cases involving serious consequences, such as potential loss of employment, imprisonment or other harm to one's family, we need to weigh the options carefully. We should not be deterred from making amends through fear of incurring injury to ourselves, but only through the possibility of causing injury to others. If we choose to delay merely out of fear for ourselves, we will be the ones to suffer. We will delay our growth and experience regression in our progress toward building a new life.

...if he gives back what he took in pledge for a loan, returns what he has stolen, follows the decrees that give life, and does no evil, he will surely live; he will not die. None of the sins he has committed will be remembered against him. He has done what is just and right; he will surely live. (EZEKIEL 33:15-16)

Regardless of our motive for taking something that is not ours, keeping it only ensures our continued bondage to those things that keep us from the Truth.

Situations which require deferred action.
In these areas, seeking additional counsel is helpful in assessing our judgment of the situation. Abruptly approaching an individual who still suffers deeply from the injustices we have done is seldom wise. In situations where our own pain is still deeply imbedded, patience might be the wise choice. Timing is important to gaining and growing from the experience and in preventing further injury.

Therefore encourage one another and build each other up, just as in fact you are doing. (1 THESSALONIANS 5:11)

Looking only for the good in each other and ourselves enables us to avoid any destructive thoughts that could impair our relationships.

> *Therefore let us stop passing judgment on one another. Instead, make up your mind not to put any stumbling block or obstacle in your brother's way.* (ROMANS 14:13)
>
> *Judging others separates us from them and prevents us from extending the love to one another that God commands.*

As we have learned, certain situations require special consideration. It is better to proceed slowly and succeed with the amend, rather than hurry and cause more damage. Here, God can be a great source of aid and comfort. He has gotten us this far, and we need to be constantly aware that our progress is greatly influenced by His presence with us now.

> *"But love your enemies, do good to them, and lend to them without expecting to get anything back. Then your reward will be great, and you will be sons of the Most High, because he is kind to the ungrateful and wicked."* (LUKE 6:35-36)
>
> *We receive God's grace without having to earn it. We must offer goodness to others in the same manner, expecting nothing in return.*

To facilitate making the amend, prepare a schedule listing the persons to contact, what you will say, how you will say it and when you will say it. Writing letters and making phone calls are acceptable ways of making amends if face-to-face contact is not possible. In some cases, meeting in person may not be the most desirable approach. The important thing is to initiate reconciliation before it is too late. Successful amends-making will produce improved relationships with those whom we have harmed and promote positive interactions with new acquaintances. Our new ways of relating will empower us to achieve and maintain healthy relationships.

> *Let no debt remain outstanding, except the continuing debt to love one another, for he who loves his fellowman has fulfilled the law.* (ROMANS 13:8)

Careful examination of our relationships with others will sometimes reveal forgotten debts. Keeping God's law requires that we make restitution.

When working this Step, we need to distinguish between amends and apologies. Though apologies are sometimes appropriate, they are not substitutes for making amends. A person can apologize for being late for work, but until the behavior is corrected, an amend cannot be made. It is important to apologize when necessary, but it is more important to commit to changing the unacceptable behavior.

Do not repay anyone evil for evil. Be careful to do what is right in the eyes of everybody. If it is possible, as far as it depends on you, live at peace with everyone. (ROMANS 12:17-18)

Seeking revenge only perpetuates distress and frustration. God requires that we return good for evil.

Occasional emotional or spiritual relapses are to be expected and should be dealt with promptly. If not, they will block our ability to make successful amends. When these relapses occur, we must accept them as signals that we are not working the Program effectively. Perhaps we have turned away from God and need to return to Step Three; or we may have eliminated something from our inventory and must return to Step Four; or we may be unwilling to relinquish a character defect and need to return to Step Six.

Do nothing out of selfish ambition or vain conceit, but in humility consider others better than yourselves. Each of you should look not only to your own interests, but also to the interests of others. (PHILIPPIANS 2:3-4)

When we inflict harm on another, we cause harm to ourselves. Our program of recovery enhances our self-esteem and enables us to love and value others above ourselves, often looking out for their best interest before our own.

Steps Eight and Nine help us bury the past. Through these Steps, we reconcile ourselves to taking responsibility for causing injury to others and for making restitution where necessary. We have a chance to redeem ourselves for past misdeeds by making amends and can look forward to a healthy and rewarding future life. We are now able to rebuild our self-esteem, achieve peaceful relations with ourselves and others, and live in harmony with our own personal world and with God.

Therefore, as God's chosen people, holy and dearly loved, clothe yourselves with compassion, kindness, humility, gentleness and patience. Bear with each other and forgive whatever grievances you may have against one another. Forgive as the Lord forgave you. (COLOSSIANS 3:12-13)

Step Nine stimulates our desire to be Christ-like. We see how His way of relating brings us peace and a growing capacity for patience, kindness and compassion.

AMENDS TO OTHERS GUIDELINES

The following is a summary of ideas and procedures that have been useful in preparing for and making the amends required in Step Nine.

Attitude

- Being willing to love and forgive yourself and the person to whom an amend is to be made.

- Knowing what you want to say and being careful not to blame the person with whom you are communicating.

- Taking responsibility for what you are going to say.

- Being willing to accept the consequences.

- Resisting the desire for a specific response from the other person.

- Being willing to turn your anxieties over to God.

Preparation

- Devoting time to prayer and meditation.

- Delaying the amend if you are angry or upset and doing more Step Four inventory work.

- Keeping it simple. Details and explanations aren't necessary.

- Remembering that the amend does not focus on the other person's part in the situation.

- Expressing your desire or asking permission to make the amend. For example: *I am involved in a program that requires me to be aware of the harm I have done to others and to take responsibility for my actions. I'd like to make amends to you. Are you willing to receive them?*

Sample Amends

- *I was (scared, overwhelmed, feeling abandoned, etc.) when _____ happened between us. I ask your forgiveness for (harm done) and for anything else I may have done in the past by my thoughts, words, or actions that caused you pain.*

I didn't mean to cause you pain. I ask your forgiveness and assure you of my intention to extend goodwill to you.

■ *I want to make an amend to you about _____. For all those words that were said out of (fear, thoughtlessness, etc.) and confusion, I ask your forgiveness. I extend my promise of love and caring toward you.*

AMENDS TO SELF GUIDELINES

The following are some guidelines to use when making amends to yourself.

Attitute

■ Being willing to love and forgive yourself.

■ Knowing what you want to say and taking responsibility for your actions.

■ Having reasonable expectations of yourself.

■ Being willing to turn your anxieties over to God.

Preparation

■ Devoting time to prayer and meditation.

■ Delaying the amend if you are angry or upset and doing more Step Four inventory work. Keeping it simple. Explanations are not necessary.

■ Remembering the amend is to yourself and does not pertain to others.

Sample Amends

■ *I was (scared, overwhelmed, feeling abandoned, etc.) when _____ happened. I forgive myself for the (harm done) and anything else I may have done in the past by my thoughts, words or actions that may have caused me harm.*

■ *I want to make an amend to myself about _____. I forgive myself for all the words that I said out of (fear, thoughtlessness, etc.) and confusion.*

STEP TEN

Continued to take personal inventory and,
when we were wrong, promptly admitted it.

So, if you think you are standing firm,
be careful that you don't fall!
(1 Corinthians 10:12)

❖ ❖ ❖

In Step Ten, we begin the maintenance segment of the Steps. We will learn how to sustain what we have accomplished, become more confident and proceed with joy along our spiritual journey. The first nine Steps put our house in order and enabled us to change some of our destructive behavior patterns. By continuing our work on the Steps, we will increase our capacity to develop new and healthier ways of taking care of ourselves and relating to others.

As we begin to experience some peace and serenity in our lives, some of us may wonder if it is permanent or just temporary. Working the Steps has helped us to see how fragile and vulnerable we are. With daily practice of the Steps, and with Christ's loving presence in our lives, we will be able to achieve and maintain our newfound equilibrium. Our relating skills will improve, and we will see how our interaction with others assumes a new quality.

At this point, we may be tempted to revert to our old bravado and believe we are healed. We may think we have all the answers and can stop here. We feel comfortable with ourselves and see no need to continue with the Program. We allow other activities to interfere and find excuses for skipping meetings and abandoning the Program. We must resist this temptation to quit and realize that giving in will deprive us of realizing the goal we have set for ourselves. We must recognize that the successes we have experienced can be maintained only if we are willing to practice the Program daily for the rest of our lives.

Step Ten points the way toward continued spiritual growth. In the past, we were constantly burdened by the results of our inattention to what we were doing. We allowed small problems to become large by ignoring them until they multiplied. Through our lack of sensitivity and skills to improve our behavior, we allowed our character defects to create havoc in our lives. In Step Ten, we consciously examine our daily conduct and make adjustments where necessary. We look at ourselves, see our errors, promptly admit them and make corrections.

While we are working so carefully to monitor our actions and reactions, we must not judge ourselves too harshly. We need to recognize that nurturing ourselves emotionally and spiritually requires daily vigilance, loving understanding and patience. Life is never static; it is constantly changing, and each change requires adjustment and growth.

A personal inventory is a daily examination of our strengths and weaknesses, motives and behaviors. It is as important as prayer in nurturing our spiritual development. Taking inventory is not a time-consuming task and can usually be accomplished in fifteen minutes per day. When done with discipline and regularity, this is a small price to pay for continuing the good work we have begun.

We need to monitor signs of attempting to manage our lives alone or slipping into past patterns such as resentment, dishonesty or selfishness. When we see these temptations arising, we must immediately ask God to forgive us and make amends. Daily practice of Step Ten maintains our honesty and humility and allows us to continue our development.

Taking regular inventory makes us more conscious of our strengths and weaknesses. We are less inclined to yield to feelings of anger, loneliness and self-righteousness if we remain emotionally balanced and gather courage as we see our strengths increasing. Our personal inventory helps us discover who we are, what we are and where we are going. We become more focused and capable of living the Christian life we desire.

❖ *Looking to Scripture* ❖

The Program's emphasis on daily inventory is based on the realization that many of us haven't developed the necessary tools for self-appraisal. As we become familiar and comfortable with personal inventories, we will be willing to invest the time required in exchange for the rewards received. Three types of inventories are recommended; each serves a different purpose. These are Spot-Check Inventory, Daily Inventory and Long-Term Periodic Inventory.

Whoever of you loves life and desires to see many good days, keep your tongue from evil and your lips from speaking lies. Turn from evil and do good; seek peace and pursue it. (PSALM 34:12)

Working the Steps trains us to be sensitive to our behavior and encourages us to seek God's will for us. As we become more adept, we turn naturally from evil and toward God.

Spot-Check Inventory

Spot-checking is stopping for a few moments several times each day to analyze what is happening. It is a short review of our actions, thoughts and motives and can be useful in calming stormy emotions. It is a tool for examining each situation, seeing where we are wrong and taking prompt corrective action. Taking frequent inventories and immediately admitting our wrongs keeps us free from guilt and supports our spiritual growth.

For by the grace given me I say to every one of you: Do not think of yourself more highly than you ought, but rather think of yourself with sober judgment, in accordance with the measure of faith God has given you. (ROMANS 12:3)

Our continuing honest assessment of ourselves will become more finely tuned as the greater truth is revealed to us. We should view each new discovery with compassion and have faith that God will give us strength according to our needs.

Daily Inventory

It is important to stop at the end of each day, review what has happened and examine our involvement to remind us that this is a daily program, lived one day at a time. It keeps us focused on the present and prevents us from worrying about the future or living in the past.

"Settle matters quickly with your adversary who is taking you to court. Do it while you are still with him on the way, or he may hand you over to the judge, and the judge may hand you over to the officer, and you may be thrown into prison. I tell you the truth, you will not get out until you have paid the last penny." (MATTHEW 5:25-26)

In the past, our pride often prevented us from making timely settlements. Living in the light of God's love helps us correct our wrongs and forgive the faults of others.

The daily inventory can be viewed as a balance sheet for the day—a summary of the good as well as the bad. It is an opportunity to reflect on our interaction with other people. In the situations where we did well, we can feel good and acknowledge progress. In those situations where we tried and failed, we need to acknowledge our attempt; for, in fact, we did try. Our failures can illuminate our errors; we can then make amends and move forward with a quiet mind. As we work the Program, we can be assured that our number of successes will continue to increase.

Therefore each of you must put off falsehood and speak truthfully to his neighbor, for we are all members of one body. "In your anger do not sin": Do not let the sun go down while you are still angry, and do not give the devil a foothold. He who has been stealing must steal no longer, but must work, doing something useful with his own hands, that he may have something to share with those in need. (EPHESIANS 4:25-28)

Delaying the resolution of angry feelings can cause physical, emotional and spiritual damage. God's grace is sufficient to relinquish any hold that negativity may have on us.

Future situations may arise that will challenge our integrity and commitment. We need to be as honest and clear about our intentions as possible. Things to consider are:

■ If we are slipping back, trying to control and manipulate others, we need to recognize this and ask God to correct it.

■ If we are comparing ourselves to others and feeling inferior, we need to reach out to our supportive friends and examine our feelings, in order to renew our own sense or self-acceptance.

■ If we are becoming obsessive or compulsive and not taking care of ourselves, we need to stop and ask our Higher Power for help, not only in determining the unmet needs we are trying to fulfill, but also how to meet these needs.

■ If we are fearing authority figures, we need to find the reason for our fear, acknowledge it, and ask our Higher Power for help in reacting appropriately.

■ If we are depressed, we need to discover the central issue that is causing us to feel withdrawn or sorry for ourselves.

■ If we are withholding our feelings, being uncommunicative or giving in to others' wants and needs, we need to take the necessary risks and express our feelings assertively.

Anyone who listens to the word but does not do what it says is like a man who looks at his face in a mirror and, after looking at himself, goes away and immediately forgets what he looks like. But the man who looks intently into the perfect law that gives freedom, and continues to do this, not forgetting what he has heard, but doing it—he will be blessed in what he does. (JAMES 1:23-25)

The work we do in the Twelve Step Program basically provides a structure wherein we can look at ourselves with honesty and lovingly accept who we are.

Long-Term Periodic Inventory

A long-term periodic inventory can be accomplished by being alone or going away for a period of time. These are special days that can be set aside for reflecting on our lives by attending a retreat or simply being in solitude. This is an important time and provides an opportunity for us to renew our intention to live a new life in Christ.

> *Therefore, if anyone is in Christ, he is a new creation; the old has gone, the new has come!* (2 CORINTHIANS 5:17)
>
> *The renewal of our relationship with Christ has brought us new life. Through His love for us, our progress to recovery will be sustained.*

This inventory can be done once or twice a year and will give us a chance to reflect on our progress from a clearer perspective. We will have an opportunity to see the remarkable changes we have made and to renew our hope and courage. We must be careful not to inflate our ego and must remind ourselves that our progress is a product of God's help and our careful spiritual growth. Long-term inventories help us to recognize problem areas and enable us to make the necessary corrections promptly. As a result of our new experiences, we sometimes find new defects as well as new strengths.

> *You were taught, with regard to your former way of life, to put off your old self, which is being corrupted by its deceitful desires; to be made new in the attitude of your minds; and to put on the new self, created to be like God in true righteousness and holiness.* (EPHESIANS 4:22-24)
>
> *The Steps repeatedly remind us that God is in charge, and that our new state of mind is grounded in what God wants for us, rather than in what we want for ourselves.*

If we sincerely desire to change our way of life, take personal inventory on a regular basis and pay attention to the sharing of other recovering friends, we will discover that we are not unique. All people get upset occasionally and are not always "right." Through this awareness, we develop the ability to be forgiving and understanding and to love others for who they are. By being kind, courteous and fair, we will often receive the same in return and can expect to achieve harmony in many of our relationships. As we progress in our recovery, we see how pointless it is to become angry or to allow others to inflict emotional pain on us. Taking periodic, regular inventory and promptly admitting our wrongs keeps us from harboring resentments and allows us to maintain our dignity and respect for ourselves and others.

A patient man has great understanding, but a quick-tempered man displays folly. A heart at peace gives life to the body, but envy rots the bones. (PROVERBS 14:29-30)

A peaceful nature enables us to be compassionate and frees the mind and spirit to seek a quality life.

The conscientious practice of Step Ten has many benefits; most importantly, it strengthens and protects our recovery. We find additional rewards in many areas, such as:

- When old behaviors reappear, they are simply repetitions of learned patterns of behavior. They reflect choices of our unconscious mind as it defended us against feelings of pain, strife, helplessness, guilt, revenge, disapproval, etc. Clinging to these patterns keeps us from achieving the spiritual growth we so desire.

- We feel safe when something is familiar to us, even though it is a negative behavior pattern or addiction from the past that may ultimately cause us pain. We use it anyway, because it is familiar to us.

- We victimize ourselves by allowing the past to occupy our thoughts. We can let go of the past by acknowledging the unmet responsibilities that created our struggle.

- Releasing an old behavior pattern can be frightening. By surrendering it to our Higher Power, we learn to trust that we will receive the needed support to develop behaviors that are more appropriate for our present wants and needs.

- We can reach out to loving and supportive friends. They are important ingredients in our recovery.

So, if you think you are standing firm, be careful that you don't fall! (1 CORINTHIANS 10:12)

As we complete Step Ten, we must not be over-confident in our recovery. Slipping into past behaviors can endanger our commitment to do God's will.

Successful working of Step Ten enables us to be genuinely sorry for our wrongs. It assists us in continually striving for improvement in our relationships with others. Learning to face our faults on a daily basis and correcting them promptly is the formula for improving our character and lifestyle. Delay in admitting our wrongs indicates a resistance to practicing Step Ten. This is harmful and will only make matters worse.

- Relationship problems diminish. Taking inventory and admitting our wrongs promptly dissolves many misunderstandings without further incident.

- We learn to express ourselves, rather than fear being "found out." We see that, by being honest, we do not need to hide behind a false front.

- We no longer have to pretend we are flawless and, thus, can be candid about admitting our wrongs.

- Through admitting our own wrongs, others may, in turn, become aware of the ineffectiveness of their own behavior. We develop a true understanding of others and become capable of intimacy.

Be very careful, then, how you live—not as unwise but as wise, making the most of every opportunity, because the days are evil. (EPHESIANS 5:15-16)

Our peace and serenity will be strengthened by the ongoing Step work we do. We now know that each day is a new opportunity to actively protect and sustain ongoing recovery.

STEP ELEVEN

Sought through prayer and meditation to improve our conscious contact with God as we understood Him, praying only for knowledge of His will for us and the power to carry that out.

Let the word of Christ dwell in you richly.
(Colossians 3:16a)

❖ ❖ ❖

As we begin our work in Step Eleven, we clearly see that Steps Ten and Eleven are the tools which will help us sustain the progress we have made in Steps One through Nine. In the first three Steps, we began to understand the seriousness of our condition and established the foundation for dealing with our problems. In Steps Four through Nine, we experienced a process similar to that of taking our car to the garage for a long-overdue, major overhaul. We devoted the time and energy required to make the necessary repairs and restore our "engine" to its proper running condition. In Steps Ten and Eleven, we have the opportunity to keep ourselves in tune by devoting time to regular service and maintenance. We learn to recognize problems, to correct them promptly, and to continually look for ways to improve our new skills for living life to the fullest. To the degree that we are willing to provide the required maintenance, we will find that our lives will run smoothly.

Prior to Step Eleven, we made contact with God in three of the Steps. In Step Three, we made a decision to turn our wills and our lives over to His care; in Step Five, we admitted our wrongs to Him; in Step Seven, we humbly asked Him to remove our shortcomings. In Step Eleven, we use prayer and meditation to improve our conscious contact with God, as well as become sensitive and responsive to His guidance. To continue our spiritual growth, we must repeat these Steps regularly.

Through the progress we have made in working the Steps, we are learning more about what we want to achieve in the Program. To protect what we have learned, we must continually seek to know God's will for us. A daily regimen of prayer and meditation makes it clear that relief from pain of the past is just a day-to-day reprieve—we must relentlessly pursue recovery on a daily basis. Those of us who have experienced the hell and chaos caused by our willful acts realize that we worshipped false gods such as drugs, sex, or money, and were often participants in addictive relationships. For us, surrendering to the Twelve Steps was not the step that led us to heaven, but was, in fact, the step that led us out of the hell that our lives had become.

Spiritual growth and development occur slowly and only through discipline. The best example of the discipline of prayer is that of Jesus as He prayed frequently to know His Father's will. In the Lord's Prayer, the singularly most important element is "Thy will be done, on earth as it is in heaven." This may be interpreted as "May your will be realized throughout all of space, time and creation. God, if it is to be done, it is for you to bring it about." As our self-esteem increases and Jesus Christ, our Higher Power, becomes a trusted friend, we grow more confident that He is present with us when we pray.

Meditation is an important way of seeking God's will for us, of setting aside our own intentions and receiving God's guidance. Meditating can quiet our minds and remove the barriers of our conscious thoughts. When properly done, this process will calm us emotionally and relax us physically. We will then release energy we normally expend keeping our emotions in high gear and our bodies tense with anxiety.

Our approach to Step Eleven will vary in intent and intensity; it indicates our commitment to a prayerful life. If we are communing and are communicating with God, His joy will infuse our fellowship and friendship with others. We will reap rich benefits. Ideally, we practice this Step daily upon awakening and retiring, to remind us that we must sincerely and humbly want God's will for us.

NOTE: Before proceeding, refer to *Guidelines for Prayer and Meditating on God's Word* on page 111.

❖ *Looking to Scripture* ❖

Praying only for knowledge of God's will for us and the power to carry it out helps us set aside our self-serving motives and interact well with others. We receive reassurance of God's presence and know that His will is for us to be restored to health. Scripture gives examples of how we will behave when we allow God's will to work through us. In Luke 6:35-38, we are told: *"Love your enemies, do good to them, and lend to them...be merciful...do not judge...do not condemn...forgive...give..."* When we follow Luke's teachings we feel peaceful and serene.

"The good man brings good things out of the good stored up in his heart...For out of the outflow of his heart his mouth speaks." (LUKE 6:45)

The goal of each of the Steps is to promote our knowledge of God and our basic goodness and value as part of His creation.

"Therefore I tell you, whatever you ask for in prayer, believe that you have received it, and it will be yours. And when you stand praying, if you hold anything against anyone, forgive him, so that your Father in heaven may forgive you your sins." (MARK 11:24)

Our belief in God and the use of prayer are the principal tools that enable the Twelve Steps to support our recovery.

Spending time meditating on God's word enables us to become better acquainted with God in the same way that we become acquainted with someone we would really like to know; that is, by spending time with Him. Meditation can be difficult in the beginning. We are accustomed to being active and may feel uncomfortable with sitting still and calming our busy thoughts. We may feel we are wasting time, instead of doing something more productive. Actually, for us, nothing could be more productive.

"Let us acknowledge the LORD; let us press on to acknowledge him. As surely as the sun rises, he will appear; he will come to us like the winter rains, like the spring rains that water the earth." (HOSEA 6:3)

Any difficulties we have in allowing God to come into our lives will be minimized as we acknowledge His presence throughout each day.

In the act of meditating, we recall, ponder and apply our knowledge of God's ways, purposes and promises. It is an activity of holy thought, consciously performed in the presence of God, under the eye of God and by the help of God, as a two-way communion with Him. Its purpose is to clear our mental and spiritual vision and let His truth make its full and proper impact on our minds and hearts. Meditation humbles us as we contemplate God's greatness and glory and allow His Spirit to encourage, reassure and comfort us.

"But when you pray, go into your room, close the door and pray to your Father, who is unseen. Then your Father, who sees what is done in secret, will reward you." (MATTHEW 6:6)

Meditation may be new to us and feelings of discomfort may arise. With practice, we will realize the value of spending quiet time in contemplation and prayer. Once we learn a technique that is comfortable to us, we will never turn away.

"Show me your ways, O LORD, teach me your paths; guide me in your truth and teach me, for you are God my Savior, and my hope is in you all day long." (PSALM 25:4-5)

Being attentive to God's guidance requires our being conscious of the unexpected gifts that come to us each day. Giving thanks for all our opportunities to serve Him heightens our sensititivy to the infinite ways in which our Lord is leading us.

In developing a routine for prayer and meditation, we seek times and places to receive God's presence and be available for Him. Some simple guidelines for learning to pray and meditate are:

- Pray and meditate in solitude. Be alone and undisturbed, so you can be totally free from distractions.

- Pray and meditate in silence, or talk quietly to God without interruptions. Outside influences disrupt your concentration and inhibit your ability to tell God your thoughts and feelings.

- Set aside quality time. Do not wait until you are tired or your ability to clear you mind is hindered.

- Listen carefully. God has messages for you, just as you have messages for Him.

- Review your daily inventory with God. Admit your wrongs, ask for forgiveness and make amends to Him as needed.

- End your session by asking for knowledge of His will and the power to carry it out.

"Ask and it will be given to you; seek and you will find; knock and the door will be opened to you." (MATTHEW 7:7)

Seeking to know His will and having the courage to carry it out are what our Lord has repeatedly instructed us to petition.

If we are progressing satisfactorily with Step Eleven by praying and meditating daily, we will see signs along the way. We will feel more at peace in our daily affairs, and will experience deep gratitude for the ongoing healing of disabled behavior. We will feel as though we have finally achieved a rightful place in the world. Feelings of self-worth will replace feelings of shame. These signs tell us that God is guiding and sustaining our recovery.

"Blessed is the man who does not walk in the counsel of the wicked or stand in the way of sinners or sit in the seat of mockers. But his delight is in the law of the LORD, and on his law he meditates day and night. He is like a tree

---

planted by streams of water, which yields its fruit in season and whose leaf does not wither. Whatever it does prospers." (PSALM 1:1-3)

If we walk in the way of the Lord, the fruits of the Spirit will appear, much as the gifts of our physical world appear in nature.

Combining prayer and meditating on God's word with self-examination is the secret to successfully working the Steps and moving toward a rewarding spiritual life. No matter how dedicated we are to recovery, we all have moments of doubt about the direction of our lives. We may even question the need to continue working the Steps. Sometimes, we are tempted to regress to our old compulsive behavior. We tend to be especially vulnerable when we feel pressured for accomplishment and expect events to follow our own time schedule. In our frustration, we seize control from God's hands and attempt to hasten the process through our own willfulness. When we do this, we are not following God's guidance and must renew the commitment we made in Step Three.

"Your word is a lamp to my feet and a light for my path. I have taken an oath and confirmed it, that I will follow your righteous laws." (PSALM 119:105-106)

We were stumbling in darkness, when through God's grace a lamp was lighted to show us the way. Our commitment is to follow the light.

Our power to implement God's will can be challenged in those moments when our lives seem to be crumbling. Again, the best example of faithfulness is the way in which Jesus persevered during the challenges of His experiences toward the end of His life on earth. The strength of His faith can be summarized by this prayer, made in Gethsemane as He was overwhelmed by what lay before Him: *"...My Father, if it is possible, may this cup be taken from me. Yet not as I will, but as you will."* (MATTHEW 26:39) During stressful moments, reflecting on Steps Three and Eleven will help us maintain our peace and serenity.

"Do not be anxious about anything, but in everything, by prayer and petition, with thanksgiving, present your requests to God." (PHILIPPIANS 4:6)

In the midst of joyful celebration or anxious conflict, through prayers of thanksgiving or sorrowful lament, our daily walk with the Lord deepens and strengthens our faith in God and the knowledge that His presence is with us.

Praying and meditating give us an opportunity to seek God's plan for us. He gave us intellect and free will, through which we think and act. As part of successfully practicing Step Eleven, we must not create excuses to delay our actions, rationalizing that we are "waiting" for God's will. Part of doing God's will is taking action, trusting that God's Holy Spirit is working through us. In unclear situations, it is sometimes wise to seek outside counsel. Revelations may come to us through other people or new experiences, as God continues to reach out to us in different ways. After careful review of the situation, our guidance may be clear and compelling or still unclear. If unclear, we must be patient—more will be revealed to us. If we cannot wait, we must select the best course of action and trust that God is with us, guiding us as we go. Our faith in His guidance will allow us to receive what needs to be revealed to us. The way we feel and function clearly indicates if God's will is being done.

"If you believe, you will receive whatever you ask for in prayer." (MATTHEW 21:22)

Keeping a diary of how God answered our prayers through individuals or new experiences is one way to document our new life in Christ.

"But the one who hears my words and does not put them into practice is like a man who built a house on the ground without a foundation. The moment the torrent struck that house, it collapsed and its destruction was complete." (LUKE 6:49)

Doubting God has consequences with which we are all too familiar. Perhaps our lack of faith caused the original despair that led us to the Twelve Step Program of recovery.

Our earthly walk with God, as exemplified by Jesus Christ, is designed to bring us a life that is filled with abundance. This is God's will for us as described in the teachings of Jesus. If we will *"...in everything, do to others what you would have them do to you..."* (MATTHEW 7:12), our daily lives will exemplify what Step Eleven means.

"Whether you turn to the right or to the left, your ears will hear a voice behind you, saying, "This is the way; walk in it." (ISAIAH 30:21)

The Holy Spirit responds to every prayer for help and guidance. His lesson for us is always unique to each situation.

GUIDELINES FOR PRAYER AND MEDITATING ON GOD'S WORD

An overview of prayer and meditation for a given day may be outlined as follows:

At the beginning of the day, review your plans and:

- Ask God for direction in your thoughts and actions.

  - To keep you free from self-pity, dishonesty or selfishness.

  - To provide the guidance needed to take care of any problems.

- Ask God for freedom from self-will.

  - To prevent making requests unless others will be helped.

  - To avoid praying for our own selfish needs.

During the day, in moments of indecision or fear:

- Ask God for inspiration and guidance.

- Reflect on Step Three and turn it over.

  - Relax and breathe deeply several times.

  - Be aware of any desire to struggle with a situation or person.

- Pray to God as often as necessary during the day.

  - *God, please remove this _____(feeling, obsesssion, addiction, etc.)*

  - *Lord, not my will, but Thine be done.*

- If possible, call a support person to identify and share what is happening.

At the end of the day, review the events that happened and:

- Reflect on Step Ten and take a personal inventory.

  - Ask God for guidance in taking corrective action.

- Ask God for knowledge of His will for you.

- Ask God's forgiveness where needed, and acknowledge that this review is not intended to cause obsessive thinking, worry, remorse, or morbid reflection.

- Give thanks to God for the guidance and blessings that were part of the day.

STEP TWELVE

Having had a spiritual awakening as the result of these Steps,
we tried to carry this message to others, and to
practice these principles in all our affairs.

Brothers, if someone is caught in a sin, you who
are spiritual should restore him gently. But watch
yourself, or you also may be tempted.

(Galatians 6:1)

❖ ❖ ❖

T he Twelfth Step completes the climb of this particular mountain. Remembering the milestones in this adventure brings
to mind the pain and joy we have experienced while accomplishing
our objective. Our experiences have been unique and individual
to each of us. We now realize that all the events of our lives have
pulled together to show us our connection to God and creation.
Our spiritual awakening has changed us, so now we have the capacity
to live our lives as an expression of God's will. An example of
this type of transformation is beautifully captured in TITUS 3:3-7:

> *"At one time we too were foolish, disobedient, deceived and*
> *enslaved by all kinds of passions and pleasures. We lived*
> *in malice and envy, being hated and hating one another.*
> *But when the kindness and love of God our Savior ap-*
> *peared, he saved us, not because of righteous things we had*
> *done, but because of His mercy. He saved us through the*
> *washing of rebirth and renewal by the Holy Spirit, whom*
> *he poured out on us generously through Jesus Christ our*
> *Savior, so that, having been justified by His grace, we might*
> *become heirs having the hope of eternal life."*

Step Twelve requires that we be instrumental in helping others
receive the message of The Twelve Steps. Many of us were introduced to this Program by someone who was working the Twelfth

Step. Now we have the opportunity to promote our own growth by helping others. Our willingness to share our commitment to recovery and our growing awareness of God's presence in our lives keep us ever-vigilant for ways to share our new confidence. This program calls us to take responsibility for the daily living out of our values. The Apostle Paul clearly instructed us in this action by saying: *"But in your hearts set apart Christ as Lord. Always be prepared to give an answer to everyone who asks you to give the reason for the hope that you have. But do this with gentleness and respect . . . "* (1 PETER 3:15)

This Step reminds us that we have not yet completed our journey to wholeness. To continue our process of growth, we must be aware that we have just begun to learn the principles that will enhance our walk with the Lord. Each of the Twelve Steps is a vital part of fulfilling God's plan for us. When our daily challenges distract us and separate us from God, we can use the Steps as tools for coping with our problems. Step One reminds us of our powerlessness; Steps Two and Three show us the ongoing need for God's help; Steps Four through Nine guide us through self-examination and amends-making; Steps Ten and Eleven help us minimize our slips and keep in touch with God. Conscientious attention to working the Steps develops in us a level of love, acceptance, honesty, selflessness and peace of mind unequalled at any other time in our lives. The hardest part of any journey is the beginning, and we have taken that step through our total commitment to recovery.

Our spiritual awakening is a gift that instills in us a new perspective. It is usually accompanied by a positive and significant change in our value systems. Our pursuit of worldly goals has been subdued and redirected; we now look for fulfillment from things of real and lasting values. For most of us, the awakening is subtle and best seen in hindsight. It is seldom a single and distinct beginning and ending. Jesus comes to us when and as He wants. We also realize it took all of this to get us here; that's why we were asleep for so long. As we awaken to the presence of God's love for us, our lives become filled with new purpose and meaning. In Romans 13:11, Paul tells us: *"The hour has come for you to wake up from your slumber, because our salvation is nearer now than when we first believed."*

❖ *Looking to Scripture* ❖

"Actions speak louder than words" is an accurate description of how we should carry the Twelve Step message to others. It is more effective to witness a principle being applied than to hear lectures on theory alone. For example, sharing our own experiences of prayer and meditation has more meaning than simply lecturing and explaining why everyone should meditate and pray. We can most effectively carry the message by sharing our own experiences of a spiritual life through working the Steps. Telling our story will help others recognize their need and encourage the growth of our own humility. Carrying the message gives us an opportunity to describe the ways in which the Twelve Steps have transformed our lives and renewed our relationship with God. Through our sharing, we can explain how our lives have been transformed by our work with the Twelve Steps.

Finally, brothers, whatever is true, whatever is noble, whatever is right, whatever is pure, whatever is lovely, whatever is admirable—if anything is excellent or praiseworthy—think about such things. Whatever you have learned or received or heard from me, or seen in me—put it into practice. And the God of peace will be with you. (PHILIPPIANS 4:8-9)

We must take action on what we know to be true. Our actions speak for us and are a clear measure of our commitment to demonstrate God's love in our lives.

Scripture contains dramatic examples of the results of personal testimony about God's interaction in human affairs. John 4:28 and John 9:17 are accounts of personal experiences with Jesus Christ and their impact on the lives of others. Those who knew the speakers were convinced of the force of Christ's presence by the changes they observed. We cannot separate Twelve Step work from our Christian walk; they are connected by our Lord's guiding hand. The action segment of the Twelfth Step is perfectly described in Romans 10:10: *"For it is with your heart that you believe and are justified, and it is with your mouth that you confess and are saved."*

Be wise in the way you act toward outsiders; make the most of every opportunity. Let your conversation be always full of grace, seasoned with salt, so that you may know how to answer everyone. (COLOSSIANS 4:5-6)

The Twelve Steps are instruments that God uses to communicate the message of Christ's healing love. When asked, God tells us how we can best convey His message to others. We must listen and act as we are led.

Jesus did not let him, but said, "Go home to your family and tell them how much the Lord has done for you, and how he has had mercy on you." (MARK 5:19)

Jesus Christ constantly praised God for His good gifts. He urges us to pray and praise our Heavenly Father without ceasing.

Working with newcomers in using the Scriptural Twelve Steps can be very rewarding. Many of them are troubled, confused and resentful. They need guidance and help to understand that the Program, through their hard work and commitment, will produce rewards and miracles that far outweigh their present pain. We must encourage newcomers to be gentle with themselves and to work the Program one day at a time. This can be a growth experience for us. As we reflect on where we were when first introduced to the Program, we see how far we have come. When carrying the message, we must emphasize that the decision to join the Program is usually made when we have suffered enough, are discouraged, are tired of hurting and have "hit bottom."

Preach the word; be prepared in season and out of season; correct, rebuke and encourage—with great patience and careful instruction. (2 TIMOTHY 4:2)

Sharing the story of our healing and recovery is the testimony which God wants others to hear. Each of us has a unique pilgrimage to relate, and some person will receive encouragement from our message.

Be imitators of God, therefore, as dearly loved children and live a life of love, just as Christ loved us and gave himself up for us as a fragrant offering and sacrifice to God. (EPHESIANS 5:1-2)

To keep the fire of our spiritual awakening alive, Step Twelve also requires that we practice the principles in all our affairs, giving out the love we have received.

Our relationship with God is the key to our success in working the Steps and applying the principles in our daily affairs. We cannot allow ourselves to drift into indifference and neglect our commitment to living according to the teachings of Christ. Scripture reminds us of the mandate to live a Christ-like life, and tells us how we will know if we fail: "No one who lives in Him keeps on sinning. No one who continues to sin has either seen Him or known Him." (1 JOHN 3:6) Life constantly reminds us that we must be prepared to face temptations and trials and, with God's help, transform them into occasions for growth and comfort to ourselves and to those around us. We must understand that we will never achieve peace and serenity independently of God's grace.

If anyone speaks, he should do it as one speaking the very words of God. If anyone serves, he should do it with the strength God provides, so that in all things God may be praised through Jesus Christ. To him be the glory and the power forever and ever. Amen. (1 PETER 4:11)

> *Through the power of the Holy Spirit, we will receive the strength to be instruments of God's healing in the world.*

Sometimes we become discouraged and lose sight of our progress. If this happens, we compare our past to our present and ask ourselves:

- Are we less isolated and no longer afraid of people in authority?
- Have we stopped seeking approval from others and accepted ourselves as we really are?
- Are we more selective of the people with whom we develop relationships, and more able to keep our own identity while in a relationship?
- Have we developed the ability to express our feelings?
- Have we stopped trying to dominate others?
- Are we no longer behaving childishly by turning friends or spouses into protective parents and being overly dependent?
- Have we become attentive to the needs of our inner-child?

Affirmative answers indicate the extent of our progress toward a healthier and better way of living.

> **Brother, if someone is caught in a sin, you who are spiritual should restore him gently. But watch yourself, or you also may be tempted.** (GALATIANS 6:1)
>
> *Because of our own struggle, we can in some way relate to the conflict others may be encountering. Being candid and compassionate in conveying the Twelve Step message may assist others in making the commitment to turn their lives over to Jesus Christ.*

An important achievement in working the Steps occurs when we become accustomed to "living" the Steps. We do this by habitually taking a problem or concern through the Steps, while acknowledging our need for God's support and guidance. The resulting peace and serenity provide a threshold of competence from which we can deal directly with the problem. Any action we take is then clearly guided by God's hand and our honest appraisal of the consequences. We can act confidently and without fear, affirming *"The Lord is my light and my salvation—whom shall I fear? The Lord is the stronghold of my life—of whom shall I be afraid?"* (PSALM 6:29)

Two are better than one, because they have a good return for their work: If one falls down, his friend can help him up. But pity the man who falls and has no one to help him up! Also, if two lie down together, they will keep warm. But how can one keep warm alone? (ECCLESIASTES 4:9-11)

The power of God's presence is increased when two or more are gathered in His name. Helping each other to know the way and keep the faith is central to the work of the Twelfth Step.

At this point, we begin to identify the many areas of our lives that are being affected by working the Twelve Steps. Our success with handling new problems is linked to our willingness to thoughtfully take action, while remembering to let go and turn it over to God. Our faith grows as we learn to relinquish control and allow God to be the director of our lives. The process is gradual, regenerative and never-ending. We slowly become more God-centered as we learn the true meaning of love, peace and serenity. Paul captured the dynamic of this Twelve Step process when he said: "Brothers, I do not consider myself yet to have taken hold of it. But one thing I do: Forgetting what is behind and straining toward what is ahead, I press on toward the goal to win the prize for which God has called me heavenward in Christ Jesus." (PHILIPPIANS 3:13-14)

"No one lights a lamp and hides it in a jar or puts it under a bed. Instead, he puts it on a stand, so that those who come in can see the light. For there is nothing hidden that will not be disclosed, and nothing concealed that will not be known or brought out into the open. Therefore consider carefully how you listen. Whoever has will be given more; whoever does not have, even what he thinks he has will be taken from him." (LUKE 8:16-18)

The Lord spreads His message through the Twelve Steps, and we are instruments for delivering it. The daily practice of these principles will confirm to others the sincerity of our commitment.

Each new day is a gift from God that we can accept and acknowledge joyfully as an answer to our prayer for serenity.

PRAYER FOR SERENITY

God, grant me the serenity
to accept the things I cannot change,
the courage to change the things I can,
and the wisdom to know the difference.
Living one day at a time,
enjoying one moment at a time;
accepting hardship as a pathway to peace;
taking, as Jesus did,
this sinful world as it is,
not as I would have it;
trusting that You will make all things right
if I surrender to your will;
so that I may be reasonably happy in this life
and supremely happy with You forever in the next.

AMEN

Reinhold Niebuhr

TWELVE STEP REVIEW

Identify a situation or condition in your life that is currently a source of resentment, fear, sadness or anger. It may involve relationships (family, work or sexual), work environment, health or self-esteem. Describe the situation and indicate your concern.

Use the following to apply the principles of the Twelve Steps to your situation.

Step One: In what ways are you powerless, and how is this situation showing you the unmanageability of your life?

Step Two: How do you see your Higher Power as helping to restore you to sanity?

Step Three: How does being willing to turn your life over to the care of God assist you in dealing with this?

Step Four: What character defects have surfaced (e.g., fear of abandonment or authority figures, control, approval seeking, obsessive/compulsive behavior, rescuing, excessive responsibility, unexpressed feelings)?

Step Five: Admit your wrongs, at least to God and yourself.

Step Six: Are you entirely ready to have God remove the character defects that have surfaced? If not, explain:

Step Seven: Can you humbly submit to God and ask Him to remove your shortcomings? If not, why do you resist?

Step Eight: Make a list of the persons being harmed.

Step Nine: What amends are necessary, and how will you make amends?

Step Ten: Review the above Steps to be sure that nothing has been overlooked.

Step Eleven: Take a moment for prayer or meditation, asking God for knowledge of His will for you. What is your understanding of God's will in this situation?

Step Twelve: How can your understanding and spiritual awakening assist you in dealing with your problem?

Are you ready for the next step in recovery?

If you are interested in continuing to use the Twelve Steps as part of your recovery we suggest that you use *The Twelve Steps—A Spiritual Journey.* It includes a format for a step-study writing workshop.

The book contains explicit, detailed writing exercises for each step on the road to recovery. The program is worked **one day at a time.**

Following is a *Sample Meeting Announcement.*

SAMPLE MEETING ANNOUNCEMENT

Step Study Writing Workshop
Based on
The Twelve Steps—A Spiritual Journey

The First Church of Santa Barbara is sponsoring a Step Study Writing Workshop for individuals who grew up in emotionally repressive and dysfunctional families. This workshop uses the Twelve Steps in a Christian context.

Beginning Date: January 8, 1992

Day: Wednesday   **Time:** 7 to 9 PM

Location of Meeting: 305 East "A" Street, Santa Barbara

Contact Person: Susanne   **Phone:** (805) 555-1212

The Twelve Steps—A Spiritual Journey is a working guide based on Bible truths, and emphasizes self-understanding and the unchanging love of God for all humanity. This book:

■ offers a tool to restore the fruits of the Spirit in your life; joy, peace, gentleness, goodness and faith.

■ provides a workable formula for confronting the past and surrendering one's life to God.

■ reaffirms the dominion of God over all of life.

■ emphasizes the relationship between The Twelve Steps and the practice of Christianity.

Meeting Format

Leader:

"Hello, and welcome to *The Twelve Steps for Christians* support group meeting. My name is _____ and I am your trusted servant for today's meeting. Please join me for a moment of silence, after which we will recite the Serenity Prayer."

Serenity Prayer
God, grant me the serenity
to accept the things I cannot change,
the courage to change the things I can,
and the wisdom to know the difference.
Living one day at a time,
enjoying one moment at a time,
accepting hardship as a pathway to peace;
taking, as Jesus did,
this sinful world as it is,
not as I would have it;
trusting that You will make all things right
if I surrender to your will;
so that I may be reasonably happy in this life
and supremely happy with You forever in the next.
Amen.

Reinhold Niebuhr

"We are a support group committed to creating a safe place for men and women to share their experience, strength and hope with each other."

"As a fellowship of men and women recovering from behaviors that have affected us in our lives, our purpose is to grow spiritually and in our relationship with God. For our guide, we use the Bible and *The Twelve Steps for Christians* to help us on our journey of recovery. We are here for our own benefit, to share our own experience, strength and hope with others. We are not here to talk about others, to condemn, criticize, or judge them. Our desire is to improve the quality of our lives as we apply what we learn from listening to and sharing with each other. Our hope is in the belief that we can succeed today in situations where we failed previously. As we place ourselves in the care of our Higher Power, Jesus Christ, our attitudes improve as we honestly, openly and willingly look at who we are and engage in healthier behavior."

"I've asked _____ to read *The Twelve Steps*."

"I've asked _____ to read the *Scripture for the Twelve Steps* after each step."

"Many of the principles and traditions of Alcoholics Anonymous are used as part of the basis of our group. We respect the confidentiality and anonymity of each person here. Remember that whatever you hear at this meeting is shared with the trust and confidence that it will remain here. **Who you see here, what is said here, when you leave here, let it stay here.**"

"We are self-supporting through our own contributions. We ask for your contribution at this time." (Take time for collection before continuing.)

"If you are new to a twelve-step support group, we offer you a special welcome and invite you to attend at least 6 meetings to give yourself a fair chance to decide if this group is for you. We encourage you to exchange phone numbers with other members for support between meetings. Phone lists, literature and information on other recovery support groups will be available after the meeting. If you have any questions, please feel free to talk with me at the end of the meeting."

"Are there any recovery-related announcements?"

"Is there anyone here today for the first time? If so, please tell us your first name so we can greet you."

"We will now introduce ourselves by first name only. My name is _____."

"This meeting is a step study using *The Twelve Steps for Christians*. The Twelve Steps represent a spiritual discipline which can provide a way out of destructive behavior and an opportunity to improve our relationship with our Higher Power, Jesus Christ."

"Today's meeting focuses on Step _____. We will read a portion of the chapter, after which we will begin our time of sharing. Please turn to page _____."

Notes to Facilitator:

- *Appendix One* contains review questions for writing or sharing on this Step.

- Leader begins the sharing by telling his or her story as it pertains to the Step being discussed. Allow a maximum of 10 minutes to share.)

- If the group is larger than 20 people it is advisable to form small groups of 5-7 people for the sharing portion of the meeting.

"Before sharing begins, I will read the **Guidelines for Group Sharing.**

- Everyone is invited to share, but no one is obligated to do so.

- Please keep your sharing focused on recent experiences and events. Focus on your personal experience, strength and hope.

- Limit your sharing to 3-5 minutes. Allow everyone in the group to share once before you share a second time.

- Please...NO CROSS TALK. Cross-talk occurs when individuals speak out of turn and interrupt one another. The group is disrupted, and focus is diverted from the individual whose turn it is to speak.

- Refrain from asking questions. Questions will be answered after the meeting so that sharing will not be interrupted.

- If you have recently used chemical substances which have had a mood-altering effect on your behavior, we ask you NOT to share until after the meeting.

■ We are not here to advise, soothe, or solve other people's problems. We can share what we have done to change our own behavior, but not what we think someone else should do."

(NOTE TO FACILITATOR: 10 minutes before closing ask for prayer requests.)

"We will now take time for prayer requests. These requests should be regarding yourself or other group members."

Closing:

"Living Free is a fellowship of (church or organization name) and is intended to complement other Christ-centered twelve-step groups. You are encouraged to attend other twelve-step recovery support groups during the week to support your recovery journey."

"I've asked _____ to read the *Milestones in Recovery.*" (Page 128)

"Reminder! What you hear at this meeting is confidential; leave it at this meeting! It is not for public disclosure or gossip. Please respect the privacy of those who have shared here today."

"Will everyone please clean up after themselves and help rearrange the room?"

"Will all who care to, stand and join me in closing with the Lord's Prayer?"

"KEEP COMING BACK, IT WORKS!"

MILESTONES IN RECOVERY

Through God's help and our work in the twelve-step program, we can look forward to achieving the following *Milestones in Recovery.*

- We feel comfortable with people, including authority figures.

- We have a strong identity and generally approve of ourselves.

- We accept and use personal criticism in a positive way.

- As we face our own life situation, we find we are attracted by strengths and understand the weaknesses in our relationships with other people.

- We are recovering through loving and focusing on ourselves; we accept responsibility for our own thoughts and actions.

- We feel comfortable standing up for ourselves when it is appropriate.

- We are enjoying peace and serenity, trusting that God is guiding our recovery.

- We love people who love and take care of themselves.

- We are free to feel and express our feelings even when they cause us pain.

- We have a healthy sense of self-esteem.

- We are developing new skills that allow us to initiate and complete ideas and projects.

- We take prudent action by first considering alternative behaviors and possible consequences.

- We rely more and more on God as our Higher Power.

Questions for Step Review

STEP ONE

We admitted we were powerless over the effects
of our separation from God—that our
lives had become unmanageable.

Step One forms the foundation for working the other Steps. Admitting our powerlessness and accepting the unmanageability of our lives is not an easy thing to do. Although our behavior has caused us stress and pain, it is difficult to let go and trust that our lives can work out well. The idea that there are areas over which we are powerless is a new concept for us. It is much easier for us to feel that we have power and are in control.

In what area of your life do you experience the strongest need to be in control?

What are the consequences of your self-destructive habits?

What difficulties are you having in recognizing your powerlessness and your life's unmanageability?

What major event in your life has caused you to realize the extent of your pain?

STEP TWO

*Came to believe that a power greater than
ourselves could restore us to sanity.*

Step Two gives us new hope to see that help is available to us
if we simply reach out and accept what our Higher Power, Jesus
Christ, has to offer. It is here that we form the foundation for
growth of our spiritual life, which helps us become the person
we want to be. What is required of us is a willingness to believe
that a power greater than ourselves is waiting to be our personal
Savior. What follows as we proceed through the Steps is a process
that brings Jesus Christ into our lives and enables us to grow in
love, health and grace.

═══════════════

List experiences that caused you to lose faith in God.

How can faith help you accept a Power greater than yourself?

What is keeping you from truly believing that a Power greater than
yourself can restore you to sanity?

Describe your inability to manage your own affairs.

STEP THREE

Made a decision to turn our will and our lives over
to the care of God as we understood Him.

Step Three is an affirmative Step. It is time to make a decision. In the first two Steps, we became aware of our condition and accepted the idea of a power greater than ourselves. Although we are beginning to know and trust God, we may find it difficult to think of allowing him to be totally in charge of our lives. However, if the alternative is facing the loss of something critical to our existence, God's guidance may be easier to accept.

———————————

Which parts of your life are you willing to turn over to God?

Which parts of your life are you unwilling to turn over to God? How does willfulness prevent you from giving them up?

How can offering your life to God reduce the stress in your life?

How do you see your life improving because of your decision to surrender to God's will?

STEP FOUR

Made a searching and fearless moral inventory of ourselves.

Step Four is a tool to help us understand our current behavior patterns and recognize our need for God's guidance in our lives. Here, we examine our behavior and expand our understanding of ourselves. Being totally thorough and honest in preparing our inventory allows us to remove the obstacles that have prevented us from knowing ourselves and truthfully acknowledging our deepest feelings about life.

What is your major strength? How does it support you?

What is your major weakness? How does it hurt you?

Which of your present behaviors is the most damaging to your life? Explain.

How does denial protect you from facing your own reality?

STEP FIVE

Admitted to God, to ourselves, and to another human being the exact nature of our wrongs.

Step Five requires that we engage in honest confrontations with ourselves and others by admitting our faults to God, to ourselves and to another person. By doing so, we begin to set aside our pride and see ourselves in true perspective. We also realize how our growing relationship with God gives us the courage to examine ourselves, accept who we are and reveal our true selves. Step Five helps us acknowledge and discard our old survival skills and move toward a new and healthier life.

———————

What can be gained by admitting your faults to another person?

What is your resistance to sharing your story with another person?

Which of your faults is the most difficult to acknowledge? Why?

How will completing Step Five stop you from deceiving yourself?

STEP SIX

*Were entirely ready to have God remove
all these defects of character.*

The task of removing our ineffective behavior is more than we can handle alone. Step Six does not indicate that we do the removing; all we have to do is be "entirely ready" for it to happen. We can become ready by faithfully working the Steps and being willing to let God assist us in removing our shortcomings. The character traits we want to eliminate are often deeply ingrained patterns of behavior. They will not vanish overnight. We must be patient while God is shaping us into new people. Allowing God be in control helps us to trust Him more completely.

===========

What do you fear by having your character defects removed?

Identify two character defects you are not ready to have removed.

Why is it necessary to learn humility before God can remove your defects of character?

What is interfering with your readiness to have God remove your shortcomings?

STEP SEVEN

Humbly asked Him to remove our shortcomings.

Humility is the central idea of Step Seven. By practicing humility we receive the strength necessary to work the Steps and achieve satisfactory results. We recognize that a major portion of our lives has been devoted to fulfilling our self-centered desires. We must set aside these prideful, selfish behavior patterns and realize that humility frees our spirit. Step Seven requires surrendering our will to God so that we may receive the serenity necessary to achieve the happiness we seek.

===

How are you benefiting from God's presence in your life?

What special blessings has God sent to you since you began your twelve-step program of recovery?

List examples that indicate you are practicing humility.

Which of your negative character traits are becoming positive? Explain how this change is impacting your life.

STEP EIGHT

Made a list of all persons we had harmed, and
became willing to make amends to them all.

Step Eight begins the process of healing damaged relationships through our willingness to make amends for past misdeeds. We prepare ourselves to carry out God's master plan for our lives by preparing to make amends. We can let go of our resentments and start to overcome the guilt, the shame and low self-esteem we have acquired through our harmful actions. Through the gift of the Twelve Steps, we have the necessary tools to overcome these damaging conditions and mend our broken friendships.

List three personal experiences that require making amends.

How will making amends help free you from resentment and shame?

How does your unwillingness to forgive others block your progress and hurt your relationship with God?

Why is forgiving yourself an important factor in the amends-making process?

STEP NINE

Made direct amends to such people wherever possible,
except when to do so would injure them or others.

Step Nine fulfills our requirement to reconcile with others. We clear our "garden" of dead leaves and "rake up and discard" the old habits. We face our faults, admit our wrongs and ask for and extend forgiveness. Making amends will release us from many of the resentments of our past. It is a means of achieving serenity in our lives by seeking forgiveness from those whom we have harmed and making restitution where necessary.

―――――――――――――――

How will completing Step Nine enable you to bury the past and improve your self-esteem?

What difficulties are you having in making amends?

Who on your amends list causes you the most anxiety?

What does making "direct amends" mean to you?

STEP TEN

*Continued to take personal inventory and, when
we were wrong, promptly admitted it.*

Step Ten points the way toward continued spiritual growth. We consciously examine our daily conduct and make adjustments where necessary. We look at ourselves, see our errors, promptly admit them and make corrections. Taking regular inventory makes us more conscious of our strengths and weaknesses. We are less inclined to yield to feelings of loneliness, self-righteousness and anger if we remain emotionally balanced and gather courage as we see our strengths increasing. We become more focused and capable of living the Christian life we desire.

———————————

List an example that shows you are relating better to others.

Cite a recent situation in which you did not behave appropriately. What did you do when you realized you were in error?

How does taking a daily inventory support your spiritual growth?

How does correcting your wrongs save you from unnecessary consequences?

STEP ELEVEN

Sought through prayer and meditation to improve our conscious contact with God as we understood Him, praying only for knowledge of His will for us and the power to carry that out.

To protect what we have learned, we must continually seek to know God's will for us. A daily regimen of prayer and meditation makes it clear that relief is just a day-to-day reprieve. Our approach to Step Eleven will vary in intent and intensity; it indicates our commitment to a prayerful life. If we are communing and are communicating with God, His joy will infuse our fellowship and friendship with others. We will reap rich benefits. Ideally, we practice this Step daily upon awakening and retiring, to remind us that we must sincerely and humbly want God's will for us.

———————————

Describe a situation where you delayed taking action because you were "waiting" for God's will. What happened?

Cite an example in which God answered your prayers through another individual or a new experience.

What do you experience when quietly praying to God?

How has your life improved as a result of working the Steps?

STEP TWELVE

Having had a spiritual awakening as the result of these Steps, we tried to carry this message to others, and to practice these principles in all our affairs.

Each of the Twelve Steps is a vital part of fulfilling God's plan for us. Conscientious attention to working the Steps develops in us a level of love, acceptance, honesty and peace of mind unequalled at any other time in our lives. Step Twelve invites us to promote our own growth by helping others. Our willingness to share our commitment to recovery and our growing awareness of God's presence in our lives keep us ever-vigilant for ways to share our new confidence.

———————————

Cite an example that shows you are "living" the Steps.

List a concern you had and describe your experience of resolving it by applying the Twelve Steps.

What connection do you see between the Twelve Steps and your Christian walk?

How do you practice the principles of the Steps in all your affairs?

The Living Free Program

The Twelve Steps for Christians is part of *The Living Free Program*, a recovery ministry dedicated to making the church a safe place for recovery. Following is a brief overview of this program.

The Living Free Program is for people who were reared in an emotionally repressive or dysfunctional family. The curriculum is based on the twelve-step process as a spiritual discipline with an emphasis on Christ-centered recovery. The program assists people in establishing and maintaining a loving relationship with God, themselves and others, and provides a safe environment where they can share their thoughts and feelings. With the grace of God, they can move from pain and denial toward healing and wholeness.

The Living Free Program sessions involve three ascending levels. The curricula include materials for individuals just beginning recovery, as well as for people in recovery who are familiar with twelve-step programs. Each level helps individuals increase self-esteem and cope with problems that affect their lives. Program participants can gain valuable insight about themselves, as they identify and confront significant issues in their lives.

Level One — Introduction to Recovery Issues
Level One introduces individuals to fundamental issues common to people in the beginning stages of recovery. The text offers wisdom and encouragement through emphasis on solid biblical principles.

TEXT: *When I Grow Up . . . I Want To Be An Adult*
A ten-week course presenting foundation material for adults who suffer from wounded childhoods. It explores way to discover our child-like nature and provides guidelines for Christ-centered recovery groups. The objective is to bring healing home to family, friends and loved ones.

TEXT: *The Truth Will Set You Free*

A 12-week course for adults who were reared in an addictive or dysfunctional family. It includes a video program with a companion workbook designed to help Christians work through unresolved grief and codependency issues in a gentle, loving way.

Level Two — Introduction to the Twelve-Step Recovery Process

Level Two is an introduction to the Twelve Steps as a spiritual discipline and demonstrates the compatibility between Christianity and the Twelve Steps.

TEXT: *The Twelve Steps for Christians*

The objective of the course is to discover the healing power of the twelve-step process when worked within a Christian perspective. The material is written for individuals who experienced trauma or some type of deprivation in their childhood.

Level Three — Twelve-Step Recovery

Level Three is an extensive 27-week course that presents the twelve-step process as a spiritual journey toward healing from childhood traumas and self-defeating behaviors.

TEXT: *The Twelve Steps—A Spiritual Journey*

This course requires that participants read each chapter and answer questions prior to attending the weekly meetings. The text contains weekly exercises for use within small group settings. Biblical references aid Christians in confronting their past and surrendering their lives to God as part of their recovery journey.

For more information call (800) 873-8384 or (619) 275-1350.

APPENDIX THREE
Self-Help Resources

SECULAR GROUPS

Adult Children of Alcoholics
Central Service Board
P.O. Box 3216
Torrance, California 90505
(213) 534-1815

Al-Anon/Alateen
Family Group Headquarters, Inc.
Madison Square Station
New York, New York 10010
(212) 683-1771

Alcoholics Anonymous
World Services, Inc.
468 Park Avenue South
New York, New York 10016
(212) 686-1100

Co-Dependents Anonymous
P.O. Box 33577
Phoenix, Arizona 85067-3577
(602) 277-7991

Debtors Anonymous
P.O. Box 20322
New York, New York 10025-9992

Emotions Anonymous
P.O. Box 4245
St. Paul, Minnesota 55104

Gamblers Anonymous
P.O. Box 17173
Los Angeles, California 90017

Narcotics Anonymous
World Service Office
16155 Wyandotte Street
Van Nuys, California 91406
(818) 780-3951

National Association for
Children of Alcoholics
31706 Coast Highway, Suite 201
South Laguna, California 92677
(714) 499-3889

Overeaters Anonymous
World Service Office
2190 - 190th Street
Torrance, California 90504
(213) 320-7941

Sexaholics Anonymous
P.O. Box 300
Simi Valley, California 93062

CHRISTIAN GROUPS

Alcoholics Victorious
National Headquarters
9370 S.W. Greenburg Road
Suite 411
Tigard, Oregon 97323
(503) 245-9629

Liontamers
2801 North Brea Blvd.
Fullerton, California 92635-2799
(714) 529-5544

National Association for
Christian Recovery
721 W. Whittier Blvd. Suite "H"
Whittier, California 90603
(310) 697-6201

Overcomers, Inc.
4235 Mt. Sterling Avenue
Titusville, Florida 32780

Substance Abusers Victorious
One Cascade Plaza
Akron, Ohio 44308

Order Form

9908	Living Free	_____	$ 5.95	_____
9906	New Clothes from Old Threads	_____	$ 9.99	_____
9907	The Truth Will Set You Free (Workbook)	_____	$10.95	_____
9007	The Truth Will Set You Free (Book & Video)	_____	$99.95	_____
9902	The 12 Steps for Adult Children	_____	$ 7.95	_____
9901	The 12 Steps—A Way Out	_____	$14.95	_____
9904	The Twelve Steps for Christians	_____	$ 7.95	_____
9903	The Twelve Steps—A Spiritual Journey	_____	$14.95	_____
9905	When I Grow Up...I Want To Be An Adult	_____	$12.95	_____

Subtotal _____

*Sales Tax _____

**Shipping & Handling _____

(U.S. Funds Only)   TOTAL _____

Visa and **MasterCard** Accepted

Bankcard No. _____

Expiration Date _____

Signature _____

* California residents add applicable sales tax.

COD orders—add an additional $4.00

** Shipping and Handling:
Minimum Charge $3.75
Orders over $25.00—$5.50
Orders over $55.00, add 10% of Subtotal.

To Order by Phone: (619) 275-1350 or (800) 873-8384
To Order by FAX: (619) 275-5729

Or send this order form and a check or money order for the total to:

Recovery Publications, Inc.
1201 Knoxville Street
San Diego, CA 92110-3718

Name: _____

Address: _____

City/State/Zip: _____

Phone: _____

144